Wild Bliss

Other Books by Lexi Blake

Evidence of Desire

Masters Of Ménage (by Shayla Black and Lexi Blake)
Their Virgin Captive
Their Virgin's Secret
Their Virgin Concubine
Their Virgin Princess
Their Virgin Hostage
Their Virgin Secretary
Their Virgin Mistress

The Perfect Gentlemen (by Shayla Black and Lexi Blake)
Scandal Never Sleeps
Seduction in Session
Big Easy Temptation
Smoke and Sin
At the Pleasure of the President

URBAN FANTASY

Thieves
Steal the Light
Steal the Day
Steal the Moon
Steal the Sun
Steal the Night
Ripper
Addict
Sleeper
Outcast
Stealing Summer
The Rebel Queen
The Rebel Guardian
The Rebel Witch

LEXI BLAKE WRITING AS SOPHIE OAK

Texas Sirens
Small Town Siren
Siren in the City
Siren Enslaved
Siren Beloved

Siren in Waiting
Siren in Bloom
Siren Unleashed
Siren Reborn
The Accidental Siren

Nights in Bliss, Colorado
Three to Ride
Two to Love
One to Keep
Lost in Bliss
Found in Bliss
Pure Bliss
Chasing Bliss
Once Upon a Time in Bliss
Back in Bliss
Sirens in Bliss
Happily Ever After in Bliss
Far from Bliss
Unexpected Bliss
Wild Bliss

A Faery Story
Bound
Beast
Beauty

Standalone
Away From Me
Snowed In

Wild Bliss

Nights in Bliss, Colorado, Book 14

Lexi Blake
writing as
Sophie Oak

Wild Bliss
Nights in Bliss, Colorado Book 14

Published by DLZ Entertainment LLC

Copyright 2024 DLZ Entertainment LLC
Edited by Chloe Vale
ISBN: 978-1-963890-08-2

Sign up for Lexi Blake's newsletter
and be entered to win a $25 gift certificate
to the bookseller of your choice.

Join us for news, fun, and exclusive content
including free Thieves short stories.

There's a new contest every month!

Go to www.LexiBlake.net to subscribe.

Acknowledgements

I always love a chance to get back to Bliss and this time is no different. Bliss is one of my happiest places and not because everything is perfect. Rather because everyone has a second chance. Even the grumpiest among us.

This book is for all the grumps out there who don't know just how loved they are.

Prologue

Sawyer Hathaway stared at the Bliss Town Hall like it was a snake that could bite him. Would bite him. Might bite him. Maybe.

He growled and was reminded he wasn't alone when a canine head came up, swiveling and looking around for a threat. The German shepherd mix was proof that things happened to him when he moved into this weird world. He'd found the dog eating out of the trash bin behind the bar he owned. She'd been skinny as hell and flea bitten and scared. He should have shooed her away, but he'd known the minute she whined and tried to grab a moldy, half-eaten sandwich that he would at least take her in for the night. He'd fed her and given her a warm place to sleep and taken her straight to Noah Bennett's animal clinic here in Bliss.

And somehow he'd left with her and a bunch of medications Noah had convinced him she needed. Now he had a dog.

He wasn't a guy who had a pet. He was a badass, a once upon a time criminal, a dude the sheriff feared. He wasn't a dog dad.

"It's okay." He reached out and patted her head. "The only threat here is to my dignity. The sheriff doesn't like me. Probably because he's an ex-DEA agent and I used to be a member of an MC that ran a shit ton of drugs. I didn't do it for the money, but I don't think the sheriff wants a rundown on how I went into a life of crime to try to save my brother."

The same brother who'd stood in front of him and told him he didn't want to see him again because Sawyer was part of a life he wasn't ever going back to. Now Wes had a wife and kid and a house in Denver, and Sawyer hadn't seen the brother he'd spent much of his life and pieces of his soul trying to protect in years.

The dog stared at him with soulful eyes. She was a good listener. She was probably the only listener Sawyer'd had since he'd joined the Colorado Horde. He'd had friends before then. Ty and Lucy and River. He'd pushed them away because of the danger he'd represented in those years and was only now finding his way back, which was precisely why he was sitting in his Jeep as the town Christmas party went on in front of him. He watched as Max Harper herded one of his kids inside. The boy. Sawyer would bet his wife Rachel had taken their oldest, Paige, with her when she came in to set up for the party. Sure enough, Rye Harper, Max's twin brother and Rachel's other husband, hustled in behind them.

Max Harper. Sawyer shook his head. "Even after all these years it's weird to think of Max as a dad. As a husband, really. He's the single biggest asshole I've ever met, and I've met Taggart. Max was born an asshole. Like the man was born without a single fuck to give. The good news is his brother seems to have gotten an adequate amount. Still have no idea how Rachel puts up with him. Not that I know her well. She doesn't exactly frequent Hell on Wheels."

Hell on Wheels was a world he understood. It was the bar his granddad had started over forty years before, and Sawyer had ended up in charge when he'd died five years back. Just in time for Sawyer to find refuge there. The bar had become the bane of his existence and his sanctuary. He worked and then went home to sleep, and then started it all over again. He rarely came into Bliss, preferring to drive hours to larger towns where no one asked questions or tried to make small talk.

No one asked about his dog or if he'd finally named his dog, and how the hell did he have a dog?

There was a tap on his window, and it took everything Sawyer had not to reach for the gun he kept close at all times—a habit mostly from those years when the world had been brutal and dangerous. Luckily he'd trained it out of himself enough so he didn't point a gun in Jax Lee's face.

The smiling dude waving at him while standing in the snow had married Sawyer's childhood friend years before. "Hey, Sawyer. How's it going? You missed the dinner party last Saturday."

It was past time to get this over with. He might be able to pawn everything off on Jax and get back in time to... Work a shift he wasn't supposed to work? Lark would get pissy with him since she rarely got to handle the bar by herself. Apparently he was overbearing or something according to his employees. Lark had been happy to send him off, perfectly thrilled to have a Saturday night all to herself. Well, and the other three employees working this evening. Lark and Sidney would handle the bar and customers, while Gil worked the fryer and Joe punched the crap out of anyone who thought Lark and Sid were on the menu. The Saturday night crowd could be rough. It was precisely why he almost never skipped one.

"Sorry, had to work." He'd gotten the evite complete with a picture of River and Jax and their big dumb dog looking cute standing in their kitchen. It was sweet and normal, and he'd known he couldn't sit at their table, and it wasn't because of the vegetarian fare. It was because he would have to sit with them and Lucy and Ty and their partner, Michael. It was because he would be the only one there alone, the only one who didn't belong. Not that he'd ever actually belonged with them. They'd formed a family over the years, and didn't every family need a black sheep?

Black sheep didn't go to family dinners.

Jax merely smiled and waved it off. "Of course, but you should know River's determined to get on your schedule. You going in? Hey, girl. How are you? Buster's inside. I'm sure he would love some company."

The dog's tail wagged madly as though she knew a good thing when it came into her life. Jax was a good thing. Sawyer was... He was the one who'd found her and gotten talked into keeping her. Would Buster like some company? River had always loved dogs, and weren't two better than one?

The idea of pawning off the pup on River actually didn't make him feel good. He'd gotten kind of used to her being around. Not because he liked her or anything. No. He didn't like having her lie her head on his lap or wag her tail when they went for a walk. She forced him to be more active. Yes, an excellent and logical explanation. He had to take her on walks and out to the bathroom, and it felt good to move more.

"I was just going to drop off some stuff." He wasn't sure why, but he'd bought presents for his friends this year. Some bug had gotten into him. Maybe because Michael and Ty had started coming in regularly with Lucy, and they always found some reason to force him to sit down for a while and share some truly greasy fries with them while they talked about what had happened up at the resort during the week. River and Jax would join them from time to time. The last year had made him…the word made his stomach turn…long. He needed to stop longing. It wasn't manly. "Hey, I should get back to the bar. Could you take some presents in for me?"

Jax's head shook, and he held up his hands, both carrying large bags. "Sorry, man. River loaded me up. Come on inside. There's turkey and dressing, and I'm sure Max is going to spike the hell out of the punch. Oh, and Stella made chocolate pies. You know since she's semi-retired no one except her husband gets chocolate pies."

It had been a long time since he'd been to Stella's. He used to go a lot as a kid. When he would play at Ty's place, and Ty's mom invited Sawyer's granddad to dinner sometimes. They would always go to Stella's and let Ty and Sawyer and his brothers sit in their own booth like big men while they laughed and shared stories of raising wild boys, as they called them. River's father would join them every now and then, and he would look over from the table he sat at with his friends to see his grandfather smiling, and the world didn't seem so awful.

A deep sense of nostalgia swept over Sawyer.

He was a long way from that boy. His grandfather was gone. His brothers were out in the world and didn't seem to care about him. Did he have to lose all his friends?

Jax's smile faded, a serious look coming over his face. "Sawyer, River misses you. It's been years, man. You can't hole up forever."

He didn't see why he couldn't. He'd holed up pretty well. And yet he found himself opening the door and letting the dog bound out. There was something magical about seeing her tail wag, her whole body bouncing around like this was the greatest moment of her life. Mere weeks before she'd growled and snapped and tucked her tail between her legs.

He could do this. He hauled the gifts out and followed Jax up to the town hall. The place practically glowed against the snow and velvet winter night. He felt weird walking into this particular Hallmark movie.

Until he looked around and realized this film would never make the Hallmark Channel's Christmas movie list since everyone was throupled up.

Threesomes were all the rage in Bliss, and he was surrounded by them. He caught sight of local rancher James Glen sitting by one of the many Christmas trees decorating the hall, his wife, Hope, in his lap, and the aforementioned vet he shared said wife with at his side. The mayor of Bliss was dancing with his wife, Laura, though their partner Cameron Briggs was plastered to her back, his hands on her swaying hips. Ah, Christmas in Bliss. He was pretty sure one of those trees was decorated with beets. Yeah, Mel Hughes would have brought the beet tree in. He glanced over and, sure enough, there was the old guy sitting with his girlfriend, who would be his wife if the man wasn't worried aliens could track him through government paperwork. He was talking to the newest trio in town. Elisa, Van, and Hale were sitting at a table with Mel—Elisa's father.

"Can I help you with those?" Callie Hollister-Wright gave him a big grin. She was a pretty brunette with shining eyes and a smile capable of lighting up a room. She had a Santa hat on her head and blinking Christmas tree lights she wore as earrings.

She was also married to the sheriff, who didn't trust Sawyer. And for good reason. "I just need to set these down and then I'll get out of everyone's hair."

Callie leaned over to pet the dog, who was drooling, though Callie didn't seem to care. "Why would you say such a thing? Come on in and stay awhile. It's cold out there. You need to warm up. Though be careful with the eggnog. Max spiked it."

"You should have known that would happen."

She straightened up, lips curling in a mischievous grin. "Well, it wouldn't be so bad if it was only Max. I'm afraid Van spiked it, too. And Ty. And then Mel added a couple of drops of his whiskey tonic…"

"Let me guess." Despite how out of place he felt, a smile crossed his face. This town was beautifully weird. "To keep the aliens away."

The old man was serious about keeping the aliens away.

"You know it's high mating season for… I don't remember what he called them, but the outcome for us is the eggnog is seriously spiked." She frowned. "It's too much. I was hoping for something sweet with a little kick, but I'll have to settle for a beer, I guess."

He didn't like the sound of that. "I thought you brought in a full bar for these things."

She nodded. "Yeah, but it's kind of a self-service thing, and I am not a bartender." Her stare focused in on him. "Not like you are. You know there are rumors you once worked at a super-fancy hotel in Denver and know how to make way more than you pretend to."

He shouldn't. He should run and run fast. The sheriff wouldn't like Sawyer mixing his wife's drinks. And yet he couldn't quite turn her away. Callie was kind to him despite knowing as much as she knew about his past. "I'll see what you have. You want sweet, right?"

"So it is true. You pretend to only know how to pour beer," she said as though she'd solved a mystery.

Sawyer placed his gifts on the big table designated for them and sighed. "I might be better than I tell people, but honestly, I don't get many requests for espresso martinis at Hell on Wheels. And I might be out of practice, so this could be terrible."

He made his way to the makeshift bar and quickly figured out his best bet was a chocolate martini. He found the shaker and was pouring it out for Callie in no time at all. Dog sat patiently beside him, her tail thumping.

She needed a name.

"Here you go." He slid the glass Callie's way.

Her eyes lit up. "It looks delicious."

Sawyer frowned. "You know I'm not the only bartender here." He pointed across the room. "Alexei literally tends the bar at your restaurant. And so does the new kid. Van."

She shrugged. "But you're here."

Jen Talbot strode up, slapping a hand on the bar and giving him a long-suffering sigh. "Thank the universe. Sawyer, I'm going to need one of those. Max ruined the eggnog, and I don't know what is in the thing Nell brought. She said it was an old recipe from her momma, and she called it winter's dew. I don't think it sounds good. She said it's the essence of winter, which is pretty much snow and cold."

Jen kind of scared him so he made a big shaker full. Like her best friend, Rachel Harper, Jen could be quite a lot to handle, but then most women in Bliss were. "Here you go. This should take care of you for a couple of drinks."

Jen took a sip, and her eyes closed. "Damn, it's good. I thought Alexei knew how to make a martini." Jen pointed his way. "You are a keeper, Sawyer..." She frowned. "I don't know your last name."

And he was okay with that. It wasn't like he was angling to get invited to dinner. It wasn't like he wanted to belong here. "It's just Sawyer."

"Okay. Maybe I don't know your first name," Jen acknowledged, and then her attention was wrenched away as two small boys ran by like whirling dervishes. "Logan Talbot and Charlie Hollister-Wright."

Both boys froze like they were playing Simon Says and Simon had said freeze.

Jen moved in front of her son, wrinkling her nose with obvious affection. "Slow down."

"Yes, momma," the little boy who looked an awful lot like Stef Talbot said.

"Yes, Auntie Jen," Charlie Hollister-Wright replied politely. And then they were off again, though slightly slower this time.

They ran past a woman in a red sweater and jeans, her dark hair flowing around her shoulders.

Sawyer stood there because something odd happened. Maybe it was the scent from whatever Nell brought. Maybe it was a contact high from standing too close to the eggnog. Maybe it was a stroke. He wasn't sure, but he could have sworn the damn world slowed down and a fucking spotlight came out of nowhere, shining down on that woman. So pretty. She practically glowed. She smiled at someone, though Sawyer didn't see who because the stroke he was obviously having made it hard to look at anyone but her. Yeah, this was a dangerous health situation. His eyes should be able to move.

In the distance he could hear music playing. Hopefully it was from the speakers and not from whatever was happening in his fucked-up head.

Had he taken a bunch of drugs and forgotten he'd done it? Should he see if Doc Burke was here? He probably was. What would he tell him? *My eyes only want to look at the new girl and damn she's pretty.*

She turned his way and looked at the martini in Callie's hands, her eyes going wide as though she'd finally seen heaven.

Or was she looking at him?

Wasn't there a broom closet in this place the Harpers had already christened? It wouldn't be the first time some adventurous tourist tried to get him alone for a memorable time. He wasn't sure why a tourist was here, but she'd probably stumbled in and everyone welcomed her because she was obviously sweet and friendly. He would welcome her boobs. They pressed against her sweater, round and tempting, and he could already feel them in his hands, feel the silk of her hair as he pushed it back so he could kiss the soft skin of her neck.

The woman started walking his way and Sawyer wondered if Ty was here somewhere and could watch the dog for a little while.

Maybe he should ask her to dinner.

Definitely a medical emergency.

"That's Sabrina. She's Elisa Leal's sister," Callie was saying. "She's so sweet. She teaches kindergarten. We all love her."

A schoolteacher?

"Elisa is my new deputy, Mel's daughter," a familiar voice said. Nate Wright's deep tones finally broke the spell. Sawyer turned, and the sheriff stood there with his wife. He wasn't in uniform this evening, but there was no way to mistake the air of authority he oozed. "Sabrina's only here for a few days. She lost her momma a couple of years back, and then she nursed her sister through cancer. She's a good one."

A good one. A sweet woman. A freaking schoolteacher, and he'd thought about banging her in a broom closet. He'd done things Sabrina Leal wouldn't be able to imagine. Now that he really looked at her he could see the way she smiled at him, expectation in her eyes.

This wasn't a woman looking for a quick lay. She would need love and affection and attention, and he had none of those things to give to anyone. The most he could give a woman was a good time in bed and a slap on the ass as she left, preferably before morning because he slept better alone.

Sabrina Leal approached the bar, her eyes on him and him alone.

She felt the pull, too. She just didn't understand what a bad fucking bet he was.

He had the sudden urge to ask her to dance.

He did not dance.

He did not play bartender for friends at a Christmas party where kids ran around and people danced and exchanged gifts like they were some sort of a family.

Sawyer didn't have a family.

"Hi, I'm Sabrina." She held out her hand like they were meeting at a fucking church social. "What's your name?"

Sawyer felt the weight of the sheriff's eyes on him, honestly the weight of the world on him, and said the only thing he could think of. "No. Nope. I'm out of here."

He strode away, not looking back. When he got to the Jeep it was only habit to let the dog in. He thought about leaving her behind, too, since someone in that warm, friendly, homey building would surely take better care of her. But then she was in her seat, and he couldn't kick her out.

Not even the baddest man in all of Bliss County would toss a dog out into the snow a few days before Christmas.

He heard someone call his name and turned the engine over.

He drove away and didn't look back.

* * * *

Sabrina watched the gorgeous man stride away. Tall and so handsome it nearly hurt to look at him, she'd felt something when their eyes had locked, but it was obvious he hadn't felt the same thing. He'd felt the opposite, apparently, since he'd run.

Everyone in Bliss was so friendly except the one man who'd caught her eye.

It had been a long time since she'd connected with a man. She'd started to tentatively dip her toe into the dating pool back in North Carolina, though she was almost certain she wouldn't be there for long. Her sister had found a home here, and if there was any way, she thought she might come west, too. Oh, not to Bliss. There wasn't even a school here for her to work at, but maybe one of the larger towns. It wouldn't be perfect, but it would be good to be closer to her sister.

"Don't take him personally," the sheriff said, moving around the bar. "I'm afraid Sawyer is not the friendliest guy in town."

"Well, you always look at him like he's about to do something illegal, so of course he's not comfortable. You have to be comfortable to be friendly," the woman Sabrina was almost sure was his wife said in a tone that let her know this was well-worn territory.

"I don't have a problem with Sawyer," the sheriff argued. "I understand him better. He's a good man, but you have to admit he's got some serious issues. He's surly and secretive and can be quite rude at times, as our new friend recently discovered."

Callie didn't look convinced but shook her head. "I bet it took a lot for the man to walk in here, and you immediately get into his space like he was going to do something wrong."

"I wanted to know what he was making," the sheriff admitted. "The eggnog is awful and probably needs to be tossed out before it poisons someone, and I'm not going to try whatever the essence of winter is. I can't find the beer, so I was kind of hoping Sawyer would make me an Old Fashioned."

"Well, you could have asked him nicely," his wife countered.

"No, I couldn't because he took one look at the new girl and ran away," the sheriff argued. He then winced and tipped his head Sabrina's way. "Like I said, Sawyer's a deep one."

He probably could sense desperation. He'd looked at her, said that girl hasn't had a date in forever, and ran the other way. She wasn't in his league looks-wise, and her mother had always been on her about losing what she called the "baby" fat. As she neither was a baby nor had she given birth to one, she had to figure it was her mom's way of "politely" calling her fat. She didn't have her sister's height or her elegant looks. She took after her father's side of the family. Short legs, big boobs, and wide hips were pretty much the only gifts her dad had ever given her. "It's okay. Though in his defense, he wouldn't have been able to pull off an Old Fashioned. There's no bitters here."

"Oh, there will be when Marie wakes up and realizes Teeny let the children decorate her like a Christmas tree," the sheriff promised. "And Sawyer... Well, I've honestly never seen the man react the way he did. I'm going to assume he had certain feelings he is not ready to deal with."

Sabrina rolled her eyes. "You think he saw me, fell madly in love, and ran because he's too damaged to ever love someone? I doubt it."

"Oh, it happens." Callie took another sip of her drink. "It happens way more often than you would think. I'm pretty sure Caleb couldn't speak for the first six months after he met Holly. I mean he could, but he didn't make much sense around her and he's got an MD."

"Sometimes I question the university who handed him his degree. They obviously didn't teach a class in bedside manner." The sheriff moved around the bar and poured himself a couple of fingers of whiskey. "Though you're right about him not being ready at the time. It took Alexei showing back up to get Doc in gear. It took Noah showing up to make Jamie look at Hope. Lots of guys are dumb."

Callie stared at him as he talked about all the other men who hadn't been ready to find the loves of their lives. The sheriff was excellent at not noticing the death stares his wife was sending him.

"Six years, Nate," Callie said with a frown.

The sheriff winced. "So all I'm saying is if he wasn't interested, he likely wouldn't have noticed you at all," the sheriff concluded after remarking on most of the trios in Bliss. "But it's probably a good thing because I don't know Sawyer is marriage material."

"I wasn't looking to marry the man. I thought I might get a Cosmo out of him." Did everyone in the world see her as some wallflower desperate to get a man?

Of course, when she'd first caught sight of him, her heart had fluttered. She'd had to catch her breath because he was a stunning man. It didn't mean she was desperate. Just a little lonely. He didn't have to run from her. It wasn't like she would have tackled him or anything. Not when it was clear he didn't want her to.

A brow rose over the sheriff's blue eyes. "Really? That is not the reaction most women have to Sawyer Hathaway."

Callie snapped her fingers. "Hathaway. And Nate's right. He is like every gorgeous bad-boy stereotype wrapped up in an emotionally unavailable package. Don't get me wrong. I like Sawyer. There's a good man under all his growly protestations, but he's not a guy I would set up with one of my friends. Now I do know some men who are looking for something more serious. We've got a couple of part-time deputies coming in. I'm pretty sure they're partners, if you know what I mean."

"Yeah, the Creede boys have stopped making fun of all the trios and started asking intelligent questions about how it works," the sheriff explained.

Callie's eyes lit, and Sabrina knew she had to shut it down and quickly. She had no idea who the Creede boys were, but she wasn't about to get connected to horny, curious dudes who would likely run like that Sawyer person had the minute he'd seen her.

"I'm not looking to be set up. I'm simply here to see my sister and then I'm heading home." Back to the house she grew up in. It didn't feel like home. It was so odd. She was sleeping in her sister's biological father's guest bedroom, and it felt warmer than the house she'd spent the last few decades of her life in. Of course her mom had never gently woken her up with the promise of pancakes and bacon. And beets. But she could handle beets. Cassidy Meyer was weird and warm and lovely, and Sabrina low-key wished she'd been the one to find out her bio dad was a short-term affair of her mom's while she was in the Army. Elisa was so happy with her new family, and it was inevitable time and distance would isolate her if she didn't find a way to stay close to her sister.

Wow. She actually was desperate, but not for some man. She was desperate to have any kind of family at all.

"I was hoping I could talk to you about that," a deep voice said. She turned and a dark-haired man stood a few feet away from her. He wore a button-down and slacks and loafers Sabrina identified as designer and expensive. "Hello, Ms. Leal. My name is Stefan Talbot and I was impressed with how you handled the kids earlier this evening."

She'd seen the kids needed some planned and organized activities and she'd taken them in hand. No big deal. "I had fun with them. Honestly, the older kids just needed some guidance about the crafts Nell and Holly set up and then they helped with the younger kids."

"You were great with them. I hear you're a teacher back in North Carolina," Talbot said, and that was when she noticed the woman standing behind him. She was almost certain the woman's name was Rachel Harper, and she was the mom of Paige, who'd proven so helpful with the younger kiddos. Rachel was watching the conversation, biting her bottom lip like it was taking everything she had not to intervene.

What was happening here? "Yes. I'm teaching kindergarten right now, but I've taught third and fifth as well."

"How would you feel about teaching in an…unorthodox fashion?" Talbot asked.

Was this obviously rich dude looking for a tutor? "I prefer a classroom setting to one on one, Mr. Talbot. If you're wanting to hire a fulltime tutor, I can give you some places to look. I'm afraid I would miss running a classroom too much."

The tutor would almost surely end up being more nanny than tutor. She knew she should probably hear the guy out since she wanted to move here but couldn't without the guarantee of a job. But she had to be honest. Her job was all she had, and she couldn't compromise on it.

"What if you could run a whole school?" Talbot asked.

She felt her eyes widen but before she could ask what he meant, Rachel Harper rushed to his side. "Not all on your own, of course. Stef, you're making it sound way bigger than it is."

"Because we're building a school from scratch," he said in low tones, as though they'd gone over this. "I'm not going to trick her."

Rachel frowned his way but was all smiles when she looked back at Sabrina. "He's making it sound like so much work. You'll have a ton of help. Everyone in town will pitch in. Paige is about to start school, and I can't stand the thought of sending her miles away every day. I want her here in Bliss."

Oh, she was starting to see the problem. "There aren't enough children in the area to support one school, much less a normal system. You would need to have elementary, middle, and high school in the same building. It's challenging but not impossible. The real problem is going to be getting funding. Is this a public school? Because funding is why most rural towns rely on bussing to larger towns."

"Money isn't a problem," Callie said with a grin. "We're going to play all the billionaires off one another. Between Stef, Seth Stark, and Caleb Burke, you'll have all the money you could want."

"Or you could say we all want what's best for our kids and we're willing to pay for it," Stef countered with a shake of his head. "Ms. Leal, I'm not trying to turn Bliss into some bigger town. I only want the kids who live here to have the best we can possibly give them. My son will be educated here. All of our kids will go to school in the town they live in. I would like for you to be a part of it. Maybe the biggest part. It would be an enormous amount of work, but think about it. You have to let your kids go every year. They move on to another class. Not these kids. These kids would be yours. A whole generation to educate."

Tears filled her eyes. A whole generation to love.

She would likely never have kids of her own, but what Talbot was offering her was the next best thing. To watch over a child from kindergarten until she sent them off to college. To be a part of their world.

"He will pay you anything you want," Rachel announced.

"Rach," Talbot huffed.

"We'll work it out." Sabrina Leal knew a good thing when it opened in front of her. A whole future flowering. She'd worried about finding a job. This wasn't a job. This was a calling. Her calling. "I'll do it. I have to finish out the year…"

"We can work remotely," Talbot said quickly as though he was afraid of losing her. "What we mostly need is your input on things like supplies and how to build the school. We'll hire some helpers, of course."

"And you'll have all the volunteers you could ever want." Rachel looked positively giddy.

"Someone want to tell me why my sister is crying?" Elisa frowned at Talbot, stepping between them.

Her sister was an Amazon of a woman. A few years older, Elisa had always protected her, sheltered her. There had been no mean sister antics or jealousy from her. Elisa had been a solid presence in her life. She'd joined the military and there had been years and miles between them, but she'd always loved her.

She got to live in the same town with her sister.

"I'm going to run the new school," Sabrina said, her voice shaking. "I mean if the fact that I'm about to burst into tears doesn't scare them off. They don't understand how much I wanted to find a way to live here with you. They don't know the gift they just gave me."

Elisa turned, and now it was her eyes shining with tears. "You're moving here? You're going to live in Bliss?"

Sabrina nodded.

"If I wasn't pregnant I would drink a whole bottle of champagne," Rachel said before turning and shouting out. "We got her!"

The whole hall erupted in cheers, but Elisa had wrapped her up in a bear hug.

"Oh, I don't have to give up my new baby?" Cassidy Meyer joined in, her husband, Mel, looking on with a big smile on his face.

Sabrina welcomed her. "I'm staying. I wouldn't want to miss your pancakes."

Sabrina stood there in the middle of the town that was to become her family and felt the love she'd been missing for years.

A brief thought of the man who'd dissed her floated through her brain, but she dismissed him. She didn't need some man to be nice to her.

This was what she needed.

This was bliss.

* * * *

Wyatt Kemp sat back, the heaviness of the night pressing in on him and the cold threatening to shake his bones.

Maybe it would be good if he looked super pathetic. Maybe Sawyer would take pity on a dude and not force him to sleep in the snow.

It was almost Christmas.

If he was back at the clubhouse... Well, it wasn't like there would be some homey, happy shit going on. Nope. Joy was not what the Colorado Horde was known for.

Years. He'd wasted years of his life because he'd tried to make his father happy and then his brother. All those years gone because he hadn't understood there was a world outside the brutal one he'd been born into. He hadn't understood it until he'd met Sawyer Hathaway.

You ever decide to get out of this hellhole, you come to my place. It's just outside of Bliss.

Just outside of Bliss, the crazy little town he'd talked about all the time. The town where Sawyer had friends and a couple of businesses he'd been forced to walk away from to try to protect his dumbass brother, who should have known better. Wes had joined the MC because it sounded cool. Wyatt had been born into it.

Damn, but he wished he'd let Sawyer save him back then. If he had, he wouldn't be standing out here in the freezing cold waiting for the man to come home, his chest aching like a motherfucker.

He hoped he hadn't bled through again.

He sat on the porch of the surprisingly large and cozy-looking cabin he'd discovered was owned by Sawyer. He'd thought about sitting at Hell on Wheels until Sawyer returned. They'd kept in touch over the years, mostly Sawyer asking him if he was ready to get out and telling him not to call him if his ass ended up in prison. Wyatt took those calls as Sawyer's sign of affection. He was pretty sure the guy didn't check up on any of his old "friends" from the Horde. They came through his bar every couple of weeks, and Sawyer was mean enough they mostly behaved. They always stayed out of town even though Wyatt had been dying to see it.

Ain't no use unless you get out of this life. All it will do is tempt a man with something he can't have. Because you cannot have the whole happy family, wife and kids thing if you're constantly under threat of going to prison.

He could, he supposed. His brother had an old lady and three kids he barely paid attention to. His brother would tell him he had it all. The family. The power. All the women he can possibly want to fuck.

Wyatt wanted more.

Of course none of it would matter if he froze to death here. What had he been thinking? Sawyer might be out with a lady. He wasn't at the bar. The nice lady there had told him Sawyer had taken the night off. He would probably be gone all night.

Wyatt was pretty sure he'd used the last of his energy to walk up this damn mountain, and now he was going to die. Freeze to death and all because he didn't have a cell phone. They'd taken his when they'd taken his bike and every cent of cash he had.

You want to leave, brother? You do it the way you came into this world. With nothing except a reminder that you are no longer family.

Wyatt took a long breath and tried to forget his "reminder." He'd survived the ceremony and hidden out for a couple of days with a woman who was club adjacent while she nursed his wounds and got him some clothes. He'd hated taking her money for the bus to Alamosa, but there'd been no other way. He couldn't stay with her because she wasn't leaving the club.

So this was the end of the road. Either Sawyer would let him in or he would die on his porch sitting in an Adirondack chair and watching the most beautiful set of stars he'd ever seen.

The sound of tires on dirt let Wyatt know he'd at least had one lucky break in all this misery.

His gut twisted because he was about to find out his fate. He was betting everything on a friendship that had been strongest years and years ago. Sawyer was kind of a dick most of the time.

Twin lights shone on the tree line in front of him, and Wyatt stood up. Sawyer was also a guy who probably shot first and asked questions never. He moved off the porch, holding his hands up.

The door opened and a big dog bounded out. Wyatt closed his eyes because he was probably about to be eaten by a guard dog. Sawyer would have the biggest, nastiest, best-trained guard dog in the world.

Wyatt managed to stay standing as the dog hit his chest. And then he felt a wet tongue on his cheek.

"Well, shit," Sawyer said with a sigh. "I probably should have taken my chance with the schoolteacher."

Wyatt opened his eyes, and the dog let its paws go back to the ground, running toward Sawyer with a happy bark. So not a guard dog. "Hey. You remember that time I saved your brother's life and you said you owed me one?"

Sawyer stepped close enough the moonlight illuminated his stark features. "You know I owe you for more than one night. You saved me, too. You finally wake up and leave the cult?"

Something eased within Wyatt. He supposed there had been a knot in his gut telling him no one would help him, that he was truly alone in the world. From the moment he'd known he had to leave, there had been a piece of himself thinking he would die. "Yeah."

Sawyer looked him over, taking in the T-shirt and track pants and sneakers. None of which fit since they'd been Lydia's ex's.

"Suppose they took everything. Your bike?"

He nodded. "A friend got me a bus ticket. I hitchhiked from Alamosa. Don't call me a dumbass because I didn't call."

"They took your cell, too." Sawyer stared at him for a moment. "How'd they take your tat? I'm betting they didn't let you laser it off. Or black it out."

"I'm okay." He had to be. There was no other way to be.

Sawyer cursed under his breath. "Acid, or did they burn it off you?"

"I'm okay." He didn't want to think about it. Or rather he didn't want to talk about it. It still hurt.

"Let's get inside. I'll call the doc. Hopefully he didn't get into the eggnog." Sawyer stepped around him, going to the door. "Don't mind the dog. She's not here forever. Just until I can find someone to take her."

The dog seemed pretty at home to Wyatt. The minute the door was open, she ran inside as though afraid of being left out in the cold. It was actually a smart idea. If he was inside, Sawyer probably wouldn't lock him out. "I don't need a doc. I'm handling it." He managed to walk in like he wasn't desperate to get warm. Cool. He was going to play this cool. It didn't matter that now he felt a little hot. Weird how he'd been cold before and now he might be sweating. "I only need a place to stay for a couple of days until I get my shit together. Maybe you could help me look for a job."

Sawyer slipped off his jacket and hung it on one of the pegs by the door. "Sure. You can get your shit together in a couple of days. And what kind of job are you thinking? Since you've been in an MC all your life."

It was stuffy in here. He took off the way too thin for this climate jacket Lydia had provided him with. A weariness struck him like a wave. "I'll find something. I only need a couple of days here, and then I'll be out of your hair. I have plans."

Sawyer stood in front of him, hands in fists on his hips. "You got no place to live, no job, no skills and you're going to...what?"

His tongue felt thick in his mouth, and his chest burned. It was like he'd held it all together with adrenaline and pure stubborn will, but now he was in this warm cabin and despite the surly attitude, he suddenly knew Sawyer wasn't going to kick him out, wasn't going to demand he kill his soul off piece by piece. Sawyer was going to be kind. It made it easy for the pain to creep back in. But also the hope. "I'm going to get a job and then I'm going to move to Bliss and find some other dumbass guy to be my best friend and we're going to find a woman to share and I'm going to be fucking happy with kids and barbecues and I'll get a truck so I can help my friends when they have to move. And my wife will yell at me to do the dishes."

Sawyer put a hand on his shoulder. "Good, Wyatt. Sounds like a good life. Buddy, you're bleeding through your shirt. Maybe we should move you to the sofa."

"I'm okay." But he wasn't. He felt the world tip and heard Sawyer curse as he caught him and maneuvered him to the couch.

Where the dog decided she could lick him healthy.

"Yeah, I'm going to need someone to get Doc out to my place," Sawyer was saying. "No, Luce, People Doc." He paused. "Unless People Doc drank the damn eggnog, and then bring out the vet. How different could it be?"

It was different, he wanted to say, but it was getting dark.

And it was okay. It really was okay.

Wyatt let go and found a certain amount of peace in oblivion.

Chapter One

Eleven months later

Sabrina Leal loved Bliss with all her heart, but she swore she was never going to get used to walking out of her cabin in the morning and being greeted by a moose.

"Bobby and Will are running late again," Del announced as she walked through the doors of the Bliss County School Grades Pre-K–12. She brushed a dusting of snow off her shoulders. Delilah was the twenty-five-year-old Stefan Talbot had allowed her to hire as a backup. Her mom was a nail tech at Polly's Cut and Curl, and she'd thought she would move out of Bliss but had been thrilled when this job had come up. She was working on her master's degree in preschool education, going to class online and driving into Alamosa to Adams State when she needed to.

Sabrina blessed the day Delilah Manning came into her life because she would never have been able to handle these kids alone. They were a joyous handful, but some of them were excellent at sneaking away. Charlie Hollister-Wright was an escape artist. "I'm sure there was an experiment they were involved in. Or they were talking to a girl. Well, Will might have been. Send them back here when they get in. I've got their lesson queued up on the main computer. Who's in for the morning session with our babies?"

It was what she called the preschool class. It was by far the largest of the classes she had. Will and Bobby Farley were her only high school students, and honestly, they were so smart they only needed someone to direct their work and bring in tutors when they had trouble. This was where having a board of directors with seemingly endless pockets came into play. She'd brought in a professor from the University of Michigan's math department to Zoom with the boys every Thursday while they were taking advanced calculus.

There was morning session and afternoon session, with lunch and a play break in between. Because the school was so small, the parents handled lunch every day. The "trios," as Sabrina called them, handled those duties. There were more than romantic threesomes in Bliss. Friendships seemed to come in trios, too. Rachel Harper, Callie Hollister-Wright, and Jennifer Talbot handled Mondays and Wednesdays. Laura Kincaid-Briggs, Holly Burke, and Nell Flanders handled Tuesdays and Thursdays. Fridays were taken care of by Beth McNamara-O'Malley and her two friends, Hope Glen-Bennett and Gemma Wells—she didn't need all those extra freaking names to remind her she's married—brought in food on Fridays. Hope was pregnant with her first child, but while Gemma had declared her marriage a child-free zone, she was actually good with the ones who weren't her own. She also declared it wasn't fair to leave her out of the whole obvious friendship-bonding thing just because her womb was closed.

Gemma was a lot. Sabrina liked her. She worked with Elisa and always had the best gossip.

"Nell and Henry have a whole lesson planned on recycling," Del said, slipping behind her desk. "Don't worry. I looked over it. It's fun, not an hour-long lecture that will put the toddlers to sleep long before their naps."

They had a toddler class and a kindergarten/first-grade class. There were also two kids in middle school and a fourth grader. It was a juggling act to make sure everyone got what they needed, but Sabrina had to admit this was the most fun she'd ever had working. There was a challenge here. Some of the kids in the area were still going to classes in Monte Vista, but a couple had already come around.

"Good." Sabrina sat back, glancing at the clock. Another thirty minutes and then the chaos would begin.

Luckily she liked a little chaos. The fun kind.

"So how did it go at Trio last night?" Del asked, not looking up from her laptop.

Sabrina sighed. The night before had not gone the way she'd hoped it would. It was stupid and she was going to get over it, but she was still thinking about the man from the Christmas party. The asshole. Mr. Nope wasn't going to ask her out, but she wanted the feeling she'd gotten when she'd seen him. She hadn't gotten it the night before. "It was nice."

Del looked up, a brow rising. "It was supposed to be hot. It was supposed to be a date."

She'd let herself get set up by her sister, who thought she might like spending time with the two deputies who worked part time for Bliss County. Knox Miller and Marshall Lethe. They normally worked in Creede but handled some late shifts for the Bliss County Sheriff's department. "They were nice."

Del winced. "So no spark?"

Sabrina let her head fall back on a groan. "No. No spark." She brought her head back up. "I don't know what's wrong with me. They were nice, but I didn't feel anything. I think maybe I can't feel anything. Maybe the whole romantic thing isn't for me."

It was why she was fixated on Mr. Nope. He'd been the first time she'd felt something for a man in a long time. She'd buried that part of herself deep, and she was still trying to get out. It wasn't like she believed Mr. Nope was something special. He was obviously not for her, but she wanted to feel a spark again.

"Of course it is. You simply haven't found the right guys yet."

Sabrina snorted at the thought. "The fact that you make *guy* plural is still so odd to me."

Del shrugged. "My mom would be way happier if she had two guys to yell at. My dad would be happier if he had a friend he could hide behind when he screws up. It's one of the reasons I decided to stay here instead of looking for a job in Alamosa or Colorado Springs after I finished my degree."

"I thought it was Stef Talbot's signing bonus."

Del's lips curled up. "Mine came from Seth Stark. And I got him to pay for my Internet for as long as I'm employed. It's so great having competitive billionaires around. But part of the reason I wanted to stay is having the option to be in a Bliss kind of relationship. Not that I have time right now. Between this job and doing all the online work to get my master's, I'm swamped. My mom thinks it's ridiculous I'm doing post-grad work. She says it's my rebellion. I think she would have been happier if I'd moved straight from high school right to a table beside her at Polly's salon."

"You didn't want to be a nail tech. I think you being dedicated to higher education is great for everyone in this town. My mom wanted me to go into the Army," Sabrina admitted. "She told me if it was good enough for my sister and her, it should be good enough for me. And that's why I had to pay every dime of college myself. She did let me live in her garage apartment, though. I paid rent, and I like to think of listening to her complain about my life as extra rent. Speaking of rent, I have to go by Marie's later today. I've got electrical issues, and I am not going to make my brother-in-law do the work for free. Marie is tight fisted, but I swear I'll get a lawyer if I have to."

She'd lived in Cassidy and Mel's guest room through the summer but wanted to be closer to the school when it opened. So she'd rented a two-bedroom cabin in the valley. The sheriff and his wife and partner were her closest neighbors. She had the most peaceful view ever and faulty wiring. She'd asked in writing for someone to come out, but Marie had been ignoring her.

"Oh, Marie isn't the tight-fisted one," Del replied. "She's the agent. Marie is kind of the go between. There are a couple of people who actually own the cabins for rent, but they all use Marie as their property manager. I know Stef and Seth both own multiple properties. Doc Burke rents out a couple of cabins around town."

"So I can yell at one of the billionaires? It's probably Doc. He forgets things all the time. If it's not someone's blood pressure reading, he ignores it." She'd figured out the town very quickly. It didn't hurt that her sister knew everyone.

"Probably," Del agreed. "Or it's one of the Texans." Her blonde bob shook. "They've been buying up land here ever since that writer broke down and ended up buying a cabin."

Sabrina knew the story well. "She's my sister's sister-in-law. Or she's married to her brother-in-law. It gets confusing when there are six people involved. And I don't think it's the Texans. They come up way too often for anything more than short-term rentals. I've got a three-year lease on mine. It's well kept, with the exception of the lights flickering on and off at the weirdest times. It's kind of creepy. I want it fixed."

"Well, you should go straight to the source," Del advised, closing her laptop and standing. "And we need to watch the weather. I've heard there's a bad storm coming in tomorrow morning. If it's too bad, I'll come by and pick you up. You shouldn't drive your sedan in this kind of storm. You need to buy a snowmobile. It's kind of like the bike of Colorado."

"Oh, I don't want you to go out of your way," Sabrina replied. "I assure you my sister will make sure I get into town okay. Or my... He said I could call him Dad. Is it weird I kind of want to call him Dad?"

"Mel Hughes? Yes, it's weird," Del replied with a grin. "Everything about Mel is weird, and he's also a great guy. He's been a dad to most of the kids who grew up here in Bliss, so I think it's wonderful he's got a couple of kids of his own now. Look, he's not your biological father, but he is your sister's. If she wants to share, I say go for it. Mel will treat you like family. Mel has never needed blood to love a person. He's got a big heart. As long as you're not an alien. Do you like beets?"

Sabrina laughed, something she did often now. "I do. And I eat them all the time. I think my blood pressure's down. So no one will think it's weird I call a man I met a few months ago Dad and a woman who has nothing real to do with my bio family Mom?"

"They'll love you for it," Del replied with a shrug. "Welcome to Bliss, sister. I'm off to teach several surly preteens about past participles. See you at lunch."

She turned and walked out as Nell Flanders was walking in. She was a pretty woman in her mid-thirties with a toddler strapped to her back. Nell believed in baby carrying. Along with a lot of other things she was vocal about.

"Good morning, Sabrina. I left Henry in the classroom to do welcomes," Nell said with a smile. "We brought the snack for the day. I made vegan muffins. I thought I'd bring one in for the teacher."

Nell knew how to make some excellent vegan food. Sabrina wasn't a vegetarian, but she also wouldn't turn her nose up at food that didn't contain animal products. She'd had Nell's tofu cake, and it was delicious. She took the muffin. "Thanks. I was going to eat a protein bar. I'm a waste in the kitchen."

It was true. She could burn water. Most nights she ate a sandwich or microwaved a bowl of soup. She was sick of protein bars.

"Well, if you ever want to learn vegan cooking, I'm your girl," Nell offered. "Now I overheard you talking about going to see Marie after school. You're having trouble with your cabin? Is it anything we can help with?"

Everyone here helped. They all pitched in. She'd already attended a party where they'd erected a barn out at the Circle G, a fundraiser for some poor dog named Princess Two, who needed a ton of meds, and been to the opening of Alexei Markov's new office in town. The Bliss Mental Wellness Center was cozy, and Sabrina was thinking about going to the woman Alexei had imported as the second therapist in the practice.

In fact, her first big town event had been a baking party for the Harper family. Apparently when someone had a baby around here, the whole community made casseroles and easy meals for the family for the first month. She'd brought important moral support to the group baking effort, all the while thinking her mother would have told Rachel if she wanted free food she should go to a church and beg. Or she would say she should have kept her legs shut.

Yeah, this was why she should go to the clinic. Her mother's voice still dominated her life, still brought a cloud over everything. She'd changed five times before her date last night because she could hear her mother's criticism of everything she put on. "Thanks so much. I will definitely think about it. As for the bad electricity, I'm going to force my landlord to take care of it. I'm going to tell Marie I won't take another day of my landlord putting me off. I might be one small part of this person's wealth, but they owe me some respect as a renter."

Nell seemed to think about that for a moment. "Well, you'll have to wait until Marie gets back from New York. She and Teeny are there because Logan and Seth's wife, Georgia, went into labor early. They'd been planning to have the baby here in Bliss, but life made their kid an Upper East Sider. I hope it doesn't affect his ideas on climate change. Anyway, I know who your landlord is if you want to talk to him yourself. Though he's on the crabby side. Don't blame him. It's only because no one's pulled the thorn out of his paw yet."

Sometimes Nell could be hard to follow. "He has a thorn?" Actually, maybe that wasn't the question to ask. "He has a paw?"

Nell nodded sagely. "Oh, yes. It comes from childhood, and perhaps the time he spent away from Bliss. He holds all of his emotions very tightly. He looks like he's made from granite, but he's not. There's a soft heart in there. I think he has abandonment issues. His father left early on, and his mom died. He was raised by his grandfather, who died a couple of years back, and his two brothers didn't hang around. But now he has a friend. I'm almost certain he knows Sawyer from his…more interesting days, but he seems like a ray of sunshine."

"Sawyer?" She kind of thought she'd heard the name before but she couldn't put a face to it. Why did it sound so familiar?

Nell nodded. "Sawyer Hathaway. He lives on one of the mountains. I could go with you to talk to him if you like."

She didn't need anyone as an emotional support human. She was an adult, and she would likely be alone all of her life. The school-marm wallflower, all things lonely woman, and it was time she accepted her independence. "No, but I would appreciate directions."

Nell told her how to get to her landlord's home.

After school, Sabrina would make her stand.

* * * *

"So we're like a Waffle House in hurricane country." Wyatt hopped down and moved to the back of the Jeep where all the supplies they'd picked up in Alamosa were stacked. The snow crunched beneath his boots. There was already a couple of inches on the ground, but according to everyone he talked to this was nothing compared to what they'd wake up to in the morning.

It was weird to think he wouldn't be spending tonight at the bar. Hell on Wheels had become as much his home as this cabin.

Sawyer popped the back open and gave him a frown. "Waffle House?"

His best friend could be dense from time to time. Although he had to allow Sawyer hadn't spent much time out of Southern Colorado.

"It's how people on the coast know if the hurricane is serious rather than media hyped. If the Waffle House closes, you get your butt out of the way. Same for Hell on Wheels. If Hell on Wheels is closed, you know it's going to be bad."

Sawyer hefted a case of bottled water. The well water they were on sometimes froze up during bad storms, he'd explained. "Well, the last thing I need is to have to deal with a bunch of drunk assholes who can't get home."

"I thought we decided we were going to call them valued customers." He was working on Sawyer's business skills. Not that Wyatt himself had any, but he was learning. He'd found the library in Del Norte and checked out books on business and self-help and finance. It had become apparent to Wyatt there were certain parts of Sawyer's surprisingly varied business portfolio Sawyer didn't enjoy running. Which was actually most of it.

Sawyer preferred to be in his workshop. It was his fortress of solitude. Wyatt was pretty certain almost no one else in his life knew how dedicated to creating furniture made of reclaimed wood the man was. He sold each piece online for ridiculously high prices but always had someone else meet the buyer.

Like being an artist would mar his terrible reputation.

Wyatt was working on that, too. Sawyer was awesome, but he had definite abandonment issues and a deep-seated fear of rejection. He'd worked a couple of psych books in, too.

Sawyer's dark eyes rolled and he headed for the cabin, the snow starting to fall in earnest. Wyatt grabbed two sacks of groceries, including the ingredients for the beef stew he was making. Sawyer also ate like crap before Wyatt came around. Well, Wyatt had, too, but he was on a self-improvement journey, and he'd been told by Doc Burke a healthy diet was important, and bar food wasn't something a man should live on.

"They're pains in my ass if they get stuck up on this mountain for the next four days. You were here during an easy winter," Sawyer explained as Bella started barking at the door as though letting them know they'd stupidly left her behind and what the hell? "Sometimes these storms can last for days, and we'll be digging out longer. It's better down in the valley. They'll be able to get around using snowmobiles, but up here on the mountain it's dangerous. If the drifts are as bad as I suspect they'll be, we'll have to stay put until they can clear the road, and that will likely be into next week."

He'd survived last winter, though he'd mostly only gone from the bar to the cabin and back. It had been months before he'd actually gone into town with Sawyer. Months later before he'd ventured down himself.

And seen the most beautiful woman in the world.

She was the new schoolteacher and very important, one of the bartenders at Trio had explained as though trying to warn him away. He didn't need to be warned away then. He hadn't been ready, but now he rather thought he was. He'd read a lot and figured out what he wanted.

Her.

And Sawyer. A real Bliss relationship.

The only problem was Sawyer was still Sawyer, and Sabrina Leal had no idea either of them existed.

But he was worthy of love and affection. Worthy of getting what he needed.

The other place he frequented was the Bliss Mental Wellness Center. Having Alexei Markov in his head was way nicer than his brother's voice. His brother told him he was a fucking moron who deserved nothing. Alexei sometimes told him he was good boy who had been twisted by elemental criminals. In a thick Russian accent.

He loved it here.

Sawyer didn't know it, but Wyatt was never going to leave. One of the things he'd learned was he had to work for the future he wanted. In his younger years, "work" meant beating the shit out of whoever his brother asked him to or getting his own ass kicked. But he wanted more now.

He hoped no one ever found out what he'd done. His last act before demanding out. His final crime against his family.

"You should be happy you have all the other businesses." Wyatt wasn't going to dive into the past. Not when the future was so happily in front of him. Once the storm passed. "Are the others going to be okay without having the bar open? Doesn't Lark have a mom in assisted living? I know Gil's wife has a job, but they probably need the money."

He was going to get the man to admit what Wyatt had already learned. Sawyer couldn't begin to accept the truth about himself unless he was willing to admit it out loud. That was the first step. He would admit he had a heart, and they could start opening it up.

"They'll be fine," was all he said as he opened the door and Bella pounced. "Damn it, Bella, down. You know your name should have been Damn It."

Wyatt had saved the poor dog from the indignity. After a month of living with the dog with no name, he'd started calling her Bella because he'd read it was a popular name for girl dogs. All the dogs in the MC compound he'd lived in had been named things like Bitch and Satan and Butthole. Bella had a more classic ring to it. "Come on, Bella. Let the mean dad in."

"I am not her dad. I'm the guy she imprinted on, and now I can't get rid of her," Sawyer groused.

Sure, he was. All complacent pet owners regularly made their dog's food themselves because the pet they didn't really want had a touchy belly. The man was in denial. Still, he couldn't say it out loud. He needed Sawyer to figure this out on his own. So he played dumb. "Sidney's got a kid. She doesn't have anyone. How are they going to be okay losing almost a week's paycheck?"

Sawyer groaned and put the water down. "Because I'll fucking pay them anyway. Let it go, man."

He would. For now. He headed back out for the case of beer they'd bought. The wind had picked up, and the snow was thick now. It was stunningly beautiful here. All of Colorado was, but here they were right on the continental divide, and this high up everything felt fresh and clean and new. Like he felt.

Wyatt let his head fall back, snow landing on his face.

"You having one of those moments?" Sawyer asked, walking past him.

"I'm just happy to be here, man." Months of therapy had cracked him open wide, and he couldn't quite stop feeling lucky, feeling like he had a real chance at something that had felt so far from him before. "I know you say this storm is going to be dangerous, but it's so beautiful."

"Well, anyone stuck out in it now is going to be a beautiful corpse," Sawyer replied, grabbing the last of the groceries and closing the back of the Jeep. "And it's not a big deal I pay them even though the bar's closed. My grandfather was smart enough to diversify. He told me to never count on one source of income. When he had money, he invested it. When his money made more money, he bought land and invested in businesses. When he died he left behind more money than we could ever need. Well, not Wes. From what I've heard he's already gone through all of his, and I have no idea what Jimmy did with his portion. We split everything three ways, with me buying out their parts of the businesses. It was lean for a while, but I'm back to being comfortable."

Damn, he hadn't meant to remind Sawyer of everything he'd lost. "Well, I'm just glad you're able to take care of your people."

"You're getting paid, too, if you're worried about money."

Of course he would go there. "I might be if you allowed me to pay rent."

Sawyer frowned. "You won't be here long, and like you said, I owe you."

It had been almost a year. They had different definitions of the word *long*. "Sure, I'm going to start looking for a rental real soon."

Sawyer's brows rose. "Really? This is a bad time to look for a cabin to rent. I think you should wait until the spring at least. And you should think about finding a place close to the bar. Even when the snow's not so bad it can be hard to get to. That little bike you bought won't handle the snow and ice the way it needs to. You should probably stay put until you have enough money for a proper SUV."

And this was why he thought his plans might work. He would spend this weekend softening the guy up and then suggest they go down to the valley and deal with some of the tenant complaints they'd recently had. He'd taken over that part of the business, too. Sawyer owned a total of five properties in the area, including his own cabin. Marie Warner was the go between and almost as surly as Sawyer. Wyatt had figured out how to soften her up, though. He went into town once a week to meet with her and sat and had tea with her and her wife, Teeny. He asked about her grandkids and how the business was going. He had a whole checklist of things to ask people to indicate he was truly interested in their lives.

The weird thing turned out to be he *was* interested in their lives. He kind of loved gossip, and Bliss thrived on it.

He wished he had more gossip on Sabrina beyond she was sweet and smart and probably dating the guys from Creede. If she was into law enforcement guys, it would make things harder, but he intended for her to never see the Wyatt he used to be. Only the man he was becoming.

"I will definitely take your advice. Besides, I liked last winter." Wyatt followed him back to the porch, but Bella had gotten out and was doing zoomies in the snow. "It was nice and quiet, and the cabin is warm."

Sawyer snorted. "You liked not getting your ass handed to you on a daily basis and not living in a place where the cops could invade at any moment and take you to jail."

All true. "I also liked playing games and learning to cook and reading books without someone telling me the state of my sexuality is tied to illiteracy. It's also nice to not listen to some dude screwing in the room next to me. The dorms there had paper-thin walls. Some of the things I heard… They were extremely wrong."

"Well, you didn't get nearly molested by a moose there," Sawyer pointed out, his lips coming up in a grin.

It had been a weird morning. Wyatt had been standing in the yard, taking in the morning air, and then there was a moose licking the back of his neck. Scared the hell out of him. "I don't know. Some of those guys got so drunk they didn't care whose bed they fell into. And one of them liked to snuggle."

Sawyer laughed, the sound booming in the quiet of the mountains. He put a hand on Wyatt's shoulder. "I'm glad you got out, brother. Come on. Let's get settled in. I'm starving. I'll see if the Internet's still up. Maybe we can play some Xbox."

Bella barked and ran past them, zooming around the cabin.

"Bella, come inside," Sawyer shouted with a shake of his head. "You would think that dog is a damn husky." When Bella didn't come back around the other side, Sawyer set down the bags and huffed. "She'll freeze out here."

He stomped off, and Wyatt took the rest of the groceries inside before heading out since Sawyer wasn't back with Bella. He hoped she hadn't run off chasing a bunny or a deer or something. The sky was getting dark, and the snow was coming down like a thunderstorm now.

He rounded the cabin and then stopped because Sawyer wasn't alone.

Standing there in the middle of the drive leading from the road down the mountain was Sabrina Leal. She had on jeans and sneakers and a coat that wasn't anywhere close to warm enough. She was shivering.

"We have trouble," Sawyer said.

Wyatt felt a smile cross his face.

This was the best kind of trouble. The kind he wanted to get into. Maybe forever.

Chapter Two

Sawyer rounded the cabin, praying Bella hadn't gotten too far. The dog was going to be the death of him one day. She had not a single survival instinct that didn't involve being so cute some dumbass human saved her. He'd caught her trying to make friends with Maurice the same day Maurice christened Wyatt's neck. The moose had some serious saliva. What he hadn't told Wyatt was the myth about the moose.

Maurice welcomed people who belonged in Bliss.

Wyatt belonged here, and Sawyer kind of dreaded the moment he found a place of his own and met a friend who wasn't a curmudgeonly asshole and settled down with some nice lady into his white picket fence life.

Actually, a fence would be a good wedding present. Nice. Ornate. He could put a pretty finish on it. He always ended up making a chair or something. He was pretty sure Ty was going to tie the knot with Lucy soon. With Michael, for some reason.

Where the hell was Bella?

The cold was getting through his heavy jacket, the snow coating everything now. He heard Bella bark and looked to the drive.

Where a woman stood, hat around her head, shivering as she reached out to pet the dog's head.

"Hey, sweetie," she said in the voice all women seemed to use on dogs and kids. It was lilting and soothing. "Is your mom or dad around?"

Damn it. He was not a dog dad. He moved in closer, ready to start a monster of a lecture because what the hell was this woman doing walking down the road wearing a light jacket in the middle of a blizzard? And she didn't have boots on. She was wearing freaking canvas sneakers. He could see clearly they were already wet and would cost her a toe or two if she stayed out here much longer. She wasn't prepared for the weather in any way.

Then her head came up, and he realized he was the one who was in trouble. So much fucking trouble.

He stood there when he should run and lock the door because that spark hit him again, every bit as strong as the first time.

The woman from the Christmas party last year was standing in the snow. In the middle of a terrible blizzard.

Her eyes widened as she looked at him. "Hi. Uhm, I'm looking for Sawyer Hathaway. I was on my way up the road but I swerved off, and now my car is kind of in a ditch and I think I left my cell phone at school."

"There's a school in Bliss?" He should have gotten together with his friends more often. Or at all. He'd pulled away from them, and now he didn't even know there was a school.

She nodded. "Yes. Uhm, could I use your cell?"

Wyatt came up behind him.

"We have trouble," Sawyer said, glancing his way. His idiot best friend was grinning.

Yeah, he might not ever tell him, but Wyatt had become his best friend. Ick. He sounded like a high school kid.

She made him feel like one, and it was a problem.

"Hi," Wyatt said like they were at a bar looking to pick up some random woman not about to make the horrific mistake of getting stuck inside a smallish cabin with her for the entirety of a blizzard.

Snowed in. They were getting snowed in, and he would be forced to be close to her and to keep his hands off her.

He pulled his cell. No bars. How could he have no bars? Wasn't he closer to the freaking satellites or whatever it was that pinged cell phone calls around?

Of course communications could be hard in a blizzard.

"Hi," Sabrina said as Bella danced around her knees. "I was hoping to get a little help."

"Absolutely," Wyatt said, hurrying toward her. "Let's get you inside first. You need to warm up."

"No," Sawyer said before he could even think about the words coming out of his mouth.

The woman's eyes flared with hurt.

Not what he'd meant to do. "I mean we only have so much time to get you off the mountain. They'll close the road soon, and you'll be stuck here."

Stuck with him. Stuck inside, trying to stay warm. If the power went out, body heat was the only way to go. Cuddled up naked under covers with those soft breasts pressed to his chest because his arms would be around her since skin to skin was also the best way to preserve warmth. And obviously sex created heat.

Nope. No way. He was not sleeping with a soft, sweet woman who would be utterly horrified at his background. Not to mention the shit Wyatt had been through. Wyatt's background would send her running.

What the hell was she doing here?

"I'll drive you back into town." Getting her home was the best move. Get her out of here and back to her own people, who likely never had to join criminal organizations so they could save their brothers. Her people were probably tourists watching the weather like it was something magical.

Wyatt looked at him like he'd grown an extra head. "Uh, if you try to get her back to town, you'll be stuck there. If you can even get down the mountain at this point." He shrugged out of his jacket and approached the gorgeous, shouldn't-be-here, big mistake woman. "Here. Come on inside and get warm and we'll figure out how to help you."

Panic. This was what panic felt like. He had stared down entire gangs of strapped dudes ready to murder him, but the idea of sharing a cabin with a petite woman sent him into a tailspin.

Because he wouldn't be able to keep his hands off her.

What if she ended up liking Wyatt?

WHO THE FUCK WAS HE?

He had to get her off his mountain. He was allergic to her or something.

"Nah. Get into the Jeep. I'll take you back down," he said, hearing the desperation in his voice. He cleared his throat and tried to sound like he wasn't a complete asshole. Which was hard because he was. "We'll get your car going once the storm clears out. I'll sleep at the bar for a couple of days. No problem."

That was friendly, right?

Wyatt rolled his eyes as he settled his coat over her shoulders. "Come on, Ms. Leal. Let's get you warm."

"My car is kind of blocking the road, actually," she said to Wyatt, not paying Sawyer any mind.

"I can handle your car," he heard himself saying as he followed them up the steps and into the cabin, Bella bouncing along like this was the greatest thing that had ever happened in the history of all time. "I can tow you all the way down."

Wyatt closed the door behind him. "Why don't you call the sheriff and see if it's even possible to get to the road at this point? I'd like for someone to know she's here."

The sheriff. Yes. There was zero way the sheriff left a sweet tourist hanging out with two dudes he was waiting for a reason to arrest. The sheriff could save him. He moved to the landline and dialed the non-emergency number. Although maybe he should call 911. Maybe they would send a chopper to rescue her.

"My sister is Deputy Leal," she said, her teeth still chattering.

Wyatt hesitated for the first time. "She's a deputy?"

Sawyer snapped his fingers, pointing Wyatt's way. "Yes. Apparently, yes, she is. I'll get her on the line."

He took the headset and walked away from the living room so the deputy's sister couldn't hear how desperate he was to get rid of her. Wyatt was starting a fire in the fireplace, and she now had a blanket around her.

"Bliss County Sheriff's Office, how can I help you?" Gemma Wells' no-nonsense voice came over the line.

"Hey, Gemma. This is Sawyer Hathaway. I own the bar on the mountain west of Nell and Henry's place."

"Yes, Sawyer, I know who you are. What can I do for you? I'm going to warn you no one's here. They're all out closing down the roads. If you're complaining about not being able to get to your cabin, well, you should have known better. Hunker down at the bar or get your ass to Nell and Henry's. They'll put you up for the night."

"No, that's not the problem. I'm at my cabin."

"Good," she said. "Stay there. We'll dig you out in a couple of days."

The woman was not listening to him. "I'm not alone. There's a woman here, and she can't stay for days."

A snort came over the line. "Are you serious? You have a hookup who waited too long to leave and now you want us to… What? Send a chopper up to save you from some one-night stand?"

"I absolutely did not sleep with her. She just showed up. I don't know why she's here, but you have to come and get her. She says she's some deputy's sister. The new one. The one who's living with Hale and Van."

"What?" Gemma suddenly sounded interested. "Are you telling me Sabrina Leal is stranded on the mountain and she's going to have to stay with you and the new guy?"

Wyatt wasn't really new. He'd been around almost… Damn. Had it been a year? "Yes. That is what I'm telling you."

"The schoolteacher is going to have to shack up with the MC boys?"

Schoolteacher? She was the new schoolteacher? He'd known she was *a* schoolteacher but now she was *the* schoolteacher. It was practically a stereotype. The sweet schoolteacher with the generous hips and soft breasts and lush mouth. Okay, maybe not a stereotype except in his wet dreams. MC boys? "I have not been in an MC for over ten years, Gemma. Do you want me to remind you about the time you ripped out Catherine's fake hair, or whatever it was you ended up clutching in the viral video we've all seen?"

Gemma had a colorful past herself. At least his hadn't been captured for the Internet.

She huffed. "It was Christina Big Tits, and it was her actual hair. And good point. Oh, there's the sheriff. Nate, Sabrina's stuck on Sawyer's mountain, and he's got his panties in a serious wad about it. Like he's a fainting, nineteenth-century virgin whose reputation is about to be ruined, and he won't be able to go to the marriage mart."

She was frustratingly sarcastic. "I am not. But you bring up a point. The schoolteacher certainly shouldn't be left alone for the weekend with two men."

A low chuckle came over the line as the sheriff took over. "Well, we wouldn't be Bliss if she didn't. So Sabrina's at your place and you want her gone. Interesting."

"It is not. I am merely trying to look out for her."

"Nah. You're trying to keep your distance. Like you did at the Christmas party last year. You know we're still talking about it. We have a couple of bets going," the sheriff said.

"I might want to change mine," Gemma said, proving they had him on speaker phone.

A pit opened in his gut. "Sheriff, you cannot leave the county schoolteacher with two dangerous men."

"Dangerous?" He could practically see the sheriff's eyes rolling. "From what I can tell the two of you are only dangerous to a bucket of hot wings. You know for a man of your reputation, you turned out to be a softie. Look, man, this storm is serious, and don't tell me I should call Del Norte and ask to borrow their chopper. It's not happening. We're in a bad situation, and you and Wyatt can take care of Sabrina. I'll let everyone know she's safe and warm, and we'll come clear the road as soon as possible. Now, if you have a serious emergency, call me. Until then, let me give you some advice on how to take care of a lady…"

"Sheriff, do you know what's going to happen if you leave her here?" Sawyer asked.

Wyatt pried the phone out of his hand. "She'll be kept warm and well fed. Don't worry about us, Sheriff. We'll take excellent care of her. We're stocked up and ready to hunker down for a couple of days. You get back to your important work and thank you." Wyatt paused and then a smile crossed his face. "You think so?" Another pause. "Well, we'll see about that. Give her sister this number so she can call. I think everyone will feel better if they can communicate. Thanks. Yes. We'll let you know. Huh, I never thought of myself as sweet. I like it. Bye, Sheriff."

Sawyer watched in horror as Wyatt hung up. "What the hell did you do?"

Wyatt started back for the kitchen. "Saved you from acting like a fool. She's a nice lady and she's here, and we're not shoving her out into the night to die. Deal with it. Also, according to the sheriff, there's always a sweet one and a hardass in relationships like this. Guess which one you are? Now, do we have any wine? She looks like a Cab girl. I think it would go nicely with the stew. I'm going to put it on and find something for her to change into. Her clothes are damp. I think maybe one of my shirts. It'll be like a dress. What can I make for dessert?"

Sawyer watched him walk away.

He was fucking doomed. Doomed.

* * * *

He was an asshole. Sabrina had zero idea how she'd managed to get here. Well, she did. She'd procrastinated for so long she had to fix the problem no matter what.

She'd thought she would have more time. The snow wasn't supposed to get truly bad until nightfall. She'd gotten caught up in talking to a couple of the parents at pickup, and she should have followed through with her original instinct to go to her sister's, steal a bottle of wine, and head home to watch *Bridgerton* for the fifteenth time. But no, she'd decided to pull up her big-girl panties and get the job done so she wouldn't think about it all weekend since she knew she definitely wouldn't get up the mountain tomorrow.

And then she'd decided it was fine. Her car could totally make it up the mountain. She'd driven in the foothills of the Blue Ridge Mountains plenty of times.

This was no foothill.

Now her car was nestled against a tree, half on and half off the road, and she was stuck with Mr. Nope and his bestie, who seemed to have gotten all the charm.

Next time she was procrastinating.

If there was any way off this mountain, she would find it. She shivered in front of the fire as both men walked back into the living room of the surprisingly cozy cabin.

The not-asshole one gave her a smile that threatened to melt her insides. He was a hottie. "Well, the sheriff knows you're here, and he's going to have your sister call. I think you should take a warm shower and change clothes and I'll get you a glass of whatever we have while I make us all some supper. We'll be warm before you know it."

"I want to know why she's here," the asshole grumbled.

"She obviously got lost," Not Asshole replied, sending Asshole a stare before flashing a movie-star-worthy smile her way.

Now he wanted to make her sound like an idiot. "I came up to find someone."

Asshole crossed his arms over his muscular chest. "No one lives up here except me. You're on the wrong mountain. You probably want the one closer to Creede. Lots of folks live there."

Not Asshole shook his head. "I live here, too. And if she got confused, it's understandable. All the mountains kind of look alike. Maybe we should all introduce ourselves since we're going to be stuck here for a couple of days."

"Days?" This was worse than she'd imagined. She was going to be stuck here with two of the most beautiful men she'd ever seen, and one of them obviously hated her on sight. Asshole, despite his assholiness, was a stunning man. He was at least six and a half feet of gorgeous man, with dark hair and eyes. And Not Asshole was his counterpoint. Sandy hair that curled slightly and angelic blue eyes. His strength was lean where Asshole was big muscles. Both of them made her feel petite and dainty, and she was absolutely neither of those things. Well, she was short and knew damn well her curves weren't exactly fashionable these days. "I need to get back to the valley. I have school tomorrow."

"No one's going to school tomorrow. Maybe Monday, but we'll still be here. You're almost three thousand feet up from town. The weather hits different this high up," Asshole said with a dour look. "We'll be about two days behind the town. Maybe I can stay in the shop."

"You are not staying in the shop. It's not heated," Not Asshole shot back.

Were they a couple? They argued like one. "I can stay out there. All I need is a sleeping bag. I don't want to disrupt whatever the two of you have going." She needed to be an adult about this. "I'm Sabrina Leal. I'm new in town. I already know his name. It's Mr. Nope."

A young adult.

Not Asshole's smile notched up. "Well, I guess that makes me Mr. Hell Yeah." He held out a hand. "Seriously, though, I'm Wyatt Kemp, and this is my friend Sawyer Hathaway, and the dancing girl is named Bella."

The dog was dancing. She seemed to be a black and tan ball of pure motion.

She took his hand despite the sinking feeling taking over her whole being. She'd been hoping Not Asshole was her landlord, but naturally her luck was running true. Warmth immediately flashed through her as she touched Wyatt's big hand. The dog sat back on her haunches, tongue lolling out as she watched the human interactions. When Wyatt let go of her hand, she felt the cold again. "Bella seems sweet. And I'm sorry for the trouble. I thought the storm wasn't coming in until later tonight. I needed to talk to my landlord about how he's been ignoring my reasonable requests."

Sawyer's frown went from what-are-you-doing-here disdain to what-the-fuck. He seemed to have an endless repertoire of frowns. "Requests? You're a tenant?"

So he was an attentive businessman. "Yes. I signed a lease months ago for the cabin on Aspen Street. I've been complaining about the electricity for a couple of weeks."

Sawyer shrugged. "Electricity's fine. It's haunted. Marie left out the haunted part in her description, didn't she? See, I thought we should disclose the whole haunted thing, but Marie is a tricky one. The valley cabin hadn't been occupied for a while, so Marie didn't tell you. Also, I haven't gotten any complaints." He turned to Wyatt, his eyes narrowing. "Have you gotten complaints?"

Wyatt simply smiled. "I bet they're on my desk at the bar. I'm so sorry. I've been swamped lately. I will absolutely get someone on it."

Was he lying to her? Why would he lie to her?

"Sure," Sawyer said under his breath. "But it won't work 'cause there's nothing wrong with the electricity. It's the ghost. Happens a lot around here. Nothing to worry about. My grandpa told me it's a friendly spirit. It likes to play around. That's all."

Was he freaking kidding? "You're saying my cabin is haunted?"

Sawyer nodded. "Yeah." He seemed to think of something, and his expression brightened for a moment. "You want to move? Because I've heard there are some nice places up in Creede."

She felt her eyes narrow. Now he was pushing all her buttons. If he thought he could scare her off, he was in for an awakening. Normally she was polite and tried to be charming, but she knew how to deal with a bully. Every teacher did. "Or I could sue you for nondisclosure of alien life-forms."

"What?" Wyatt asked, his angelic eyes widening.

She wasn't about to get lost in those eyes. No way. She focused all her mad-teacher energy on Sawyer. "Check it. It's on the books. In the town of Bliss, Colorado, it is illegal to sell or rent property without a full alien life-form disclosure. They have a form and everything. Did you file with the city?"

In this case the "city" was Cassidy Meyer, who kept impeccable records.

He stared at her for a moment. Yes, he was definitely giving her a you're-a-moron frown. "It's a ghost not an alien. Granddad thinks it's probably the guy who originally built the place back in the eighties. Definitely a ghost."

He needed to understand she was not playing this game with him. "Oh, it'll be an alien by the time I'm done. Blinking lights? Alien interference. The crackling sound I keep hearing? The alien ship must not have all its sound dampeners on. The fact that the lights go out for precisely two minutes every day at 7:02 p.m.? Aliens keep a tidy schedule, my friend. I will type up a report, and I assure you my new dad will take you down. I'm not joking. I'll tell my dad you sold me an alien stronghold and he will never stop."

Sawyer actually took a step back. "Mel? Are you talking about Mel Hughes? He doesn't have any kids."

Wyatt sent him a what-the-hell look. "Do you listen to anyone? The new deputy is his bio kid, and Mel's adopting this one. I mean in theory. I don't think he's legally adopting her. You need to get on Nextdoor sometime."

"What is Nextdoor?" Sawyer seemed deeply confused. "I don't have a next-door neighbor. The closest I had was Michael, and now he lives in the valley. Hey, we could probably get to his cabin."

"We are not taking her to that ramshackle piece of crap. It doesn't have heat, and I'm pretty sure it's got a nest of possums living there," Wyatt countered.

She was not staying with possums. Though they would likely be nicer hosts.

She needed one good thing to come out of this debacle of a day. Her car was wrecked, and she was stuck with this duo of temptations reminding her of just how school-marm wallflower she'd become. "Are you or are you not going to fix my electricity? I can have my future brother-in-law do it, but you are going to pay him because you are the landlord, and fixing things is your responsibility because the cabin is your asset, not mine. You should understand if you do not live up to your end of the bargain, beyond bringing my new dad into the scenario, I'll bring in my friend Nell, who will help me protest your many infractions of the Bliss County code." She gasped, exaggerating it for the drama. "You know, I'm almost certain I saw a Reticulan Grey in the backyard, and he was obviously dumping toxic waste in the river. And all because of you."

"You are really fucking mean. I did not expect you to be so mean." Sawyer seemed to think the problem through. "Well, put like that I suppose I will pay for someone to tell you there's nothing wrong with the electricity, but you have to promise not to sic Mel on me. Or Nell. Those two are a team up no one needs."

So at least she'd won one thing. "Excellent. Now I'm going to take a shower and then I will lock myself into whatever spare room you might have, and you won't see me again until I walk out of this place. Call me when the snow melts, asshole."

She turned and started to walk away and realized she did not know where she was going. The cabin was cozy, but it wasn't as small as her own.

"The bathroom is the second door on the left, and you can stay in the guest room," Sawyer said. He was staring at her again, likely trying to figure out a new tactic to get her out of his house. "It was my room when I was a kid. The bed is small, but the mattress is new. The sheets are in the dresser. You should know Bella usually sleeps in there."

"Bella is welcome." At least she would have a companion.

"I, uhm, I suppose I will make you a tray and put it outside your door." Wyatt's smile had amped down. "Let me know if you need anything else. We'll leave you alone, of course."

He turned and walked toward what she suspected was the kitchen.

Sawyer's brow had furrowed. "He was looking forward to having company. Now you made him sad. You know we don't get many guests."

"I can't imagine why."

"You're going to starve because you don't like me?" Sawyer asked, every word a challenge.

"I have a protein bar," she announced. "And I think half a Snickers. And also, I could probably use a cleanse. I've been around some toxic people lately."

He moved into her space, but Sabrina held her ground. "He's not toxic. Wyatt's been through more than you can imagine, and he wants to be a good host. Don't be stubborn."

Sawyer Hathaway had not one ounce of self-awareness. "The problem isn't him. The problem is you."

He loomed over her, his expression softening and making her breath catch. When he wasn't frowning he was stunning. Who was she kidding? He was always stunning.

"Yeah, I get that a lot. I'm sorry. I had a bad reaction to you."

Bad didn't begin to cover it. "Clearly. Look, I don't know why you disliked me at first sight…"

"Didn't. Pretty much the opposite." He was staring down at her like he wanted to memorize her face. "Saw you, wanted you, knew I shouldn't have you, so I escaped."

"Escaped?" Now she did step back. She had no idea what he was doing, but she wasn't about to let it happen. "What exactly did you think I would do to you? Jump your bones? Try to force you to go to a hotel with me?"

He shrugged, and his eyes spent way too much time on her lips. "It happens. Usually I'm up for it, but you… I can't explain it but I felt something and I didn't like what I felt. So I took myself out of the situation because you looked soft and sweet and I thought there was zero way you would be able to handle a man like me."

"A man like you? Arrogant and rude? I know exactly how to handle a man like you. You throw him out with the trash and then you don't have a problem anymore."

His lips curled up. "See, this was the part I didn't catch. The mean part. I like it."

He was so frustrating. "Let me get this straight. You realized I can't leave and you can't leave, and now you think because we're stuck here we should... What?"

"I think we should start over," Sawyer admitted. "I think you should take a shower and change into dry clothes, and then we'll sit down and have dinner made by a former one percenter who got out and now for some reason wants to be the world's best host. He's serious about hospitality and making things nice. His family, well, think of them like a violent cult. He wasn't allowed much contact with the outside world, and when he finally got out, I'm pretty sure the first thing he watched was Top Chef. It imprinted on him. I'm also pretty sure he's the one who didn't tell me about the complaints since I know for damn certain nothing gets past Wyatt. Which makes me think he wanted this to happen."

She was confused. "Wanted me to get into a car accident and get stuck here?"

"No. Wanted you to come out and meet me in person, where he would almost certainly be because he's my shadow these days. Or maybe I'm his. I don't have a lot of family anymore so Wyatt's pretty much it."

"Family doesn't have to be blood," she replied, not liking how she was already warming up to him again.

"As you're learning with Mel and probably Cassidy," Sawyer allowed. "Now that I think about it the last time she came out here to do her biannual check to see if the...I don't remember the name of the damn things...mating spaces were laid out, she mentioned her new baby. I thought she got another dog or something."

"It's the Neluts." How weird her life had become. She knew exactly what he was talking about. "According to Dad, they have a biannual mating schedule, and they come to Earth to do it, so to speak. They're seafaring. Star faring. They live on spaceships. They like to mate in mountainous regions for religious purposes."

"And you're a weirdo." He said the words with a smile.

Yep. It was way better when he frowned. "You're a bully."

A startled expression took over his handsome face, and the man actually looked hurt. "Am not. I don't like bullies. I'm sorry. Again. Not something a bully would say. I am maybe not so good at handling certain emotions. Like most of them, with the exception of annoyance and anger. I'm excellent at those. Everything else I'm a little slow at. But I can come around. So how about you join me and Wyatt for dinner and we'll see where the night goes from there. I mean apparently they're not sending a chopper up to rescue you from my clutches."

"I don't think you're going to clutch me."

He seemed to consider her statement. "How about I promise no clutching. Unless you ask me to."

"I'm not going to ask you." Her stomach rumbled. "But I will have dinner, and I won't make Wyatt eat alone with you. I bet you don't even compliment his cooking."

"I eat it," he said like that was supposed to be enough.

What did poor Wyatt have to go through? And what was a one percenter? Sawyer said it like she should know what it meant.

"I'm taking a shower now," she announced. "I don't suppose you have anything I could change into."

"I'll get some of Wyatt's clothes. They'll be too big, but they won't fall off you. I'll leave them on the bed." Sawyer stepped back. "And Sabrina, I'm sorry if I hurt your feelings. It wasn't my intention, and despite my reputation for being an asshole, I don't like to run around hurting women's feelings. Which is why I didn't talk to you the night of the Christmas party. If I'd talked to you…would you have been polite to me?"

"Of course."

"Then you might have been safe," he said.

Again with the confusion. "Safe? And I'm not now?"

"I haven't decided. The mean thing throws me off."

Such an odd man. "You are safe from any interest from me, Mr. Hathaway. All I want from you is to fix my electricity and to let me stay here until someone can come get me. I'll stay out of your way and you can stay out of mine."

"Somehow, I don't think that's going to happen, sweetheart."

"Oh, and a third thing." She leaned in, giving him her best sit down and do your work and stop talking stare. "Don't call me sweetheart."

She turned and walked away, Bella hard on her heels.

It was going to be a rough couple of days.

Chapter Three

Sawyer walked into the kitchen, his sparring session with the luscious Sabrina Leal playing through his head.

And his dick.

"Dinner will be ready in about a half an hour," Wyatt said in a tight voice, not looking up from the stove where he stood, stirring a pot.

He was good at stirring a pot. "Did you or did you not ignore the requests Marie sent over because you wanted to force a meeting with Sabrina?"

Wyatt sighed. "I wanted to meet her, but I didn't want to come off like some weirdo. She doesn't go out a lot, and I couldn't come up with a reason to go to the school. I considered adopting a kid."

"What?"

Wyatt shook his head. "Well, I considered paying a kid to say he was like my younger brother or something, but then I realized how it would probably look so I didn't do that. Then she started asking about the electricity and voila. Here she is. I will say I didn't think she would end up getting stuck here. I thought she would come to the bar and then I would apologize and offer to get her a drink to make up for things, and sure, I'll come look at your electricity."

"You're not an electrician," Sawyer pointed out.

"Which is why we would have to spend time together," Wyatt replied. "We would have to find someone, maybe talk about how to solve the problem. We won't now because you suck."

He wasn't going to argue about the state of his personality. He'd been born this way. "You're just as good as an electrician since it's not the electricity."

Wyatt huffed. "No. Apparently it's an alien."

Damn, when she'd flushed and leaned toward him his dick had tightened and his world had kind of tilted on its axis. He hadn't expected her to push back. In his head he'd formed a fully detailed version of her. Sweet. Probably wanted a family. Wouldn't ever accept a man who'd been arrested as often as Sawyer had. Wouldn't want to hang out in some dingy bar in rural Colorado. Wouldn't be able to stand up for herself so he would end up walking all over her because he was an asshole who needed a woman who could put him in his place. "Yeah, we're going to have to figure something out or Mel really will be on my ass. And I don't even want to mess with Nell. I thought maybe when she had a baby she would chill or not have as much time to protest, but she just brings the baby along. I swear she taught her baby to cry on cue."

Wyatt sighed again, stepping back. "Well, I suppose she's locked herself in the room. I'll find a tray or something."

"She's promised to come out to dinner."

A brow rose over Wyatt's blue eyes. "She did?"

"We talked after you left. We've agreed I'm an asshole." It wasn't the only thing he'd agreed to. "And apparently I'm not supposed to call her sweetheart."

Wyatt went still, staring at him like he was working through some problem in his head. "You called her sweetheart?"

"Yeah."

"Okay, maybe we should go over a couple of things," Wyatt began. "Why were you such a massive ass to her? I've never seen you be so rude to a woman who wasn't drunk off her ass and trying to cop a feel."

It happened way too often at Hell on Wheels.

Wyatt waited for him to say something.

See, this was why he didn't do friends. Or roommates. They expected a guy to talk way too much. Wyatt had been pretty easy in

Wild Bliss

the beginning. They'd communicated mostly through grunts and the occasional *want a beer?* They'd talked about how Wyatt could help with the bar and eventually the businesses Sawyer had inherited, but then the therapy had started. Freaking therapy. "Look, I saw her and things got weird and I didn't like it."

"You saw her and things got weird. Weird, how?" Wyatt's eyes went wide. "Holy shit. You love at first sighted."

Sawyer pointed a finger his way. "Abso-fucking-lutely not. I do not do the love crap. I saw her and thought 'hey, there's a gorgeous woman I'd like to spend some time with. In bed.' If I'd seen her at Hell on Wheels, I'd probably have done exactly that. I would have brought her up here and had a hot night and sent her on her way. But we weren't in my world. We were in Bliss, and I don't belong there."

Wyatt's head shook. "Why do you think you don't belong there? I don't get it. Everyone's so nice."

"They're nice, but at some point they'll figure out what we did in the past and then it won't be so nice," Sawyer explained.

"They know. I mean the sheriff talked to me. He told me I should let him know if my brother ever shows up," Wyatt replied.

For a man with Wyatt's rap sheet, he was awfully naïve. "He was warning you. He was telling you he'll be watching you. Like he watches me."

Wyatt thought for a moment. "I don't think that's what he meant. I know cops, man. I've been around all kinds of cops, and Sheriff Wright was simply letting me know he's here. He spent time undercover in an MC. He knows what it's like. And he knows there's not always an easy way out. Especially if you're born into one. He's the one who told me to go see Alexei."

It bothered Sawyer. "And it's why I told you it's a bad idea. Alexei is probably telling the sheriff everything."

"He wouldn't. Alexei knows where we've been. He wouldn't betray me, and I don't think the sheriff would ask." Wyatt turned back to his stew. "Anywhere I go, my past will follow me. Do you really think we don't belong here?"

He didn't understand what he was trying to say. "No, we don't belong down the mountain. *Here* is exactly where we belong."

"Do you think I scare them when I go into town? Is that why you usually drive all the way to Alamosa for supplies?" Wyatt asked quietly.

Sawyer leaned against the sink, hating the fact he'd put a look of sorrow on his friend's face, but they had to acknowledge the truth. "No. I don't think you scare them. But I also think we're not getting invites to dinner or town parties. Look, Wyatt, I'm not saying they're going to show up with torches and pitchforks."

Wyatt frowned, and his eyes narrowed. "Holy shit. They're not afraid of us. You're afraid of them."

What the hell? "I am not."

Wyatt's head nodded as though he was confirming some long-held belief. "The way you were afraid of her. You said it yourself. You felt weird. What if weird means emotional? What if your version of weird is an emotional connection to a woman you've never felt before? You're afraid of being rejected so you reject people first."

He should never have taken him into town. He definitely should never have let him see Alexei Markov. "I am not afraid of rejection. I don't care about anything. Now we have to talk about how we're going to handle our guest for the next few days. You like her."

Wyatt looked like he didn't want to change the subject, but he went with it. "Yeah. I like her a lot."

"You don't know her."

Wyatt shrugged, obviously not bothered. "I know enough to know she's kind and funny, and she's good with pretty much everyone she meets. She's excited about being here in Bliss, and she wants to go ice skating but she obviously needs someone to help her get through her first winter here. She doesn't even have a real coat. I'm surprised her sister hasn't taken her shopping, but then she's been super-busy with the school. She stays late most nights."

Holy shit. This was worse than he thought. "Have you been stalking her?"

Wyatt frowned. "No. I just… I just am sometimes going the same direction and sit close to her at Trio, and I mean it's not like I don't have ears and stuff."

Sawyer pointed a finger his way. "You have to stop. The sheriff won't put up with it if he thinks you're stalking the women of Bliss."

Wyatt had the good grace to blush. "I'm not. It's only the one woman, and it's not stalking. It's intense interest with a dash of eavesdropping. Nothing more."

And there it was. He was neatly trapped. It was plain to see if he didn't seduce Sabrina Leal, Wyatt would end up in prison.

His brain was really going that way. The part of Sawyer still thinking with his brain knew this was what could only be called bargaining. The dick part didn't care. The dick part was more than happy to bargain away because he'd found a road leading him straight into Sabrina's pretty panties. And he wasn't doing it for love or any other bullshit. He was doing it because he owed Wyatt.

And so his brain and dick made the bargain. "You know she can never be anything more than a couple nights of fun."

Wyatt's gaze turned distinctly suspicious. "Is this the part where you tell me no teacher is going to ever want to build a life with two former criminals and we should accept the fact that all we can ever be is fun sex for her?"

He finally got it. "Pretty much. And it's not just the teacher part. Her sister is a deputy with the county. She's literally law enforcement. I'm certain she's already seen your rap sheet."

"I wasn't convicted of anything," Wyatt argued.

"Only because the MC had an excellent lawyer," Sawyer pointed out. "Sabrina will be horrified when her sister hands her your records, and don't think she won't if she finds out her little sister is involved with two shady characters."

"I'm not shady anymore. And I think you're wrong about the sheriff. I actually think he likes me. He called me the sweet one. Said there's always one in a Bliss partnership, and it's obviously me." Wyatt stopped. "Wait. Do you think they think…"

Sawyer was going to have a serious talk with the sheriff. "They don't think we're a couple. He's talking Bliss nonsense. It's something Stella said a couple of years ago. She believes every Bliss male partnership consists of an asshole and what she calls the sweet one, meaning the one the woman they select can walk all over. It's bullshit."

"So I really am the sweet one," Wyatt said, his lips curling up.

"Well, we both know I'm the asshole." He was comfortable with it. He was even oddly comfortable with the idea of sharing a woman with Wyatt. For the short term, of course. "Look, it's obvious to me you want this woman. Physically, I want her, too. And now I think she might be able to handle what I need. She's different than I thought she would be, so if you can accept the reality of the situation, I think we can talk to her about a suitable arrangement."

Wyatt sighed. "You want to offer her sex."

"It's all we can offer her."

"Because she's a schoolteacher and we're unconvicted former criminals," Wyatt finished. "There's not a lot of redemption in this world, is there?"

Sawyer wished so much she hadn't shown up on his mountain. "I'm not saying you can't find a woman and settle down. I just don't think it's going to be her."

"You didn't say *we*," Wyatt pointed out.

"Because I'm more than willing to share a woman for sex, but I'm not going to have a relationship with one. I'm not built for it." He wasn't the kind of man who talked and shared, and that was what women needed. He could give them sex and help them out from time to time, but it was all he was good for.

Wyatt nodded, seeming to come to a decision. "All right. How about we make a deal? We're honest with her. Honest about who we are and what we want, but we're not going to hit her with it all at once. We've got a couple of days with her. Let's have a nice meal and see where it goes." Wyatt stared at him for a moment as though trying to read his mind. "You want to put it all out there, don't you?"

Sawyer shrugged one big shoulder. "I think it's best, but I'm going to let you steer this ship. I'm only here for the sex."

"And if she doesn't want only sex?" Wyatt asked.

"Then you should probably see her on your own, but be brutally honest with her before she says yes. Her sister will give her the report on you at some point. It'll hurt so much more if you wait." Sawyer had a feeling it wasn't going to come to that. "But I think she's interested. There's real heat between us, and I don't think she'll be able to stay away. Her sister is in a ménage. She's got to be curious. I'll be less of an asshole, and maybe she'll get cold and need some body heat."

"I will take the lead and if she's…amenable…I'll date her on my own." Wyatt grinned. "Amenable means agreeable. I've been doing word of the day. I think I'll bring up my interest in education. It's something we have in common."

He turned back to his stew.

Bella came bounding in as Sawyer heard the door to the bathroom shut and lock. The dog bounced in front of him and then ran toward the back of the house and then to Sawyer.

"Bella likes her. She's doing her 'someone I like locked me out, and can't you bust through so I can be with my friend' dance," Wyatt said.

Yeah, everyone in his household liked the new girl.

It had been easier when his household was made up of him and no one else.

But he had to admit, it had been way less fun.

* * * *

Wyatt was determined to not act like a creepy stalker. His stalking—if one could call it that—was friendly. If he thought for a second she would be offended, he would stop. She might get offended if she knew how his eyes were drawn to the deep *V* of her shirt. His shirt. She wore one of his white undershirts, and it looked damn good on her.

She was wearing his clothes, and the deeply buried caveman inside him liked it. The pajama bottoms were too long and she'd had to tie them around her waist, but she still looked awfully pretty sitting across from Sawyer at the dinner table they almost never used.

It felt right to have her here, and he was going to prove to Sawyer this could work.

"This is good." Sabrina gave him a smile before she ate another spoonful.

"It's Sawyer's mom's recipe." He'd been perfecting it. Since he no longer spent his days beating the shit out of people, getting the shit kicked out of him, or lying to the police about both, he'd found the joy of hobbies. He'd tried a lot of things. The Bliss County Recreation Center was a lush field of learning. He hadn't been good at macrame, but he'd been damn good at the self-defense class where they'd used crochet hooks to—as the teacher explained—incapacitate a son of a bitch. He'd ended up teacher's pet in that one. But the cooking classes and the book club were what really got him interested. "I added some bone broth to give it an added layer of flavor."

She smiled again, and his dick tightened. "Whatever you did it's excellent and exactly what I needed. I can't believe how cold I was."

"You're on a mountain more than ten thousand feet above sea level and it's almost winter." Sawyer had been quiet since she'd entered the room, but naturally now he found something to needle her about.

"She's new to town," Wyatt said pointedly. "She obviously hasn't had time to shop. I'll…" This might be too early to start gently taking control of certain aspects of her life like her comfort and safety. But he wanted to. He wanted to be the one to ensure she had everything she needed. When he'd first come out of the MC, Sawyer had told him he needed to find his vocation. Wyatt had been forced to look the word up because vocabulary wasn't a big thing in his family. Vocation meant job, but it could also mean calling. The longer he was in her company, the more he thought taking care of Sabrina Leal might be his vocation. "I'm sure her sister will take her."

Sabrina winced. "She did. I'm afraid I'm getting a hearty lecture from my sister and the men she's engaged to. She took me to the Trading Post a couple of weeks ago and I bought a heavy coat and boots, but it didn't seem like it was going to be so cold today. She told me there was a storm coming, but I'm going to be honest, I didn't think snow."

He understood. "Because you've never had to live through a Colorado winter."

"But snow is rain when it's below freezing," Sawyer pointed out utterly needlessly.

Sabrina's jaw clenched. "Thank you. I had no idea. I'll write it down so I don't get it confused again."

Why? Sawyer rarely talked. Why had he decided to change his persona now? He could be his normal surly, silent self and everything would be fine. He was going to have to drag Sawyer's ass kicking and screaming into this relationship. "I had a hard time with my first winter here."

"I thought you were from Colorado." At least she didn't keep the look of disdain in her eyes when she switched her focus to him. It seemed reserved for Sawyer, so maybe Wyatt still had a way in.

"I am." He took a sip of the Cab he'd found stashed away in the back of the pantry. Normally he was more of a beer guy, but he was spreading his wings. Or more importantly trying to make a good impression since Sawyer was making the worst possible one. "But I'm from eastern Colorado. It's like Kansas lite. It gets cold, but the elevation isn't what it is here in the mountains."

"It's flat," Sawyer added.

"I know what he meant by Kansas lite," Sabrina replied with a long sigh.

Wyatt sent Sawyer a look he hoped conveyed what an ass he was making of himself.

Sawyer sat back, looking strangely bewildered. Damn. Was the guy actually trying? What if Sawyer simply didn't know how to carry on a conversation with a woman that wasn't about what they wanted to drink or how they liked it in bed?

He needed to find common ground between Sawyer and Sabrina or he was definitely going to fail on this quest.

"So what made you want to go into teaching?"

Both Wyatt and Sabrina's heads turned because Sawyer had asked the question, and his tone had been almost polite.

The dude *was* trying. Holy shit. He really did want Sabrina. He should have known the minute she'd gotten up in his face and shown how not afraid of him she was that Sawyer's dick would win. He didn't do soft and sweet. But what if he could have a combination of softness and steel? A woman he could be vulnerable around, who would also put him on his ass when he needed it.

"I always liked kids," Sabrina said, caution clear in her tone. She buttered her cornbread. "Before my mom left active duty, we spent most of our time on military bases. The opportunities for babysitting were endless once I reached a certain age. We also had some mixed-ages classes. I liked the format. I think it's oddly more natural than kids only spending time with other kids who are exactly their ages. When I chose to go to college instead of into the military like my mom wanted me to, she basically said she wouldn't help me unless I was going for a degree where I was practically guaranteed a job. Teaching was on her short list, and lucky for me, it's what I wanted to do. She still didn't pay for tuition or anything, but she gave me thirty bucks a week for food and stuff."

"How did you survive on thirty bucks?" Wyatt asked.

Sawyer grunted, taking a sip of his beer. "You buy ramen

noodles and figure out how to make a pound of ground round last for days. Condiments are your friend. Get the cheapest burger you can at a fast-food place and load up on packets of condiments."

Sabrina smiled Sawyer's way for the first time. "I ate a lot of tacos. There was a place off campus where you could get ten tacos for ten bucks, and I would split it with a friend and then we had dinner for two or three days. I still had some hot sauce packets hanging around when I moved. It was so ingrained in me I kept doing it even after I had a good job."

Wyatt was confused. "Why didn't your mom give you money?"

"Because she didn't agree with her life choices," Sawyer said. "Didn't you listen?"

Asshole. "I did but I don't understand."

"I think you should," Sawyer shot back. "Your father sure as hell didn't give you the option of going to college. Hell, he pulled you out of high school when he was legally able to and put you to work for the club."

A flush of shame went through Wyatt. Sabrina was a schoolteacher. She valued education, and he didn't have much of it. "I got my GED. I had to do it on my own."

Sawyer shrugged like Wyatt had made his point. "See. That's what she had to do."

"She wasn't the kindest woman," Sabrina said quietly. "My mother had firm beliefs on how the world worked, and any time I challenged those beliefs I was punished in some way."

Sawyer pointed Wyatt's way. "See. Same." He set his beer down. "Oh, did you think because she seems so nice and sweet her parents must be, too? Or is this one of those I don't understand how the outside world works and I think it's all puppies and roses?"

Yep, there was more of the shame. "I know how the world works. I was confused."

"You don't, buddy, or you would be more cautious." Sawyer nodded Sabrina's way. "We had to get him a social security card when he started working. At twenty-seven."

He wished Sawyer would stop talking. "My family... Let's say they believed in staying off the grid as much as possible. I did, in fact, have a social security card and a driver's license. But they weren't real. I had to have a lawyer find my birth certificate. I'm glad

I had one."

"Your past doesn't matter," Sabrina said with a smile. "Isn't that kind of what this place is about? From what I can tell, a lot of people came here looking for a second chance. I'm trying to find a truly supportive family. I'm trying to clear my head of my mom's voice. I have twenty-eight years of listening to her tell me everything will go to hell if I'm satisfied even for a moment. She thought happiness was an affront to fate or God or whatever you want to call the universe. If a person wasn't humble and miserable, they weren't doing something right."

"In my world if a man wasn't screwing over everyone outside of his family, he wasn't a man at all." Wyatt could relate wholly. "Did she ever tell you that you're beautiful? I don't say it because I'm trying to get something out of you. I'm saying it because I know how it feels to get ground under the boots of someone else's damage, and what helps is hearing the truth. Sometimes you have to hear it over and over until you believe it."

Her eyes were suddenly shining in the low light from the dining room sconces. "That's kind of you."

"He's not being kind. He's telling you the truth." Sawyer was studying her. "But you don't know it, do you? Like he doesn't get he's smart. You should stop listening to those voices. Just shut 'em down."

Her eyes rolled, and she picked up her napkin, dabbing at them. "Another to write down. Forget your trauma. So, Sawyer, who's your terrible parent?"

He seemed to think about the question for a moment. "I guess my dad. He left when I was four, though, so I don't remember much about him. My mom was lovely, and my grandfather was the best man I know."

"Then how did you end up being such an asshole?" Sabrina asked.

Sawyer's lips curled up. The big bastard did seem to like it when she was mean. "I was born that way, I guess. So you're telling me you don't care about anyone's past?"

"I'm telling you I don't think a person's past matters if they're trying to be better." She turned Wyatt's way. "I think it's wonderful you got your GED. I don't need to run a background check to make new friends. My mom would have done it. She was suspicious of everyone. I would rather concentrate on the here and now. Wyatt, what is it you do for a living? I know Sawyer rips off his tenants."

"I do not." Sawyer finally seemed a bit offended. "Your rent is perfectly reasonable for the valley."

"It's not reasonable for a place where the electricity needs fixing," Sabrina countered.

"I told you it's a ghost." Sawyer snapped his fingers as though remembering something. "Grandad used to tell the tenants to play Creedence Clearwater Revival once a day and the ghost finds it soothing. I think maybe it puts him to sleep or something."

"That is the most..." Sabrina began.

Wyatt needed to take control or they would fight the rest of the night. "I handle some of Sawyer's business work. His grandfather left him the bar and properties and a couple of other businesses. I do all the accounting. It's the one thing my father and brother did value about me. I'm good with numbers and detail-oriented work."

She focused on him. "Really? Do you use a spreadsheet? I could use a couple of lessons. The new system Stef Talbot had installed is hard to navigate."

Now she was talking his language. He would learn the system from top to bottom if it meant spending time with her. "Absolutely. I'm good with spreadsheets."

"He's not great with passing on complaints, though," Sawyer grumbled under his breath.

Wyatt kicked him under the table. Sawyer grunted.

Bella, who'd been laying under the table at Sawyer's feet, thought it was a signal it was time to play. Her head came up, tongue lolling out as she stared at the stew.

"She's so cute. How long have you had her?" Sabrina asked.

"Since she showed up and wouldn't leave." Sawyer went back to sipping his beer. "Tried to turn her over to the vet, but somehow she ended up back in my Jeep along with a dog bed, food and water bowls, and a collar."

"He didn't give her a name for the longest time." Wyatt was beyond relieved they weren't going to go into his child and young adulthood this evening. His childhood was a horror story for another time. "I moved in and finally couldn't handle him calling her Dog all the time. So I went on the Internet and searched for most popular dog names and Bella seemed nice. I wonder why Bella, though. I love the name, but why is it so popular?"

"*Twilight*," Sabrina replied with a brilliant smile. "Your dog is named after the heroine of a popular book."

Sawyer snorted.

"I did not know," Wyatt admitted. He'd never heard of *Twilight*. He wondered if she liked it. "Maybe I'll give it a try."

"Oh, I want in on that book club," Sabrina shot back. "I bet you've never read a book like it."

"He hasn't read many books at all," Sawyer said with a huff. "He's definitely never read *Twilight*."

Was Sawyer trying to make him look bad? "I read all the time. I like to read."

Sawyer turned his way, surprise plain on his face. "Dude, I was talking about before. You weren't exactly a big reader. You didn't have time between…"

Wyatt stood up. It was obvious this wasn't going the way he wanted it to. "I need to check on the dessert. I made some brownies. They should be almost done."

Maybe if he wasn't in the room, he could reset the conversation. He pushed through the swinging doors separating the kitchen from the small dining room, holding his bowl and spoon.

Was he doing the right thing? Despite what he'd said to her, he meant to seduce her. They had days and days before anyone would be able to get up here. She didn't have anyone in her life. There was nothing keeping her from enjoying a brief affair.

She didn't know he meant to make it far longer than brief.

Of course it might never get off the ground if Sawyer had anything to do with it. He seemed determined to paint them both as poorly as possible.

Or he's trying to get all the bad stuff out of the way.

She'd said she didn't need to know about his past.

Because she thinks you were in an isolated, probably weirdly religious cult.

She was right about the cult part. His father's MC ran much like a cult, only they worshipped money and power rather than any deity.

He set the bowl in the sink and took a long breath. He had kind of sprung this whole thing on Sawyer. He should have sat down with him and explained his plan. Wyatt was self-aware enough to admit he hadn't because he'd known what Sawyer would say. Absolutely no. He would have told Wyatt to pursue her on his own if that was what he wanted. Oh, Wyatt knew if he'd said it was only about sex, Sawyer might have high-fived him and told him it was go time. It wasn't like they hadn't shared a couple of women over the past year.

But he had the strongest feeling it would be more than sex with Sabrina. He was serious about her, and it meant he had to find a way to get Sawyer serious about her, too.

He knew most people would tell him to leave Sawyer behind, but there was another instinct playing through Wyatt. It told him if Sawyer didn't come with him, he would be alone for the rest of his life. Despite being an asshole of the highest order, Sawyer Hathaway was also one of the most generous men he'd ever met. He owed Sawyer. He liked Sawyer. He liked Bliss and how the people here lived their lives.

He wanted all of it. Wanted it badly enough he was willing to fight for it. If he had to fight a little dirty, he was okay with that, too.

He checked the brownies and pulled them out because they were done. He hoped they weren't sitting in absolute silence, but maybe it was for the best. Maybe he'd been wrong to push so hard at first. They needed a night to relax and settle into the situation. In the morning, he could charm her. He had no illusions they would spend the next couple of days in bed. No. The next couple of days would be spent getting to know each other, seeing if she wanted to date them.

No matter what Sawyer said, he didn't want some secretive affair with her. He wanted a normal relationship, wanted to be a part of the town with her. Sawyer was wrong. His background wasn't so bad no one wanted him in Bliss. The sheriff knew and thought he was the sweet one. The sheriff wasn't freaked out by his past.

Of course the sheriff didn't know all of his past. The sheriff only knew the actual records. There was so much not contained in those reports.

If his brother ever discovered what he'd done…

His dark thoughts were broken by the sound of the phone ringing. At least the landlines were still working. He moved over to pick up the handset, pressing the button to accept the call. "Hello?"

"Hi, this is Deputy Leal. I'm looking for my sister."

Despite the fact that mere moments before he'd been thinking about his good relationship with law enforcement here, he felt his spine stiffen. "Hello, Deputy. She's having supper right now. I'll go and get her for you."

"This is Wyatt, right?" the deputy asked.

"Yes, ma'am. Wyatt Kemp is my name, Deputy."

"And mine is Elisa," she replied. "Is she okay? Gemma didn't tell me much more than she's stuck on the mountain with the MC boys."

He did not like the nickname. "Neither one of us has been in an MC for a long time. We're out of the lifestyle."

There was a pause on the line. "Sorry about that. Gemma doesn't have much of a filter. Is my sister okay? I have to ask you because she won't tell me. She'll say whatever it takes to make me comfortable, and I need to know if I should risk trying to make it up there."

"She's fine. She's not used to driving in this kind of weather, and she did have a little accident."

The deputy gasped. "An accident?"

He probably should have set the conversation up better. "I think she hit a tree, but she's perfectly fine. We got her a warm shower and dry clothes, and she's got a room for the night. I'm pretty sure it locks if you're worried about it."

She was quiet for a moment. "I wasn't worried about you or Sawyer hurting her, Wyatt. Sawyer's grumpy, not violent. And you've become everyone's go to when it comes to taking advantage of young, strong men. Do you think we don't see you helping Teeny unload supplies or making sure someone else elderly in Bliss gets across the street okay? Look, I know you've got a rap sheet, but I also know how you grew up. You're trying. Don't let the badges fool you. This police department is genuinely concerned with the good of everyone in town. We get to know people. So that's why I'm going to ask you to be careful with my sister."

"Of course."

"Because I've seen the way you look at her."

Wyatt stopped. "I don't... Okay, I like her."

"And there's nothing wrong with liking her. She's a likable

person, but she's new here and she's getting her feet under her. Go slow. Give her a chance to get to know you. She's not the kind of woman who throws herself into a relationship," Elisa explained. "And that is all the sisterly advice I'm going to give you. Be nice to my sister and we'll be good. Now can I talk to her?"

It wasn't a conversation he'd expected to have, but it had gone pretty well. "Of course. She's in the dining room. I promise we're ready for this storm. She'll be fine here." He pushed through the doors, and the first thing he saw was Bella licking stew off the floor.

And the second was Sawyer on top of Sabrina on the dining room table.

"I think she's going to have to call you back, Deputy."

Nope. He wasn't getting anything he'd expected today.

Chapter Four

Sabrina watched Wyatt walk away and the minute the doors closed to the kitchen, turned on the asshole. The big, gorgeous asshole, with pitch black hair and a jaw made of granite. And seriously sexy shoulders.

None of which made up for the fact that he was a massive ass.

"Are you trying to make Wyatt feel like crap? Because I think you succeeded. I thought you two were friends." She rather thought they were more, but they hadn't said anything. The idea they were a couple made it even worse.

Sawyer turned her way, brows rising over his deep brown eyes. "We are. I wasn't trying to make him feel bad."

How could he not understand what he'd done wrong? "You tried to make him look uneducated."

"He is. Did you hear the part about the GED?" Sawyer's brows formed a *V* over his eyes. "It's not like he went to college or anything. Neither did I. You should know I'm not very educated before you make any decisions."

What was his point? She didn't know there were any decisions to be made, but she ignored it. "What I heard was the part about him working hard to make up for something that wasn't his fault. He got his GED despite the fact he didn't have any support from his family."

Sawyer's eyes found his beer. "I know he worked hard. I was only teasing him."

"You were bullying him."

His eyes came back up, a flash of annoyance there. "No, if I was going to bully him I would have done way worse. Look, Sabrina, I don't know where this outrage is coming from. I thought we were just talking. I thought you should probably know we're not in your league when it comes to the smarts stuff. You should be aware. Though he does read quite a bit. It's kind of annoying. He reads a book and thinks he knows things."

"Yes, knowing things is what happens when you read a book. It's kind of the point." What exactly did he mean? "Why should I be aware? And why would you think I need someone to be in my league? I'm not snobby. Smarts are about more than a formal education. You need to be nicer to your partner."

Partner was a good word. It was one of those middle of the road words with the potential to mean any number of things.

"I know there's more to life than college, but…" Sawyer seemed to stop, his body going oddly still. "Partner? What do you mean?"

What did she mean? Panic flashed through her. She shouldn't have used the word *partner* because she'd started thinking they were a couple. Oh, Wyatt had told her she was beautiful, but he was only being kind. These were grown men, not boys. There was zero reason for them to live together unless they were…together. Was it hard to be a couple in rural Colorado? Was that why they weren't open about it? Teeny and Marie seemed to be fully accepted. But then she had a student who didn't feel like he could come out to his parents. She hadn't been here long enough to truly understand all the ways Bliss worked. It might be why they lived on this mountain and didn't seem to spend much time in town. "I mean you're partners. It's okay. I don't have a problem with it."

He leaned forward slightly, seeming to get serious. "Look, I have to be honest with you. We've definitely done it, but it's not like we're formally partners, though I do think it's what Wyatt's angling for. I just can't give it to him. The sex, yes, but you should know I'm not great with anything long term. I'm not built for it."

Poor Wyatt. Her heart ached for him, but there was something calming about having the truth out there. She didn't have to worry she would make a fool of herself. She knew the boundaries, and she and Wyatt could be friends. Though she might advise him to leave the glorious grump and find a kinder boyfriend. "You should be honest with him about what you want. How long have you been together?"

"He's been here almost a year," Sawyer replied. "We've done it probably four times. I'll admit I don't do it the way I used to when I was younger. Ty and I used to do it all the time. Like we would walk into a bar, and it was a free for all. I'm getting way pickier as I get older. There's a time and a place, you know. I'm worried Wyatt wants more than I can give, and that's something you should think about when he inevitably talks to you."

Was she about to become their therapist? And was he talking about the Ty her sister sometimes worked with? The EMT? They were exes? Well, Sawyer seemed to have a type. Hot and charming. "You want me to tell him you don't want something long term with him?"

Sawyer sighed like he was happy she understood. "I want you to think about what he can offer you and how hurt he might get if you dive into something physical with him."

She was so confused. "I don't see what I have to do with the fact that you've only had sex with your boyfriend four times this year."

Sawyer's eyes widened and his jaw dropped, and then the most brilliant smile came over his face. "Baby, we're not gay. We're both straight. We're trying to figure out how to seduce you. That's what I meant by partners. Given who your sister is and the fact you live in the valley, I assumed we were using the word in the same way."

The world seemed to stop. He...Wyatt...they... "I'm sorry. What?"

Sawyer was giving her his "you're a dumbass" stare. "He likes you."

She set her spoon down because she wasn't hungry anymore. What was Sawyer trying to do? "We just met."

"You might have met him recently, but he's seen you and liked you. It's a dude thing. See, we don't actually have to know a woman to know we want a woman. Same thing for me, but I thought you weren't the kind of woman who could handle me. Now I know you're mean." The last was said with a smirk that lit his whole face with arrogant charm.

What the hell was going on? Ah, maybe Wyatt wasn't the only one Sawyer was bullying today. She wasn't sure why the man had taken one look at her and disliked her, but she wasn't going to take his abuse. "That's not nice of you, but it's easy to see you're not a nice man."

"I never hid my personality." He actually seemed happy she understood. "I'm not nice but I can be kind, and I can be good for certain things."

"Like humiliating the women you take a dislike to?"

"What?"

She stood up, placing her napkin on the table. "I don't have to sit here and listen to you make fun of me. I am well aware I'm not some bombshell."

He stared at her as though pure willpower could keep her standing where she was. "Sabrina, why do you think I ran? And I did. I took one look at you with your soft eyes and hips I could hold on to, with all that hair, and a mouth I knew I'd want to kiss, and I ran like a fucking coward. Why do you think I ran? Do you think it was because I saw you and said no, I don't want to know her? It would have been far easier to simply be polite to you and then never speak to you again. Instead, I made an ass of myself the likes of which the town below us still talks about to this day. I took one look at you and knew I wanted to fuck you, but I also made a few assumptions about you."

She couldn't believe what she was hearing. "Assumptions?"

He stood slowly, unfurling his tall, muscular body like the gift it was. "I assumed you were the type of woman I stay away from. Innocent. Sweet. Nice. The kind of woman who would slap me if I offered her a hot night or two in bed. The kind who would never consider letting me touch her because I run a bar and I used to be a criminal. Think about the last part as you're standing there looking like you could eat me alive."

He used to be a criminal? She stashed those words away for later perusal. There was too much going on for her to handle it all. She had to focus on the immediate threat. "Not true. I'm not...looking at you like I want you."

"You're looking at me exactly the way you did the night I ran,"

Sawyer said, his eyes narrow.

"I was only trying to get a drink." It was the lie she told herself every time she thought about that night. Which was way too many times.

A low chuckle came from Sawyer. "Sure you were. You only wanted a drink. You didn't want me. You shouldn't want me. If you were as smart as I think you are, you would run the way I did."

There was one problem with the scenario. "I can't. If I leave, I'll probably die."

"And that's why you're going to fail, baby," Sawyer said in a low tone that stroked over all of her senses. "You're making all the wrong choices, and it's going to get you straight into bed with two men you have zero business fucking around with. Do you have any idea the things we want to do to you?"

Wyatt and Sawyer? Both of them. At the same time. Four hands on her. Two pairs of lips caressing her skin. The thought took her breath away. She wasn't sure why she was so shocked at the notion. A few days before she'd been on a date with two men looking for a Bliss-style relationship, but she hadn't felt this wild thrill of anticipation. Along with the thrill was the utter fear he was making fun of her. There was no way big, sexy Sawyer had been plotting with gorgeous Wyatt on how to seduce her schoolteacher self. "Stop it."

"I'll stop it if you tell me you don't want me. Make me believe it, Sabrina. Otherwise, you are fucking doomed, baby. You should have played it sweet, but no, you showed me your claws and I liked them."

She had to force herself to breathe. "You're being cruel now. You don't want me. Wyatt doesn't want me."

"Wyatt took one look at you a couple of months ago and has been following you around ever since, and it's played hell on my ability to get laid. Turns out despite all my trying to not fall into the whole Bliss-sharing thing, I genuinely prefer to have a partner. When Wyatt showed up I thought, good, while he's here I'll play the field a little. We only had a couple of women before he caught sight of you, and now he's a fucking virgin saving himself for his wedding night, and the thought of going out and finding my own one-night stand holds no appeal at all. However, the thing that does hold appeal is spending the next couple of days snowed in here with you, fucking this feeling I have out of my system. What do you say, Teach?"

"You want to sleep with me?" Sabrina couldn't believe she was asking the question.

One big shoulder shrugged, and he was far too close to her. So close she could feel the heat coming off his big body. "If we fall asleep, I won't mind, but this isn't about sleeping. This is about getting you out of my system because we can't work."

"I never said I wanted a boyfriend." But hadn't she taken one look at this man and wanted to know him? In any way she could. She'd been wrong about him. He wasn't someone she could date, but she was stuck here with him. It was a terrible idea. Terrible.

"Good." Sawyer seemed oddly satisfied. "Do you want a lover? Not forever. Just a couple of days and then we go our separate ways, and when we see each other we can be friendly."

"I don't think you can be friendly to save your own life."

He loomed over her, his hand coming up to stroke her chin so she had to look up at him. "Probably, but maybe I won't need to run every time I see you because I'm afraid I'll do this."

His head lowered and her breath caught in her chest as his lips brushed over hers.

How long had it been since she'd felt lips on hers? So damn long. She'd thrown herself into her work and starting her career, and then her mother had been sick. Then her sister. She'd forgotten how to live and this…oh, this made her feel so alive. Her hands went to his waist, and she wished there wasn't a flannel shirt between them. Her impulse was to pull it out of the encasing of his jeans so she could feel warm skin.

Sawyer groaned and backed her up against the table as his tongue came out, running over her bottom lip and demanding entry. She gave it to him, her heart rate tripling as his tongue stroked inside. Warmth pooled in her pelvis, and she could feel her pussy softening up. One kiss. It was all it took for this man to get her wet and ready for sex when she hadn't even felt the need in years.

"Let me in," Sawyer said, the words rumbling against her lips.

"I already did." She'd opened her mouth for him. She didn't want him to stop. Time seemed meaningless right now. So did anything outside of this room. It didn't matter. What mattered was getting him to kiss her again.

He picked her up and set her on the dining table. She heard something hit the floor, but it didn't matter because he kissed her and eased between her legs. "This is what I want. Let me in, Teach."

She didn't respond. Couldn't because his tongue was in her mouth again, boldly invading and stroking against her own. Somehow her arms ended up wrapped around him, and she felt her back hit the table, her legs around his hips. And there it was. Proof the man wasn't lying. His cock was rock hard against her pelvis.

His hand stroked against her hair as he kissed her.

This...this was what she'd waited for all her life. This feeling. This was more than lust, less than love. This was addiction and pleasure and life.

"I think she's going to have to call you back, Deputy."

Wyatt's deep voice broke through the haze of desire Sawyer had created around her. She gasped and started to push at his big chest.

Sawyer stood up, turning his partner's way. "Sorry. I didn't hear the phone ring."

Wyatt offered her the phone. "It's your sister. She's worried about you. I'll clean up the kitchen and see you two in the morning."

Sabrina scrambled to get off the table. What the hell had she done? Bella seemed to be the only one happy about what had happened since she was currently cleaning the floor of the stew they'd spilled. She grabbed the phone like it was a lifeline. Wyatt simply turned and walked back into the kitchen.

"This isn't over, Teach," Sawyer said. "I'm going to go find out what got Wyatt's panties in a wad. You talk to your sister, and then we'll figure out what we're going to do."

He didn't wait for an answer, simply turned and walked away.

"Sabrina?" Her sister's voice came from the headset.

Tears pierced Sabrina's eyes. What had she done? She put the phone to her ear. At least she had her sister to give her advice.

She was going to need it.

* * * *

Sawyer should have known it would all go to hell. Though he hadn't expected Wyatt to send it there. One minute he'd been so close to heaven and then... Well, he wasn't even sure what had happened.

Why hadn't Wyatt maneuvered himself in? Sawyer was almost certain Sabrina would have accepted him. She'd been so fucking responsive, so ready to take everything he wanted to give her.

He heard Sabrina say hello to her sister as she retreated to the back of the cabin. Likely to lock herself in her room.

Coward.

Now he did understand her actions. He knew why she'd retreated. The question was what had happened to his partner.

Bella licked the floor where the bowl had spilled. She'd already gotten everything in the bowl, but she wasn't about to leave any deliciousness behind. Sawyer kind of understood the dog. He wished he'd had a chance to lick Sabrina. He reached down and grabbed the bowl, putting it back on the table. "Wish me luck, Bella."

Sawyer pushed through the kitchen doors. Wyatt stood at the sink, the window in front of him dark with night, though he could see the snow was still falling. "Dude, what is your damage?"

Wyatt turned on him, his jaw tight. "My damage? Are you kidding me? You knew how I felt about her and you tried to fuck her anyway. Was this your way of showing me it can't work?"

He was pretty shocked by Wyatt's hostility. Were they even watching the same show? "I have spent all night trying to make it work. What are you talking about?"

Wyatt pointed a finger his way. "I'm talking about the way you've cut me off at the knees at every single turn. Every time she asked me a question and I answered, your ass had something to say about it. Always negative."

Had he been? "I was being realistic, Wyatt. Look, I wasn't trying to…"

Wyatt wasn't listening. "You tell her how dumb I am."

"I didn't say dumb, but I didn't want her to think we're college graduates or something." Now that he thought about it there might have been a better way to let her know about their differences.

"You tell her how shitty my family is."

"Your family is a literal crime syndicate," Sawyer pointed out. "Not any way out of shitty there, buddy."

"And then when you've driven me off, you get her on the table and start to fuck her?" Wyatt's tone was low and angry. "You couldn't go to the bedroom or something? I suppose it would have taken me longer to find you if you'd had any amount of respect for her."

"That's what I'm trying to tell you," Sawyer insisted. "I totally respect her. She's mean and she thought we were gay. I get it. We're adult men living together. No biggie. But I wanted to show her we aren't, and just saying it didn't feel strong enough."

He'd needed to drive the point home, and he would have. With his dick.

Wyatt had gone still, his expression blank. "She thought we were a couple?"

Sawyer shrugged. "Like I said, we're roommates, and not many dudes our age have roommates."

Wyatt nodded as though confirming something in his head. "She thinks I'm weak."

His head wasn't very smart. "What?"

"I did too much girl shit."

Sawyer was deeply confused. "Girl shit?"

"Cooking. Trying to ask polite questions. I talked about fucking brownies." Wyatt huffed out a laugh that held no humor. "Naturally she thinks we're gay and I'm the wife."

Sawyer took a deep breath and didn't follow through on his first instinct which was to call the motherfucker out for being an asshole. This wasn't about Wyatt's feelings. This was all the bullshit his family had taught him. Wyatt had required some deprogramming, and it looked like he needed a reminder. "Cooking isn't girl shit. We need to eat, too, and you're good at it. Brownies are delicious, man. I keep this place clean because I like it clean, not because I'm getting in touch with my inner woman. All the shit your dad and brother told you was woman's work was because they're too lazy to know how to take care of themselves. Housework should be done by anyone who lives in a house. You want a relationship with a woman, not to find a woman who'll do all the shit you don't want to do. You want a partnership, and you've worked to learn how to be a good one. You're upset, but you can't let those voices take over, man. You know they're wrong."

Wyatt took a long breath, his eyes closing. When he opened them again he seemed calmer. "You're right. I'm sorry. I struggle to figure out what's right and what's crap my family shoved down my throat so I wouldn't see how wrong we all were."

Sawyer nodded, happy the drama level seemed to be coming down slightly. "Exactly. Dude, you told me your brother said accounting was for beta men. Numbers, being smart enough to handle your own money, is for lesser men. Your family is fucked up. Stop letting them seep in and destroy everything. There's no alphas or betas. We're not a fucking werewolf pack. Some people need to be told what they are. You are not one of those people. You get to be Wyatt. You get to like cooking and accounting and still be a strong man."

Wyatt's head fell back, and when it came up again it was clear Sawyer had gotten through to him. He was surprised at the wave of relief he felt. "You know for a self-proclaimed feelingless asshole, you're a good friend, Sawyer."

Yeah, he didn't like how that made him feel either. Kind of warm. He was going to ignore the whole feeling thing. "Now can we talk about what happened? Maybe you don't know how these things work. I thought I'd taught you. When one of us gets the woman we both want on her back, you join in, not interrupt."

Wyatt's head shook. "What the hell happened? I got the feeling you two low-key hated each other when I walked out."

"Hate is a strong word. I definitely don't hate her. I explained why I had the reaction I had to her in the beginning. I also let her know I would be open to spending the weekend in bed with her. Both of us. Then she did this thing where she said she wasn't attracted to me, but she kissed me back, and then it went the way these things go."

"With you nearly fucking her on the dining room table." Wyatt sighed. "We need to do better. Again, I'm sorry. I had a bad reaction. I got jealous because I thought she was choosing you over me. Which is fine if that's what she wants."

"We haven't given her the option yet," Sawyer pointed out.

Wyatt winced. "Isn't it a little soon to ask her if she wants to go to bed with two men?"

"I'm going to be honest with you. This weekend is all I'm willing to commit to. I wasn't lying to you. I can't be in a relationship like the one you want. I don't even want to be in a relationship." He didn't. He was happier alone. Though happy wasn't the word he should use. Comfortable. He was more comfortable alone. Except he'd liked the last year of his life. It had been nice to have Wyatt around. But he wasn't about to bring Sabrina in when he knew how people would react.

Wyatt stared at him for a moment. "You really don't want to date her?"

The idea of him holding hands with a woman and taking her to Stella's for dinner and then dancing at Trio was ludicrous. "I don't have time to date."

"Not everyone will leave you, Sawyer."

He wasn't doing this. "I mean what I'm saying. I would love to spend this weekend with her, but a weekend is all I have in me. If you want to try to see her afterward, then that's your thing. I'm going to be open and honest with her about what I'm willing to give. And if you don't want to, I'll understand and I'll back off."

He didn't want to. Every cell in his body shouted at him because he couldn't conceive of never touching her again now that he had. Once he'd spent real time in bed with her, she would be out of his system, and he would be able to be friendly with her. Then it wouldn't matter if she chose to date Wyatt. Though he still thought it was a bad idea.

Wyatt was wrong. He wasn't backing off because his brothers had both left and didn't seem to give a shit about him. He wasn't staying away from close ties because his mom had died and then he'd watched his grandfather's body and mind slowly decay. He simply knew himself and was realistic.

"All right."

He wasn't sure what Wyatt meant by those two words because there wasn't much inflection behind them. "So you want me to back off?"

"No," Wyatt replied. "Let's talk to her. Be honest. See if she maybe is interested in a hot weekend and in getting to know me better. You're only here for the sex. I'll take care of her. She moved her whole life to Bliss. She's got to be curious. Her sister's in this kind of relationship. I can't imagine she doesn't want to try it, but hopefully she'll also be open to dating in a more conventional way. Or we can find another guy."

Wow. Those words had him standing up straight and for reasons he did not want to think about right now. Or ever. "You can't bring in some random guy. You have to have a partner. You don't, like, audition for a third. The guys have to be long-time friends."

Wyatt's brows rose in question. "Like Alexei and Caleb?"

"Okay. They weren't exactly friends." Caleb had pretty much hated Alexei. Or so he'd heard. It wasn't like he sat around gossiping about the town citizens. He sometimes happened to be in the room where his servers were gossiping. Or he overheard Lucy and River talking about it.

Wyatt wasn't done. "From what I understand, Michael didn't know much about Ty when they started dating Lucy."

Now he did know about that particular threesome. "Ty screwed up with Lucy or they wouldn't have needed Michael at all. Michael kind of slipped through the cracks, and now they can't get rid of him."

"They're happy together," Wyatt shot back. "I'm keeping my options open, and you should understand if you decide to be stubborn, you don't get a say in what happens to us after you're gone."

What did he mean by gone? "Well, I didn't say I was leaving. I kind of live here."

Wyatt's eyes rolled. "You are so literal. I'm saying if you're out, you don't get a say in what I do when it comes to Sabrina."

Sawyer wanted to argue because sometimes he thought Wyatt was a baby bird except with muscles and a rap sheet, but he was right about this. "All right."

Wyatt seemed to ready himself for battle. "So we're going to walk out there and ask her to sleep with us while we're snowed in."

"Or I could just kiss her and then we don't have to talk about it." He didn't see why they had to be so formal. He'd told her what he wanted. She'd let him lay her out on the dining room table. Talk over. "This time, you come in from behind. Like kiss her neck or something."

"We're talking to her. I need verbal confirmation of consent," Wyatt replied with a long-suffering sigh. "Buck it up, Sawyer. I'm in charge of this. I know that's going to be hard for you, but this isn't some tourist we're picking up. I like this woman."

Sawyer liked the tourists. They tended to be nice ladies. Well, he thought they probably were. It wasn't like he spent a lot of time with them.

He would be spending days with Sabrina.

Maybe this was a bad idea. Locked up in a cabin with a woman he had no business being friends with, much less lovers.

But Wyatt was walking out of the kitchen, and Sawyer found himself following.

This was going to be a train wreck.

Or an amazing night. He wasn't sure which one he hoped for.

Chapter Five

Sabrina closed the door to the bedroom she would be using while stuck in this cabin. This room. Not Sawyer's. What the hell had she been thinking? "Hey, sis. I'm fine. I didn't understand how quickly the storm would get bad and I tried to run an errand before I went home."

"Run an errand?" her sister asked. "On Sawyer's mountain? There's not much up there. Did you get lost? Did you forget the turnoff to Dad's place?"

She knew exactly how to get to Mel and Cassidy's. "No. It turns out Sawyer is my landlord."

"He is? Huh. I thought Marie handled it for you."

Her sister didn't know everything about Bliss. "She's only the agent and she's out of town. I really wanted to get the electrical system looked at."

"I told you Hale would do it. He's not going to charge you," Elisa insisted.

"He shouldn't have to," Sabrina countered. "My landlord should do it, and he should pay Hale if he does the work. It's not fair. He's agreed to let Hale look at it. They can sort it all out when the storm's over."

"Wyatt said you had an accident." Elisa sounded concerned.

"It's minor." If she didn't convince her sister, she would try to get up the mountain. "I wasn't going very fast, but my tires slid and I ended up hitting a tree and getting stuck. I had to walk to get to Sawyer's place. Though I didn't know it was Sawyer's place. I mean, I knew it was Sawyer. I just didn't know Sawyer was Sawyer."

"Oh, no. What did he do?" Elisa asked. "You're talking like you did in high school when you had a crush but didn't want Mom to know because she would inevitably talk you out of trying to date because all men are evil and no relationship ever works out."

Did? What had Sawyer done? Well, he'd awoken her sleeping beast because she'd kind of thought she was done with sex. Even as she'd gone on her last date, her heart hadn't been in it. Sex was awkward and so far not worth the embarrassment. She'd had exactly two lovers, and neither of them had been the stuff of romance novels. She wasn't sure why she thought it would be different.

But she did.

"I'm flustered. It's been a rough day, but I'm fine and the guys are nice. They said I can stay here until the storm passes. I need to call Del. She's going to have to open the school on Monday. Sawyer told me we likely won't be able to get off the mountain until Tuesday."

"That's what Nate told me, too," Elisa admitted. "I can try to get up there on a snowmobile if you need me to."

She wasn't going to risk her sister's life because she'd made a fool of herself. "I'm fine. Like I said, I'm safe and warm. I will admit it's awkward to be here with two strangers."

Elisa was quiet for a moment. "So I haven't talked about this because I didn't think anything would come of it. Sawyer's not exactly your type."

"Do I have a type? I kind of thought my type was only found in fiction." It was what she feared.

"Fair," Elisa conceded.

"What haven't you told me?" She wasn't sure she wanted to know.

"There are a couple of times I've heard people talk about what happened last year at the Christmas party," Elisa began.

She knew this story well. "He was an asshole to me."

"He behaved out of character," her sister countered. "I don't know the guy well, but he's always calm. I've had to go out to Hell on Wheels and handle a few situations. Sawyer's not exactly friendly but he's a solid guy, and he's not rude without provocation. Everyone in town still talks about how he reacted to you."

She had no idea the people were still talking about that night. She'd thought only she and Nate and Callie had noticed. "He told me it's because he's attracted to me and he doesn't want to be. So he's not merely rude. He's cruel."

Now her sister seemed genuinely taken aback. "I'm surprised. He's not known for lying. Quite the opposite. He's brutally honest. What's going on up there?"

She shouldn't have said anything at all. Except she kind of needed advice. "He kissed me."

"Sawyer did?" Elisa asked with a gasp, and Sabrina could hear her boyfriend Van say something in the background. "Van wants to know if Wyatt's there, too."

"He was in the kitchen."

"Van thinks that was a dirty play on Sawyer's part because Wyatt's been following you for months," Elisa said. "Really? And you didn't mention that to me? Sabrina, according to Van, Wyatt makes puppy-dog eyes your way, and he got sad when he saw you out with the Creede boys. Hang on."

"Hey, Brina," Van's deep voice came over the line. "So when you come into Trio and Wyatt's there, he always gets the server to change his table so he's closer to you. However, when he saw you on your date, he sat at the bar and talked to me all night about this woman he's interested in but hasn't been able to approach yet. He didn't say your name, but I knew who he was talking about."

Everything her sister's boyfriend said confirmed what Sawyer had told her. "Why didn't you say anything?"

"Uh, I'm going to give you back to Elisa."

Elisa huffed. "Coward. Okay, I did know Wyatt was interested, but he and Sawyer, well, they have complicated pasts."

Like she didn't know that. "He said he used to be a criminal."

"From what I understand, he was in a rogue motorcycle club for a few years," Elisa explained. "Do you know what a one percenter is?"

"I've seen *Sons of Anarchy*. Something like that?" She'd seen the previews at least.

"Pretty much but worse. The Colorado Horde is bad, Brina," Elisa said, her tone grim. "But from what Nate told me, he went in to try to save his brother. He got out when his brother went to jail because he took things too far and got caught. You should know Wyatt's older brother is the current president of the MC."

"But they both got out." It was all in the past.

"Yes, and Wyatt's adorable," Elisa agreed, "but you should know there's another side to him."

She wasn't sure where her sister was going. "Everyone has a dark side."

"You don't."

"Of course I do," Sabrina said with a sigh. "I just don't show it, and the violence I would do would likely always be to myself."

"Sabrina."

"No. I'm not saying I'm in a bad place, but I have been, and I managed to get out of it. I've had dark thoughts. Men who want to truly take advantage of a woman don't lay out all the bad facts and then try to convince her to sleep with them. They pour on the charm." Now she could clearly see what Sawyer had been trying to do. Warn her. Wave all his red flags. "He told me he wants to sleep with me while we're stuck but he won't date me afterward."

"Wyatt said that?" Elisa asked.

"No, Sawyer." What did Wyatt want from her? The situation was bizarre, but she couldn't help but be tempted. "Elisa, tell me I'm naïve for thinking about telling them yes."

A pause came over the line before her sister spoke again. "Do you think you're getting a love relationship out of this?"

She was being realistic this time around. "No. I think I'm going to get an orgasm, and I would really like an orgasm, sis. I've never had a real one before."

"You can't be... I suppose you can be serious," Elisa said with a sigh. "I know it couldn't have been easy trying to date when you were living with our mom. And then I needed you."

She could hear her sister getting emotional. Elisa had gone through breast cancer with surgery and chemo and radiation. Sabrina had taken care of her. She couldn't let her think anything but the truth. "I wouldn't take any of it back. I was so grateful I could be there for you. Not a second, Elisa. I wouldn't change anything."

"But you don't have anyone to take care of now. You deserve some wildness," her sister said, sniffling. "You deserve some joy, and I won't think any less of you if you take it. If you can take what he's willing to offer and nothing more, then it's not a bad idea as long as you're careful."

"Trust me. I have zero interest in Mr. Hathaway outside of his very hot body and what seems like his well-honed skills," Sabrina admitted. "He's not someone I would want to spend time with in the real world. I don't know about Wyatt. The crime-family thing is a bit off-putting, but I also think he seems incredibly nice."

"You don't have to make any decision except whether you trust them enough to spend a weekend with them. If the sex is bad or you decide you don't want them anymore, it could get awkward."

Or if she was bad in bed. She had to assume Sawyer had a ton of experience. Wyatt, too, since he was stunningly beautiful. And they'd done this together before. Though apparently only a few times. They were still probably good at it. She wasn't even sure she could have an orgasm.

A huff came over the line. "I know what you're thinking and stop. You're not bad at sex. You just haven't had a lot of it. I think you'll find most men have low bars when it comes to sex. If you're willing and enthusiastic, they'll be happy. I can't believe we're talking about this. Are you sure you don't want me to set you up with someone…"

"More in my league?" Sabrina asked.

"Not what I meant," Elisa said quickly. "I meant a couple of guys who would maybe fit better into your life. I think if you give Marshall and Knox a chance, you'll see how great they are. One date doesn't mean a thing."

She didn't want to argue with her sister. She also didn't need permission. Her sister thought she needed to move right into a permanent relationship, but Sabrina wanted to go a little wild for once in her life. There had been no spark with her sister's coworkers. They were great guys, and maybe she would be able to have a more open mind once she'd settled in. But for now there was only one experience in the world she wanted to have.

Even if it was the worst mistake she'd ever make. "You're right.

I'm being silly."

Her sister was quiet for a moment, and Sabrina knew she was thinking about how to handle her. "You're not being silly. Sabrina, I'm worried you're not built for an affair like this."

Her sister didn't think she could handle having sex. Probably didn't think she had those urges. She loved her sister, but somehow in that moment her sister sounded more like their mom. It wasn't fair or right, but as Elisa talked about how she needed a man who would enjoy her lifestyle all she heard was how boring she was. How in a box she'd become. She'd moved her whole life for a fresh start. Not all relationships had to be forever. She'd skipped the part where she had fun with no expectations, where she lived in the moment. "Thanks, sis. I'm sure you're right. I'm going to get some work done. Maybe some reading."

"I feel like I'm letting you down," Elisa said.

"Not at all." Could she blame her sister? She was trying to protect her. "Don't worry about me. I'm fine and in my right mind. The truth is Sawyer himself told me it would be better to not indulge this insane impulse."

"It's not insane. It's just... I think you're risking your heart, and I would hate to see it broken."

By Sawyer? No way. He was a walking vibrator in her head. But she was never going to tell her sister. This was going to be her secret. Something for her and no one else. "Not going to be a problem. Good night. I'll see you on Tuesday."

"I'll call you before then." Her sister's voice had gone low, concern plain. "If there's any way for me..."

She needed to shut that shit down now. If she was doing this, then she wanted all the time she could have. "Do not waste resources and put yourself in danger when I'm perfectly fine. I'm not joking, Elisa. I will see you on Tuesday. Good night."

She hung up before her sister could argue with her. Elisa had been extremely nonhelpful. She'd basically mirrored Sabrina's own emotional state, pinging back and forth between good idea and terrible idea. Somehow hearing it from someone else made her decision clear.

So maybe she had been helpful. If Elisa hadn't flip-flopped and made her see how ridiculous she was being, Sabrina would still be questioning herself. Instead, she carried the phone back toward the living room. She'd expected to find them in the kitchen, expected to have to figure out what Wyatt had been so upset over since according to everyone this was exactly what Wyatt wanted.

Instead, they stood in the living room, side by side. A pair of absolutely delectable treats, the kind she'd never been offered before.

She wasn't in their league, couldn't even begin to keep up with them sexually.

But damn she was going to try.

"Sabrina, we would like very much to have an open and honest conversation with you," Wyatt said, the expression on his gorgeous face so serious.

Had he been watching her? Waiting for a good time to ask this question? And Sawyer's eyes went right to her breasts. If he wasn't lying, then he wanted her. It felt like he wanted her.

An ache opened inside of Sabrina, one that could only be filled by them.

"I want you to understand if you say no, it's one hundred percent cool. If you feel uncomfortable, I'll find a way to make you comfortable. There's no pressure," Wyatt was saying.

"Uh, if she says no, it's totally going to be awkward," Sawyer muttered under his breath.

He was not an optimist. She was done with talking. Words didn't do a damn thing for her right now. She'd overanalyzed everything her whole life. Now she wanted to feel.

Sabrina walked straight up to Wyatt and went on her toes and pressed her lips to his.

* * * *

Wyatt had been about to tell Sawyer to shut his mouth when Sabrina was suddenly all up in his space, her breasts pressing against his chest and his cock immediately at attention. He was so shocked he stood there for a moment, letting her soft lips brush over his.

"I've been told you might like me," she whispered.

Okay, so now he wasn't so pissed at Sawyer, who'd almost surely told her his secret since he'd been excellent at hiding it. "I think you're gorgeous, Sabrina."

Her hands found the tops of his shoulders and her eyes came up, staring at him with an innocent lust that damn near flattened him. "I think you're gorgeous, Wyatt. I don't want to admit it because it's going to go straight to his already big head, but Sawyer's not bad himself."

Sawyer snorted.

This felt more intimate than anything he'd had before. "He's not as egotistical as he seems. He's hiding a bunch of unprocessed childhood trauma. And adult trauma."

"I processed it all," Sawyer argued. "I don't need to write a double album about it."

He felt his lips tick up as he stared down at Sabrina. She was beautiful, with lush lips and wide eyes and a nose he wanted to drop a kiss on. It felt right to be here with both of them, safe and warm in this cabin. "He's talking about my musical preferences. When I lived with my family, it was all screaming rock songs. Turns out I like Taylor Swift."

"I do, too," she said with a grin. "So you mentioned we should have a talk. How about we skip it and I say yes?"

All he needed was a yes, but he found himself deeply enjoying talking to her. Flirting with her, his hands finding the curves of her hips. "How about I take your yes and run with it? If we talk, Sawyer will go into all the ways he's damaged and can't possibly have any kind of a human relationship outside this cabin."

She turned her head slightly, and Sawyer shrugged.

"He's not wrong," Sawyer said.

She winked his way. "I promise I won't ask for a ring unless it fits around your neck and I can strangle you with it. After, of course."

"After," Sawyer said, moving in beside them. "Did I mention how mean you are?"

It seemed like every time Sawyer managed to get the super-sweet woman to take a swipe at him, his interest went through the roof.

"You bring out the bad in me," she said and then looked back to Wyatt. "How does this work? I've never... I mean I have..."

"You've never had this kind of sex," Wyatt concluded. "It's pretty much the same except with four hands on your body."

"And there are two dicks," Sawyer added as though she wouldn't be able to figure it out.

"No, there's one dick and then there's Wyatt," she shot back and went on her toes.

She was fucking perfect. He lowered his head, letting his mouth find hers as Sawyer groaned and moved in behind her. Wyatt kissed her for real this time, allowing himself to take control. He moved one hand up to cup the back of her neck while the other wrapped around her waist, pressing her against him. He let his tongue run over her plump bottom lip and then inside when she flowered open for him.

"I was only trying to make her understand we'll both want her," Sawyer said, his voice deep and thick with arousal. "I didn't want her to think we would like whisk her off to one of our bedrooms and she'd only be with one of us. We're not switching off. If we're doing this, we'll all stay in the big bedroom for the weekend."

Her eyes looked a bit glazed when Wyatt let go of her mouth. "Yeah, I got that part. My sister's boyfriends don't pass her off to each other on a nightly basis. They're all in one big bed. I have to say, it sounds nice."

"It is nice." He intended to make it so nice for her she would overlook the fact that Sawyer was an ass who was going to fight this tooth and nail for a long time. Eventually he would come around. At some point, Sawyer would think it was nice, too. "But you know what's going to make it even nicer?"

Sawyer was already turning her his way, getting his mouth on hers so she couldn't answer.

"Getting you naked." It was time to take charge. This was where he felt the most in control. When he was with a woman, giving her pleasure and affection, taking care of her needs.

This was everything he'd wanted since the day he knew he was going to find a way to leave the club. By any means necessary.

She made the sweetest mewling sound as Sawyer seemed to try to inhale her. No matter what the asshole said, he was so into Sabrina. Wyatt had known him a long time, and he'd never seen Sawyer react to a woman the way he was now. Wyatt watched as Sawyer turned her fully toward himself, his hands cupping that luscious ass of hers.

They looked good together. She was small and curvy to Sawyer's blatant masculinity.

Wyatt sat down on the couch, willing to watch the show now that he understood he wasn't being left out of it. He'd let all those old voices play with his head, and he wasn't going to do it again. He was in a good place now, and he was going to enjoy it.

Damn, but he was going to enjoy her.

Sawyer finally let her breathe, turning her around so she faced Wyatt. "He wants to see you naked. I want to see you naked, too. I want to be naked with you most of the next couple of days, so you should be aware."

"It's cold," she said but with a breathy laugh that went straight to Wyatt's dick.

"We'll keep you warm," Wyatt promised. "Now let me see you. Do you have any idea how long I've wanted to see you stripped down and naked for me?"

"Apparently since the first time you saw me." She seemed to stop and lose a bit of the confidence she'd walked into the room with. "I heard a rumor, but it might not be true."

"You were sitting in the park with your sister and you were drinking coffee. Black with two sugars. I had been walking back to my bike. I had some errands to run." He'd had to see Doc Burke to check on the burn wounds he'd taken. He'd been aching, and then he'd seen her. "You were sitting there and you laughed. I love the way you laugh. And then I saw you and I thought you were the most beautiful thing I'd ever seen."

She took a moment before she replied. "I know I shouldn't believe you."

"He's not smart enough to lie," Sawyer snarked.

Sabrina turned and frowned at him. "You need to stop teasing him. He's obviously smart. You said he grew up rough, and he's managed to make something of himself. He got out. That makes him smart."

He wasn't sure about how smart he was, but he deeply enjoyed the way she defended him. He knew she was going into this whole encounter with Sawyer's words in her head. She thought she could spend the weekend with two bad boys and get out with a smile on her face and the town none the wiser.

He was going to make sure she couldn't walk away.

"I sat down on the bench across from you and you never noticed me. You were far too busy talking to every kid who walked by," Wyatt continued. "Your eyes would light up and then you would talk to them and give the kid a high five or a hug. You seemed to know exactly how to handle them all."

"I was new in town, and someone clearly had called around and said I was in the park. And the moms and dads brought out all their kids to meet me," she said wistfully. "It was a lovely way to start to get to know everyone."

"I had also just moved here, and seeing you sitting there made me sure I'd done the right thing," he said. "But I'm sure Sawyer would say I'm going too fast, so let's concentrate on getting you naked because I assure you I wanted to see you that day, too. Whatever you've heard it's true. I haven't been able to stop thinking about you. So be brave and hand Sawyer your shirt. Though you should know I like seeing you in my clothes. I'll be sad when you're back in your own."

"Your disappointment will have to wait, because like I said, we're keeping her naked." Sawyer's hands went to the hem of her shirt. "Let's go, baby. Wyatt's right. We're taking too long."

Wyatt had wanted to have a long discussion, but it was clear something the deputy had said to her sister had done the trick. It was good to know her sister didn't have a problem with him. Sawyer was wrong. The people of the town seemed to like them both, though they did think Sawyer was kind of a dick most of the time.

Sabrina's arms went up as she allowed Sawyer to drag the shirt over her head, and she wasn't wearing a bra. Wyatt's dick tightened again, almost painfully, but he was ignoring it because watching her blush under his gaze was everything. Her breasts were round and full and tipped with pink and brown nipples that hardened as she stood there. She was far more beautiful than he'd imagined. And he'd imagined a lot.

Sawyer's big hands came from behind and cupped those lush breasts. She gasped and then her eyes closed and she leaned back into him, biting her bottom lip.

How long had it been since she'd been adored the way they were going to adore her tonight?

He'd watched her, carefully listened to how people spoke about her, had gotten to know what they thought about her in town. Sidney Carmichael adored her on every level. She worked at Hell on Wheels and her kid was in one of Sabrina's classes. Sidney practically worshipped the ground she walked on.

So he'd known she was smart and kind.

Watching her handle Sawyer was a revelation, though.

Watching how she melted against him made Wyatt want to join them. But he had a point to make. He was perfectly willing to go with the flow, to put others' needs in front of his own. There was one place he needed control.

"Off with the pants, Sabrina."

Before she could follow his orders, Sawyer's hands were moving, thumbs hooking onto the waist band of the too big for her pajama bottoms and tugging.

"No underwear," Sawyer said with a low chuckle. "I'm surprised."

"It's in the wash," she replied, flushing beautifully. "You didn't give me any."

"Don't have any panties laying around, Teach," Sawyer admitted. "And I might throw yours out altogether. You won't need them."

Her chin came up, and she turned on Sawyer, pointing a finger his way. "Don't you dare. I will need them. Do you understand what I will do to you if you leave me pantiless come Tuesday morning?"

"He's baiting you, sweetheart. He likes it when you get mean." Wyatt liked the view of her gorgeous ass. "I'll save your undies. Now come here and sit on my lap and I'll explain to you how the rest of the night is going to go."

Sawyer's lips curled up. "You should do what he says. He's kind of bossy when he's horny. The good news is he's totally chill the other ninety percent of the time. Now kiss me before he makes you pay him all the attention."

Sawyer dragged her close, his hands going straight to her ass, cupping her cheeks while he inhaled her. Their mouths moved as they kissed, bodies tight against each other.

Then Sawyer pulled back, and one hand went around her torso as the other scooped her knees up. He lifted her easily, cradling her against his chest.

Sabrina's eyes had gone wide. "You picked me up."

"Don't say it," Wyatt warned.

"I'm too heavy. You could hurt your back." She said it.

"Now you've done it," Sawyer said with a wince. He walked with her, not showing a single sign her sweet weight bothered him at all. Because it wouldn't.

Sawyer deposited her onto Wyatt's lap, and he suddenly had a bundle of soft, sweet femininity in his arms. He wanted to roll her over on the couch and cover her with his body. But he had a point to make.

"Sabrina, I won't listen to you talk badly about yourself. I won't allow anyone else to either, but definitely not you. You are gorgeous and made of curves I find so fucking sexy. I assure you Sawyer and I could carry you around all day and never feel your weight."

"You're sweet," she said with a shy smile.

"Here's the not sweet part," he offered. "I'll give you this one. You didn't know the rules. Now you do. Say it again and I'll spank that sweet ass of yours."

Her mouth came open but her eyes had gone soft.

Score one for him. He'd known damn well she would be sexually submissive. She probably needed it. She seemed like the kind of woman who put everyone else in front of herself, who deep down worried any kind of pleasure was selfish. So he would give her a place where it wasn't until she could understand how much she deserved a man's adoration. "Spank me?"

He felt his lips curl up as he smoothed back her hair. "Yes. I'll turn you over my knee and I'll stroke my hand over your cheeks, and then when you're not quite sure what I'm going to do, I'll smack your sweet flesh until it's pink and you're hot and your pussy is dripping with arousal."

She bit her bottom lip. "See, now it doesn't sound like a threat."

"Oh, it is," Wyatt promised. "But the best kind because I think you'll like it. If you don't, then it's off the table. But, baby, I don't want to hear you talk badly about yourself. Call Sawyer an asshole all you like. Tell him he's a rude prick, but don't say anything about yourself."

"That's fair," Sawyer agreed because he was pretty self-aware.

"You're like some of the other guys in Bliss, aren't you?" Sabrina asked.

"If you're talking about whether I'm into the D/s lifestyle, not in any formal way. It's for fun, baby. If you're asking if I need to be in control during sex, pretty much, yes. I have some things I went through as a younger man, and I'm still processing them, but I don't know if I'll ever be willing to do certain things. Even things I would like to do to you, so I know it's not fair."

Her gaze softened, and she put a hand to his cheek. "What things, Wyatt?"

He shook his head. "Not tonight. I want tonight to be about you."

He didn't want to tell her his secrets—would never tell her all of them. Not tonight. Not until she knew him better. He had to prove he wasn't the man his father and brother had tried to make him be. And it started with pleasure.

When he leaned toward her, her arms went around him and he knew he'd won.

For now.

Chapter Six

Sabrina felt alive in a way she was pretty sure she never had before, and she knew this was a mistake of massive proportions.

She was still going to make it.

She was sitting on the lap of one of the two hottest men she'd ever met, and he kissed like a dream. Wyatt's tongue stroked hers even as his hands did the same, finding her curves and leaving a trail of arousal everywhere he went.

"I'm going to get things ready," the other hottest man she'd ever met said. Sawyer was standing over them, and he'd gotten rid of his shirt. His muscular chest was on display, and it made Sabrina want to run her hands all over him. He smiled down at her as though he could see her desires on her face. He leaned over and kissed her forehead, a sweet gesture that felt completely contradictory to his normal taciturn nature.

Her heart softened, and this was why it was such a bad idea.

She was pretty sure her sister was right and she would be emotionally involved with them by the end of the weekend, and Sawyer had made himself plain.

"Come on, Bella," Sawyer said, and she realized the dog had been sitting there watching them.

Wyatt brought her attention back to him. "He'll feed her and put her in her crate for the night. Tell me how you like it."

It. Sex. He was talking about sex. Well, of course he was since she was naked in his arms. Completely naked. While there was a storm outside, it was warm in here, the fire's heat caressing her skin, though it was the fire they'd stoked inside her really heating her up.

One weekend. It was all she would have with them, so she was going for broke. "I don't know, Wyatt. I'm going to be honest. I haven't had a ton of sex. I've only dated a couple of guys, and it wasn't anything to write home about. I've already felt more intimate with you than I did any of them."

A brilliant smile crossed his face. The man could light up a room when he wanted to. "It's because I talk a lot. Sawyer's going to say I talk too much, but it's good to talk during sex. How will I know if you like something or want to try something if you don't tell me?"

"I think I might like to try the spanking thing," she admitted. The minute the word spanking had rolled out of his mouth, she'd felt her whole body tighten with anticipation. She'd read about it in romance novels and had always wanted to ask Elisa if she'd tried it.

But she hadn't.

"We can try anything you want," he promised.

"As long as you're in control." She said the words more as a reminder than an admonition, but she saw a little hurt go through him. "I like you being in control, Wyatt. I think that might have been the problem before. No one was in control. I don't know what I like because so far, outside of this evening, I would have told you I don't really like sex at all. Now I think I wasn't with men who took it seriously."

"I'll tell you what I like." Wyatt's hand came up and cupped her breast. "I like spending whole evenings like this. You naked and sitting on my lap while we watch a movie or talk. If you're cold, we'll wrap you in a blanket, but my hands will be on you. I'll kiss you every now and then and play with your nipples and rub your clit to remind you how this ends. With me inside you."

The man knew how to talk. She definitely would have said talking about sex would be awkward and it would be better to simply do it, but he was making her reconsider everything. She could feel the swell of his erection against her ass. "How will you…take me together? At the same time."

His fingers started playing with her nipples, exactly as he'd promised. Fire seemed to lick through her, making her squirm. "Yes, we'll take you at the same time, but, baby, we've got to work our way up. I don't know if it happens this weekend. I don't suppose you've had a bunch of anal sex."

And there it was. Yup. She was talking about butt stuff. "Never."

"Does it scare you?"

"A little, but I think I'm ready to try scary things. Especially since I happen to know a couple of women who tell me it's amazing." Her sister didn't really tell her. She simply walked around with a smile on her face all the time, glowing in a way she never had before.

"We'll get you ready." Wyatt's eyes were on her mouth. "I think I'd like you to get me ready now. Take my shirt off, Sabrina."

He released her, allowing her to slide off his lap. She leaned over, realizing how close the position put her breasts to his mouth. She slowly unbuttoned the flannel shirt he wore, and every now and then she would feel his lips brush her breasts, tongue flicking out to stroke a nipple. Sabrina groaned but kept up the task she'd been assigned. And realized he was wearing layers. This would have been infinitely easier in the summertime.

But then she wouldn't be stuck here with them.

He held his hands up when it was time to drag the T-shirt over his head.

And she got her first look at his chest. His muscular, ruined chest.

He winced when she stepped back. "Yeah, I probably should have warned you about that. I had an accident last year. Got hit with a blowtorch. It's fine now. I can keep the shirt on if you want. I know it's…"

Oh, she wasn't playing with this man. "Don't you say it. If I can't say it, you can't. It's not ugly. I was just surprised. Blowtorch? How do you accidently get hit with a blowtorch?"

"Maybe it wasn't so much of an accident. I don't want to talk about the past tonight," Wyatt said with a weary sigh.

She didn't want to pull him down into a place she understood well. Regret. Pain. The wish things had gone differently.

"Unless it bothers you," Wyatt offered.

"Do I get to spank you?"

His lips split in a brilliant smile, and he reached out, pulling her back down into his arms. "Like I said I've got some boundaries that might not feel entirely fair, so how about we find another way I pay for my sins."

He flipped her so she was flat on her back and he was between her legs, denim rubbing against her pink parts. Then he was moving along her body, his eyes on her as he pushed himself down. He moved until his mouth was right above her pelvis, hovering above her pussy.

Her heart rate ticked up, whole body going tight with anticipation. Was he going to?

Yes. He was definitely going to.

"How about if I get insecure and start saying bad shit about myself, I owe you," Wyatt offered. "I owe you this."

Heat poured through her veins as Wyatt licked her clitoris. He parted her labia and ran his tongue along her most tender flesh. Her head fell back on one of the pillows as he ate her pussy like a starving man.

"Now that is a pretty sight," a deep voice said.

She opened her eyes and Sawyer was standing beside them, watching Wyatt work her pussy.

"I bet you taste like heaven, Teach," Sawyer said, pulling at the buckle of his belt.

Desire overwhelmed her. She was a woman used to living in her head, used to allowing all the worries of daily life to invade on every moment of her existence.

She couldn't think of a single reason why this wasn't the best idea she'd ever had. Not one. Actually, she couldn't get her brain to form a single thought except one.

More.

Wyatt licked her pussy in long strokes before sending his tongue deep inside, spearing her the way his cock eventually would.

"Give me your hand," Sawyer ordered.

Without thought she lifted her right hand toward him as Wyatt continued to fuck her with his tongue. She glanced at Sawyer and gasped because he'd chucked his jeans and stood there totally naked, every inch of him muscled and perfect. His cock stood at attention, thrust up from a nest of neat dark hair, and he brought her hand to it.

"He's going to be on you in a heartbeat once he wrings an orgasm out of you. He won't even wait until we're in bed," Sawyer explained. "So I have to get what I can. Stroke me."

She wrapped her hand around his big cock, loving the feel of soft flesh covering hard muscle. Sawyer's hand covered hers, directing her.

Sabrina rode the wave, letting Wyatt pull her one way while Sawyer pushed her another. Somehow it wasn't chaotic. Somehow they managed to find a beautiful rhythm, matching each other and making it all run smoothly.

"You feel so fucking good," Sawyer muttered, his hand tightening around hers as he picked up the pace.

"You *taste* so fucking good." She heard Wyatt's words rumble against her pussy and then he sucked her clit between his lips, and she knew she was done for.

She felt Sawyer's cock swell in her hands as the orgasm overtook her.

Nope. She'd never had one before. Not a real one. She'd had little pleasures, mostly given by her own hands, but this was something so different. This encased her and shoved the rest of the world out, blanketing her in pleasure as surely as the snow outside covered the world.

Sawyer groaned, and she felt the warmth of his release cover her fingers as she pumped his cock.

Wyatt rose from her pussy, getting to his knees and shoving his jeans down, releasing his own cock.

He was so beautiful. Every bit as masculine as Sawyer, but in a unique way. Lean muscle to Sawyer's linebacker presence. His cock was long and hard in his hand as he stared down at Sabrina, her arousal still on his lips.

Sawyer released her hand and reached to the table, grabbing something he tossed Wyatt's way. "Thought you would need that."

Condom. She watched as Wyatt tore open the package and with shaking hands rolled the condom over his cock.

Sawyer sank down on the couch across from them, not bothering to put his clothes back on.

Her whole body felt liquid as Wyatt spread her legs and settled between them. His face was a mask of desire as he leaned down and kissed her.

He wanted her. So did Sawyer. It wouldn't last but it didn't matter. She had this moment. This weekend. She could remember it forever and remember how for a brief moment she was everything she wanted to be.

She wrapped her legs around his waist as she felt his cock press against her. Sawyer being in the room made it perfect. He was sitting there watching them, no jealousy at all in his expression. When she looked over at him, he winked her way, his hand stroking his cock again.

He was waiting for his turn.

She wasn't this woman. She wasn't the kind of woman who could handle two men. Except she was. This weekend she was. She could go back to being Ms. Leal when the snow melted, but for now she was dedicated to simply being theirs.

She gasped as he pressed himself inside. His hands held her tight as though he was afraid of losing her. She could have told him she wasn't going anywhere. She wanted to know. Needed to see this through and take all the memories they could make in this short, stolen period of time.

He kissed her again, focusing her on him and the feel of his cock stretching her. She was so full of him, so surrounded by him, and with Sawyer's gaze on her she felt like he was with them, too.

Wyatt kissed her over and over, giving her time to adjust. When her hands found his waist, slipping down to cup the cheeks of his ass, he groaned and pulled away slightly.

"You feel so good," he said against her ear. "So fucking good."

He pulled out and then thrust back in, and Sabrina couldn't help but tighten herself around him, wanting him as close as possible. This was the intimacy she'd always craved, this feeling that they weren't separate at all in this moment. Wyatt moved in and out, his cock rubbing against her sweet spot. She felt her whole body—so loose only moments before—tighten in anticipation. She'd been sure this part would only be for him. She'd known she would take the closeness and affection while they had their pleasure, but she felt desire spark through her again.

Wyatt picked up the pace, and she went careening over the edge, the orgasm catching her off guard and taking her breath away. Wyatt seemed to go wild, his hips thrusting over and over as his cock moved inside her. She tightened her hands on him, riding the wave to a perfection she'd only found once before. Moments ago, with him.

Wyatt fell on top of her, and she loved the feel of his weight. A deep sense of peace invaded her bones as he kissed her neck and ran his nose along her skin. He breathed her in, like he was trying to memorize her scent.

He smelled like sex and pine and the warmth of a fire in the middle of winter.

He smelled like home.

Sabrina shook herself out of the thought. She wasn't falling into the trap. This was exactly what Sawyer had told her it was. Sex, and it was grand.

She forced the emotion out of her head, concentrating on the needs of her body. She kissed Wyatt and then grinned Sawyer's way. "So what do you say we take this to the bedroom?"

Sawyer stood. "I say that's the best idea I've heard in years, Teach."

Wyatt kissed her one more time and then rolled off her. He kind of hit the floor in an ungraceful move because he hadn't bothered to completely take off his pants. Wyatt laughed, his face young and carefree as he rolled over. "Guess I was too eager. But don't worry. Next time I'll do it right, girl."

He'd done it perfectly, but before she had a chance to tell him, Sawyer moved in and lifted her up into his arms. "You got her dirty. I'm going to clean her up. We'll see you in bed, partner. How about you bring those brownies in? I get the feeling I'm going to be hungry."

Wyatt stood suddenly, pulling his jeans up and looking utterly delicious. "My brownies."

He ran off toward the kitchen.

And Sawyer carried her away.

It was going to be a sweet night.

* * * *

Sawyer was surprised at how much he felt for the woman in his arms. He'd watched her with Wyatt, and something deep inside had clicked. Like someone had turned a switch he hadn't known previously existed. It scared the fuck out of him, but he wasn't going to let this night go by without having her.

He had days with her, days and nights before he had to acknowledge the fact that they wouldn't work in the real world. The real world was snowed in and couldn't get to them right now, so it could go fuck itself.

He carried her through the cabin he'd grown up in, into the room he'd taken over when his grandfather had passed, and into the bathroom he'd spent a shit ton of money redecorating.

Sabrina's eyes widened as she took in the surroundings. "This is beautiful."

He couldn't help but grin. "Unlike the rest of the place?"

"That's not what I meant."

He set her on her feet. "I know. This is one of the rooms I spent cash on after I inherited the place." He moved to the big shower. It dominated the room. Sawyer had hand selected the rock wall and the stone flooring. "This used to be about a quarter the size and had nothing but an old sink, toilet you had to jiggle the handle to get to flush, and a bathtub I'm pretty sure Granddad found at a junkyard. He did his decorative shopping at the junkyard. Come here."

She stood in the middle of his dream bathroom looking slightly nervous and awkward and still sexy as hell.

"Sabrina, I came all over your hands. The least I can do is wash you up," he offered. He didn't worry she was changing her mind. The way she looked at him told him she wasn't searching for an exit ramp. She simply wasn't used to walking around naked in a strange man's house. "Come here."

He turned on the shower, setting the temperature and the steam levels.

"This is amazing, Sawyer." She let him lead her inside and breathed in the steam. "Is that...?"

"Lavender," he replied. "The shower has a couple of scents it releases. I didn't actually pick them. They came with the package, but I find the eucalyptus is helpful when I have a cold and the lavender... Well, women like the lavender."

Her lips curled up. "Is this your secret? You lure women into this lush bathroom to make it easier to seduce them?"

He felt the water warming on his back, and he stared down at the gorgeous teacher. "I've actually had very few women here. This place, well, I grew up here. It feels a little sacred to me. I updated a couple of things after my grandfather passed. This bathroom was one of them because Granddad was stingy when it came to money. I didn't even know what showers were until I stayed at Ty's place when I was a kid. I thought everyone had to bathe in cold water and fit three boys into a tiny space to get ready for school. I vowed one day I would have a real bathroom and a workshop. Everything else stayed pretty much the same until Wyatt complained about the stove and the refrigerator."

"What was wrong with them?" Her hands found his waist, and the talk was doing what he'd hoped it would. She was relaxing. She was focused on him. She hadn't even noticed he'd placed a string of condoms on the shelf containing the soap and shampoo.

"Grandad found those in a junkyard, too. I'm pretty sure they were from the sixties. You had to be real careful because the stove got hot to the touch when it was on. And the freezer, well, it had zones. Some of them were way too cold so your food froze, and some weren't cold enough so it spoiled. It was always an adventure, but Wyatt wanted to know his food wasn't going to go bad or be frozen, and he's been burned enough so we bought new ones."

Her eyes went soft. "Someone burned him. He didn't want to talk about it, but I can't imagine it was an accident."

"It wasn't, and he'll tell you the story when the time is right. You have to know he's out of that life now. The burns on his chest were payment for leaving. You don't get out of an outlaw MC without pain. There are men I've met who I would say they'll go back, but Wyatt isn't one of them. He's a solid guy." He owed it to Wyatt to let her know what a good man he was. She could trust him. Even if she could never trust Sawyer.

She put a hand on Sawyer's arm, right over the black box where his Horde tattoo had once been. "And this was yours?"

The room was starting to steam up, so he eased her closer, invading her space. "I had it easier than Wyatt. I wasn't born into it. I went into the club because my brother was a moron, and someone had to watch over him."

She breathed in the steam. "Did you save him?"

"Sort of. I made sure he didn't die, but when I had the chance to keep him out of jail, I didn't take it. I thought it would prove to him

110

this wasn't the right life. And it did. He did his time and now he's in Denver with his wife and child, and he's happy from what I can tell." He didn't know. All he knew was Wes didn't want to have anything to do with him, and that was fine.

He'd gone into the MC to try to save his brother, and now his brother was on the straight and narrow and had his white picket fence, and there was no place for his unsavory bar-owner brother who lived on a mountainside. He didn't want his new friends to know where he'd come from, and Sawyer was proof of his wild youth.

Wes deserved his white picket fence and two point five kids. And so did Sabrina, which was why he would absolutely let her go at the end of this weekend.

Her eyes had a wide, soft look, letting him know she was about to go all sweet and sympathetic. Sympathy was the last thing he wanted. He did the only thing he could do. He leaned over and kissed her. So much better. When his mouth was on hers he felt like he had something he could give her, something she needed. Her mouth opened under his, and then the steam wasn't merely coming from the shower.

She was so fucking small against him. So petite and sweet, and he agreed with Wyatt. She should get her ass smacked when she talked bad about herself. He wasn't all aboard the BDSM train the way Stefan Talbot was, and he'd never dipped his toe in it the way Wyatt had started to, but smacking her pretty ass held a strong appeal.

There would be time enough to play later. Right now his cock was tightening, letting him know that little orgasm he'd had wasn't going to cut it. He wanted inside her. He let his tongue play with hers. He felt her hands on his hips as she pressed her body to his. Her breasts were crushed against his chest as he pulled her closer and let the water slide over them.

He got his hands on her, loving how soft her skin was, how her breasts felt when he cupped them. He adored the moans she made as his thumbs brushed over her nipples. Before long he was kissing his way down her body. Caressing her neck and shoulders, licking at her nipples and dipping into the hollow of her sweet belly button.

"Spread your legs."

Sabrina gasped because Sawyer hadn't been the one giving the order. She should probably get used to Wyatt popping in. Sawyer had known he would show up at some point, and he would likely get pretty bossy.

However, he agreed this time. "Spread your legs."

Sawyer leaned over and ran a finger against her pretty pussy. Soft and warm and very pink. She smelled like lavender and sex. He licked and sucked and played with her pussy while Wyatt moved in behind her, holding her up and giving her balance. Wyatt's hands played with her breasts while he whispered into her ear. Sawyer couldn't hear, but he knew what his partner was saying.

She was beautiful.

She was sexy.

They wanted her so badly.

All true.

Sawyer dragged his tongue over her pussy and was delighted with the gasp and squirm she gave him.

"You hold still," Wyatt growled. "You let him have you any way he wants. That's what this weekend is about. We get to have you, to bring you to orgasm again and again. You're going to be our sweet little fuck toy. Do you want to be our fuck toy, Sabrina?"

He half expected the smart teacher to tell him to go to hell. Wyatt always had to push. But Sabrina nodded.

"Yes," she said, and she didn't whisper the word. She said it out loud. Like she meant it. Like she really wanted it.

He could have ignored this pull of attraction if she'd stayed the soft, sweet teacher he'd thought she was. But she was kind of a badass bitch, and it did something for him. His cock was aching, and he didn't want to wait another second.

Sawyer stood and grabbed the condom he'd placed on the shelf earlier. His freaking hands were shaking.

He wanted her.

He wanted her way more than he wanted to want her.

He looked back, and Wyatt had taken advantage of the situation to turn her toward him, kissing her deeply. They already looked like a couple. There was zero awkwardness between them, as though they'd touched and everything between them fell into place.

The universe could be so fucking cruel because Sawyer didn't see how it could work, how she wouldn't get hurt by coming into their world.

And still he couldn't stop. He couldn't not take these days with her.

He shoved out all the worry. He wanted one fucking night where he didn't think about how he would fit into her world, where he only knew she was in his and she was safe. He would go right back to reality in a couple of days, but not now. Now was all about the three of them, and for now Sawyer was a part of it.

"Hey, don't hog the girl." It was his turn, damn it. Hopefully by the end of the weekend they could maybe take her together and have one perfect memory, but for now, he wanted to be with her.

Wyatt's smile was utterly satisfied. Like a man who knew he was going to get exactly what he wanted. He was obviously certain he could tempt Sawyer.

Then Sabrina opened her eyes and bit that full bottom lip of hers, and Sawyer knew it would take everything he had to let her go come Tuesday. She was his walking wet dream, and tonight he could have her.

With a low growl, he moved into her space and picked her up, relishing in the gasp that came from her throat. He pressed her against the wall of the shower and spread her legs wide. He captured her mouth with his, tongue plunging deep in an imitation of what he was about to do with his cock. Her legs went around his waist, hands grasping at his shoulders as she kissed him back, giving him all her sweet passion.

"Sawyer," she said as he pulled away slightly.

"Sabrina," he replied, staring into her eyes. He didn't need to look down to know where his cock was. It was right there, right where the fucker wanted to be.

"Please."

Her breathy plea was all he needed. Sawyer thrust up, penetrating her deeply with one long pass.

Her eyes widened and she held on tighter, legs clenched around him as though she was afraid to let him go. He could have told her he wasn't going anywhere. There was no place he wanted to be but right here in this moment with her.

This was heaven.

His whole body felt electric. He'd had a lot of sex, but this felt like something more. He let his body lead him. His brain would only question everything, but his body knew exactly what he needed.

Her.

Sawyer pressed her hard against the wall as he fucked into her over and over again. Something about knowing Wyatt was watching made it all the hotter.

Sawyer kissed her over and over, feeling drugged with the sex and the intimacy, with simply being here with them. With being a part of a "them." He'd never thought he would be, but this felt perfect and right.

He angled his hips up so he could find her sweet spot and knew the minute her nails dug into his shoulders that he'd managed it. She gasped and held on as he stroked into her again and again, until he felt her pussy spasm around him, giving him exactly what he wanted.

His eyes damn near rolled back as the pleasure took him, but he was determined to watch her, to take in every moment of her pleasure. Every sound, and the hard feel of those nails sinking into his skin, proving she was as fierce as she was sweet, that she was an excellent match.

He slammed into her one final time, giving up everything he had.

Pleasure and peace. It was what she brought him.

"Baby, he dirtied you up again," Wyatt said with a *tsk* in his tone. "Come here. I'm going to make sure you're clean."

Sabrina's hands had gone gentle, stroking down his back as she stayed right where she was, against the wall with his dick still inside her. "I don't think he means that."

It was good she was starting to understand them. He kissed her again, something he almost never did. Fucking, yes. Kissing, no. He wasn't the type of man who simply kissed a woman over and over again because he couldn't get enough of her.

Yet here he was.

He didn't want to let her go but he did. He backed up, ensuring her feet found the floor as he stepped into the spray of the shower. Now he kind of wished it was cold. He was already heating up for her again.

Wyatt immediately stepped in, and his mouth was on hers in a heartbeat.

Sawyer took a long breath and realized he was in serious trouble.

Chapter Seven

Sabrina woke up on Monday morning feeling a bit sore and a whole lot satisfied.

Two days of pretty much nonstop sex would do that to a girl. It made her wonder what sexy shenanigans they would get into today. They had another whole day together, and she was certain those two men wouldn't waste it.

She yawned and stretched and wondered where her love gods had gotten off to. The clock told her it wasn't exactly early, so she would bet her men had decided to let her sleep in while they started work. Living in a cabin like this wasn't as easy as her mom's home in North Carolina. Sawyer would check on the generator, ensure they had enough dry firewood. Wyatt would start breakfast and coffee.

How had she lived for years in the two-story her mom had bought after she'd left the Army and never truly felt at home? She didn't even realize it. Not feeling cozy and safe, like nothing bad could ever happen here, had been normal to her. Until she'd come to Bliss.

The heavenly smell of coffee wafted through. Soon there would be bacon and eggs and toast.

She got on her knees, looking out the window over the big bed in the room they'd shared during these stolen days. It had a view out to what she considered the backyard, though it wasn't like there was a fence or anything. It was a window to an almost magical world. Everything was still white and shining in the sunlight. Every now and then she would look out one of the windows and see a moose or deer or elk ambling across the snow-covered ground. She'd caught sight of bunnies hopping back to their lairs. Bella would bark at all of them as though welcoming them to her world.

There was a line of footprints leading from the large building in the back toward the cabin. She couldn't tell if they were coming or going, but she bet she knew where Sawyer was this morning.

She would miss this place.

One more day and then she would have to go back to the real world.

The door opened and Wyatt walked in, carrying a mug. "Good morning, sunshine."

He was so beautiful. His golden hair curled slightly around his ears and he smiled that breathtaking smile of his. She could practically feel the man's arms around her.

She worried she would always be able to feel them.

"Good morning." She didn't bother to bring the sheet around her chest. They'd spent so much time naked it didn't bother her anymore. "Is Sawyer out in the shop?"

She'd been into the building Sawyer called his shop. It was full of all kinds of tools capable of severing various body parts. Or building furniture.

There had been a lot of sex, but also a lot of talking. She'd learned Sawyer's hobby was building furniture from recycled wood. According to Wyatt, he spent hours and hours out there. He'd built the beautiful dining room table and the ones in the living room she thought were fascinating. He'd built the rocking chairs on the porch she hadn't sat in because it was too cold. But she could see how nice it would be to sit there in the warmer times and watch the beauty of all this nature around them.

Wyatt handed her the mug and sat on the edge of the bed. There was a bit of wariness in his expression now. "Yeah. He's been there since dawn, I think. I already took him a thermos of coffee. He might be a while."

"It's his thinking place, isn't it?" At first Sawyer had been completely focused on her, but last night, she'd noticed him pulling away. He hadn't come to bed with her and Wyatt, telling them he needed to take Bella out for a walk.

"It's his hiding place," Wyatt corrected. "I'm afraid he's going to be in there most of the day."

"Because he knows I'm leaving tomorrow, and he hasn't changed his mind." She hadn't expected him to, but it hurt her heart. Over the last two days she'd grown to like Sawyer. He was taciturn, but it was simply who he was. It was like having resting-bitch face. He had active-asshole personality syndrome. Deep down he was a good man, a kind man, but one with walls he had no interest in tearing down.

"I don't know." Wyatt's big hand came out to cup her cheek. "I think the fact he's hiding is actually a good sign. He likes to think about things. If he'd completely made up his mind, I think he would be in here getting as much sex as he possibly could before he has to let you go."

"You can't push him into this," Sabrina warned.

"If I don't, then how will I get what I want?" Wyatt asked. There were moments when she could see the lonely boy he'd been.

"What do you want, Wyatt?" She needed to hear it. They'd played around it. She knew they wanted to take her together, likely tonight. She needed to know if Wyatt wanted more than double penetration.

"I want to see if this thing can work between all three of us," he said quietly, his eyes staring right into hers, holding her gaze with quiet sincerity. "I'm crazy about you, Sabrina. I know it sounds dumb, but I saw you and I knew I'd come to Bliss for a reason. But, baby, we should talk about my past. I might have been able to stay out of jail, but it wasn't because I didn't commit crimes. There will be people who don't think I'm good enough for you."

She didn't care about them. "I don't live my life by anyone's opinion but my own."

"Not even your sister's?" Wyatt asked.

She'd thought about this in the last couple of days. Oh, she'd told herself she would live in the moment, but she couldn't help but think about the future. "I love my sister. She doesn't get to choose who I spend my time with. I have some questions for you. I've been thinking about what's been said over the last couple of days, and I'm pretty sure I've been able to put together some puzzle pieces. Sawyer went into the MC because his brother was an asshole who didn't even appreciate how Sawyer was willing to put his life on the line to save him."

One side of Wyatt's mouth quirked up. "That is accurate."

"And you were there because your father was the president, and then your brother took over when he died. From what you've said it sounds more like a cult than a motorcycle club. You were raised in their world. Did you even know what you did was wrong?"

"Did I know running drugs and guns was wrong?" He seemed to think about the question for a moment. "I suppose I didn't when I was young. It was the family business. I went to school, but I was taught to keep to myself. The only kids I was allowed to play with were the other MC kids."

"They isolated you. Like a cult." She'd heard Sawyer use the word to describe Wyatt's childhood. At first she'd thought he was exaggerating, but as she'd pieced some things together, she'd come to realize how accurate it was.

Wyatt's hand came out to brush back her hair. "But I did know later. I knew what my father taught me was bullshit. I figured out there was a whole other world out there, and Sawyer's the reason. The years he spent with the Horde changed my life. He taught me I didn't have to be this asshole who cared about nothing but loyalty to a bunch of other assholes. I didn't have to accept I would likely spend half my adult life in jail. He gave me the courage to get out, but I did do things I'm not proud of."

She didn't want him to think she was a saint. "We've all done things we're not proud of. I once kept a library book for three weeks overdue and I didn't even pay the fine because the check-out guy liked me. I flirted with him so he would clear my three dollar and forty-two cent fine."

"Uhm, baby. We are not the same." But there was a smile curling up his lips, and he brought her hand up to kiss it. He sighed. "I promise you I've left my family behind, and I won't ever go back. I paid my debts to the Horde and I'm free. I have a decent job and I'm planning on taking some business courses at the college in Alamosa. I'm good with numbers, and I like the work."

"Good. Then maybe I can use you sometime." Given the

situation she was in with the school being so rural, she had to jump on any expert she could find. Caleb Burke was already signed on to teach Will and Bobby's anatomy course.

His expression turned wolfish. "Baby, you can use me anytime you like."

"I meant at school." The man really did have sex on the brain. "Right now I'm doing all our bookkeeping, and I hate it. Marie said she would handle it but she kind of scares me, and I think she might be the kind who questions every expenditure. She said she didn't understand why we needed so many tissues when all the kids could just wear long sleeves and use those."

She was almost sure Marie had been joking, but there was enough doubt she had to consider she wasn't.

"I would be more than happy to help you, but maybe you should talk to the school board," he offered with a wince. "I want to be upfront. I don't want to be your dirty little secret. That's what Sawyer thinks we should do. Or I should do. Date you but not in a way anyone could see. He thinks I'll ruin your reputation, and he might be right."

She needed to make a few things clear to him. "Sawyer sees the world through poop-colored glasses. His hot bod houses the soul of Eeyore."

"I think he would say he's being realistic. He doesn't exactly fit in."

She'd thought about this, too. She'd been in Bliss for months. Not once had anyone said "hey, stay away from the dude on the mountain. He's trouble." They did wonder why he didn't come to any of the town functions. She'd heard Rachel Harper complain because she had friends she needed to set up and Sawyer was single and uninterested. His disinterest clearly frustrated Rachel's inner matchmaker. "Only because he doesn't want to. I've heard a lot about how he's the baddest man in Bliss. Do you know who says it?"

Wyatt nodded. "Sawyer."

"Exactly. He sees what he wants to see because he's not willing to risk getting hurt. No one in town thinks less of him for trying to save his brother. Now I have heard they think less of him because of his wine selection. Boxed wine shouldn't be the only option," Sabrina explained and then sighed. Just because she understood the man didn't mean she could change him. "I don't think he's going to turn around. So the question becomes are we a packaged deal? Do you think you would want to date me if Sawyer won't?"

This was the question she'd been afraid to ask. She'd started this whole weekend with the knowledge that it wouldn't be forever. But what if Wyatt had been honest with her? What if he hadn't been trying to get into her panties and he really did have a thing for her? She definitely had a thing for him and didn't see why they wouldn't explore the connection between them. Unless he only wanted a woman Sawyer wanted, too.

"Sabrina Leal, you are not getting away from me. I worked too hard to get you right where I wanted," he said, kissing her palm. "Marie did bring me the complaints. I'm pretty sure they got lost on my desk."

"You asshole." But she said it with a smile. It was nice to be pursued. It made it easy to make the decision. "And don't worry about the town. If they could forgive Alexei Markov, who literally brought an entire Russian syndicate down on their heads once and then an assassin, they'll forgive you for being born. You didn't have a choice. And when you did, you got out. You're kind of in the best place possible for second chances."

"All right, then. I'll stop with the warnings. And you'll stop going out with those deputies," he said. "I didn't like watching you with them."

Such a stalker. They would have to work on the behavior. "They were nice."

"But they weren't for you," he said solemnly. "I'm for you. Sawyer's for you. Even if he's too stubborn to admit it."

She needed him to be sure. "You have to be ready for him to never change his mind."

"How about you? You okay with just you and me?"

She was more than okay. "I am. I'll be honest, I've wondered if Sawyer wouldn't be interested in joining us from time to time, but I don't know if I can handle a relationship like that for very long. Wyatt, you should know I went a little wild this weekend, but I want a marriage at some point. I want a family. I'm not saying you have to ask me to marry you. But I would like to date someone who is open to the possibility."

"I am open to the possibility." He leaned over and kissed her forehead. "And I hope you remember I'm new to this whole dating thing, so I'll probably get some things wrong. We didn't date in the MC. There were two kinds of women..."

She shook her head and put a finger to his lips. "Nope. You can keep all those explanations. I'll handle our dating life. How about we have dinner at Trio tomorrow night? Ooo, or I could come to Hell on Wheels."

"Trio it is." Wyatt kissed her, brushing his lips over hers this time. "There's actual food at Trio. All we have is fried stuff. It's starting to affect my gut. Trio sounds like the perfect place to go for our first date. Everyone will know we're together, and they'll stop trying to set my girl up."

"Well, I'm glad to hear that since you seem to have skipped a couple of phases," a deep voice said from behind the closed door. "Of regular dating. Like coming over to meet the girl's family before you spend a weekend together."

Sabrina screamed and coffee went flying as she tried to duck under the covers because the voice had come from right behind the closed door, and it had not been Sawyer.

"Sorry, sweetie. I wanted to come up and check on you," Mel said from the hallway. "Cassidy and your sister have been real worried about you. I reminded them you're a smart, capable woman, and Sawyer and Wyatt are good men. But your sister is worried they'll take advantage, and Cass is real worried about alien activity. You're of a breeding age, so we have to be careful. Now I told them the Neluts won't be looking to mate for another couple of months, and Sawyer's granddaddy was always real careful about making sure this place wasn't attractive to them. That's why there's always wildflowers around. They can't stand the smell."

"My fake dad is here," Sabrina whispered. "And I'm naked."

Wyatt ducked under the covers with her. "We can stay here. Maybe he'll go away."

Mel proved he wasn't going anywhere soon. "Elisa wanted to come up herself, but I explained if she was on the back of the snowmobile, we wouldn't have any place to put you. And hers isn't rigged right to get all the way up here. It's better in the valley."

"He's not going away." She'd told her sister she wasn't going to go wild. And then she'd gone wild, and now she felt like a teenager who'd gotten caught.

"Is he going to kill me? Is that what fake dads do?" Wyatt asked.

"Sabrina, you okay in there?" Mel asked.

"Yes." She had to handle this like the adult she was. "Yes. I am fine. I was straightening up in here and I'll be out momentarily. I wasn't expecting company. Elisa said no one would be able to get me until Tuesday."

"Like I said, those county vehicles don't have the get up and go mine has. It's the small nuclear engine I got from some friendly... Well, see, they don't like the term space pirates," Mel began.

Sabrina winced as she pushed back the covers. "Sawyer's going to kill me. I got coffee everywhere."

"I'll handle it," Wyatt said, rolling off the bed. "I'm surprisingly good at laundry. I've never met a girlfriend's father before. Okay. I've never actually had a girlfriend in the traditional sense. Just a bunch of club whor..."

She gave him her best schoolteacher finger. "Do not finish that sentence, Wyatt Kemp."

"Yes, ma'am. What I meant to say was my relationships before this were mostly transactional." His lips shut, and he handed her the clothes she'd been wearing the day she'd joined them. She'd made do with their T-shirts and sweats she had to tie around her waist.

It hadn't been hard since she hadn't worn clothes much. She'd cuddled with them under blankets while they watched movies and lounged on Sawyer's lap while they sat by the fire and talked. They'd seemed endlessly interested in her stories from the teaching battlefield.

How was it already ending? She pulled on her clothes with shaking hands. Only a few moments before she'd told Wyatt she accepted Sawyer wasn't going to stick around, but now, faced with it, she had to tamp down some panic.

She wasn't going to be the woman who didn't take a man at his word. She wasn't going to push Sawyer. She certainly wasn't going to sit around and hope he changed his mind.

"It's okay." Wyatt had pulled a shirt on and got into her space. "So your dad knows. Let's stop calling him fake because it's obvious the feelings are real." He grinned. "See, I'm learning feelings are important and about more than anger. The therapy's working. I'm going to see if Mel would like to join us for breakfast."

It was probably better than hustling him out of the house and pretending nothing had happened. Wyatt's calm helped her balance. "Okay. I'm going to use the bathroom and I'll be right out. Wyatt, you can tell him we're dating but maybe…"

"You and I had the most wonderful weekend. I'm so grateful you got stuck here because I fell hard for you. And Sawyer worked in his shop. That's all anyone needs to know." Wyatt kissed her forehead and walked off to handle Mel.

She could so fall in love with him.

But she worried she would always miss Sawyer.

She took a long breath. Reality was back, and she had to face it. At least she wouldn't be doing it alone.

* * * *

Wyatt made sure his shirt was straight as he walked out of the bedroom where he'd spent the absolute best days of his life. The weekend had been everything he could have hoped for.

With the exception of Sawyer being such a scaredy cat. He'd known the minute he'd woken up and realized Sawyer wasn't in bed with them, his partner was in his shop pretending he wasn't freaked out it was Monday and they only had one more day with Sabrina.

Except they didn't because they were whole-ass adults who didn't have to stick to some arbitrary date they set. Just because they weren't snowed in anymore shouldn't mean they had to end this amazing experiment.

He took a deep breath and opened the door. There was a tall, somewhat gaunt man standing in the hallway wearing overalls and boots and a coat, a trucker hat on his head. He appeared to be in his late sixties but still had a lean strength no one could deny. He hadn't been formally introduced, but he did know the man's name. "Hello, Mr. Hughes. I'm Wyatt Kemp."

He held out a hand.

Mel's eyes narrowed. "Are you?"

He wasn't sure where that came from, but Wyatt answered. "I am."

"Are you sure?"

"I mean, yes. It's the name my parents gave me. They never indicated I was someone else." He wasn't sure where this dude was going. "Should I get Sabrina? She's perfectly fine."

"Is she?" Mel stalked toward him, a flask in his hand. "Now I told everyone we have a few months before we have to worry about the Neluts pestering our women for babies, but that doesn't mean a single male couldn't find his way here and try to get a head start on the others. Drink this."

He was pretty sure he shouldn't drink anything he didn't know the ingredients of. Was Sabrina's adoptive dad trying to kill him? "Sir, I think you should understand my intentions toward Sabrina are entirely honorable."

"Yes, your people think it's honorable to continue your DNA lines by any means necessary," Mel replied.

Or he was insane.

"It's beet juice, buddy," a deep voice said and Sawyer rounded the corner. "It's perfectly safe. Unless it's his tonic, and then you're in for a pretty wild couple of hours. I swear he puts peyote in it."

Mel frowned, a deep furrow above his brows. "I do not. I would never use sacred peyote except in the proper religious ceremonies. People just forget how to make excellent whiskey. With some medicinal properties. Has he ever taken the beet?"

"I actually am not great with vegetables." He'd grown up with carnivores. "I could do a nice salad. Or some corn."

With a lot of ranch. He bet Sabrina was a nutritionally balanced kind of woman. He would work on it. He could probably get used to broccoli and green beans.

"Sabrina, we need to get out of here," Mel said, raising his voice. He turned back to Sawyer. "You need to be careful. I've had some disturbing reports about new technology allowing aliens to impregnate human males."

Sawyer snorted. "I will be careful."

"I'm sorry, what?" Wyatt was awfully confused.

"We need to leave why? I'm pretty hungry," Sabrina said, walking out of the bedroom. She caught sight of Sawyer and smiled before she realized he was avoiding her gaze. "Good morning, Mr. Hathaway."

Sawyer nodded her way. "Ms. Leal. I was going to change." He seemed to remember he was about to walk into the room Sabrina had walked out of, and he was a coward who didn't want the weird dude to know he was sleeping with his daughter. Nope. He was leaving Wyatt to take all that craziness. He pointed to the guest room door. "In here. In my room. Where I sleep."

It took everything Wyatt had not to roll his eyes as Sawyer ducked into the guest room where absolutely none of his clothes were so he wasn't sure how the man was going to change. He would probably hide out until the threat had passed.

So that was how he was going to play it. Well, he should have known. And he was pretty sure no one was going to believe it. But it wouldn't matter because Mel was staring at him like he was... Well, some kind of alien who wanted to spread his seed far and wide.

"He's not a Nelut, Dad." Sabrina walked up to the man and took the flask, turning back to Wyatt. "It's beet juice. It's gross, but you will drink it so my father doesn't think I'm having an alien baby he's going to have to protect from galactic invaders."

"He wouldn't just, like, take care of it?" This was the most bizarre conversation he'd ever been in. And he'd been around criminals trying to figure out which stuffed animal was the best to hide meth in. Also, he was putting off the moment when he had to drink Mel's juice thing.

"Take care of it?" Mel's shoulders went back. "Of course I would. It would be half human." Then his eyes flared. "Oh. I know what you mean. What kind of monster do you think I am? My own Cassidy gave birth to two halflings, and they're the best boys you'll ever find. What is wrong with him?"

The last question was directed to Sabrina, who shook her head and handed him the flask. "Everything will be fine if you drink this."

"Isn't this a question of bodily autonomy?" He was learning new things all the time, and one of those things was he shouldn't be forced to drink if he didn't want to. Downing a six-pack before lunch had been one of the ways to show masculinity in the MC.

Sabrina's voice went low. "It's a question of if you ever want to see my body again. Naked."

He drank the juice. The teeniest, tiniest bit.

Mel stepped back like something bad might happen. He gave it a moment.

Sabrina took the flask and handed it back. "There. He's human, though I thank you for protecting me. Now let's go and have some of his perfectly normal breakfast. I'll see if we have some turkey bacon. You know pork isn't good for your heart." Sabrina turned Wyatt's way. "And thank you for indulging my dad." She went on her toes and kissed his cheek before whispering in his ear. "Slip him two pieces of real bacon when I'm not looking and he'll be yours forever. Mom is on a health kick."

She went back down on her feet and turned and joined her dad, looping an arm with his. "Come on and I'll get you some coffee. Is the valley passable again? Did Delilah open the school this morning?"

"Everyone decided two snow days would be acceptable," Mel was saying as they walked away. "But you should know every parent in the valley wanted to make sure you're okay. Elisa fielded several calls about whether we should send a chopper up here to get you."

Sabrina laughed, the sound magical to his ears.

She was important to the town.

He was going to make damn sure he didn't screw it up for her.

He started toward the dining room. The door to the guest room opened and Sawyer stood there, glancing down the hall to make sure the coast was clear. "I don't think it's a great idea to let Mel know what went down this weekend."

That ship had sailed. "He caught me and Sabrina in the bedroom, so I think he probably knows."

"He knows about you and Sabrina," Sawyer pointed out. "Not about me and Sabrina."

"You think the town is going to believe Sabrina was here and you didn't touch her even though she obviously touched me?" Wyatt asked.

"I think we can talk to Mel and explain maybe he shouldn't mention anything at all. He's a good man. He knows how to keep a secret."

"He thinks aliens are real."

"I don't know they're not. According to the rumors, Mel worked with Elisa's mother, who was an Army intelligence agent. The word is he might have been CIA. Like black ops CIA," Sawyer said with a straight face. "The kind no one ever talks about."

"Well, then he's terrible at keeping secrets because he explained alien mating to me," Wyatt pointed out. "Look, man, don't hurt her like this. Act normal. If you don't, she'll think you're embarrassed you slept with her."

Sawyer straightened up. "I'm not."

"I know you're not," Wyatt conceded, "so act normal."

"Maybe she's embarrassed she slept with me. Did you think of that?"

Wyatt sighed. "You could ask her." He needed to give the man some space. He couldn't solve the situation by pushing him. It would be solved by having Sabrina around a lot to tempt him. "Or not. It's fine. I'll let Mel know Sabrina only had eyes for me. She wasn't even interested in you."

"No one is going to believe that." Sawyer frowned.

"Which way should I handle this, brother? Are we going for humiliation? Or do we keep up your reputation as an asshole and tell everyone you turned her down?" He was being completely unreasonable. It made Wyatt hopeful. Sawyer was always steady. He didn't care what anyone thought. Except he didn't want anyone to think Sabrina didn't like him.

Sawyer growled. "Fine. She turned me down. It doesn't matter. The only thing I care about is her being safe and happy. I've got to find a way to get her car off my mountain. I'm going down to look at it now that the snow's stopped. I'll take Bella with me."

"Bella is cuddled up in front of the fire, and she's going to want to hang out and wait for Sabrina to drop bacon," Wyatt pointed out. "Or feed her leftover eggs from a spoon when she thinks you're not watching."

Sawyer sighed. "She's going to ruin that dog."

And yet Sawyer hadn't stopped her. Not once. "If you wait and have breakfast with us it will likely feel more normal to Mel. He'll probably believe nothing's wrong and you're just a friend."

"And when I look at her like I want to lay her out and make a feast of her?" Sawyer asked.

Now they were getting somewhere. He'd been waiting for days for Sawyer to talk honestly. "Man, I do not get this. Come on. You care about her. She cares about you. Why all the tough act? I know you think you'll end up being bad for her, but why borrow trouble? Instead why not make the decision to not be bad for her."

It felt like the simplest thing to do.

Sawyer's head shook. "That might be the most naïve thing I've ever heard you say. Do you think I wanted to be bad for my brother? Do you think I want the shit that happens in Hell on Wheels to happen? I'm a magnet for bad shit, and I'm not going to bring it into her life. At some point it's coming back to bite me in the ass, and I'm going to make sure she's well clear of the damage."

"Or you could understand bad things happen to everyone, and it's better to have people you love around you when it does." Again, a truth that should be simple.

"Would you put her in your brother's way?" Sawyer asked.

The very idea of Sabrina being in the same room as his brother sent a chill down his spine. "Of course not. I would make sure he couldn't get to her. But it doesn't matter because I'm out of the life."

"You might be done with the life, but it's rarely done with you," Sawyer said gravely. "And that's why I should stay away."

The subtext was obvious. If Sawyer's past was dangerous, then Wyatt's was beyond. Sawyer had gotten out on fairly good terms. Wyatt had paid in blood and sacrifice and sin. At least they thought he'd sinned, and if they ever found out…

Which they wouldn't. He'd been careful. He hadn't left the life so he could be alone and miserable. He'd left so he could have a life, and part of the life he wanted was finding a family. Sabrina was part of his family. He knew it deep in his bones. She was important. Sawyer was important. But he couldn't force Sawyer to see it. "I'm going to date her. I wish you would join me because she has feelings for you, but even if you never touch her again, I'll be there for her. Now come out and have breakfast and explain her dad to me. Then I'll help you see what we can do about getting her car down the mountain."

"Oh, Dad told me Long-Haired Roger is going to come and get it tomorrow. He or Elisa will take me to school tomorrow morning," Sabrina said breezily as she walked past them. She stopped and gave Wyatt a kiss on the cheek. "Don't forget what I said about the bacon. Between that and proving you're not trying to force me to incubate baby aliens, he will adore you. He's actually easy to get along with.

Good morning, Sawyer."

She gave Sawyer a brief nod and then walked into the bedroom.

Sawyer's eyes followed her, his jaw going tight. It was obvious he hadn't liked being left out.

Which was precisely why Wyatt's evil plan was going to work.

He gave Sawyer a pat on the arm and went to ensure his potential future father-in-law got some forbidden bacon.

Chapter Eight

Sawyer waved as Long-Haired Roger pulled away, starting to tow Sabrina's car down the mountain.

It had been a day and a half since she'd left, and he was fairly certain she'd already sent Wyatt a number of texts. They weren't having trouble communicating at all. He'd heard his partner talking on the phone with her late the night before. Luckily Wyatt had put his cell on speaker so Sawyer had been able to hear her voice, listen in as she described her day of lesson planning and talking to her sister. Apparently, she'd decided to tell Elisa she was having dinner with Wyatt because they'd had such a lovely time together being snowed in. She'd told Elisa they'd talked and played games and watched movies. She'd talked about the lovely meals they'd prepared together.

She hadn't mentioned Sawyer even once.

She apparently hadn't told her sister how he'd fucked her at every given opportunity. She'd skipped the part where she'd lain in his arms and talked about her job and how much she loved it while he'd kissed her and stroked her breasts and memorized every fucking word she'd said. She hadn't mentioned how those movies they'd watched almost always had to be paused so she could ride his cock while she blew Wyatt's.

How he'd been planning to lay siege to her tight asshole had her dad not shown up and snowmobiled her away. He was entirely certain that motor wasn't legal.

"Maybe I should have driven it down and taken it to her myself." Wyatt stood beside him, watching the tow truck slowly make its way around the curve.

The road up the mountain had just been cleared, and Wyatt was already planning how he was going to get into the valley tonight for his date. Sawyer was pretty sure if the road crews hadn't cleared it, Wyatt would have walked down. Or called up Mel and begged for a ride. He'd caught Wyatt looking up books about aliens. The little fucker.

"Roger wants to take it in and have a look at it," Sawyer reminded him. Wyatt was like a kid with his first crush. Or a man who knew he'd found a good thing and wasn't about to let it go. "He'll take it to the school or have Jesse or Cade deliver it back to her cabin. Trust me. They'll take care of her."

"Should I pick her up? For the date." Wyatt tugged his gloves back on as Bella bounced around in the snow. "I should pick her up. She said we should meet at Trio, but I should pick her up."

"The valley is fine." Sawyer turned back to his Jeep, parked fifty feet away. They'd come down to help Roger out. Naturally Roger had brought his tiny chihuahua, bundled up in a dog coat and tiny boots, and Sawyer had spent most of his time trying to ensure Bella didn't sit on the thing and squash it. That dog was Long-Haired Roger's baby. Sometimes he wondered if Roger had ever tried to breastfeed when it was a pup. "The roads are clear. She's got a meeting in town before dinner, so it's easier for her to meet you there."

Wyatt made it to the passenger door and sent him a look. A look that let Sawyer know he'd said way too much. "So you listened in?"

Sawyer sighed. He was out of practice. "You're loud."

"I was in my bedroom."

"Which is next to the living room," Sawyer pointed out.

Wyatt nodded. "Sure. I'll try to be quieter. Especially when I have her over."

What? Have her over? No one had said anything about having Sabrina over. Was he supposed to watch them date? Know not to come home when there was a sock on the door? There was an easy solution to the problem. "Shouldn't you stay at her place? Also, this is your first date. I don't think you should be thinking in terms of staying overnight with her."

A snort came out of Wyatt as he swung himself up into the cab. "I think last weekend counts as a first date. We spent two and a half days together. This is simply our first public outing."

"The town will think it's a first date," Sawyer groused, and he wasn't sure why. Well, he was. He just wasn't sure why he felt the way he did.

Left out. Abandoned.

It had, in fact, been his idea not to join them in the whole let's-be-normal-and-date thing. Well, normal for Bliss. The whole only dating one person thing would put them on the outer corners of normal in Bliss. They would have to hang with Nell and Henry and Marie and Teeny. Cassidy and Mel.

Huh, the town weirdos really were a little weird. It said something when Marie Warner was the most normal of the group.

The point was, he knew he'd made this decision. So why did it rankle?

"Good. I want everyone to know we're dating, and maybe then people will stop trying to set my girlfriend up," Wyatt said with a shit-eating grin on his face. "It'll put those deputies on notice. She won't be going out with them again. They texted her while she was here. Did I mention it? They actually texted her and said they would be willing to risk life and limb to come get her and take her home."

Those Creede boys definitely knew a good thing. The truth of the matter was there was a dearth of women who wanted to settle down here in Bliss, so when they showed up they tended to be popular. "Be careful around the deputies. The sheriff's okay, and I think Elisa and Cam are fine, but I don't know the Creede boys. They've only been working shifts since Logan left and Cam went part time."

He could never be sure about law enforcement. Some of them simply looked at him and decided he was a criminal. If the deputies who wanted Sabrina didn't mind playing a little dirty, they could fuck with Wyatt.

Another reason to stay away. Sawyer whistled, and Bella bound down the road and without missing a beat, leapt into the back of the Jeep. She hit the seat and shook the snow off her big body, sending it all over the place before she snuggled down into the thick blanket he kept there.

It was supposed to be for emergencies, but somehow it had become a dog bed.

"Hey, girl. Did you have fun playing with Princess Two?" Wyatt reached around and petted the dog, whose tail thumped happily.

Sawyer shut the door and put the truck in drive, starting down the road toward the bottom of the mountain and Hell on Wheels.

Wyatt might have nothing better to do with his time, but Sawyer had a business to deal with. He needed to get the bar up and running now that the sun was out again. He would probably have to take over the shit Wyatt had been doing. The accounting stuff he hated. But could he count on Wyatt to still want to work when his head would be down in the valley? How long would it be before he started staying in the valley full time?

"You're such a good girl," Wyatt was saying.

Would Bella miss Wyatt if he moved out? *When* he moved out?

What if Wyatt asked to take Bella with him? It wasn't like Sawyer hadn't told him a million times it hadn't been his idea to get a dog and he didn't even want a dog. And he'd complained about the dog taking up space and having to feed her and getting mud everywhere.

Wyatt wouldn't want Bella. Right?

"You know she's my dog." Why had he said that?

Wyatt sat back, turning toward Sawyer. "Yes. Bella is yours. Uhm, should I not tell her she's a good girl?"

Bella's head came up like she understood the question and was deeply offended at the thought of not being told the truth.

Because she was a good girl.

"No." Sawyer kept his eyes on the road. Up ahead he could see the taillights of the tow truck as it rounded the corner. "Just wanted to make sure it was clear."

Wyatt huffed. "You want to make sure I don't run off with your dog when I inevitably leave you."

"Not what I said."

"No, but you felt it," Wyatt countered.

This. This was why he didn't talk. Talking always got a man in trouble. When one kept one's mouth shut, no one asked questions. Oh, sure he'd get the "is anything wrong" question in the beginning, but after a few taciturn nos, people usually stopped asking.

"You think I'm running off with Sabrina and now I'll steal your dog and you'll be all alone." Wyatt somehow managed to make the words sound like an accusation.

"I absolutely did not say anything of the kind." He hit on the one thing he could hang on to. There had been one disagreement they'd had all weekend long. "I want it known Bella shouldn't be fed scraps. I don't want you taking up Sabrina's bad habits. It's not good for her belly."

Bella whined. Like the damn dog knew he was talking about all the treats Sabrina had been sneaking her and they would never come again.

Or she was reacting to his harsh tone.

"Sure," Wyatt agreed.

They were silent for a moment. A nice moment. A peaceful moment.

"You know I'm not abandoning you, right?" Wyatt asked, his tone soothing.

Why was Roger taking so fucking long? Sure it was a dangerous road and he was in a large, unwieldy vehicle towing another vehicle, but he could pick up the pace. "You seem to be ready to stay forever. You were only supposed to be around a couple of nights, you know."

If he'd offended Wyatt, he couldn't tell. Wyatt merely adjusted his seatbelt and relaxed back. "Well, I wouldn't have stayed if your place wasn't so nice. I think you might be lonely if I left. It's almost like you fixed the cabin up for a family."

Where the hell was that coming from? "I did not. The only thing I renovated was the bathroom. I wanted a proper shower."

He'd explained his reasons. Childhood trauma. The second bathroom he'd added was also from the childhood trauma of sharing one bathroom with five people at times. Humans weren't meant to live that way.

"And you redid the kitchen," Wyatt pointed out.

He forgot so many things. "Because you whined so much."

"And built the dining room table," Wyatt continued.

"I like to build things." He wasn't sure what the man was going on about. It was a hobby. It wasn't like longing or shit.

Wyatt wasn't through. "And the coffee table, and I would be

surprised if it was your grandad who bought the plates and glasses."

"I got a deal at the Restaurant Depot in Colorado Springs." Why was Wyatt poking at him? Even assholes needed plates. Matching ones. Pretty ones.

Wyatt's shoulders shrugged. "Well, all I'm saying is the place is nice. Way nicer than anyone would think."

It had been so much better when they barely talked. He should let this go. Let it go, and Wyatt would stop talking if Sawyer shut his yap. "What is that supposed to mean?"

"All I'm saying is people would be surprised how nice the place is since you seem determined to make them think you're some kind of hermit with no care for anything except..." Wyatt seemed to think for a moment. "I actually don't know what they think you care about. The bar. The businesses. Money. They think you only care about money. Holy shit. You're modeling yourself after Scrooge."

And they'd ventured into the ridiculous. "I am not."

"Is it from the one with the Muppets or McDuck?" Wyatt asked, proving he'd skipped high school English.

"I am not Scrooge." He wasn't. He didn't really care about money, but what the hell else was he supposed to do besides work? It was what his grandfather had taught him. The only time he'd been away from work was the year and a half he'd followed his idiot brother around. "And don't start calling me Grinch either."

"Why not?" Wyatt asked with a shrug. "According to your reputation around town you hate Christmas."

Damn it. He ran out of a Christmas party shouting *nope* one time and this was what he got. "I don't hate Christmas. I just don't think about holidays much. For a bunch of years my friends weren't around during the holidays. After my grandfather died and my brothers left, I depended on my friends, and then they were gone, too. Ty worked two jobs. Lucy dealt with her family, and they were a handful. I used to spend time with River and her dad, but he died and she went on the run with Jax when the CIA was trying to catch him and vivisect him."

"I'm sorry, what?"

It was good to know Wyatt hadn't figured out everything, but Sawyer waved him off. "Long story. That dude's from another universe, and it's dangerous there. But it's all good now. They're all happy and back in Bliss."

Wyatt just kept going. "But you didn't spend last Christmas with them. I should know because we split a rotisserie chicken, can of green beans, and a six-pack of beer."

"Like I said, they're all happy. They don't need me hanging around." One more turn and he would be at the bar and he could go hide in his office.

Actually, his office would make a nice hidey-hole for a couple of days. The rate Wyatt and Sabrina were going they would be married by Thursday and have two point three kids next week. Then they wouldn't even think about the surly asshole who shared their bed for a weekend.

What the hell was wrong with him?

"You genuinely think you hanging around them would drag down their happiness?" Wyatt went into a soft tone Sawyer had begun to think of as his therapist mode.

They were not going there. "Maybe *I* don't like being around them. Maybe I can't stand all the white picket fence boringness of making popcorn and watching movies and talking about what happened at work. You know what happened at work? Nothing. Lucy dealt with some rich asshole and Ty saved a life and River and Jax took some tourists on a raft. Why should I care? And they'll be having babies soon. Oh, they talk a lot about babies. What the fuck do I know about babies except they poop and cry and I don't want any."

Most of the time he didn't. Sometimes he thought it wouldn't be terrible to have one. Maybe two. Three was too much. Three made one of them an asshole, and then the other two hated him.

Shit. Was this about his childhood?

Did he actually have abandonment issues?

"Do you?" Wyatt asked. "Do you hate being around them?"

Of course he didn't. He missed them. Hell, sometimes he even missed Michael—Lucy and Ty's partner. He was quiet, the kind of man you could nod at and stand silently and drink a beer around. Now that he thought about it, he and Michael might have never exchanged more than twenty words in the whole time he'd known him.

Michael might be his favorite person.

"It doesn't matter. Look, I know you're trying to psychoanalyze me so stop." He made the last turn and watched as Sabrina's car was towed onto the highway. It was a crappy car. A sedan had no place here in the mountains. She needed something with four-wheel drive. Something that could handle the weather and the turns and terrain. "You need to get her a better vehicle."

"Uhm, I don't know I'm in a position to buy her a car." For the first time in days, Wyatt seemed unsure of himself. "I don't have much saved up. I left the MC with nothing but the clothes on my back. I used everything I made in the last couple of months on the bike I got from Jesse and Cade."

"I meant help her get a new one. And teach her to drive." Out of the corner of his eyes he saw Wyatt's hand go up. "Damn it. Fine. I'll teach you and you can teach her."

Wyatt's brow furrowed. "I can drive a bike, but I'm not good with cars yet. It's a different skill set."

"How did you plan to get to your date tonight?" Had Wyatt thought this through? Or had he been distracted by boobs? "Are you going to follow her back on your bike? And when you asked if you should pick her up, did you mean throwing her on the back of that piece of crap you bought? Do you have a second helmet?"

"I was going to give her mine," Wyatt admitted.

"Now that will get you in serious trouble. There are no helmet requirements for anyone over eighteen, but Nate will find a reason to pull you over. You'll find yourself in Doc's office, and he's got pictures and x-rays, and the stories the man can tell." Sawyer didn't fuck with Doc Burke, and when he rode a bike, he definitely put on a damn helmet.

"She probably shouldn't be on a bike," Wyatt said, his shoulders coming up.

This was what he needed. This was the wedge that would make Wyatt see what a terrible idea all of this was, and then they could go up to the ski lodge and sit in the bar and find a ski bunny who wanted nothing more than a good time. He didn't have to lose his friend. "You can take the Jeep. I'll have someone drive me back at the end of the night if you're still out."

"Really?" Wyatt sounded hopeful again. "I'll be careful."

"If you stay with her, make sure to text me. Someone can pick me up and take me to work." Or he would stay in the office tonight. It wouldn't be the first time he'd slept at the bar. Damn, did he have dog food? He was pretty sure he had dog food.

Where Roger had turned left to go into the valley, Sawyer turned right and could see the bar up ahead. The lights weren't on yet, but the place was so familiar he always seemed to see it with its neon red and blue blinking arrow. His grandfather told him the arrow brought in the customers.

His grandfather would have liked Sabrina.

Sawyer pulled into the parking lot and noticed the back door by the trash bins was standing open. Lark walked out, wearing jeans and her coat, a cell phone at her ear.

That was when his cell buzzed.

She looked up, and a visible sigh went through her.

Something was wrong. Sawyer cut the engine and was out of the truck as his longest-running server jogged up to him.

"Hey, boss. You know how you always say we have to make sure there are no holes in the walls because the rats will come in looking for warmth?" Lark frowned. "This time they were looking for cash and booze."

"Is everyone okay?" Wyatt asked, Bella at his heels.

"Are they still here?" He didn't want to think about what could happen to his servers if they came across some assholes trying to rob them. "You know what I said."

Bella joined Lark, rubbing her head against the server's thigh. Lark nodded as she ran a hand over Bella's head, seeming to get comfort from the gesture. "Yes. Give them anything they want if I can't get to your office and lock myself inside. I know, boss."

His office was something of a safe room. The door was steel reinforced and had an electronic lock. It also had a way out. His grandfather had often kept large sums of cash and wanted protection.

Joe walked out. He didn't bother with a coat. The big guy didn't wear one even in the coldest weather. He was six foot four inches of pure muscle. "They were gone by the time we came in. Likely for more than a day given how cold it was in there. They knocked over some tables, took the hundred you leave in the register and a couple of bottles of the cheap stuff. Dumbasses didn't find the twenty-one-year-old Scotch you keep for Taggart."

He kept a small stash of more expensive stuff for the rich Texans who liked to walk on the wild side when they visited their vacation cabins. There was a reason he kept a hundred in the register. "They didn't find the safe?"

"I can't be sure they even looked for it." Joe put a hand on Lark's shoulder, which let Sawyer know she was more freaked out than she was letting on. "I don't know this was anything more than a couple of kids looking for a thrill. They took some cheap booze and knocked over some of the tables. Hell, as far as I know they were caught in the storm and needed shelter, but they're assholes about it."

"And what happened to the security system?" It wasn't like he simply locked the door and hoped for the best.

"It was going off when we got here, but I think the wireless got knocked out in the storm," Lark said, sounding more sure now. "The physical alarm works on batteries, but the part that pings your phone requires the Internet to work, and it's been up and down even in the valley. I called the mayor's office, and they said they expected things would be back up and running sometime this morning."

His cell started to ping. Apparently the mayor had someone working on it. Likely the Farley brothers. They were far faster than any professional group, though they would likely have to hack some systems. It was the way things tended to work in Bliss. Sure enough, he had a notification his security system had gone off. Helpful.

"Should I call the sheriff?" Wyatt asked.

Technically they were on unincorporated land and Wright didn't have jurisdiction. Practically, he knew what he had to do. "Yeah. Insurance won't pay unless there's a police report, so give them a call. I don't suppose the security cameras were working."

"They were off and on because electricity was spotty. I told you we needed to upgrade the generator," Joe said with a shake of his head.

He would never hear the end of it.

"Hey, Gemma. This is Wyatt Kemp out at Hell on Wheels. We had a break-in over the weekend and were hoping someone could… Yeah, he knows I'm calling," Wyatt said. "He's standing right here. Well, Sawyer might not think he needs the sheriff's office involved, but I assure you the insurance company is going to…"

Sawyer sighed. Sometimes his reputation made things difficult.

He walked into the bar that had been in his family for over fifty years. At least the break-in would take his mind off the fact that the sweetest woman in the world was once again firmly out of reach.

* * * *

"Hey. Sorry I didn't see you yesterday." Elisa walked into the office, tugging the hat off her head. She was dressed in her khaki uniform, her hair pulled back in a neat bun. "There was a nasty accident coming into town, and it took forever to get it all figured out, and then there was the paperwork. By the time I got home, I thought you would be in bed. Then Hale let me sleep in because I got home so late, and I missed you this morning. So I thought I would catch you before school starts."

Sabrina felt a smile cross her face. "It's almost one."

Nell Flanders and Holly Burke were with the younger kids for lunch so Sabrina could have an hour of admin time. Will and Bobby almost always went home for lunch, but they'd brown bagged it today and were helping Del with the older kids.

"Yeah, I missed that, too." Elisa put her hat down on the desk and took the seat in front of Sabrina's desk. "It's been a day. I'm sorry I didn't come get you myself."

Sabrina sat back. "No, you sicced Dad on me. Or did you mean to sic him on Wyatt and Sawyer?"

Elisa's brows rose. "Did I need to sic him on Wyatt and Sawyer? He wouldn't tell me anything beyond you were safe and you had dinner with him and Cass last night. And he told me the electricity problem you went up to complain about isn't Sawyer's fault."

It was good to know Mel Hughes didn't simply report back to his bio daughter. He was the dad she'd always longed for. Even if he was a little weird. "Don't tell me it's an alien."

"He says ghost," her sister countered. "Apparently Dad also believes in the afterworld."

Sabrina groaned. "It doesn't matter. Sawyer's agreed to pay Hale to fix it."

Elisa nodded. "I'll let him know." She went quiet for a moment. "What happened? Don't give me the BS you did on the phone."

She'd spent a good part of the day trying to decide how to handle her sister. She'd talked around things during their brief phone call.

She'd discussed the situation with Wyatt, who'd told her he'd back however she wanted to play it.

She didn't want to play.

"It was the most amazing weekend of my life."

Elisa took a long breath and seemed to decide on how to proceed. "So you slept with them."

It was surprisingly easy to tell her the truth. "I did. It was amazing and I'm okay. We talked, too. We spent real quality time together. They're amazing men."

"You know about…" Elisa began.

She needed to stop her sister before they got too far along. "I know about Wyatt's childhood. I know he grew up in a world we can't imagine, and Sawyer was the one who got him out. Not directly, but Sawyer's time with the Horde affected Wyatt on a base level. He taught Wyatt how to value himself enough to leave."

"I haven't heard the full story, but then it's not like Sawyer talks a lot," Elisa admitted. "I think I've had one conversation with him, and it didn't include a bunch of words. It was mostly nods and grunts. So you're with them now?"

"I am with Wyatt. Sawyer was a lovely weekend, but we're not a good match." She rather thought they were. When she was around Sawyer talked more, opened himself up. But she couldn't force him to see that she was good for him. She knew damn well Wyatt was good for her. He made her smile, made her look forward to something besides work. She liked how he was embracing the world. He'd told her he was going to the library to pick up a copy of *Twilight* so he could feel closer to Bella. She was looking forward to discussing sparkle vampires with him.

He was adorable and sexy, and he made excellent brownies.

And that thing he did with his tongue…

"Are you sure you want to make decisions based on one weekend?" Elisa asked, her brow furrowing.

"How long did you need with Van and Hale?" Her sister was being a hypocrite. She pretty much met her men and started seeing them exclusively. She had two boyfriends roughly two days after she'd hit town. Sabrina had taken months to find her men.

Though she hadn't actually gotten both of them.

Would she mourn Sawyer forever?

141

The truth of the matter was she should be grateful Sawyer hadn't put up a fuss about her dating Wyatt. It was obvious the men of Bliss took their partnerships seriously, but Sawyer had simply nodded and wished them well.

Had the rejection hurt Wyatt's feelings, too? Would he mourn the loss of Sawyer?

Sabrina shook the idea off. Wyatt knew what he wanted. It wasn't like Wyatt and Sawyer wouldn't be friends. Wyatt still lived with the man and probably would for a long time. They were going to take it slow.

Unlike her sister.

"It was like a week." Elisa sighed. "As long as he makes you happy, I'll be happy."

"Are you sure?" She wanted to make a couple of things clear to her sister. "I know you've worked almost all your life in some kind of position of authority."

"And I'm marrying two guys with really interesting histories." Elisa's lips curled up, and she got the secret smile she always had when she was thinking of Van and Hale. "Van's parents carted him all over the country. We're pretty sure he was accepted into two actual cults. No formal schooling until he was an adult. He's been arrested a couple of times. Hale's not exactly what I would call a people person… Huh. When I think about it we kind of shop at the same store, sis."

Sabrina laughed. "I guess so."

Elisa leaned forward, reaching out and putting a hand over Sabrina's. "Hey, you know I'm here for you no matter what. Whether I like the guys you date doesn't matter, and the last thing I want is to stand in the way of your happiness. You could have heard Van and Hale's backgrounds and put up a wall, but you didn't."

She hadn't even thought about it. All she cared about was how her sister felt. Luckily, she liked her future brothers-in-law. "Because they're great guys."

Elisa sighed and sat back. "Mom would have. Mom would have done anything she could to get rid of them. I can hear her sometimes asking me why I'm trying. I already had one divorce. Why do I think this time it'll work? She would have pointed out every flaw in them."

"Because she didn't believe any guy could be great," Sabrina replied. "You can't listen to that voice. Mom put so much of her own trauma on us. There's not a piece of advice she gave us not steeped in her own self-loathing. I spent way more time with her than you did. You very smartly got the hell out when you could. I stayed home because I was scared."

"She raised you to be scared," Elisa pointed out. "She wanted you to take care of her. She knew I would leave, but she thought she could keep you around to be her caretaker. So she taught you to be afraid."

Sabrina's gut tightened even thinking about her mom. "And to not trust my own instincts. To not believe anything good could happen to me. And when you got cancer after she died, I felt like she was right."

"It was bad timing," her sister said quietly.

"No. It was great timing because it was caught early and you're safe and healthy today. That's what I figured out. Mom only looked at the bad things that happened and not how we could make it better, learn something, grow from how we handle the tough times. She constantly turned in on herself." Sabrina had been to a therapist when Elisa had first been diagnosed and she'd known her time as caretaker wasn't over yet. She'd nursed her mom and then sister, and talking about how she felt had helped open her eyes. She understood why she'd done the things she'd done in the past. "Our grandparents weren't warm and loving. She didn't have any siblings. She was alone and she learned to be that way, learned to think bad things happened because the universe wanted them to happen to her. It's an odd form of control. A way to make things all about herself so she never had to worry about anyone else."

Elisa's head shook. "If the universe is out to get her, what's she really going to do about it? That's not control. It's an unwillingness to put in any effort to change."

"Sometimes change isn't possible. I like to think Mom's affair with Mel was her trying to change." Meeting Mel had been a revelation. She would never have imagined her mother with a man so kind. "He's so unlike the men she was normally attracted to, and I'm not talking about the alien stuff. Mel is kind and caring. He's thoughtful."

"And he scared her. She wasn't used to having someone openly care about her and she didn't trust it, and then she was pregnant," Elisa admitted.

"You know she once told me she never wanted kids." It had been a late-night revelation a few months after her mother's initial diagnosis.

Elisa huffed. "Great thing to tell your kid."

Sabrina shrugged. "She'd had a couple. *In vino veritas*. The point is, she had you and then she had me. She never loved my bio dad but she went out of her way to be with him. I wonder if there wasn't an act of hope in that."

"In dating a dude she didn't love and having a child with him when she knew it wouldn't work out?" Elisa asked, brow rising.

Her sister didn't connect emotional dots well. "In giving you what she never had. A sister."

Elisa stopped, her jaw tightening. "You think she had you so we would have each other?"

It might have been the kindest thing her mother had ever done. "I think it's possible. I like to think it's the one hopeful thing she did. We were left with very little, and then you got the diagnosis and we didn't break. Why didn't you break?"

A faint stain pinkened her sister's cheeks, a sure sign she was getting emotional. "Because I couldn't let you down."

Sabrina's answer was the same. "I didn't break because I couldn't let you down either. So here's where we make the choice. You already did. You chose not to let the past hold you back. You chose to embrace everything you found here in Bliss. No matter what happens in the future. I'm doing the same. I'm embracing this new family you brought me into with so much gratitude. I can't tell you what it felt like to have Dad pick me up."

Even though it had sucked to leave Wyatt and Sawyer early, knowing Dad cared enough to come get her had warmed her heart.

"Because no one ever did it for you before," Elisa said with a sigh. "Because Mom would have told you to suck it up, but Dad would never leave you alone if he had the choice."

"And I'm not his biological child." Yet he'd accepted her so easily. Far more easily than either of her bio parents.

"I don't think that means much here," Elisa pointed out. "What I've found is Bliss is a place where people go when they need something different. Where blood isn't the only way to make a family. Where we can be who we are, and as long as we're kind we'll be accepted."

It was why she loved it here. "Yes. It's kind of like paradise, though sometimes the locals don't understand what a good thing they have."

A laugh huffed from her sister. "We're back to Sawyer."

Yep. They were back to Sawyer. "I understand so many things about him, but not this. Why does he think people don't like him? I guess the better question is do people like him?"

Elisa thought before she answered. "From what I've been told, Nate didn't understand the reasons he was in the MC before. Nate used to be a DEA agent, and he spent years embedded in an outlaw MC. It was rough on him, so when he found out Sawyer was a former member of one of the worst clubs he had to deal with, Nate wasn't exactly friendly."

Sawyer did seem hesitant around law enforcement. Wyatt oddly didn't. "And now?"

"Now, he's had a couple of years to calm down, and Sawyer's helped on some cases," her sister explained. "He also helped out one of the former deputies, Marie's son, Logan. He got into trouble a few years back. I think it was serious, and Sawyer came through for him. Nate won't talk about the specifics, but he thinks Sawyer is a solid guy now. And Nate thinks Wyatt is a goofball who had zero business being in an MC in the first place."

"He didn't have a choice." Sabrina wondered how he'd survived a couple of those years. He told her he'd been initiated at eighteen, and it had gone downhill from there.

"We all know that." Elisa sat back, crossing one leg over the other and regarding her sister seriously. "But you should know the past comes back and bites us in the ass when we least expect it. Be ready for it, and know you have a family around you. We'll be there for you no matter what."

Which was why this could work. "I know, and it's why I'm following my instincts."

"Is your instinct to take no from Sawyer?" Elisa asked.

It wasn't. When she sat with the problem and asked herself what she should do, she went back completely on everything she'd said before. That had been her fear speaking. What did her hope think about the situation? "My instinct is to fuck the man until he can't imagine not being in my bed."

Elisa grinned her way. "And that's a problem, why?"

Sabrina wasn't the only one doing a one eighty today. "I thought I was too delicate to have a simple sexual relationship with a man."

"I did not say that," Elisa announced with a shake of her head. "I said I thought you were too emotional to want nothing but sex from a man. Sex isn't all you want from Sawyer. You like him."

Sometimes she wished she didn't. He was complex. He was going to be such a hard nut to crack, but here she was. "I do. I'm surprised, but there are layers to the man I didn't imagine, layers that go so well with Wyatt's. He's practical to Wyatt's dreamer. He's oddly artistic. He's grumpy as hell, but I think it's because he expects to be alone for the rest of his life. His grandfather was. His grandad lost his wife and then his only daughter, and he had to raise three teenaged boys alone. But I can see so plainly Sawyer wants more. He just doesn't know how to get it. Or if he's willing to let himself have it."

"So give it to him for a while and see if time and proximity can change his mind," Elisa offered. "Tell him you're willing to sleep with him and date Wyatt, and he doesn't owe you anything more than a good time in bed."

Sabrina felt her eyes widen. "Who are you?"

Elisa chuckled. "I'm a woman who is learning to trust in her sister's seemingly endless strength. I'm sorry I was so…like our mom the other day. I was worried about you getting your heart broken, but I forgot how you can't feel joy if you don't also feel sorrow. Mom thought she wouldn't have to feel grief or loneliness if she never loved or needed anyone. I think the only thing in the world worse than grief is emptiness. Go after what you want, Brina. Be ruthless if you think you're good for him. And if he breaks your heart…"

The thought didn't terrify her the way it used to. A broken heart could be mended. An empty one couldn't. "I'll have my sister to hold me while I cry. I'll have Cassidy making me tea and cakes, and Dad will threaten to bring the Neluts down on Sawyer's ass."

Her sister shook her head. "He means that literally. I got a big lecture on how they impregnate males. It was terrible. I can't unsee it. There were slides."

Sabrina laughed. "I'll make sure to let Sawyer know to avoid all aliens. But seriously, I won't want revenge on him. I want a shot with him because I don't know if Wyatt will be completely happy without him, and I know damn straight Sawyer will never be happy alone. At least if I get my heart broken, I'll have had some spectacular sex."

Elisa's grin went wide. "Who would have guessed the boring Leal girls would be so wild?"

"No one. Not a single person."

"I want you happy, and happiness sometimes requires risk, so I say go for it," her sister pronounced. "I would take you shopping and get you some sexy clothes, but we live here and our options are limited. We'll have to fly to Denver for a weekend and go shopping."

It would be a fun way to spend a weekend, but she wasn't sure she needed it. "He seems to like me no matter what I wear. Attraction isn't the problem. Getting through all of his walls is."

"Wear him down, sister," a practical voice said.

Sabrina looked up, and Rachel Harper stood in the doorway, a baby on her hip.

Callie Hollister-Wright was beside her and managed to look sheepish. "Sorry. We came by to talk about the lunch menu for next week and didn't want to interrupt."

Sabrina gave the women her best teacher stare. "Didn't want to interrupt or didn't want to miss a word?"

Callie winced, but Rachel simply strode in. "The second part. So you're going to take Sawyer down? Are you sure because I have…"

Rachel could be a wrecking ball when she wanted to be. "I am not dating anyone but Wyatt Kemp. I am thoroughly taken, so don't set me up with anyone. Move on to Delilah."

Elisa stood and grabbed her hat. "I will let you get back to work, sis. Rachel, Callie."

They both acknowledged her sister as she walked out.

"Fine," Rachel said, shifting the young boy to her other hip. The youngest Harper simply yawned and laid his head on his mom's shoulder. "I've been waiting for someone to come in and take Sawyer in hand."

"In hand?" She knew? She'd taken him "in hand" several times.

"She means she wants to be able to get things out of Sawyer without actually having to talk to him," Callie corrected. "Like whenever anyone needs something from Max, they go straight to Rachel, or when people think Nate's in a bad mood, they come to me."

"Speaking of, I am not paying that ticket," Rachel informed her friend. "You tell Nate if he needs a new copy machine, he can ticket Stef."

"You were going twenty miles over the speed limit," Callie began and then waved her off. "We've talked a lot about how Sawyer could spruce up the bar and maybe have a better wine selection."

"And a girls night," Rachel said, taking a seat.

"Doesn't Callie own a bar?" She knew the answer since she was going there tonight. For her date.

"Yes, she does, and you know how crappy it is to have a girls night when the husband of one of the girls is the bartender?" Rachel asked. "We get lectures on singing too loud and drinking too much, and oh, Rachel, don't dance on the tables. It's not hygienic. I am the mother of three children under the age of seven. I do not need Zane Hollister being my daddy."

She was thinking about the look on Sawyer's face when she proposed a girls night free for all at Hell on Wheels. It would probably go blank, like he couldn't conceive the words had come out of her mouth.

But girls night could be fun. "Well, I have to convince him first. He's made himself plain."

"Did he or did he not take advantage of the storm to get into your panties?" Rachel asked.

"He did," Sabrina confirmed.

Callie sat down beside her friend. "Sawyer wouldn't have slept with you if he hadn't really wanted you. I've known Sawyer for a long time. He's younger than me but we were in school together for a couple of years. He's very straightforward."

That was part of the problem. "Yes, he is and he's told me what he wants."

Rachel waved the thought off. "He's also dumb as a post when it comes to most things. The man thinks he's the baddest dude in town. Sure, buddy. Maybe if you want to keep that schtick up you shouldn't run around helping old ladies get groceries in their cars or haul your ass out to the alien highway to ensure Mel's watch posts are secure and he won't break a leg on the ladders. Max and Rye were planning to check them out, but Sawyer was already there working away. I would say he hates all of us, but he's always nice when I'm around him."

"He thinks everyone is scared of him," Sabrina explained. "Because he was in an outlaw MC."

Rachel snorted while Callie laughed.

"Sure, we're scared," Rachel said, patting her son's back. "I've probably killed more men than Sawyer."

Rachel went there often. It was a bit intimidating. "Okay, so how do I get him to understand he's not unwelcome?"

A long look passed between Callie and Rachel.

"I think the men of the town will have to do some of the work," Callie replied. "You do what you have to do to get Sawyer to see how nice it would be to have people in his life. And the best plan of action is having sex."

Rachel smiled. "A lot of sex. Oh, and if you can do the whole 'I don't care about labels or stuff' thing, it drives men like Sawyer crazy. If you convince him you do not care about locking him down, he will be so desperate to be locked down."

"I would normally say Rachel is wrong, but I know Sawyer, and I think it'll work on him," Callie agreed. "He can be contrary."

She wasn't sure what they meant by the men having work to do, but she did agree Sawyer could be a little perverse.

The good news was she could talk to Wyatt about it. He hadn't wanted to leave Sawyer behind. He'd been all in on the Sawyer could join them in bed idea.

Her date this evening was going to be interesting.

Chapter Nine

"I don't think it was the generator going out." Cameron Briggs looked down at the laptop on Wyatt's desk.

Wyatt was starting to get a nasty feeling in his gut. Something wasn't right. He could feel it.

"But it did go out." Sawyer stood in the doorway. He'd been on edge ever since the sheriff and Deputy Briggs had driven up, but he was more chill around the deputy. The sheriff was currently talking to Joe and Lark about what they'd seen when they'd gotten to the bar this afternoon.

Briggs had checked out the security system. "Yes. Someone fucked with it. It's got some wires cut."

Sawyer waved him off with a sigh. "Nah, it's freaking raccoons. They love to chew on anything they can find, and given how cold it's been, it's not surprising they found a way in."

"Did they grow opposable thumbs and learn how to use wire cutters?" Briggs asked.

"I assume not," Wyatt said, ignoring Sawyer's perfectly normal explanations.

"What?" Sawyer strode away, obviously going to check on the generator.

"Joe must have missed it." Wyatt pulled up the security records.

Briggs was excellent with a computer, from what he'd heard. The deputy had been a white hat hacker for most of his adult life.

"It would be easy to do since the wires they snipped were interior." Briggs stepped in front of Wyatt's desk. "Do you have any footage from yesterday? Anything right before the cams went out?"

Wyatt pulled up the security system. He was good with a laptop, too. It was the one thing his father had been willing to let him study when he'd shown some talent. He'd been allowed to take some classes, and they'd brought in a hacker to teach Wyatt how to do various jobs that would help the club. He knew how to change records and steal money. How to launder money.

Sabrina knew all of those things in an academic fashion.

How would she handle it if she had to really face what he'd done in the past?

"I looked through it, but I couldn't find anything." Going through the footage they did have was how he'd occupied himself most of the afternoon.

"They had to be inside to take out the generator," Briggs pointed out. "Sawyer was smart. He brought it inside a couple of years back because Maurice kept knocking into it. He doesn't like the sounds it makes when it's running."

Wyatt wasn't certain they should give a moose so much power, but here he was. He found the footage he was looking for. "Are you going to try to figure out who broke in? I thought we needed a police report for insurance purposes. Joe thinks it's probably some kids."

"I'm not so sure about it," Briggs said. "Kids wouldn't be so thorough about covering their tracks. If it was someone who got stuck, they wouldn't want the cameras off. They would want the security system to trigger because it would mean someone would come looking and rescue them. They would also likely be around. You know I had a thought." He pulled his radio out. "Hey, Gemma. Could you pull up the highway cams from yesterday around four p.m.? The cams going from Bliss toward Hell on Wheels. Sure thing. Thanks."

"That will be helpful." Wyatt was impressed with how thorough they were being. "We can see who was in the area at the time. But I still think this is kids. Or assholes who realized no one was watching the place. They did steal the money from the cash register."

"What if the point wasn't robbery?" Briggs asked.

"If it wasn't robbery and it wasn't because of the storm, why would anyone break into a bar? I suppose there are people out there who break shit for fun, but they didn't vandalize the whole place." He'd been surprised at how little damage was done. It had been somewhat halfhearted. They'd taken the money in the till and a couple of bottles of cheap whiskey, and for what? "Why would they go out of their way to make sure the cameras were off if they weren't going to rob the place?"

"Assholes." Sawyer walked in, a fierce frown on his face. "Do they have any idea how much cutting that wire is going to cost me? If I can even get a damn electrician out here. I might have to buy a whole new generator."

"Or you can get one of the Farley brothers to do it," the sheriff said, walking in behind him. "Will rewired the bread oven at Trio for us a couple of weeks back. Kid hadn't done anything like it before. Just looked it up on the Internet and had it working in hours. Give a genius a YouTube video and you'll be surprised what he can accomplish."

"Sure. His mother's going to let him come hang out at Hell on Wheels for a couple of hours," Sawyer muttered.

"Those boys tend to do whatever they want since their dad told them they could have a car if they could build one from Long-Haired Roger's unused parts," Briggs commented with a grin. "Looks like hell but the engine runs. I'll be sad when those boys go off to college. The schoolteacher says she thinks she can get them into an Ivy League school."

Sabrina. The mere mention of her name made him sit up straighter. "I bet Sab…the schoolteacher would give them extra credit for helping out. Like an engineering project."

The sheriff snorted. "Is that how you're playing this?"

"Playing?" Briggs asked.

"Oh, yeah. You weren't around. Sabrina Leal got caught on the mountain and had to spend three whole days with these two," the sheriff said.

"Two and a half," Sawyer corrected and then seemed to realize he'd said something out loud he'd probably meant to say only in his head. "Her dad came and got her."

And Sawyer had been pissed he'd missed his last night with her.

He had to convince Sabrina that leaving Sawyer out was a mistake. He knew if they had more time together, Sawyer would fall into place. Oh, he wouldn't make an announcement or anything, but one day it would simply be normal for the three of them to be together, and there would be no going back.

She was worried he would break her heart, but Wyatt was going to make sure she understood it would be worth it. He would take care of her no matter what.

They were a team.

It was so fucking good to have a team.

Briggs's brows rose and he nodded. "Ah, so we think..."

"Sabrina is my girlfriend," Wyatt announced. He wasn't sure why he'd hesitated. It wasn't like they weren't going out together in a public place this evening. "I've been crazy about her for a while now, and I used our time together to convince her to give me a shot. So I will absolutely ask her if one of the twins wouldn't mind trying to fix the wiring on the generator."

"She's not mine." Sawyer spat the words out like he had to get them on record or the world would explode.

Wyatt didn't bother to hide his eye roll this time.

"I mean, she's Wyatt's." Sawyer nodded, obviously trying to get his proverbial feet under him again. "I wanted to make it clear to everyone since no one in this town seems to be able to handle a woman on their own. Wyatt can. He is."

Now the sheriff was the one rolling his eyes. "Sure, Sawyer. You would never do the threesome thing. Never."

"No," Sawyer argued. "I wouldn't do the relationship thing. I'm not a relationship guy. Teach is a nice lady. She should be in a good relationship."

The sheriff whistled. "Well, I'm glad to know you care."

"But I don't..." Sawyer began and then grunted, a frustrated sound. "Look. She's a nice lady and she's dating my friend, and good for them, and the town should be happy for them and leave it be."

Briggs huffed out a chuckle. "Well, that'll be a first."

Wyatt wasn't sure what he meant, but he needed to get them back to the subject at hand. The afternoon was moving toward evening, and he needed time to get ready for his date. He looked down at his laptop where he'd managed to pull up the footage he needed. "It's here, but all I'm getting is a gloved hand turning the camera down."

The sheriff frowned Sawyer's way. "The camera is movable?"

Sawyer sighed. "It's old. I know I should have upgraded, but I'm not good at installation, and you know how hard it is to get anyone out here. The system my granddad put in worked so I didn't replace it."

"It's over twenty years old?" Briggs asked, a look of horror on his face.

Sawyer shrugged. "If it ain't broke."

"Well, it's broke now." The sheriff's head shook. "I'll send over a couple of options and either Cam or I will help you install it. I think we can get way better coverage for you. I wish the back of the place had more than one camera on it. You're up against national forest land. Anything could come out of there."

"Why would you help me?" Sawyer asked.

"Because I don't want to be the one to have to clean up bodies if something goes wrong out here," the sheriff shot back. "Is that a good reason? Is it better than telling you I'm the sheriff of this town and I worry about you and your employees being so isolated here?"

"The bodies' thing works for me," Sawyer replied. "Sure. Let me know what my options are, and I will be grateful for the help."

Brigg's brows rose. "What happened to him?"

The sheriff shook his head. "We'll talk about that later."

"Or we could not," Sawyer insisted. "I don't want anyone to talk about me."

The radio buzzed, and the deputy picked it up. "Hey, Gemma. You got what I need?"

He stepped away as Gemma started to speak.

"Look, I'll take the help with the security system," Sawyer was saying. "But only because I've got Lark and Sid working here, and sometimes Sid brings her kid in because that worthless piece of crap baby daddy of hers won't pay for babysitting so she can work."

"Stef, Rye, and I helped Bill at Mountain and Valley upgrade the security out there," the sheriff admitted. "We're here for this community. I know you're not in town, but your employees mostly live in Bliss."

Wyatt backed up the camera footage. There wasn't much to see, just a gloved hand, but something about it caught his eye, made some instinct deep in his gut flare to life.

"I know I've been an asshole to you at times, but I hope we're past that now," the sheriff continued. "I appreciate everything you do for the people around you."

Not the way to handle Sawyer, but Wyatt didn't pause to correct the man. He did pause the video. It was grainy and slightly out of focus. They definitely needed better cameras. It was a miracle he'd gotten this good a feed from the sucker.

"I don't do anything, Sheriff. Look, if the help comes with an obligatory hug and singing 'Kumbaya,' I'll let the darkness take us all," Sawyer replied in his Sawyer way.

Something about the glove. It was black leather, but there was stitching on the edge. It was barely in camera range, nothing more than a line of red, a curl of it.

Like the end of an "e." Like the end of the word *Horde*.

There were a couple of pieces his brother considered part of the "uniform." The vest with patches, steel-toed boots, and gloves his wife made with the words *Horde* on one and *Forever* on the other. Wyatt had worn them every time he hopped on a bike since he was eighteen.

He burned them along with his vest the night he left.

An icy tendril flicked down his spine.

"No hugs, I promise," the sheriff said, sounding defeated. "It's really because I think you're a fuckup and I don't want to have to clean up after you."

Sawyer actually smiled. "I can handle that."

He was overreacting. Wyatt forced himself to take a deep breath because the truth of the matter was he couldn't tell from so little evidence. There were surely other people who wore gloves with red embroidery on them. It might not actually be red. It was so close to the camera it was hard to tell.

What if this wasn't about robbery? What if it was about revenge?

"So Gemma found some footage we'll look into." The deputy rejoined them, slipped his radio back onto his belt. "We've got some bikers coming up this way about twenty minutes before the cams went down."

"Bikers?" Sawyer's body was suddenly straight, his shoulders going back. "What were they riding?"

"Harleys. Custom from what Gemma said, and she actually knows her stuff. Her husbands build custom bikes," the deputy explained. "She said they were expensive."

"And?" Wyatt knew there was an "and" in there somewhere. He trusted Gemma's husbands. Jesse and Cade had built the bike he'd bought a couple of months ago. They would know.

"She said they didn't look like tourists," Briggs admitted.

"Fuck," Sawyer cursed under his breath.

"Any reason you can think of for your brother to come bother you?" the sheriff asked. "You left on decent terms."

"If you call them burning his tat off decent terms," Sawyer muttered, his eyes coming up, gaze finding Wyatt's.

The sheriff whistled. "So they weren't happy about you going, but you paid the price they demanded. Why would they bug you now?"

"He is the guy's brother," the deputy pointed out. "Some brothers are assholes who play practical jokes on each other. Maybe he came in thinking he would see you and catch up on stuff and when you weren't here, he decided to mess around."

"When I left, I was told I was out forever. I believe the words my brother used were *cast off*. I'm not to be acknowledged by anyone in the family." Wyatt had been cool with it. He'd never wanted to see any of them again. "I don't know why he would do it, and I'm not sure I'm sold on it being my brother. There are plenty of MCs out there and even more dudes who ride bikes around for fun. Some of them cause trouble."

But not many who wore those particular gloves.

Not many who could have a real reason to fuck with him.

He couldn't know. His brother couldn't possibly know what he'd done the night he'd performed his final act for the club. No one could know.

"You're right," the sheriff agreed. "We'll take a look at the traffic cam footage and see what we can come up with. In the meantime, I'll get this report finished so you can have insurance come out and start a claim." He tipped his hat. "Sawyer, I'll get you the info on the new systems."

Sawyer nodded. "Thanks, Sheriff. Deputy Briggs."

They walked out, leaving him alone with Sawyer.

"It's not my brother." Wyatt refused to believe it. There was no reason for his brother to come after him. They'd made their deal. He'd paid the price.

Oh, but you didn't. Did you? You made him think you paid that price in sin and blood, but you tricked the devil, and you've always known if he ever finds out...

If his brother ever learned what he'd done, everyone Wyatt cared about would be in trouble.

He was being paranoid.

"Okay," Sawyer said, sitting down across from him. "But if it was, why would he be here?"

He couldn't tell Sawyer, couldn't tell anyone.

"I'm not sure," Wyatt said quickly. "What would even be the point in coming into the bar and throwing around a couple of chairs? It's not how my brother does things. If he wanted a meeting, he would demand a meeting. He would have left something."

"Did you check your desk?"

"How would he know?" But he was already opening the top drawer.

Bile rose in his throat because there was a card. It was red, the color the Horde used.

Wyatt pulled it out and slid the card from the envelope. It was a birthday card. The kind you would buy for a kid. There was a puppy with a hat on decorating the cover.

Wyatt opened the card.

Happy belated birthday, brother. Need you to figure out some of the accounting stuff you left behind. Turns out the new guy can't get into a couple of the accounts. I tried to see you last night but you weren't home, and my bike won't take me up the mountain you're living on. So I'll send someone by tonight. Make sure you're available. We can do this the hard way or the easy way. Tell Sawyer I said hi.

Wayne

He was screwed, and he wasn't about to take Sabrina down with him.

* * * *

Sawyer looked at the card and managed to stifle the growl he felt in the back of his throat.

Those fuckers had come into his bar? They'd thrown his chairs around and helped themselves to the emergency cash? They were threatening his friend?

"You do something with the accounts?" Sawyer knew Wyatt had been trained to take care of the club money. It would be an excellent—if dangerous—way to fuck with them.

"No," Wyatt said quickly. "I would never touch a dime of it. It's all coated in blood. I didn't take any money from the club, and I did nothing to hinder their use of the accounts. When I left I didn't want any excuse for my brother to come after me."

"But you did something."

"Nothing he could know about," Wyatt replied, and his jaw firmed stubbornly. "Please don't ask me about it. I made promises."

So this had something to do with his conscience. Likely he'd helped someone his brother would have a problem with. Sawyer could understand. "What do you want to do?"

"I want to wake up and it's two days ago and it's still snowing," Wyatt said.

Sabrina would still be in bed, and he could curl himself around her. They would make love to her and then tease her about all the sexy sounds she made, and Sawyer would lay his head on her chest and listen to her heartbeat while she ran her fingers through his hair.

He wouldn't touch her again. She'd made herself plain. Once the weekend was done, she would be with the man who wanted a relationship with her. Not with Sawyer.

And now he had proof right in front of him. Proof he'd been right all along. The Horde wasn't finished with Wyatt. "I'm afraid time travel isn't in the cards today. So we have to figure out what our options are."

"I call my brother and tell him I'll come home," Wyatt offered. "I'll do the job and then we'll be done."

"I don't think it's going to work. Do you even know his cell now?" If Wayne Kemp hadn't changed his habits, he would discard his personal phone every couple of weeks."

"I can call the clubhouse. The number never changes," Wyatt said resolutely.

"Okay. You can, but I think your brother came into town for a reason." Wyatt wasn't thinking straight. He was panicking, and Sawyer needed to bring him back to reality if they were going to get through this without any of the cleaning problems the sheriff had mentioned. "He wants to let you know he can still get to you. Can still get to me."

"Then I'll leave," Wyatt offered.

Sawyer sighed. "And he'll send in his boys to beat the shit out of me until I tell them where you've gone."

"You won't know," Wyatt promised.

"Look, dude, I love a good time as much as the next guy, and while it's been a while since I got the shit kicked out of me, I'm older now and I don't think I'll heal up as well as I used to. So how about we don't." He'd hoped to never be touched by this life again, but here he was. Wyatt needed to be reasonable. Unless he was willing to go off the grid and hide, his brother could find him.

Wyatt's hands came down on the desktop, disrupting the normally orderly desk. "I didn't mean for this to happen."

Sawyer felt for him. Wyatt had done everything he could. He was enjoying the simple life. He should be able to, but fate could fuck a guy over, and this was precisely why he couldn't have a relationship with Sabrina. She might be mean, but once she saw what their lives could be like at times, she would run the other way. And she would be right to. She should be safe, and she would never be safe with either of them.

Although it wasn't like he himself had been sticking his fingers into the MC pie recently. He'd gotten out, and Wyatt was his only connection. He'd managed to get a reputation for not allowing criminal shit to happen in his bar. He got a lot of bikers in, but there was a reason outlaw MCs called themselves one percenters. Most motorcycle clubs consisted of dudes who liked riding around with their friends and seeing the country in a way you couldn't from a car. They were dads and brothers, and lately moms and sisters and businesspeople who thought riding a Harley was a walk on the wild side.

He probably should think about adding champagne to the menu. He'd had a group of women come through a couple of weeks before who'd asked for mimosas.

His clientele was changing.

Sabrina liked mimosas.

"He's threatening you." Wyatt was staring at the card. "It's why he mentioned your name. He wants me to know he can get to the people I care about. It's how my brother works. He wants more than a couple of accounts."

"He needs to be taught the meaning of the word no." Sawyer wasn't about to let Wyatt get pulled back in because Wyatt was worried he could get hurt. He was a big guy. He could handle himself. "Look, I don't think we should panic. Very likely the reason he came in person is he doesn't want anyone listening in. You know how paranoid they are about money."

It was precisely why Wayne had wanted Wyatt handling everything. He wanted someone he trusted implicitly, and that had been his own brother. The brother he could scare. The brother who'd been raised to be obedient.

It had to bother Wayne he couldn't handle his own brother. Sawyer wondered if it had caused some questions about his leadership. It would rankle.

"If I do this thing for him, do you think he'll leave me alone?" Wyatt asked, though it seemed like he knew the answer.

"It depends on whether he decides you're an easy target or a hard one." Sawyer was a practical man.

"Sabrina makes me an easy target," Wyatt said softly.

"She does, but your brother doesn't know about her." He seriously doubted Wayne Kemp was in on the Bliss gossip grapevine. His men would be holed up somewhere waiting to show up tonight. "Yet."

"He knows I'm living with you. He knows where I work. If I start dating Sabrina, he'll figure it out, and the next time he wants something from me, he'll use her to get it." Wyatt finally said the truth.

"We don't know for certain." It was weird. He knew he should be nodding his head and agreeing because Wyatt was finally getting a grasp on reality. He found himself reluctant to kill all his dreams.

Because they were normal, ordinary dreams. Dreams that should have been his right. The right to live the way he wanted, to love the woman he wanted to love. To be himself. It felt wrong to give it up because his bully of a brother wanted to get his way. Again.

"I do." Wyatt glanced at the clock. "I know exactly what my brother can do to a woman, and I won't let it happen to her."

He picked up his cell, and Sawyer worried whatever he was about to do would wreck Wyatt for a long time. "How about we think this through?" He was the voice of reason, why? "Call Sabrina and let her know something came up and you can't make it tonight. Tell her about the break-in. Explain you need a couple of days. She'll understand."

"And what happens when Wayne shows back up in a month or two?" Wyatt asked, a dark look coming into his eyes. Sawyer remembered that look. He hadn't seen the tight expression on Wyatt's face since he left the MC. "If he figures out how I feel about her, he'll threaten her any time he needs something from me."

"So you go through life alone because you're worried your brother will hurt anyone you care about?" Sawyer understood the idea on a base level. People were trouble. Stay away from people. But it bugged him now.

He was kind of tired of being alone. It wasn't like he was going to start joining social groups, but he liked having Wyatt around.

He liked having Sabrina around, and if Wyatt was with Sabrina, then Sawyer got to be Sabrina adjacent. He wanted to be Sabrina adjacent.

"I don't know." Wyatt shook his head and took a long breath. "I didn't expect I would have to deal with him again. I'm a little shaken."

"Of course you are, but you're not thinking straight. You're panicking, and I don't think you have a reason to panic. Sabrina isn't some random chick you met in the clubhouse. I'm not saying those women don't deserve protection, too, merely pointing out they don't usually have it. Sabrina does. She's got an entire sheriff's department who will look out for her. She might be your weakness, but she's not a soft target. And she's also not a shrinking violet. You need to talk to her and explain the situation."

Wyatt nodded. "Yeah, I should talk to her. We're supposed to meet in an hour and a half. I can figure out what to say by then. I get what you mean about her sister being a deputy, but Elisa can't be around all the time."

"Dude, Sabrina lives in the valley. People in the valley look out for each other." He wasn't sure why he was pushing this. A couple of days before he would have done almost anything to keep Sabrina out of his life. He'd known he wasn't good for her, and Wyatt wasn't either. Now he was sitting here with actual proof he was right slapping him in the face and he was arguing.

Because he'd figured out she might be able to handle him, might be the person who could draw him out and make him comfortable with her so he didn't have to be alone.

"And they'll get hurt, too," Wyatt replied. "My brother can be ruthless when he wants something. I'm trying to imagine what he could do to someone trying to defend Sabrina. Elisa might know how to handle herself, but what if Nell or someone like her is there and tries to intervene?"

Sawyer chuckled at the idea. "Then they'll get to know Henry's serial killer side real fast."

Wyatt snorted. "Yeah, sure. Henry Flanders is a killer."

How little he knew. "Henry Flanders is ex-CIA, and you seriously shouldn't fuck with his wife. He's the most patient dude in the world about anything but his wife and daughter and the protection of the town he loves. If you're worried about Callie, she's got two former DEA agents who would take apart anyone who tried to touch her. And Rachel... Well, Rachel scares me all on her own. She's always trying to get another notch on her I Shot a Son of a Bitch club membership. The women of this town are fierce, and they won't take well to some asshole bikers threatening people. If Wayne wants a fight, Bliss will give him one."

"Which is why I should think about leaving." Wyatt sat back, a defeated look on his face.

Overdramatic bastard. "Can we get through tonight and see what he wants? I'll send Lark home early. It shouldn't be crowded. I can handle the bar, and we'll have Joe and Gil. Can you get the cameras back online? I want records of what happens."

In case he needed to call in Nate. He wouldn't involve the sheriff if this was a case of Wayne needing a password.

But he didn't think it would end there.

Wyatt moved his fingers over the keys of the laptop. "Yeah, I'll get it done, and I'll make sure my brother has no reason to pull anything shady. I'll give him what he wants and then we'll figure out what to do from there."

Sawyer had a couple of things he needed to do, too. He stood and moved to the door. At least Wyatt wasn't talking about dumping Sabrina and going on the run anymore. Giving him something to do—that was the key. "So you'll call Sabrina?"

Wyatt was right about leaving her out of the meeting tonight. There was zero reason to put her on Wayne's radar at this point. But Sawyer didn't want Wyatt to get lost in the planning and forget to let her know. He wouldn't want her sitting there looking all pretty and having to deal with the slow recognition she'd been stood up.

Wyatt didn't raise his eyes from the laptop. "I will definitely let her know how things are going."

There was a piece of Sawyer that thought those words sounded ominous. An instinct whispering something was going on in Wyatt's head and he wouldn't like the outcome.

But he was real good at ignoring it. What would Wyatt do? He might be way overly dramatic and scare her, but then they would all sit down and figure this out.

He would only be there because it was his bar. So he should definitely be involved in the discussion because it was his bar and Wyatt lived at his house. Cool. That made sense.

Yeah, it was easy to shove aside the voice telling him to talk to Wyatt some more. What was hard was not getting excited at the prospect of Sabrina needing him. Of them both needing him.

He might not have to give her up. Not yet.

Sawyer walked out feeling oddly hopeful for once.

Chapter Ten

Sabrina looked down at the text she'd just received and felt her stomach drop.

Hey, I was going to let this go, but I decided to be a nice guy and give you the heads up. I'm not coming tonight. The weekend was great, but I'm not interested in seeing you again. I like my women a little wilder. Good luck out there.

She read it again. And again.

They'd talked hours before and Wyatt hadn't given her a single hint he was anything but excited about their date. He'd talked about which burger he would order and asked if she would want to dance with him.

Not once had he told her he was thinking about dumping her because she wasn't "wild" enough.

Tears threatened to blur her vision.

This wasn't Wyatt.

She texted back.

Hey, what's going on?

She waited a couple of minutes, hoping to see the little circles that would tell her he was writing back. Impatience took over.

Wyatt, you need to talk to me.

A *message not delivered* sign appeared under her text, and she noticed it wasn't the same color it had been before. All of the previous messages had appeared in blue and the one she'd last typed was now in green.

Had he blocked her number?

He'd slept with her for days, told her how much he wanted her, and then blocked her number?

She would have slept with him anyway. But that fucker had basically made her fall in love with him. He'd told her how perfect she was for him, how great they could be together, and it was all a lie.

Or was something else going on?

"Hey, can I get you a drink? I feel like the first bottle of wine should be on the house since I know what happened at school today." Callie Hollister-Wright wore a Trio T-shirt and jeans, her dark hair pulled back in a ponytail.

Charlie and Zander, Callie's twin boys, had taken hide and seek to a whole new level today. They'd been playing with the younger kids and managed to hide in the ceiling. They'd damn near given Del a heart attack, but Sabrina had excellent hearing and they couldn't contain their glee at freaking the teacher out. "They're good kids, but I think I will have a drink. Vodka tonic."

Callie's brows rose in obvious surprise. "I thought you were more of a white wine girl."

Should she even stay? It might be a better idea to leave and drink alone at her place with the freaking ghost.

How was she going to tell her sister she'd been a complete idiot? That she'd been played?

She should have known. This shouldn't come as a complete surprise to her. It was how her life worked. What the hell had she been thinking? She wasn't even close to their league looks-wise, and neither of those men would want a schoolteacher for a girlfriend. Sawyer had been plain. Wyatt had lied.

"Vodka tonic it is," Callie said with a nod. "I will be right back."

Callie hustled off, and she saw her stop at a booth to her left. Callie leaned over as though whispering to whoever was in the booth.

Everyone would know because she'd been stupid enough to

announce it to the world.

Sabrina Leal—schoolteacher extraordinaire—had told the whole town she had a boyfriend, and he hadn't even shown up to their first date.

She was not going to cry.

Well, she would, but she wouldn't do it here.

When she got home she would cry her eyes out and figure out how to put on a brave face when her dad asked her how things were going with Wyatt.

Her dad? Was she an idiot for calling him her dad? He wasn't. He was Elisa's dad. Sabrina's father had never wanted to see her. He'd left and never looked back. He hadn't sent her birthday cards or called to see how she was. He'd walked out and left her with a cold, unemotional mother.

"Hey, aren't you supposed to be on a date or something?" A familiar blonde slid into the seat across from Sabrina. Gemma Wells was dressed for a date night in a white silk blouse, a rope of pearls around her neck and her makeup done perfectly. "Your sister mentioned this was a big thing for you."

Gemma worked with Elisa. She supposed it wasn't shocking Elisa had mentioned her sister had a date since it rarely happened. She had to be set up with guys. She couldn't find her own.

Her brain sought for any other explanation than the truth. But there wasn't one. Lies would only get her into more trouble. "He changed his mind."

"Changed his mind?" Gemma asked.

"Who changed his mind?" Holly Burke turned in her seat. She was at the table to the side of Sabrina's booth, and she wasn't alone. There was a large man with longish dark hair, a slightly smaller one with gold-blond neatly cut hair, and a baby girl in a high chair. Alexei Markov, Caleb Burke, and their little girl, Amelia.

Sabrina should have remembered Bliss wasn't a town where people kept to themselves. They weren't in high tourist season, so everyone inside the cozy pub was a local and everyone would be interested in gossip about the new girl.

She'd kind of wanted it when she'd thought Wyatt would be here. She'd wanted to sit in Trio with her hot guy and know everyone was talking about the new couple in town.

Pride goeth before the fall. She could hear her mom say the words, see the judgment in her eyes.

Had it only been a couple of hours before that she'd sat with her sister and promised to ignore those voices? She sniffled and forced a smile on her face. "Wyatt was supposed to meet me for dinner, but it turns out he has other things to do. It's okay. I don't mind eating alone."

The big Russian leaned over, his head cocking to the side to look around his partner. "Wyatt Kemp? He asks you to dinner and does not show? We are certain he is all right and has not had the accidents?"

She wasn't sure why Holly's husband was so concerned. Alexei wasn't the doctor in the group. Dr. Burke was, but he showed zero interest in anything but getting Amelia to eat her dinner.

"Oh, it was no accident." A bit of anger was starting to thrum through her system. There had been no need at all to tell her he cared about her. He could have had his weekend of sex and fun and she would have gone on her merry way. She wouldn't have opened herself up the way she had. They both could have come out of this thing with whole hearts, but some men needed a trophy.

It wouldn't be her tears.

"It was not?" Alexei stood and moved close to Holly, who had turned her chair.

Callie came rushing in with her vodka tonic. She placed it in front of Sabrina. "There you go, sweetie."

"Damn. Did my kids drive you to drink, Teach?" Max Harper stopped as he was making his way across the dining room. She'd seen the Harpers sitting with Nell and Henry and their baby as she'd walked in.

Sawyer called her Teach. He growled it when he wanted her attention on him. Said it softly when he kissed her. Winked at her as he said it when he was feeling playful.

Damn it, they were going to get her stupid tears.

Max's eyes widened as though he'd realized he was in the room with something terrifying. He backed up even as Holly stood and started toward her.

Sabrina felt tears rolling down her cheeks.

Max's horrified expression deepened, and he started walking

away. "Rach, we're going to lose her, but it's not my fault. I think Alexei said something to her."

"I do not be saying anything to her except questions," Alexei replied. "She is obviously in a state of emotional distress."

Rachel ran onto the scene with Nell on her heels, both women looking at her like a disaster was unfolding right in front of their eyes. "What's happening? She was fine earlier. She was great." Rachel's eyes narrowed. "I'll kill the little fucker."

He wasn't little, and he really knew how to do the other part. He was an excellent fucker. Maybe she was bad at it. She had to tap the brakes because this scene was getting out of hand. She was creating a gossip wave she didn't know how to ride out. "I'm fine."

Sabrina took a long drink. And managed to not cough because someone had poured that sucker strong. There was a lot of vodka and not much tonic.

Gemma was nodding. "Good. Drink up, girl. I found it is so much easier to beat down who I need to when I get enough vodka in me."

"You aren't beating anyone down," Jesse McCann said from his seat in the booth behind them. He'd craned his neck to look over.

He wasn't the only one. Sabrina realized a whole lot of Bliss was in Trio, and they were all looking her way with the exception of Caleb, who was still trying to get his daughter to eat something. He was currently trying to use the airplane method, but Amelia's landing strip was stubbornly closed to all carrots.

"I will beat down whoever I like," Gemma shot back.

"Jesse, I thought better of you, sir," Nell said, shaking her head. "You know I do not condone violence, but Gemma is not a puppy for you to command."

"No, she's my sub," Jesse argued.

Cade Sinclair stood up, a grin on his handsome face. "Oh, I have been living for this. Go on, Nell."

"Nell knows the obligations of a submissive." Henry had joined his wife and held Poppy against his chest. The baby was wide eyed and looking around the room like this was the best entertainment ever. "And she also understands there is a time and a place to discuss such things, and it's probably not in the middle of Trio. I take it one of the MC boys fucked up? Was it Sawyer?"

Sawyer had been open and honest about what he wanted, and it wasn't long term with her. It made her ache but she could handle his rejection because it had always been out there. Wyatt had lied, and his lies made her more than sad.

His lies made her angry.

"It was Wyatt, and this is why I am concerned," Alexei explained.

"I would have thought it would be Sawyer," Max replied. "Well, hell, that makes it way easier. I'm pretty sure I can beat the other guy down. He's not as big as Sawyer. You want me to beat him down for you, Teach? Or do you want Gemma to do it? I know she looks like she wouldn't, but there are videos proving she can. Though I don't know Wyatt has enough hair for her to pull."

"Oh, I'll pull more than hair," Gemma vowed.

"Slow down, people. We need to think this whole thing through. Perhaps we should protest Wyatt." Nell looked thoughtful, as though trying to decide how many signs to make.

"Stop," Sabrina said, sniffling again. She had to get control of this situation. She wasn't sure she could think of anything worse than a Nell-led protest of her getting dumped. "No one is beating Wyatt down or protesting. It's fine. We spent a nice weekend together, and he changed his mind about seeing me again."

"He came by and told you he didn't want to see you?" Holly asked. "He dumped you right here in Trio?"

Sabrina shook her head. "No."

"He called you?" Callie asked.

Was it worse? She wasn't sure. Maybe the text had been a kindness since she didn't have to see him again. "No."

Except she did because he wasn't moving, so he would be around. She would see him and know he hadn't even cared enough to tell her in person he'd changed his mind.

Rachel's eyes narrowed. "Do not tell me he sent you a text telling you he wouldn't be making it to your first date. To the date he promised you after you spent all weekend with him. Do not tell me that."

Max's head shook. "Seriously don't tell her. She might explode. We've been doing real well, and I haven't even been arrested in over a year, so she's got an unhealthy amount of rage with nowhere to put it."

Rye walked over, holding the baby like a football he needed to protect. "Guys, you're leaving me alone with the kids, and they do math now. They know I'm outnumbered. What the hell is going on? Ethan already slobbered all over Max's burger."

Max looked at his twin. "Rach found out the woman she loves above all others got dumped by the new guy via text, but only after she spent the weekend riding him like a horse she was training."

Rye's eyes widened. "I can handle the kids."

He ran.

"Wyatt better like the food at Hell on Wheels." Callie joined Rachel and Nell, their solidarity clear. "Because he is never coming here again."

"Stop." The last thing she wanted was a scene. Though it was nice to know there were people who cared. "This is nothing for anyone to worry about. I'm fine. I thought we had made a connection, but it appears it was one sided. There's no need to blackball the poor man. It simply didn't work out, so I'll move on."

"In a car that rolls over his body." Gemma advised.

"I can drive it," Rachel offered.

"I don't believe we should violently assault the man." Nell was looking at her like she was a baby deer with a broken leg and Nell was going to nurse her. "We should merely show our distaste with his actions by singing outside his house for a period of no less than twenty-four hours and perhaps bombarding him with texts about inappropriate things. It might teach him what texting is for."

"Everyone stop," Alexei said with a shake of his head. "This makes no sense. Look, I am not allowed to talk about certain things."

"Because Wyatt's his patient." Doc said, finally joining the conversation. Amelia had grabbed the spoon.

"Caleb," Alexei admonished.

"Well, everyone knows, and I'm not his therapist. I'm the guy who sits behind him at Stella's for breakfast who has to listen to him drone on and on about how he wants to be good enough to date someone like Sabrina Leal." Caleb took a spoon to the face without missing a beat. When Amelia laughed at her own antics, Caleb stuffed a piece of banana in her mouth. "What Alexei can't say is there has to be some other reason for the aforementioned emotional change in Wyatt because that man is into you. He's crazy about you, and it would be out of character for him to hurt someone like this."

"I would not be able to be saying these things because of patient privacy," Alexei said with a frown.

"But it's accurate?" Holly asked.

Alexei nodded. "I will be calling him tomorrow. Something is wrong."

They weren't listening to her. "He changed his mind. He liked the idea of me, but then he actually spent time with me and he doesn't like me. I guess he said all the stuff about us dating to make sure I didn't cause a fuss when I left. He also might be a little intimidated by Mel."

"He should be intimidated by me," Rachel said, an unholy gleam in her eyes.

"He should be intimininadated by me, too, Momma." At some point Paige had joined them. She stood there in her pink jumper, hands in fists on her hips. She was Rachel's mini-me, and she had her momma's rage down pat. "Ms. Leal is the best teacher, and no one should hurt her. I will kick him in the shins. No one treats my teacher bad."

"Badly." She was still a teacher, after all. "It's no one treats my teacher badly, Paige."

"His leg's going to feel badly when I kick it." Sometimes Paige didn't want a lesson.

"You are not kicking anyone," Max said with a huff.

"Aunt Nell, Daddy is patriarching me," Paige proclaimed.

"Huh. I wonder if it has anything to do with Hell on Wheels getting robbed," Gemma mused.

"What?" Someone had obviously buried the lead. Sabrina turned to Gemma. "What do you mean someone robbed Hell on Wheels? No one told me."

"Well, I didn't think I should. We're not terrifically close, and I kind of thought the guys would tell you. Or your sister, though now that I think about it, she wasn't on duty when we got called out there," Gemma admitted.

Sabrina didn't care about why she hadn't known. She did however have some questions. "What happened? Is everyone okay?"

Gemma waved the concern off. "Everyone's fine. Someone broke in while the storm was going, and we're pretty sure it was a group of bikers making a mess. I tracked them via traffic cams. Though we should call it something else because it's not like we get traffic out here. We should call them road cams."

Bikers? "Like his family? Gemma, this is important. Could it have been his brother?"

Now all eyes were on Gemma, and she seemed to realize she was the center of attention and wasn't sure she liked it. "Uh, I don't think so. He didn't say anything if it was. You know the Horde is based in Colorado Springs. It's hours from here. I doubt they would drive all that way to steal a couple hundred bucks and some cheap liquor."

"Well, cheap is all Sawyer has," Max added unhelpfully.

Alexei stepped closer. "Sabrina, if there is even the hintings Wyatt's brother is trying to contact him…"

"He would want me to stay away." A thrill of hope sprang through Sabrina. Was this Wyatt's way of trying to protect her? Oh, the hope was suddenly squashed by anger again. "He would rather break my heart than tell me what's happening?"

"It's just like a man," Paige announced. "Don't worry, Ms. Leal. Me and Charlie and Zander will get him."

Callie's eyes went wide, and she looked down at Rachel's mini-me. "I think we should leave the twins out of this."

It was time to start taking control. If she was right and Wyatt had done this to "protect" the little woman, he was about to find out exactly who the little woman was. And she was not going to have her students turn into a vigilante gang.

"I never leave Charlie and Zander out of anything, Miss Callie," Paige declared. "They're my best friends and we love Miss Leal because she is the best teacher in the world. We can take this Wyatt guy down. I bet he's never even had a snake in his bed."

Rachel gasped.

Max shrugged as though he should have expected it. "It's fine. She won't put a venomous one in."

"Paige Harper," Sabrina said in her best teacher voice, "you will not put a snake in Wyatt's bed."

Paige nodded. "It would be hard. I don't know where his bed is. So I'll slip it into his boot when he's not looking. See, this is where Charlie and Zander come in. They're real good with distractions."

"We're going to need bail funds," Callie said under her breath.

"Paige," Sabrina said, reaching a hand out to Paige. "My darling girl, what is the most important thing we can be?"

Paige's little mouth formed a flat line as though she wanted to argue, but she huffed out her response. "Kind."

"Even when people are not kind to us, we have to remain true to being the people we are. It doesn't mean you let someone walk all over you, as Mr. Kemp is going to learn this evening, but it does mean we don't seek revenge over hurt feelings. We talk about our feelings. Also, it would be unkind to the snake." She got a nod from Nell for that last bit of advice. "I am going to talk to Mr. Kemp, and no matter the outcome, we'll be polite to each other."

"Yes, ma'am," Paige replied. "I hope it works out for you, and I won't kick him next time I see him. But only for you."

"She is a miracle worker," Max breathed his wife's way.

"I told you," Rachel shot back. "Paige, could you please go help Papa with your brothers? I'll be right there."

Paige nodded and walked away, her ponytail swinging.

"Well, see now I think I should go beat the shit out of him," Max said with a shake of his head.

Sabrina pointed his way. "Do you need the same lecture I gave your daughter?"

Max snapped to attention. "No, ma'am. You should handle Wyatt in your kind way."

"Perhaps we should talk tomorrow in my office," Alexei offered.

She wasn't going to wait so long. But then she also didn't need five concerned parents following her to Hell on Wheels. She stood up and grabbed her purse. "I will call him tomorrow after I've calmed down and ask if we can meet up. Thank you all for your time. I will see you at school tomorrow."

They all watched her warily as she walked away.

She made it out to her car when Gemma came rushing out behind her.

"Hey, Sabrina," she said as she caught up. "You know I'm a lawyer, right? I got my Colorado license last year."

"Good for you." She wasn't sure why Gemma thought she needed to know her career status. Her brain was already on the fight she was about to take on.

Had Sawyer told Wyatt breaking her heart would be the best way

173

to ensure she stayed away? They would talk about that, too.

Gemma frowned, arms crossing over her chest. "You're not going home. You're going to Hell on Wheels to take that man's balls. I heartily agree with this plan, though if anyone asks I had no idea. If you need to do shady shit, don't tell me so I can defend you. It'll be fun. All I've done so far is file crap for the city. I would love a murder case."

She wasn't going to kill him.

Just maim him a little. And hope Paige Harper never heard the tale.

* * * *

Wyatt looked up at the clock, his heart clenching as he realized she was probably still sitting at Trio looking pretty as hell, and she now knew she was all alone.

Had she left the restaurant when he'd blocked her?

Hey, what's going on?

They were likely the last words he would hear from her. Not anger and rage. No promises of retribution. She'd been worried about him. He'd been as big an ass as he could be and she'd wanted to know what was going on because she couldn't quite believe he would hurt her like that.

Now she knew. Blocking her would put all doubt to rest. The next time he saw her, he would be cold. He wouldn't acknowledge she existed.

And in a few months, he would leave Bliss since it looked like Sawyer was right and his brother wasn't going to let him go easily.

Sawyer slid a beer in front of him. He was sitting at the end of the bar, turned slightly since he was waiting for the moment when the door opened and his past came back to haunt him.

Did his brother know what he'd done and all of this was some elaborate plan to draw out the punishment? He wouldn't put it past Wayne to come up with some elaborate retribution. It would include some emotional torture.

Of course if Wayne knew, there would be way more than

emotional torture. There would be pain until he couldn't handle it a second more and he gave up everything he'd done.

The one thing he was absolutely certain of was his sins wouldn't touch Sabrina.

"How did she handle it?" Sawyer passed off two more beers to Lark, who walked off to take it to table twelve.

"It was fine." He hadn't explained to Sawyer that he wasn't going to take his oddly reasonable advice. This wasn't a reasonable situation, and if Sabrina knew he was in trouble, she would want to help. Helping in this case might cost her mightily. "I don't think she took things too seriously, either. She was only being polite."

A brow rose over Sawyer's dark eyes. "The woman let us play with her asshole. She wasn't being polite. She was into us. You, in particular."

He'd been right the first time, but Wyatt had given up his dream. There would be no happy threesome, no settling into the sweetest, most fun town he'd ever been in. He wouldn't be everyone's helpful friend, wouldn't play with the kids and the dogs and help out when someone needed strong arms.

He would leave as soon as he could and never look back, and when he got to the next place he would keep to himself. He wouldn't put anyone else at risk.

"She wished me well and said everything is cool." Let that be the end of it. He didn't want some weird fight with Sawyer before he had to deal with his brother.

Dark eyes narrowed. "You're lying."

Wyatt huffed. "It's none of your business."

Perhaps pointing out he was being nosy would get the man to back off. Sawyer was the most misanthropic person he knew.

Of course he only knew what to call Sawyer because Sabrina had a wide vocabulary and liked to share it with the world.

"Uh, it's absolutely my business because if you didn't do what I told you to do, we're going to have a serious problem," Sawyer replied.

"I solved the problem."

"How did you solve the problem?" Sawyer was insistent. "Did you give her some weird drug that makes you forget things? Did Jax have any left? Because unless you erased last weekend, she's going to show up at some point in time. Look, if you did give her a drug, people are going to come after you. We need to make it clear you're the only one responsible for that particular action because there are some boys from Texas who will take offense, and I don't want to mess with them."

When had Sawyer developed a sense of humor? It was a really inopportune time to develop a dry wit. "Of course I didn't do anything to harm her physically. I'm trying my best to ensure nothing hurts her."

"But you didn't tell her what was happening? You came up with some reasonable excuse for why you couldn't join her this evening. Right?"

Sawyer was going to kill him tonight. "No. I didn't. I told her thanks for the sex but I wasn't interested in seeing her again and then I blocked her. So now she knows exactly who I am and she'll stay away."

Sawyer groaned, and his head fell back. "Damn it."

He didn't have to say anything else because the doors opened and four familiar men walked in. They were all wearing jeans and T-shirts and black leather vests proclaiming their full membership in the Colorado Horde.

Sawyer straightened up. "Doug. He's your brother's second, right?"

Wyatt nodded. "The big one is Doug. The tallest one goes by Murphy. You probably remember the asshole in the back."

He was the one looking around, checking all the exits and eyeballing who was where in case he needed to beat the living shit out of someone. It was what Brutus did best.

"Yeah. I had more than a run-in with him," Sawyer said. He called over to Lark. "Time for you to take a break."

"But I just had a break," Lark argued.

"My office. Now. Lock yourself in," Sawyer ordered.

Lark nodded, seeming to know when the boss meant business. At least he wouldn't have to worry about her.

"What can I get you, boys?" Sawyer asked.

Wyatt didn't recognize the fourth man, but he was big and brawny and looked like he ate nails for breakfast. So his brother had replaced him with another enforcer.

Doug's gaze was on Lark's backside as she strode away. "I was hoping she would take our orders."

Wyatt bet he had. All of these men would treat her like she was on the menu. Precisely why Sawyer had sent her away.

Wyatt watched as the only two other customers in the place seemed to feel the shift in the air.

A couple of regulars who came in from Creede stood and threw some cash down and walked out.

So they were alone.

At least no one else would get hurt.

"She's taking a break," Sawyer announced cooly. "So why don't you boys get your business done and we can all get on with our evenings."

"Not very hospitable of you, Sawyer," Doug said with a sneer. He slapped the new guy's chest and pointed Sawyer's way. "Jeff, this here is Sawyer Hathaway. He rode with us for a while, then his brother did a tiny stint and he couldn't handle it. I don't know, Hathaway. I think you would have done well in prison. Pretty boys are popular there."

"I'll never find out," Sawyer replied smoothly. "I'm a simple barkeep now."

"I doubt you're anything simple," Doug said, looking Wyatt up and down. "You get your brother's message?"

"He's not my brother." Wyatt intended to make things plain to these men. "He made himself clear when he burned the tat I never asked for off my chest. But I did get the message the president of the Horde sent me. I gave you all the account numbers. I didn't leave a damn thing out."

"Well, your brother...excuse me, the president of the MC, seems to think you did, so you either need to take a look at these accounts or pony up the three hundred K we're missing," Doug announced.

His temper threatened to flare.

"Oooo, looks like little brother is getting mad," the new guy said. "I'm so fucking scared."

Brutus leaned over and whispered something in his ear that had Jeff frowning.

"Seriously?" Jeff asked.

"Once saw him take out eight guys by himself," Brutus replied.

"There's a reason his brother's not here." Sawyer had come from behind the bar. "They call Wyatt the Berserker. He's perfectly calm until he loses it, and then we're lucky if he doesn't kill someone."

Wyatt hated the nickname. He'd definitely hated the way his father had slapped him on the back and called him a real man the first time he'd beaten a man near to death. He'd been sixteen, and one of the older bikers had hit him and called him a bunch of names that would get the man canceled. Wyatt had seen red. He hadn't even remembered his first fight, but his father had pushed him for more.

It was a side of himself he'd hoped he'd left behind forever, a side he'd never wanted Sabrina to see.

"Did you bring the laptop the new guy is using?" Wyatt didn't want to talk about the past. "I left the one I used. Tell me he didn't try to get a new one. No one in the MC really knows computers."

His brother recruited for other skills.

Jeff stepped up. "I know a little, and I brought this piece of crap you left behind. It's useless. I barely managed to find the other accounts."

Wyatt took the laptop from Jeff and opened it. The dumbass hadn't even changed the password. He knew exactly what was wrong. "There are two accounts I didn't keep with the others. They're behind a wall, but I left instructions on how to get around it."

"If you didn't hide it, I wouldn't have to get around it," Jeff shot back.

"I have to hide it because it was earned through criminal means and needs to be laundered before the club can use it, dumbass," Wyatt replied, touching the keys with purpose. The faster he got them what they needed, the sooner he could go back to mourning Sabrina.

Doug grunted. "Well, he's not wrong. Sawyer, why don't you get us all a couple of beers while Wyatt finds the info we need."

"He'll be so fast you won't have time for a beer," Sawyer replied. "Besides, you already stole from me so fuck you."

Brutus frowned. "Well, you weren't here so what else were we supposed to do?"

"How about not fucking breaking in?" Something nasty was rising in Wyatt's gut. His brother was playing games with him. He'd done everything he was supposed to do—Wayne thought he'd done everything he was supposed to do—and this was how his brother kept a deal.

His brother had already cost him everything. Being born into his family had cost him a normal childhood. It caused him to be arrested for the first time when he was freaking ten because kids needed to pull their weight in his father's narrow-minded world. This life had denied him an education, individuality, any form of freedom, and now it cost him the one woman in the world he'd ever truly wanted.

"How about not being a little pussy." The new guy had a couple of inches on Wyatt and probably fifty pounds of muscle. "Look, I don't care what they call you or if once you got in a decent punch or two. You're a momma's boy pussy, and now you're going to get the job done and you're going to hand over everything you owe your brother and then you're going to serve us some beers and introduce the nice young lady the big guy sent away and then maybe, if she satisfies us, we'll go away. Otherwise, my needs will change and I'll require some violence."

"Wyatt." Sawyer's tone was a warning.

Somewhere in the background he heard the front door opening, but it was a distant thing. What was far more immediate was the buzzing in his ears.

Everything. These motherfuckers had cost him everything and they wanted more. They thought Lark wasn't a person. She was nothing but a doll to play with and toss away. No one outside the Horde mattered. They were kings, and peasants were there for their pleasure.

He hated them.

"Wyatt Kemp, we are going to talk," a familiar voice said.

"I fucking told you," Sawyer ground out. "Sabrina, you need to leave. Right now. You go back down to the valley and forget you were here tonight."

Sabrina was here. She'd walked in the door. It didn't hit his brain the way it should.

"Now we're talking," the new asshole was saying. "Me and Brutus can take this one and Doug and Murphy can play with the brunette." He walked right up to Sabrina—his Sabrina—and put a hand on her. "You and me are going to have some fun."

And Wyatt saw red.

Chapter Eleven

Sawyer had known everything would go to hell the minute Wyatt told him he hadn't taken his reasonable advice. See, this was precisely why he didn't go to the trouble of giving advice. No one ever took it. When he'd learned Wyatt had broken up with Sabrina, he'd known her pretty ass would show up and likely tonight.

She couldn't have picked a worst time.

Sawyer started to move toward her and the asshole who'd put his hands on her. It had been the sight of Sabrina in danger that threatened to take a nasty scenario and push it into ultra-violent territory. Sawyer wanted to kill the fucker, and he didn't have Wyatt's trauma responses. If he didn't deal with the situation, Wyatt might actually kill the man.

Which would be fine except then Nate would have to do paperwork, and he hated paperwork.

Sabrina stood there, staring at the man who'd probably spent more time in jail than she'd spent alive, and there wasn't a proper amount of fear on her face. She needed to keep her mouth closed and let him handle this situation. Talking to this guy on any level would do nothing but make things worse.

It was going to be okay. Sabrina was likely terrified, and fear would make her very submissive. She'd never been in a situation like this before. He would pick her up, lock her away with Lark, and deal with the situation. All she needed to do was not make things worse.

"Sir, I am not here to find a date, nor am I here to be manhandled," she stated in the sweetly bossy tone she used.

He was going to spank her. He finally understood the appeal. Oh, he'd gotten the whole "get his hands on her pretty ass" thing, but the spanking he was thinking of went far deeper. When he spanked her, she would feel his fucking will. She was putting herself directly in harm's way, and he was going to make it clear to her how unacceptable it was.

He glanced over and Wyatt had shoved the laptop away, his eyes going dark and a flush rushing across his skin. He had seconds to defuse the situation. He'd actually seen Berserker Wyatt, and it wasn't pretty.

"Hey, she's mine, and you better take your hands off her." A man like the one in front of Sawyer only understood things in brutal terms. "Mine, you motherfucker. Do you understand what a claim means in our world?"

"I understand you're not in our world," the asshole shot back and pulled her in closer. "That makes anything you have fair game."

"I don't think she's Sawyer's," Doug said, looking from Sawyer to Wyatt. "And isn't that interesting."

Wyatt unleashed a yell and went for it.

Sawyer barely got to her in time. He pulled her away right before Wyatt tackled the way bigger than him guy and started to go to town.

This was going to get wild. He had to pray these guys didn't pull weapons.

"You are in so much trouble," he growled as he held her tight.

"Wyatt," Sabrina called out even as she struggled in Sawyer's arms.

"Stop it," he ordered. He was going to have to drag her all the way to the back room.

In the background Sawyer heard one of the other biker gentlemen speaking. "Wyatt, shit, man, you need to calm down. You don't want to do this."

"Well, he fucking does now," Sawyer said with a long huff. "I warned you."

"How were we supposed to know he had a whore?" Doug asked.

"And one he's serious about."

Wyatt rounded on Doug and punched the fucker right in the face.

"Wyatt, please stop," Sabrina yelled. "It doesn't matter what he says. It's only words. I don't care."

She was clawing at Sawyer's forearm, trying to get him to release her, but he held tight. "He does, and you can't talk to him now. There's no talking him down. Let me get you somewhere safe."

"We can't leave him." Sabrina sounded tortured.

"You're going to do exactly what I tell you to do," Sawyer whispered, wincing when Doug got in a hearty gut punch. At least the first guy seemed to be unconscious. "Do you understand me? He never, ever wanted you to see this part of him, and he's going to be devastated. But he'll be more devastated if you get hurt."

"He's outnumbered," Sabrina insisted. "You have to help him."

"No, I have to get you out of here." Sawyer started to drag her away from the bar and toward a hallway leading to the back of the building.

"Please," Sabrina begged. "Please help him." She put her arms up against Sawyer's and tried to twist out of his hold. She'd definitely had some self-defense training.

But not enough since she gained absolutely no ground.

"Sabrina, I swear I'll spank you if you try that shit on me one more time." Sawyer dragged her closer to the office, closer to safety.

"I'm not afraid of you," she shot back and then brought her kitten heel right down on the bridge of his foot, sending pain flaring through him.

It was enough to cause him to shout out and let go of her.

She took off, running to get to Wyatt as Sawyer winced and moved after her. She picked up a bottle of tequila sitting on the counter and wielded it like a baseball bat. She swung out, striking one of the men attacking Wyatt across his broad back.

"You leave him alone," Sabrina shouted, and she was reaching into the crossbody bag on her hip.

She was going to kill him. His heart thudded in his chest as the biker turned from Wyatt and brought his fist up to punch Sabrina. It could kill her. He could see it plainly in his head. His massive fist could crack her skull. Sawyer threw himself bodily in front of her, taking the punch across his chest as he knocked her out of the way.

Wyatt yelled and jumped on the asshole's back.

The whole world felt like chaos as Sawyer hit his knees on the hardwood floors and winced at the pain shooting through his body.

This was why he didn't have friends.

Friends got a man into trouble.

He had to get Sabrina out of here, damn it. This whole situation had gone deadly. He wasn't completely certain Wyatt hadn't killed the first man. He was still on the ground.

Sawyer got to his feet as Doug finally pulled a gun, pointing it Wyatt's way.

"Don't make me do this, Wyatt," Doug growled. "I don't want to kill you. I don't have what I need out of you yet, but I'll fucking do it. I'll take your head back to your brother and he'll have to be satisfied with that."

The world seemed to slow because Sawyer was absolutely certain he was about to watch Wyatt die, and then likely Sabrina.

Then it would be his turn.

He'd always thought he wouldn't care. Life was something he'd endured for so many years, but in this moment, he wanted…more.

More life. More friendship—even if it was annoying—more her.

So much more her.

He had to get to Sabrina. Wyatt would want him to give Sabrina the best chance she could have. If he could get her out of the bar, she could run for the valley. Nell and Henry's place wasn't too far away, and Henry would protect her. Henry would get Nate.

He never thought he would want to see Nathan Wright darken his door, but here they were. He would give almost anything to see Nate and Cam rushing in to save the day.

Sawyer forced himself to move because Wyatt wasn't capable of backing down at this point, and it was going to cost him everything.

Doug shouted again and then aimed right for Wyatt's head.

Sabrina stepped in behind Doug, and she had something in her hand. Doug's full attention was on the threat he knew about.

He never saw Sabrina coming. He didn't know Sabrina apparently carried around a freaking stun gun.

She touched the stun gun to the back of Doug's neck, and the man's body seized and he fell to the floor. It gave Sawyer the chance to tackle Brutus, who'd decided Sabrina was a threat and had started coming at her. He wasn't sure where the fourth guy had gone. Sawyer used his forward momentum to slam the bigger man against the bar, hitting his head hard against the wood. Brutus got in one good punch before Sawyer took his head in hand and slammed it again as hard as he could since the dude was absolutely thick skulled.

"Smart move, babe," Sabrina said. "Do you want me to stun him, too? Just to be certain? And what do you want me to do with this?"

Sawyer felt his eyes widen as he turned and Sabrina had her stun gun in one hand and Doug's semiautomatic pistol in the other. Though she wasn't holding it right. She grasped the handle between her thumb and forefinger as though the thing was rancid and she was looking for a place to toss it.

This was how he died. Not in a fight. Sabrina was going to give him a heart attack. And yet, he'd liked how she'd called him babe.

Would she still call him babe after he'd smacked her ass until she couldn't sit properly? He might find an exotic plug and torture her rectum until she wouldn't even think of pulling this shit again.

She glanced back at Wyatt, who was now covered in blood and looked like he might turn into a werewolf at any moment. She didn't even blink. "Hey, sweetie, the other one ran away and he's hiding in the men's room. Do you want to handle him? I can do it, if you're too tired. I have pepper spray. And bear spray. I know I'm supposed to use it on bears, but I think it'll work on him, too."

She was freaking calm.

Wyatt's jaw actually dropped. "What did she say?" He shook his head as though trying to clear it. His face fell as he looked around the room. "What happened?"

She'd managed to shock Wyatt out of his episode. It was a relief because Sawyer worried he was going to have to fight to get him back. Sawyer moved around to the bodies on the floor, disarming them all so no one woke up and started shooting. In the distance he heard the sound of sirens. Lark had gotten scared, and he didn't blame her. She'd done exactly what she should have. She'd probably been watching on the CCTV cams and decided to risk Sawyer's anger to save their lives.

She would find his anger was going to be directed somewhere else. Somewhere like Sabrina's backside.

He didn't want to think about the ramifications of what came next. Not with Sabrina. It was fucking inevitable. She'd walked in when everyone had told her to stay away. At least for tonight she would be his again.

No, he was worried about what happened when Wyatt's brother learned his plan had failed and in the most spectacular and unexpected way. There would be retribution.

"What do you think happened?" Sawyer used his boot to poke at the first asshole who groaned and proved he was still alive.

"I think Wyatt had a moment when he disassociated from his everyday personality and turned to violence because he has unprocessed childhood trauma." Sabrina actually smiled. Like this was just a fucking normal day. "You did good, honey. I don't think you killed anyone. But you should handle the guy in the bathroom. He was rude, and he did not fight fair. He was sneaking up behind you until I hit him with a saltshaker to the head. I used to teach softball to my students back in North Carolina. I was an excellent pitcher."

Sawyer put a hand to his brow because his left eyebrow had developed a sudden twitch.

Sabrina was going to drive him utterly mad.

"Did I hurt you?" Wyatt stood feet away from her, his hands clenched in fists as though he didn't trust himself not to touch her.

Sawyer was starting to think Wyatt wouldn't have a choice. Sabrina seemed to have decided what she wanted, and she was proving herself to be a woman who didn't change her mind.

"Of course not," Sabrina said, her tone going soft. "You would never hurt me." She frowned suddenly. "Well, not physically. We're going to talk about how much words hurt later on tonight, but I do believe the sheriff is here so you should ensure the last criminal doesn't get away. Sheriff Wright will take them to jail, and then we're going to have a long talk."

"You should leave," Wyatt said, his eyes not quite meeting hers.

"I'm not leaving." She set all her guns on the table closest to her. She got into Wyatt's space, forcing him to look her in the eyes. "If you're going to break my heart, you do it in person, and you better make me believe, Wyatt, because I'm not being left behind because you're afraid of what your brother might do to me. You need to hear me. If you are doing this to protect me, don't. I might decide your brother is between me and what I want, and I'll find a way to go after him."

"Sabrina." Wyatt's eyes had gone wide. "You can't."

"Watch me." She went on her toes and brushed a kiss over his cheek. "Now go and make sure that asshole isn't getting away."

Wyatt turned and walked back toward the bathroom.

"Boss? Is everything okay?" Lark and Gil stood in the hall leading to the office. "I got scared and called the sheriff. I'm…"

"Don't say you're sorry." Sabrina was absolutely the bossiest thing he'd ever seen. She walked right up to Lark and put a hand on her shoulder. "You did the right thing. I know Sawyer is reluctant to deal with the authorities because he thinks it makes him look hot being a bad boy, but there is certainly a time and a place to call the sheriff, and this is definitely one of those times."

"I do not." What the hell was she talking about?

She turned slightly to look back at him, her lips curling up. "Well, then you must be afraid of the sheriff."

"I fucking am not." Why were they discussing this? They had half dead bodies all around them and a world of hurt coming and she was poking him.

So fucking mean.

Wyatt got a kiss. He hadn't gotten a kiss.

"Then it's the other," Sabrina said with a shrug as she moved closer to him. "The point being you're not going to be mad at the young lady who made the reasonable choice to call in the sheriff."

Who was here. Sheriff Wright strode in, his gun up and ready, followed by Elisa Leal, who matched his energy.

"Hey, sis, we're all good," Sabrina said like she was inviting her friends over for tea and not to clean up a bunch of bodies.

Wright's gaze moved around the bar. "You do this damage, Sawyer?"

"He certainly did not," Sabrina said primly. "Wyatt had a reasonable reaction to a gentleman insinuating I take cash for my favors, and then I took out those two with my personal stun gun, and Wyatt is dealing with the last one in the men's room, I believe."

The sheriff got on his radio. "Gemma, could you call EMS? We're going to need Ty to look over some of these guys. Have Doc come out, too. One of these dude's has what looks like an ostrich egg on his noggin, and apparently there was some electrical play going on."

Sabrina's sister looked her up and down, proving the Leal women handled a crisis with cool precision. "That's not even your sluttiest outfit. You can look way more whorelike. The stun gun worked well, huh? This one is still twitching. I told you it was a good investment."

"I didn't get to use the bear spray, though." Sabrina sounded deeply disappointed.

He was going to have to go through her bag since it seemed to be full of weapons.

But the best weapon she had was her sassy mouth because he was pretty sure at this point she could handle his shit. Probably better than any woman he'd ever met.

It was a temptation he might not be able to avoid.

Although she was going to get a full dose of him tonight, and it might be enough to send her running.

"Hey, how much trouble are we looking at?" Nate kept his voice down as Elisa started securing the prisoners.

He'd expected Nate to take him in, too, but the sheriff seemed to not need much of an explanation. There was also something about the way the man used the word "we" that eased some of Sawyer's anxiety. "They didn't get what they wanted, and Wyatt's insulted them. His brother will react."

"You okay?" Nate asked. "It had to be pretty rough for someone to call me out."

"It was touch and go. Wyatt lost his shit when one of them put hands on Sabrina," Sawyer admitted. It was odd, but he didn't feel the desperate need to clam up around the sheriff. It was kind of nice to have him here.

"Is this why he stood her up tonight?" Nate asked, keeping his voice low. "He worried?"

"Beyond worried, but I don't think Sabrina is going to take no for an answer," he replied as the door opened and Wyatt drug the last of his brother's men out by his collar.

Wyatt stopped when he caught sight of the sheriff. "Sorry. Sabrina told me I had to finish the job. I suppose she'll be satisfied if I give this jerk up to you. He was hiding in one of the stalls, and I'm pretty sure he peed himself. So much for the horrible Horde."

"You have no idea what's coming for you," the asshole snarled. "Wayne is going to show you who's the boss. He'll take you all down."

Elisa stopped, staring at the man Wyatt shoved toward the sheriff. "That sounded like a threat."

"It did indeed," the sheriff agreed. "I couldn't tell, Deputy Leal, if he was talking about us or someone else."

"Oh, it totally felt like us," Elisa replied. "He was definitely letting the sheriff's department know his group is going to target us. Probably was talking about the whole town."

As Elisa started to put cuffs on the guy, he frowned the sheriff's way. "This bar ain't on incorporated land. We checked. No one protects these assholes. They're on their own. This arrest ain't legal."

Wayne needed to train his men better. "Did you think this is the Wild West? Of course I can call the sheriff and have you arrested for assault."

"Then why ain't he arresting Wyatt? No one laid a hand on anyone until Wyatt went wild," the man replied as one of his friends began to groan.

Wyatt's hands were suddenly in his pockets, his eyes on the floor.

"Oh, I assure you I had hands laid on me, and Wyatt was merely attempting to protect me," Sabrina announced, joining him and threading her arm through Wyatt's. "I can assure you Wyatt had no intentions of violence until they threatened to do terrible things to me."

The sheriff finished hauling up Doug, who was still twitching. "And what was Sawyer doing?"

"Oh, he was attempting to get me to safety while Wyatt dealt with the threat," Sabrina replied. "He didn't understand how competent I am at defending myself." Her head turned until she had him in her sights. Her lips curled into the meanest fucking smile. "He knows now."

His cock tightened at the thought of how he was going to handle her. "I do. I know now exactly how strong you are, Sabrina. I also know you don't follow directions well, which we're going to talk about."

Elisa's eyes went wide, but she never took a hand off her prisoner. "Uh, should I hang around? I could get Cam to come in for a while."

"Why would you?" Sabrina didn't seem to notice how stiff Wyatt was. She cuddled closer to him. "I assure you I can handle anything Sawyer wants to do…discuss with me."

"Sure," the sheriff said with a knowing smile. "Leal, I think your sister knows what she's gotten herself into, and I suspect she's going to need some alone time to deal with the situation. Sawyer, I advise you to shut down for the night and come by the station tomorrow so I can take some statements."

"I'm not pressing charges," Wyatt said and moved away from Sabrina suddenly.

"I am," Sabrina announced.

"Damn it," Wyatt said, turning to her.

The sheriff was right. They needed to deal with this alone. "We'll come by in the morning, and we're shutting down for the night. Thank you, Sheriff."

He sent Sabrina a stare he hoped got his point across. She needed to keep quiet until they were alone.

She simply gave him a serene smile before turning to the sheriff. "Yes, thank you so much, and Elisa, I'm fine. I think Wyatt and I have things to talk about."

"I'm not worried about Wyatt," her sister explained. "But Sawyer's got a certain look in his eyes."

Sabrina strode over to the bar and picked up a bottle of tequila. "His eyes are going to be the only thing he uses on me unless we come to another arrangement. What do you say, Sawyer? Are you going to lecture me? Give me a whole bunch of words like you're my daddy?"

"It won't be words, baby," he nearly snarled but only because she was pushing his every fucking button.

"Ooookay." Elisa nodded. "'Night then. See you tomorrow."

The door opened again and one of the deputies from Creede strode in. He was a tall man with youthful good looks. He was the all-American hero type.

He'd dated Sabrina.

"Hey, I just got the call," he said. "Knox is out in the car.

Gemma said you needed backup." His gaze caught on the gorgeous girl at the bar who'd poured herself a shot of tequila. "Sabrina? Oh, god. What happened? Are you okay, sweetheart?"

Wyatt growled.

He did not need this shit again tonight. There was only one way to handle the situation, and it was oddly easy. He'd tried to find a way out. He'd done his level best, but she had no sense of self-protection, and she was going to have to handle it from here on out. "Our girlfriend is fine, Deputy. These men threatened her but her men took care of it."

The deputy's expression fell, but Sabrina looked like a cat who'd lapped up all the cream. "Yes, they did."

The sheriff and his deputies took out the trash, and Sawyer prepared to lay down the law.

* * * *

Wyatt wasn't sure when he'd lost all control. Oh, he knew he'd lost physical control the minute the asshole had laid hands on Sabrina. He'd gone to the place he had in childhood when he couldn't handle the world and he had to fight for his life. It was a place his father and brother had pushed him to time and time again. He would start normally and then he would look down and there would be blood on his hands and bodies on the floor.

Sabrina had watched him lose his shit.

And then complained he let one get away.

Yeah, that was the moment he should have known he'd lost all control. Every bit of it.

"What the hell were you thinking?" Sawyer rounded the bar after locking up for the night. They were finally alone. Sabrina had already poured herself another shot, and she lined up two more glasses.

Wyatt was sitting at one of the tables, utterly unwilling to get close to her again.

She had no idea what she'd started, no idea what trouble they were all in.

"I was thinking the man I care about was in trouble," she replied.

"I broke up with you." He wasn't sure where his plan had gone wrong. His fists ached but not half as much as his heart at the thought of what his brother's men could do to her now that they knew he cared about her. "I was plain about it. I don't want to see you again."

Sabrina poured the shots. "Sure. You don't care and I'm not wild enough and you always freak out and become a rolling ball of violence at the thought of another man laying hands on any woman of your acquaintance."

She had him there.

Sawyer pointed a finger his way. "I told you it wouldn't work, but that's another lecture for another day." His attention centered on Sabrina again, his jaw tight. "I want to understand what the hell you thought you would do walking in this bar the way you did. Do you understand the words *situational awareness*? Can you put them together for me?"

He'd never actually seen Sawyer so upset. Not even when his brother had gotten arrested. Sawyer was always cool under pressure, but he'd lost it tonight, too.

He'd also announced to the world Sabrina was theirs.

For the first time, Sabrina flushed slightly and looked the tiniest bit uncomfortable. "Well, how was I supposed to know they weren't the regular clientele? This place is something of a biker bar, from what I understand. How am I supposed to tell the difference between everyday, fun-loving bikers who enjoy cheap beer and the criminal ones?"

Sawyer's eyes rolled, and both he and Wyatt tapped their chests on the left side. "Patch."

Yep, they were on the same page.

Except he felt something building between Sawyer and Sabrina, something he wanted to be a part of but he couldn't now because he had to leave. It was the only way he could protect them all.

Unless it was already far too late.

"Patch? You mean the little scout thing they had on their vests?" Sabrina asked. "I thought it was like a Boy Scout patch."

Sawyer's brows rose. "You thought they were Boy Scouts?"

She bit her bottom lip and looked so fucking sexy it hurt. "Well, not when they opened their mouths. Sawyer, I'm sorry I caused a problem, but I'm not sorry I came here tonight. Wyatt was wrong to do what he did. He doesn't want to break up with me. And the truth of the matter is you don't want to keep your hands off me either.

You're both scared of things that would be better to deal with now and get out of the way so we can figure out if we can be happy together. I know it's a hard word for you. So how about we use the word you do understand. Content. I think you could be content with me and Wyatt if we can get past this whole thing with his brother and you can deal with your abandonment issues."

"How are you going to deal with the flat of my hand on your naked ass?" Sawyer growled.

Sabrina's breath hitched. "I'll probably cry and curse your name until you fuck me, Sawyer."

Wyatt stood up. "Do either of you understand what happened tonight?"

Sabrina's expression softened. "I understand you had to face something you hoped you never would again. Wyatt, don't pull away from me. You were wrong to try to push me away. I'm not fragile. I'm not going to break down because you have to beat the crap out of some guys who deserved it. Though I am going to ask you to be prepared for a couple of the kids in my class to kick you in the shins. I tried to explain to Paige it wasn't necessary, but she can be stubborn. And Charlie and Zander tend to do what she says. Maybe you should wear shin guards for a couple of weeks."

What the hell?

Sawyer threw back his head and laughed.

But Wyatt got into her space, putting his hands on her shoulders and barely stopping himself from shaking some sense into her. "This is not a joke."

Her hands came up, and the minute she touched his face he wanted to hug her. Warmth seemed to spill from her into him, a calm sense telling him they could handle anything. "I know. I'm so sorry he came back into your life. But he was always going to, and you're not alone now. You have Sawyer and you have me and you have this town."

The town he was coming to love? He knew he'd made this very argument to Sawyer, but now that the actual threat was here, all he could think about was how nice they all were to him. How they had kids and futures, and his brother could take it all from them. Maybe they would win, but if Wayne wanted a war, he could do a shit ton of damage before they took him down.

He could hurt the kids Sabrina taught. The ones she loved and centered her world around.

He could definitely hurt Sabrina.

"Don't," Sabrina said, her chin coming up and showing the stubborn expression on her face. "Don't you sit there and pretend like I matter when you're willing to leave me. If you care about me, you should be willing to let me stand beside you. I'm not some meaningless sex toy. I'm not some doll you hug for comfort. I'm a whole real human being who could be part of your life if you allow me to be."

"He could kill you."

"I could get hit by a car tomorrow," she argued, tears welling in her pretty eyes. "I could have a heart attack. I could get cancer like my sister did. The truth of the matter is I'm going to die someday, and there's nothing you can do about it. But you can choose to live whatever life I have with me. Be brave, Wyatt. Don't let them take your whole life from you."

Every word drove into his soul. Was he doing what she'd accused him of? Was he treating her like a toy and not the brave, resourceful woman she was? But how could he put her in danger? How would he ever live with himself?

"Wyatt, it's done," Sawyer said, moving in closer, his arms over his chest. "She's on their radar, and there's not a damn thing you can do about it except spank her ass red and take out all of your tension on her pretty pussy. And her mouth. And maybe her asshole, if she's ready."

Sawyer wasn't helping. "You're supposed to be the voice of reason. You're literally the person who told me this was a bad idea."

"It is, and we're going to have to deal with it, but my grandfather always told me when fate walks in, there's not a hell of a lot you can do." Sawyer stared at her, his hand coming out to stroke her hair. She leaned into his touch. "The night I saw her for the first time, you showed up on my doorstep. I don't think I ever had a choice. I think you two might be my fate. And that sucks for you. I thought I could help you avoid it, but you're both stubborn assholes, and you might be stuck with me now."

"Not if I leave tonight," Wyatt vowed.

"With what?" Sabrina asked, her eyes wide and guileless as she looked up at him.

Sawyer snorted. "I knew you were up to something. What did you do, brat?"

Wyatt wasn't sure what she could have done. Until he remembered how she'd brushed up against him as the sheriff and his deputies had hauled off his brother's enforcers. He stepped back and felt for his wallet. His back pocket was completely empty. And he didn't have the keys to his bike. Shock flashed through him. His sweet schoolteacher had rolled him? "Where is my wallet, Sabrina?"

"You can have it and your keys back when you're willing to be reasonable and not make emotional decisions that could harm all the people you care about." She went back to her tequila as though she hadn't taken almost everything he owned. "Until then consider yourself in time-out."

The idea of spanking her held a lot of appeal. "I can hotwire the bike, Sabrina."

"Maybe, but what are you going to do about the tires?" Sabrina asked. "I asked Lark to let the air out of them. While y'all were cleaning up, Lark and I decided you shouldn't make big decisions right now. Apparently Lark has been going to a textile arts class with Callie and she's heard the whole story about how Callie trashed Zane's bike so he couldn't sacrifice himself in a burst of male drama."

Sawyer took a shot of tequila and lifted it Sabrina's way. "Every word out of your mouth is going to be accounted for tonight."

"Am I wrong? You guys have one gear. The minute things go wrong you're tossing yourself on the fire. Be creative. There are other ways to solve problems," she argued. "Sometimes you have to take away options so students can learn how to do things differently."

"I am not one of your students." Wyatt wasn't sure if he was angry or… No one had ever fought for him with the singular exception of his only real friend, the man who'd called it all fate. Certainly no woman had stood in between him and danger. Not his mother. Not any of the women he'd called aunts.

"You're lucky because I would have notes," Sabrina said.

"She is asking for it, brother. Now I realize she's been begging for it since the day she set eyes on us." Sawyer tipped back the shot, downing it in one go. He slapped the glass on the bar. "She's got us in a corner. If you run, all you're doing is leaving me alone to take care of her. Your brother's going to do what he's going to do, and leaving us alone helps no one at this point except you."

"I'm not doing this to help me. Maybe if I go to him, offer myself up." Wyatt was looking for any way out of the trap. It was a trap he wanted to be caught in so badly, but he didn't see how it ended well.

Sawyer's hand went to the back of Sabrina's neck. "And when he wants to torture you? You think he'll simply smack you around? The man literally burned the skin off your chest and you still walked away. I don't think your own physical pain is going to do it for him. So he'll come after Sabrina, who will be down a protector."

Sabrina sighed as Sawyer tightened his hold. "I'll still have you and my sister and Mel and Cass, and don't discount Paige Harper. The kid is mean. Oh, and Henry. Nell will give him a lecture about humane assassinations, but they're serious about Poppy's education."

Why wouldn't she listen? "This is not a fucking joke."

"No. It's not, but you sacrificing yourself solves nothing," Sabrina said. "And we can't fix it tonight, but we can do something else. We can let this awful night lead us to something good. Wyatt, I think I'm falling in love with you and with Sawyer, even though I know he gets a little sick when he hears the word. So we'll say I'm used to his face and it would be annoying to have to find another lover."

Sawyer grinned. "You speak my language, baby. Back at you."

Were they right? Was there anything he could do about this tonight? It appeared she'd cut off all avenues. It wasn't like there was a handy bus station he could walk to.

He could call his brother and turn himself in and the only effect would be to put Sabrina in greater danger.

He needed to talk to someone, but he was pretty sure Alexei's office was closed for the night.

So what else was there left to do?

She was falling in love with him? He was already madly in love with her. In love for the first time in his life. He knew what he wanted. His friend. Their lover. Eventually their wife. He wanted to live with Sawyer and Sabrina right here in Bliss, where he could help Mel fight aliens and join Nell in whatever protest she happened to be involved in. He wanted to go squatching, even though he wasn't sure what that was, but Max Harper made it sound fun.

He wanted to be normal. A guy who loved his family.

"But we're going to have a long discussion about how you behaved this evening." Sawyer stood, looming over her. "Because you could have gotten killed tonight. You could have made everything worse. I'm not playing or joking, Sabrina. You nearly gave me a fucking heart attack tonight, and you're going to pay for it."

"I'm not afraid of you," she replied.

From what Wyatt could tell, she wasn't afraid of anything or anyone.

"You're not going to be able to sit tomorrow," Sawyer vowed.

Sabrina walked over to the bar. She leaned over, offering up her backside, her palms on the railing. "I think you'll find I can work while I'm standing."

Sawyer groaned. "If you're not joining us, you should go up to the house because this is going to get wild, brother."

He watched as Sawyer approached her.

Was he going to walk? Could he make the long walk up to the cabin, leaving them behind, leaving behind everything he wanted?

For one night, he could have it. It wouldn't work. He would find a way to save them both, but maybe Sawyer was right and they could have this one night. She'd made it so he couldn't go anywhere, couldn't try to solve the problem tonight, so why not indulge himself?

Before he found a way to kill his brother and end the threat.

It might be a better plan than sacrificing himself. If he killed them all, she would be safe.

Wyatt unbuckled his belt.

He wasn't going anywhere. Not for the rest of the night.

Tomorrow he would figure out how far he would need to go to save them all.

Chapter Twelve

Sabrina knew she'd won this battle the minute she heard the clink of Wyatt's belt hitting the floor.

She also knew damn well the war wasn't over because she'd seen the look in his eyes. She rather thought Sawyer had made his decision and would be grumbly but steadfast.

Wyatt was still thinking about how to sacrifice himself, and she had to ensure it didn't happen.

Tonight it would be easy because he would be focused on torturing her in the sweetest way.

She held her position, hands flat on the rail of the bar.

"You ever spanked a woman?" Sawyer asked.

Sabrina wanted to know the answer. She turned slightly and saw a gorgeous Sawyer frowning her way.

"You, eyes front," he ordered in a deep tone. "Your sass is not required."

But her sass was exactly why she was here in the first place. Still, she knew she'd pushed both men far beyond their normal boundaries for the evening. They were overstimulated and needed a safe space to deal with all the emotions of the night.

And apparently their safe space was her ass.

"Yeah," Wyatt replied. "There was this... Well, we shouldn't go into it around Sabrina."

"There was a woman?" She wasn't good at staying quiet. "I don't mind you talking about your past relationships. I had one boyfriend who said he was into spanking, and I got excited until I realized he wanted me to spank him. Not that there's anything…"

A hard hand came down on her ass, the force shoving her forward. She had to balance to stay on her feet.

"Absolutely not," Sawyer announced, his hand still on her cheeks. The other found the nape of her neck. "You will be still and take what we give you. You've misbehaved all fucking night long, and don't tell me you didn't know. You knew damn well I wanted you safe."

"I made myself very plain," Wyatt added.

He was wrong. "No, you lied to me and hurt my heart and wouldn't allow me to serve my primary function in this relationship which is to stand beside you and care about you. So I had to go to a secondary function which is kicking the ass of anyone who's trying to hurt my man."

"Not helping your case," Sawyer grumbled. "And you didn't kick them. You stunned them. There's a difference."

"I'm only trying to say Wyatt's past doesn't bother me." She needed to make it plain. "Neither his past with the MC he grew up in nor his past relationships."

"Relationships?"

Sabrina knew she'd miscalculated when she heard the arrogant tone come out of Wyatt's mouth. He was always sweet with her. She'd never heard him sound surly and mean, but here they were. He'd had a foot back in the world he'd tried to run from and it was affecting him. "I don't care about your ex-girlfriends."

Sawyer was busy pulling up the skirt she'd carefully donned for her date. It was a flowy thing, something she could dress up or down. This evening she'd taken off the cardigan she'd worn to school over a slightly fussy white blouse in exchange for a V-neck sweater that showed off the curves of her breasts. She'd also put on some lacy undies because she'd never planned for their date to end at Trio.

"I never had a girlfriend, Sabrina," Wyatt continued as Sawyer shoved her skirt up, exposing her backside. "When I was fifteen my father assigned one of the club whores to rid me of my virginity."

"What?" This wasn't something Sabrina was going to sit idly by and listen to like it was a fun story of his youth. "He had someone rape you?"

Wyatt stopped. He'd moved into her line of sight. "Why would you think that? I was a teenaged boy."

"Being a boy doesn't mean you wanted it."

Sawyer's hand softened as he caressed her. "I've told him this, too. You have to understand we're deprogramming all the crap they shoved into his head. I know. I'm usually the problem, but I was just born stubborn. My grandad would have killed anyone who tried to touch me against my will. It's not the same for Wyatt."

"My dad wanted to make sure I wasn't something he didn't want me to be," Wyatt admitted. "But I don't want to think about it tonight. To answer Sawyer's question, yes, I have spanked a woman. Several of the club whores enjoyed bondage and kink, and I learned how to please them. Those relationships were perfectly consensual. Yes, Sabrina, we called them whores and they served the MC. They were women who thought they might become old ladies, but once you fucked every guy in the MC, that possibility was kind of gone. For the men I grew up with, there are two types of women. Wives and whores."

He sounded so remote. Only the feel of Sawyer's warm hand on her skin kept her from standing up and trying to protect herself. Sawyer was there, telling her everything would be okay. Letting her know she was beautiful and had nothing to hide from them. It made it easy to ask the question she needed to ask, the one that would tell her how far away Wyatt truly was. "Which one am I?"

His expression softened. "You don't belong in there in any way. You're Sabrina. Those women… They were who they were. They were stuck in bad choices and believed they didn't have a way out, and some of them enjoyed it and wouldn't trade their lives for anything in the world. There are no categories for women."

He wasn't far away at all. "And you're Wyatt and so much more than any group of people would box you in as. You make the decisions."

His eyes narrowed. "Do I? Because it seems like I made a whole lot of decisions tonight no one honored. Where is my wallet, Sabrina?"

It had been a calculated act on her part. She'd known it could bite her in the ass. "You can have it back after you've thought about your actions."

She'd been planning to give the man a lecture on hurting the people he cared about and how thoughtless it was to send a text when the situation obviously required an in-person discussion, but that particular line of thinking was cut off by the serious smack of Sawyer's hand against her cheeks. Pain flared and her eyes watered and…damn, but her pussy clenched. Heat sparked through her, sending waves of warring sensation through her body.

"Wyatt, I don't actually think you're in a place where you should spank her. You've been through too much," Sawyer said, his hand back to caressing her. "But there is something you can do. Why don't you go to the office and in the closet there's a bag. You'll know what to do with it."

Ominous words. She had to catch her breath. "What does that mean, Sawyer?"

Wyatt walked away, his boots thudding against the floor.

"I'm going to give my partner something to do. Wyatt's fought enough this evening," Sawyer said before delivering another bone-rattling, pussy-shaking slap to her ass. This one had her going on her toes.

"What's he going to do?" Sabrina asked through clenched teeth. The pain rapidly morphed to something else, something that left her jangled and disjointed and wanting. This was why they called it torture.

"That is for me to know and you to find out, Teach," Sawyer whispered. "But he can't do it while you're wearing all these clothes. Give me these panties. You won't need them."

She felt his fingers slide under the waistband of her undies, dragging them down her legs. She lifted them in turn so he could get them off her and then gasped as she felt the heat of his breath on the skin of her rear.

"Damn, this is a pretty ass, and I like how pink it is now," he said.

"Sawyer," she began because while they'd kind of played around, he hadn't put his face there.

A flash of pain had her gasping again. He laid five quick,

stinging slaps to her right cheek before she felt something nip at her.

Holy wow, he'd bitten her. Bitten her ass.

And she'd kind of liked it. The pain had made her fingers curl around the curve of the bar.

"You stay put or I'll tie you up, Sabrina," he vowed. "You wanted me, well, this is me, Teach. When you make me insane—and I don't think this is going to be the last time you do it—I'm going to take my pound of your pretty flesh. Unless you're scared or I hurt you in a way you don't enjoy, you take it. You smile and say *yes, Sawyer* because right now you aren't in control."

She was always in control, always thinking about how her actions affected others. She was in charge of so many young lives, and the town was dependent on her for the most important thing of all—their children's futures.

She realized what she'd found with these two men the weekend they'd spent snowed in. She'd thought it was sex and affection and a wild side she hadn't known existed. But it was more. She'd found a space where she didn't have to be in control, where she could be taken care of.

Her mother had rammed it into her head that she should trust no one to take care of her. Certainly no man. Men left, according to her mom.

Mel wouldn't have left. Oh, he wouldn't have married her mom, but he wouldn't have left Elisa. And when her mom had married Sabrina's dad and history had played itself out, Mel would have been there. It wouldn't have mattered she didn't have a drop of his blood.

She didn't have to make decisions based on her mother's life. She had to go with her instincts, not the lessons taught to her. Her instincts told her these men were important.

These men were worth the heartache if things didn't work, worth the pain that would inevitably come because nothing lasted forever.

"Yes, Sawyer."

She felt him lean against her, felt the rough edge of his incoming beard as he nuzzled her. "Are you sure, Sabrina? I made a claim tonight, and it'll be hard to take back. I'm not smooth. I fuck up a lot. I'm not what you would call emotionally available."

He was wrong. "You're better than you think you are. Do you want me to keep quiet about how I'm feeling?"

"No," he admitted. "I don't like it when you don't talk to me. Even if it's because I didn't talk to you. I don't like talking, but I like it when you do it."

She'd always known. He was a bit slow, but it was okay. "I can talk enough for both of us and I'm sure, Sawyer. I'm sure. It's why I put you in a corner and made you claim me."

She'd known what she was doing, though she hadn't been certain it would work. Sawyer needed a reason to change. He was a creature of habit. He clung to his habits even when they didn't make him happy. But he could change. The fact that he let Wyatt stay with him was proof, and he was happier with Wyatt around.

He was happier with her around, too, so she was going to have to get used to his preoccupation with her backside. He seemed to like to spank and kiss it, which is what he was doing now.

"You sealed your fate for the time being, but you can always change your mind. I said what I said because I want the sheriff to know I'll take care of you, but no one in town is going to be surprised if you dump my ass later on. Let's get through this crisis and we'll figure things out on the other side."

He couldn't simply move forward. He had to do it incrementally. "So you want me to stay with you while we figure out how to help Wyatt?"

He got to his feet and then his big hand was on her arm, hauling her up and pulling her against his chest. "I don't want you to stay with me. I demand you stay with me. You aren't going anywhere on your own until the danger is over. You'll have a bodyguard. It can be me or Wyatt or your sister or anyone who I approve of, but the minute you don't follow orders, you'll find yourself in a cage, and I'll be the one holding the key."

Her heart softened because he was telling her everything she needed to know. He was scared to lose her. He cared, and he wasn't going to let her go. "I promise."

Sawyer stared down at her and then he growled and slammed his mouth over hers. His tongue swept across her lips and then into her mouth, dominating her even as he pushed and pulled, dragging the rest of her clothes off and tossing them to the side. Somehow she went from fully dressed to having only Sawyer's hands on her skin, and she didn't care. She was completely naked and pressed against the bar, Sawyer's cock against her pussy, and it felt perfect.

And Wyatt said she wasn't wild.

"Damn," a low voice said.

Sabrina turned her head and Wyatt stood by the bar, a small bag in his hand. Gone was the worried expression he'd been wearing, replaced with a look of lust.

This was what they needed. Her instincts might not always be correct, but Sawyer's seemed on point tonight. They didn't need to talk. They didn't need to sit down and hash things out in an intellectual way. They definitely didn't need to discuss their feelings.

They needed to revel in them in a physical way. She told her kids to use their words, but there were also times to put them away, times when words didn't convey enough.

She held out a hand, and Wyatt hesitated for the barest moments before his jaw firmed and he strode to her.

"This isn't over, Sabrina," he said, his voice taking on the husky tone he used when he was getting serious about sex. And then he was kissing her while Sawyer moved away, ceding his place.

Wyatt's tongue caressed hers, his hands pulling her close and winding down to cup her ass so she could feel how much he wanted her.

"Did you clean it?" Sawyer asked.

Wyatt's mouth came off of hers for a moment. "Yes. And I warmed up the lube, but all I could find was regular lube. I think she deserves the hard stuff."

Well, he had her attention. "Hard stuff?"

Wyatt's lips curled in a smirk. "Yeah, baby. When you trash my bike and hide my wallet, you should have to take the ginger lube."

"Why would lube have flavors?" Sabrina hadn't gotten this deep with her sister. They'd had some serious sex talks, but not one had covered tasty lubricants.

"You wouldn't eat it, Teach," Sawyer said with a chuckle. "The oil released by the ginger would make your asshole burn."

"Burn?" She wasn't sure she was ready. "I think I'll take more spankings, please. Or we could do like a really brutal oral, perhaps."

Wyatt stared at her for a moment and then his head fell forward, leaning against hers. "You're going to kill me, Sabrina."

She brought her hands up to hold him there. "I don't want to kill you. I want to live with you. I want to be with you."

"Well, you're with me for the foreseeable future," he said, his voice slightly tortured. "You have to be. There's no other choice. As for your punishment, it starts now."

"Sorry, now that I know how much punishment she can rack up, I'll make sure to keep a solid variety of exotic lubes. Ginger is only the beginning." Sawyer sounded…weirdly happy. "We can have so much fun."

So all she had to do to get Sawyer to toss out his inhibitions when it came to relationships was to let him torture her asshole. Awesome.

"Give me the plug," Wyatt commanded. "We'll have to settle for this. Sawyer's right. I'm too emotional to really spank you tonight, but tomorrow I'll have processed the trauma you put me through and I'll be ready to thoughtfully smack your ass for everything that went on this evening."

She was so glad he'd had some therapy. Also she was glad Sawyer didn't keep ginger around. Of course that might change if Rachel Harper had her way and he got more serious about craft cocktails. She might need to give it some thought.

Then she wasn't thinking about anything except the fact that someone parted the cheeks of her ass, which meant two men now had a perfect view of a piece of her anatomy she'd never seen before.

What if it was hideous?

"Damn, she's pretty," Sawyer said, and she could feel him kneeling behind her. "She's going to be so tight."

"She's only taken a couple of fingers up until now. Let's see how she handles a plug." Wyatt sounded calm and centered.

She'd been expecting a plug. This was something she'd gone over with them. They hadn't been able to take her together because they'd needed time to prepare her. When Sawyer had told her he wasn't staying with them, she'd thought she'd lost the chance.

"See, now I think I was way too nice when I warmed this up," Wyatt complained. "I should have made you take it icy cold, but my soft heart defeats me every time."

She felt the sensation of warm lube coat her delicate flesh and she shivered. Vulnerable. She was so vulnerable like this, and the feeling was what made everything so intimate. Her vulnerability was balanced by her trust in them. She could be open with her body and they would honor her, would give her the affection and pleasure she longed for.

She wasn't sure she longed for the jangly sensation she got when she felt the tip of the plug rim her.

"Hey, relax." Sawyer was beside her now. "Let him work that sweet plug in your ass and then we'll show you a preview of how it's going to feel when we take you together. It's how we'll keep him here with us. We'll hold out on him while your little asshole gets used to a plug. He wants to take you together."

"Like you don't," Wyatt complained while working the plug over and around and back again.

"Never said I didn't. I didn't think it could work because I'm an asshole and hard to live with. Turns out Teach here isn't some sweet thing I'll run over without meaning to. She likes to stun men for fun, and I'll remember that. After she stuns me a couple of times for being a jerk, I suspect I'll learn my lesson."

"I didn't do it for fun." She whimpered when Wyatt started to push the plug. Yep. It was one strange sensation. It wasn't pain, exactly. It was pressure, and also there was a need inside her to push against it, to take it in one go.

"Like you didn't have fun, you bad, bad girl." Sawyer whispered the words against her ear but she felt his hand move under her hips, fingers sliding toward her pussy.

"That's right, baby," Wyatt encouraged as the plug slid in deeper before he pulled it out again. "Relax. Sawyer's going to help you."

It was the perfect distraction. How the hell could she think about the plug in her butt when Sawyer's big fingers were sliding over her clit?

"I don't think we have to worry about her enjoying it," Sawyer chuckled. "She's so fucking wet. She liked her spanking and she's enjoying the plug. She'll love it when we fuck her pretty ass."

She hadn't realized how aroused she'd become, but Sawyer's fingers easily slid over her clit, pressing down and rotating in perfect time with the plug fucking her. She moved her hips, finding the rhythm they set and letting go of anything but the sensation they brought out in her.

The plug was hard and smooth, and despite the warmth of the

lube there was a slight chill to it where Sawyer's fingers were all heat and strong flesh. He rubbed her clit over and over, and Sabrina felt softness well inside her, a rushing wave of pleasure that engulfed her even as she felt the plug slide deep inside.

She felt boneless as she sagged over Wyatt's legs.

"And now she's ready for a little fun. You need to clench, baby, because if you lose this plug, I'm going to let Sawyer spank you all over again," Wyatt promised.

She barely had time to heed his words before she was being lifted up by Sawyer.

Her night was far from over.

* * * *

Contrary to what most people might believe, Sawyer kept a clean bar. But no bar was so clean he would let her kneel on the floor. Nope. His Teach would be horrified. Oh, right now she was all drugged on adrenaline and orgasms, but when she woke up in the morning she would give him a lecture on the dangers of bacteria, and he wanted to avoid lectures.

But he damn sure wasn't about to avoid getting her in between him and Wyatt, and no turns this time. Nope. After the day they'd had, he was going to push her every boundary.

And he was going to check the sturdiness of his pool table.

They should have gone up to the house. Or he should put a couch in the office. Yeah, he would have to do that because Sabrina had made her bed, and the least she deserved was a couch.

The pool table was going to have to make do.

He set her on her feet, and Wyatt immediately moved in behind her.

"Hands on the railing, legs apart." Wyatt was quite bossy tonight, but then the guy had been through some shit. "I'm serious, Sabrina. Don't lose the plug."

Her head turned Wyatt's way. "Have you tried keeping a plug in your butt while being carried across a room? We're going to have a talk about gravity, Mister."

He was totally…oh, shit. He'd almost thought the word. Almost. He was totally going to hang out with her for the rest of their lives because he wasn't rude and he wouldn't kick her out. And if it became ruder to not marry her than to marry her... What's a guy supposed to do? Would he fight her if she wanted, say, a couple of kids? Yeah, probably, because he would be a terrible...

Except he wouldn't. He would be a fucking good dad. He'd been an excellent brother. Maybe he didn't talk as much as he should, but, hey, the kid would have two other people in his or her life who would never shut up. He would be totally necessary if the kid wanted to shove his or her feelings down deep and pretend they didn't exist.

He did have a place in a family.

He wasn't planning on starting one tonight though. He pulled a condom out of the kit Wyatt had brought out and handed it to him. "Suit up. I'm going to make sure our pretty teacher can't lecture us for a while."

"What do you mean?" Sabrina asked. "And seriously, how am I supposed to keep the plug in?"

"Clench, baby," he advised as Wyatt chucked his clothes in a hurry.

Sawyer was down to his jeans and boots, and both had to go. He kicked off his shoes and dragged his jeans and boxers off. Sabrina had found her position. Feet on the ground, hands palms down on the railing, and ass sticking out so Wyatt could get between her legs and show her how tight she could be.

Not anywhere as tight as she would be when she was riding one of them while the other fucked her ass, but it would do for tonight.

And he wanted to feel her mouth on him. He wanted that glorious take-no-prisoners woman to take his cock and suck and love and lick it and then swallow down absolutely everything he had to give her.

She gasped when he climbed onto the pool table and got to his knees in front of her, stroking his cock so he was hard and ready. "Right here?"

He grinned. It was weird. He was using muscles he hadn't before he'd met her. "Right here. Right now."

She bit her bottom lip as Wyatt moved in behind her. "You're giving me a lot of tasks to do at the same time, guys."

"Good thing you're a multitasker." He wasn't listening to complaints. He'd had an awful fucking night. It would more than likely lead into a couple of super dangerous and dramatic days. He had to go into the sheriff's office and talk to people in the morning. It was all her fault since if she hadn't shown up, they likely would have handed over the codes Wayne wanted and... Hell, those guys wouldn't have just walked away, but it was more fun to blame Sabrina for everything. There were some plus sides to having her around. "You take me, Teach. You take me or he'll stop doing what he's about to do."

Wyatt had his hands on her hips, steadying himself as he started to penetrate her.

Sabrina's eyes went wide. This was why he'd played with her clit. Not only had it taken her mind off the plug Wyatt had worked into her ass, but it had gotten her ready for sex. He'd known damn well Wyatt wasn't in the mood for a ton of foreplay. They could play with her all night, but this first time would be quick. It would be a way for Wyatt to purge his system of all the anxiety he'd felt this evening.

Wyatt needed this. They all did, but Wyatt needed to be reminded they were all alive and together, and it would be stupid to not be together in this.

Sawyer was not a man who liked to admit when he was wrong because he was almost always right, but Sabrina might have said some truths to him. The sheriff hadn't swaggered in looking to arrest them all and let the system sort it out.

He'd been more than fair. Nate had...trusted him.

It was a weird feeling and one he didn't want to dwell on right now.

He had more important things to do.

"Damn, she's so tight," Wyatt groaned.

Sabrina bit her bottom lip, her fingers curling around the railing. "You're too big."

Wyatt's lips curled up. "No, I'm not. I fit real nice. Sawyer, I don't know how long I'm going to last."

"You'll last long enough to give her an orgasm," Sawyer ordered. "Play with her clit. She's incredibly sensitive. Sabrina, take me."

"I thought you were punishing me," she whispered as she leaned over and licked her tongue over the head of his already weeping cock.

"Should I be getting all these orgasms? Oh, that feels so good."

It would feel even better when they were both deep inside her. "He's going to stop if you don't take care of me."

She lowered her head and lightly sucked him behind her lips, the sight making Sawyer groan.

"And punishment is a word we use to let you know we weren't happy with how you behaved," Sawyer admitted. "I wouldn't ever spank you if I didn't think you would enjoy it. It's not truly punishment so much as you giving comfort to the men you terrified."

"Nah, let's call it punishment. She was a naughty, naughty girl, and now she has to make up for it." Wyatt used his free hand to smack her ass. "Now she's going to learn what happens when she defies us."

She was going to learn how many times she could orgasm. He wasn't sure Wyatt understood what he was doing.

Sabrina grinned as she licked the drop of arousal that had appeared on his dick. "What he said. I get it, babe. You are totally right, but the fantasy is way hotter."

Oh, he could play, too. He wrapped a hand around her hair and pressed his pelvis up. "I said take me, Teach. You're not in charge here. You're in a fucking detention, and you're going to stay there until I'm sure you've learned your lesson."

She groaned around his cock as she pulled him into the heat of her mouth. Her tongue whirled around him.

Did his sweet schoolteacher like to play dirty? Did she want to be his sex toy in the bedroom and his partner outside of it? He'd kind of always thought he'd have to pick. He'd thought he would never get the chance to pick because no woman would want to handle his crap for long.

He stroked her hair as Wyatt started to fuck her, the rhythm of his thrusts forming the tempo of her own. She let Wyatt push her and pull her, drawing her mouth on and off Sawyer's cock. He watched as his overheated dick disappeared behind those luscious lips of hers only to reappear as Wyatt pulled back. She whirled her tongue around and around the head, the tip rubbing the indention on the underside of his cockhead. He was going to see fucking stars soon.

Like everything Sabrina did, she sucked cock like it was her job and she was ready for a promotion.

It was disconcerting to feel something other than lust or gratitude for a woman he was in bed with. Those were simple emotions, and what was going through his brain was complex.

He wanted her because she was warm and safe and knew how to give a man everything he could possibly need.

He wanted to walk away from her because he didn't trust this feeling. Safety was an illusion. Safety and warmth could go away in a heartbeat.

Damn it. He was not getting into this. He was willing to cede the argument that maybe…just maybe he had…it made him slightly ill…abandonment issues. But they were not going to ruin his blow job.

Her eyes softened like she could feel what was going through his head, and then she scraped her teeth lightly against his skin, bringing him back into the moment.

She was hot when she was being sensitive to his feeling. One feeling. Only one. He could shove the feeling away and concentrate on how good her mouth felt. How hot and sexy she was. How nice it felt to know he would wake up with her in the morning.

Fuck it. She was turning him into… He wasn't even sure what he was turning into, but it was weird and he wasn't sure he liked it.

She sucked him hard, taking him to the back of her throat and then groaning as she obviously found her pleasure. Wyatt let out a little shout, and then Sawyer was going over the edge. He held her head, forcing her to take all of him as he filled her mouth. All thought flew away as he rode the wave of his orgasm, the sensation pulsing through him like a heartbeat connecting to her own.

Yeah, he'd thought that.

Sabrina leaned back, swallowing and then licking her lips in the most outrageously sexy way. "Well, if I'd known all I had to do to get you two to double team me is use a stun gun on a couple of guys, I would have done it way sooner."

He heard the sharp sound of a hand smacking flesh, and she whimpered.

"Don't remind me," Wyatt said, stepping back. "I just calmed down. Now I need a beer."

He could use one, too. "Make it two."

"Three," Sabrina said as Wyatt made his way to the bar. And

then her eyes widened and she grimaced.

Sawyer couldn't help but grin. "You lost the plug?"

She nodded and looked so adorable.

Yep, he was fucked. He was going to have to find a way to fix the mess because he was rapidly coming to the conclusion he didn't want to live without either one of them.

Chapter Thirteen

Wyatt stood at the edge of the woods, snow clinging to his boots, hoping he'd made it out of the cabin without waking Sawyer or Sabrina. He'd gotten the text he'd been waiting for hours after they'd finally gone to bed. Sabrina had fallen asleep against him, but at some point she'd turned and ended up with her head on Sawyer's chest.

It had been his first lucky break of the entire last twenty-four fucking hours.

He'd slipped out of bed and gotten on his laptop. He'd finished the job because there was zero way his brother didn't show up and soon.

He didn't want Wayne to decide to meet him at the cabin. He didn't want Wayne to know there was a cabin at all.

So he'd texted his brother and told him to meet him at Hell on Wheels if he wanted his accounts.

As he'd suspected, his brother had told him he'd be there in half an hour and not to be late.

He'd known the fucker was in town and probably seething since he wouldn't be able to get his people out of jail until tomorrow.

He'd known the fucker wasn't back in Colorado Springs.

The purr of an engine let Wyatt know it was time to come out of the shadows.

Would his brother finally take a knife to his throat? Hadn't he been expecting it since the moment he'd told Wayne he wanted out and he would do it one way or another? He'd told his brother he would either let him go or Wyatt would go to the police and hand over everything he had on the club.

That was when they'd made their devil's bargain. The one that could cost Wyatt everything.

As he stepped out of the tree line and onto the gravel of the parking lot, he realized he hadn't gotten out alone.

Bella walked up beside him, her tongue lolling out of her mouth as she took her place at his side.

"How did you get out?" They hadn't put her in her crate because they'd been far too busy taking Sabrina to the bedroom to deal with coaxing Bella in. Then when they'd taken a break, Wyatt had fed her and then gotten pulled back into sex.

Naturally the dog said nothing, simply looked up at him and wagged her tail.

"Go back." He said the words even though he knew damn well she wouldn't obey him. No one obeyed him tonight.

He felt under his jacket where the small pistol lay against his side. Could he do it? Could he kill his brother in cold blood?

Yes. To save Sabrina and Sawyer he could certainly do it, but he had to be careful because if one attempted to take down the monster, one better not miss.

The sound of at least two other engines told him tonight wasn't going to be his night unless he wanted to die, too. Which he would consider, but first he would give his brother a chance.

There was nothing to do but walk out and pray Bella didn't get hurt. The alternative was to go back to the cabin, and Wayne would certainly find the trail if he looked for it.

Wyatt stepped around the back of the bar, moving to the front parking lot as the motorcycle headlights came into view. Funnels of light that always preceded the darkest part of his life.

Bella headed the other way, disappearing back up the trail. A wave of relief went through Wyatt. She'd probably seen a squirrel or a rabbit and would spend the next hour chasing it. The good news was she'd been distracted, and he didn't have to worry about her until it came time to head back to the cabin.

If he headed back to the cabin.

This might be the right time to disappear. Though it was made far more difficult by Sabrina's actions. He didn't even have his freaking wallet.

But he'd walked away with nothing before.

He held his hands up because he couldn't be sure his brother's men wouldn't take any shot they had.

Luckily they kind of needed him alive for the time being.

The neon sign was dark and when Wayne parked and turned off his bike, the others followed suit, and they were left with only the moonlight to illuminate the night around them. He wasn't sure what phase the moon was in but it was still bright and shining, and it would be dawn soon. Wyatt stared across the parking lot. Wayne had brought three men with him, though he couldn't see their faces. Yet. He knew his brother's build. Even in shadow he could pick Wayne out. He'd always been the monster in Wyatt's life, the shadow turning everything dark.

"You want to explain yourself, brother?" Wayne didn't care for pleasantries.

Probably because there wasn't anything at all pleasant about him. "Your men came in and got handsy with some of the women in the bar. This isn't Horde territory."

Wayne whistled, and his head dropped forward. "Let me guess how it went. You decided some chick who's probably got a triple digit body count was actually the Virgin Mother and you did that crazy killer thing you do. Anyone dead?"

He wondered how Wayne didn't know. "No one called you?"

"No," Wayne shot back, moving in closer. He pulled leather gloves off his hands, and Wyatt could see his brother was now sporting a longish gray beard. He looked more and more like their father every day. "Which is why I'm here. I need to know if you and the traitor killed my men."

If Sawyer was a traitor simply because he wanted to leave, he wasn't sure what Wayne would consider his own crimes to be. "No one is dead. One of the servers got scared and called the sheriff. This isn't Horde territory, so the law around here did its job. They're being held overnight in town. You'll probably be able to bail them out in the morning."

Wayne seemed to consider the scenario. "Someone bail you out?"

Wyatt had to admit it surprised him as well. He'd expected the sheriff to act like he was an animal and take him in. He was surprised no one had to fight him to make him stop. All Sabrina had to do was be there to get him to calm down. "Didn't have to. The sheriff took my word about what happened."

Wayne adjusted the cap on his head. "You mean the sheriff took Sawyer's word. You don't talk much after you lose it. Now if I remember correctly, the town down there belongs to Sheriff Wright. Nathan Wright. Former DEA agent Wright. Why would Wright take your word for anything? Or Sawyer's."

"I haven't been in trouble since I got here. Neither has Sawyer. And we weren't the only witnesses," Wyatt explained. "You should know Zane Hollister's here, too. This town is full of ex-law enforcement."

In the moonlight, he saw a brow rise over his brother's dark eyes. "You think that'll save you? You think they'll help you out once they know who you really are?"

His gut clenched but he didn't back down. He knew what his brother was talking about, what was always hanging over his head. "I think if they figure out who I am, they'll definitely find a way to come after you."

"For that particular crime? Well, I had nothing to do with it, but you sure did." Wayne nodded toward the bar. "You going to invite me in? Have you lost all your manners?"

"You never taught me manners, and no, you can't come in. We're closed for the night. I'm not here to drink with you and pretend this is some kind of family reunion. I'm here to give you the account codes so we can be done. If your men hadn't been such sexually molesting assholes, this thing would be over and you would have your money and wouldn't have to spend some of it on bailing them out."

Wayne stared at him for a moment. "You took out all four men? Or did Sawyer get his freak on too?"

In this he didn't have to lie. "Sawyer didn't touch them. It was all me."

And Sabrina. Actually it was half Sabrina, but he was never telling that story to his brother. The men would keep quiet too because they would never let it be known a five-foot four-inch curvy schoolteacher had taken them down without breaking a nail. But they would still mention her.

"I often wonder what you could have been if you hadn't been such a pussy," Wayne spat out with disdain.

"We'll never know," Wyatt replied.

"Oh, I have an inkling." His brother looked him up and down. "You look good. You look taken care of. You got a woman? I would bet Sawyer isn't the one putting meat on your bones."

He hadn't eaten much back then. The last few years in the MC he'd kind of wasted away. Now he realized it was due to depression and anxiety, and when he wasn't dealing with those things, he ate like a horse. "I'm learning to cook."

Wayne's eyes rolled. "Of course you are. So this thing between you and Sawyer is… I mean, you're the girl, right? I always knew Sawyer was a lightweight and you probably swung both ways, but the thought of the two of you together kind of makes me sick."

If his brother wanted to believe he and Sawyer were lovers, it was fine with him. It might throw him off the scent when it came to Sabrina.

"It can make you sick all you like, asshole," a deep voice said.

Fuck a duck. Sawyer was leaning against one of the big cedars lining the back of the parking lot, Bella at his side.

Had he been betrayed by the dog? Had Bella run back and gotten Sawyer up? And he'd given her treats…

There were suddenly a whole bunch of guns pointed Sawyer's way, and the big guy's hands came up.

"I'm unarmed, assholes," he said. "And the dog's a sweetheart. She's only dangerous to ground meat and my knees when she tries to trip me. I'm serious. You want to see me go all John Wick on your asses, hurt my dog."

"You're all about protecting your dog and not your lover?" There was a nasty challenge in Wayne's tone. "That's sad for my brother. I'm sure he thought he was gaining a protector."

"Wyatt doesn't need one," Sawyer replied, his hands coming down as the weapons were holstered again. "Wyatt's good at taking care of himself."

"He seems to think he's good at taking care of you." Wayne was all masculine taunting now, as though he thought if he pushed them enough he might get the fight he truly wanted. "He was telling me how he's learning to cook."

"And he's reading a lot." Sawyer moved closer. He wore a pair of pajama bottoms and a hoodie Wyatt would bet wasn't covering a shirt. He'd obviously dressed with haste since he had on a set of slippers instead of the boots he would normally wear. Wyatt knew those slippers had been a gift from his friend Lucy the year before. He never wore them outside the house. "He started *Twilight*. Picked it up at the library last time he was in Del Norte."

The men behind Wayne snorted.

Wyatt wasn't about to be shamed for his reading choices. It was good. He was almost finished and would be moving on to the next book in the series. It would be fun to talk about it with Sabrina. Well, it would have been if his asshole brother hadn't shown up to ruin his life. Now Sawyer was being a jerk, too. It was just his night. "I wanted to know about Bella's name," he said under his breath before turning back to his brother. "I've got the account numbers you need on a drive along with the codes. They were all there, just hidden, as they should be since you're a criminal organization and law enforcement is pretty good with computers these days. I took a look through the system your new guy brought. He's sloppy with the laundry, if you know what I mean. I would watch him."

The new guy was the asshole who'd started this whole fucked-up mess of an evening. If Wyatt could get him executed with a few truths, all the better for the world.

"Does law enforcement have my laptop now?" Wayne's voice had gone dangerously low.

"No. We didn't disclose the reason your men had for coming to visit," Wyatt explained, and now he realized how lucky/unlucky he'd been. Though if Wright had the laptop, there would likely have been a disturbance at the sheriff's office, and someone could have gotten hurt.

"I've got it." Sawyer moved back to where he'd been standing and retrieved the small tote bag he'd left there. "One of the reasons I came down was to give you this. Can't have it hanging around."

Wyatt felt his face flush. He'd forgotten the damn laptop. The one in the cabin where Sabrina was sleeping. At least he hoped she was sleeping and didn't show up like a warrior princess to save the damn day.

"He can be forgetful," Sawyer said, handing the bag over. "Now, you have what you came for. I need to know this is over."

Wayne took the bag, handing it off to one of his men. "It could have been if Wyatt had kept his temper in check. An ex-DEA agent has my men. We could have avoided this."

"They won't talk, and Wright's not one to do what it would take to make them talk." If there was one thing he'd figured out about the sheriff it was that the man was fair. He wouldn't engage in the kind of torture Wayne would use to loosen up lips. "Pay their bail and I'll see if I can't get the charges dropped so we can all move on."

"I'm not so sure about Wright," Wayne countered. "Once a DEA agent and all. But I'll have our lawyer up here in the morning. Wyatt, you do understand what I'll do to you and your boy toy here if you're lying to me."

Sawyer huffed. "I'm not the boy toy. He is obviously the boy toy. I'm like a… What do they call them? Bears. I'm like a bear. A grizzly bear. He's a teddy bear."

It was good to know Sawyer was having fun. He chose to ignore the sarcasm. "I'm not lying. I want you gone. It's all I've ever wanted."

"So all this time I thought you wanted out because you were too weak to handle our lifestyle. Instead it was because Sawyer turned you," Wayne said, and there was no way to miss the disgust in his tone.

Wyatt wasn't sure what to say, and he half expected Sawyer to punch the guy and the whole scenario to go off the rails again.

Sawyer sighed and obviously braced himself. And then his arm went awkwardly around Wyatt's shoulders. "Don't make this less than it is. Your brother is a…" Sawyer took a long breath. "Very good boyfriend."

He had totally underestimated Sawyer. Oh, he'd known the man had nothing against sexuality of any kind, but he'd kind of expected him to proclaim his masculinity.

But then when a person was comfortable with his masculinity, he didn't need to herald it from the rooftops. He didn't need to play into entrenched gender roles to feel like a man.

Bella sat down in front of him like she was posing for their yearly Christmas card.

Ooo, getting a Christmas card might continue to throw his brother off the scent. Although there was one problem. "But could you keep it quiet when you go pick up Doug and the guys? We're not exactly out in town. I've even got a girl I see so no one suspects."

Sawyer's hand tightened on his shoulder, though Wyatt couldn't tell if it was a *you're a dumbass* squeeze or *keep it up, buddy*. He was sure he would find out in a couple of minutes.

"Yeah, it was our friend your guys tried to molest tonight," Sawyer added. "She's been good to us, and that's why Wyatt lost his shit."

Definitely *keep it up, buddy*.

Wayne stared at them like he wasn't sure he bought it, but then he nodded. "Well, I'll let you two get back to your evening. I meant what I said, Wyatt. If I ever find out you've been talking, we're going to have a problem, you and me."

Wyatt stood stiffly, watching as Wayne got on his bike. The sun was starting to come up as they revved their engines. Pinks and golds streaked over the sky as they drove away.

"I'm a beard now?"

Sawyer's arm dropped as he turned Sabrina's way. "I told you to stay in the cabin."

She seemed to have been hiding behind the tree line. She was wrapped in one of Sawyer's coats, her legs bare against the chill and feet covered in oversized socks and Crocs. Her hair was kind of wild around her head, and she yawned. She was unkempt and so sexy it hurt to look at her. "I'm not so great at following directions."

She moved to Wyatt.

"You better get good at taking a spanking then," Sawyer said with a frown. "They could have seen you and then all of Wyatt's work would be trashed."

She moved into Wyatt's space, wrapping her arms around him. "It won't work, but it's okay. Though I have to wonder if I'm your beard, why is it my backside that's sore? It doesn't seem fair."

Wyatt knew he should protest, should tell her to stay away from him, but he couldn't hold back. He needed her warmth far too much. He wrapped his arms around her. "Sorry, baby. It was the only way I could think of to counter what Doug is going to tell him. If he thinks I'm involved with Sawyer, he'll come after him if he feels the need."

"And I'll be ready," Sawyer shot back. "But we have to make things clear. I am absolutely the bear in this relationship."

Sabrina chuckled and yawned as she stepped back. "I don't think anyone is going to mistake you for a twink, babe. Come on. Let's get some coffee going. I have to be at school in a couple of hours."

And he had to be at the sheriff's office soon. He watched as Sawyer took Sabrina's hand and started to lead her back up the road toward the cabin as Bella dashed behind them.

Everything he cared about was on that road.

He had to ensure they survived no matter what.

* * * *

"You're going to a school board meeting?" Lucy looked at him like he'd grown two heads.

Sawyer staved off a yawn. He hadn't gotten a ton of sleep between all the sex and then Wyatt thinking he was a ninja and trying to sneak out. A loud ninja. A forgetful ninja. And then there had been breakfast and taking Sabrina into work, and he'd gone to the sheriff's office to give his recollections of the night before.

He needed a nap.

Lucy had caught him as he'd headed out of the sheriff's office. Wyatt's statement was taking a while, and he couldn't head back to the bar without him, so he was going to take the time to run a couple of errands. He had a list he needed to pick up from the Trading Post. Apparently women didn't use bar soap on their hair. And he'd caught her trying to shave those gorgeous legs of hers with his razor.

So if she was going to stay with them for a while, she needed some stuff. Would Marie laugh her ass off if he asked her what kind of shampoo Sabrina might like?

Of course now he had two women to talk to since Lucy wasn't alone.

"Sawyer Hathaway at a school board meeting?" River Lee smiled up at him. "I can't believe it. Do you think the place will burn down when he enters? Is it like a church and he's a demon?"

Lucy frowned and slapped her best friend on the arm. It was a familiar gesture, one he'd seen many times during their shared childhood. "Don't tease him."

He didn't see a problem. "Nah, she's right. It'll probably cause a minor earthquake, though I seem to have survived going into the sheriff's department."

Cameron Briggs had been the one to take his statement, and he'd been professional and easy to deal with. All in all, not how he'd thought the interview would go. He'd envisioned getting grilled under harsh lights or something and the law enforcement officer would try to trip him up and get him to admit some terrible crime because he was Sawyer Hathaway and they wouldn't believe he could do anything that wasn't criminal.

Huh. It did sound a little dramatic.

Lucy's eyes went wide. "I heard. Ty said he had to go down to the sheriff's office and check on some bikers last night who'd gotten pretty beat on. Are you okay?"

He should have known they would come looking for him. They were always nosing around…

They cared about him. He needed to stop fucking around and say things that were real. Lucy and River and Ty cared about him, and they had for years. He was the problem. He was the one who hated change and shoved people away when things didn't stay exactly the same as they had before. It was good River had gotten married to a man who adored her and Lucy and Tyler had gotten their shit together, even if they'd needed a six-and-a-half-foot, at one point could have been mistaken for a Sasquatch lawman to do it.

He stopped and gave Lucy what he hoped was a reassuring smile. "I'm fine. Wyatt's fine. Sabrina's fine."

River studied him, her head tilting slightly as though she wasn't sure what she was seeing. "Why are your lips doing that? Should we call Ty? Or take him to Doc's. He's having a stroke."

Such a brat. A guy smiles once… "I am not having a stroke. And last night was a blip. Wyatt's brother needed some information, and he sent the wrong people to get it. They're all out on bail this morning, and now the lawyers can work through it." He thought of something. "Oh, hey, if anyone comes around asking if I'm sleeping with the teacher, I need you to tell them I'm in a committed relationship with Wyatt and would never cheat on my man."

Lucy's jaw dropped open. "Holy shit. He *is* having a stroke."

"I'm not having a stroke. It's to protect Sabrina," Sawyer explained. "Wyatt's brother's guys got a good look at her and he's worried they'll use her as leverage, so when he met with Wayne last night he mentioned it wasn't Sabrina he was in love with. It's me, and Sabrina's a friend who helps us cover the relationship so the town doesn't know we're lovers. But I need the town to know we're lovers. Well, fake lovers."

No one in Bliss would blink an eye if he'd walked down Main Street holding Wyatt's hand. Love was love was love in Bliss, but they were also excellent at going along with a plot. Especially if said plot meant protecting someone they all cared about.

They would do it for Sabrina. Not him. Maybe for Wyatt.

"But you're sleeping with her, right? Not with Wyatt? The Wyatt part is the fake part?" River asked, and then her head shook and she flushed. "I mean it's fine if you are. It's lovely. I just... You were into women when we were growing up. Like in them all the time. I'm pretty sure you slept with all of the cheerleaders at our high school."

And a whole lot of the pep club members, and both French horn players. They'd been startlingly good at oral. "I'm not sleeping with Wyatt." It wasn't entirely true. "I am, but we're sleeping sleeping, not not sleeping sleeping. I'm not doing him is what I'm trying to say."

"But you are doing Sabrina Leal?" River seemed to require clarity.

Well, it wasn't like he could keep it a secret. Wayne might buy the whole Sabrina as a distraction thing, but no one in Bliss would. It's not like Sabrina would keep it a secret. "Yeah. Apparently she's my..." It was hard to say. It was just a word. He'd used it before. He was sure he had. He'd even said it yesterday, but these were his closest friends. He mumbled his way through. "Girlfriend."

Lucy leaned in. "What? I didn't catch that. You're whispering, Sawyer."

He glanced around to see if anyone was listening. "Girlfriend. She's my girlfriend. And she's Wyatt's girlfriend. We're sharing her."

River's face lit up. "This is the best news I ever heard."

Lucy nodded her way. "It is. Sawyer is dating the schoolteacher. I always thought you would go for a… I don't know. I didn't see you with a schoolteacher. Don't get me wrong. Ms. Leal is gorgeous and smart and charming, but I guess I didn't see you involved with someone who wears so many cardigans."

"She wasn't wearing one when I did her on the pool table last night," he said. It was kind of nice talking to his friends.

Lucy stopped for a minute. "Like on the pool table or like using the pool table as leverage? I'm trying to work the physics out in my head."

He thought about it. "Both."

River shook her head. "Nope. There's math and there's girl math and then there's sex math, and we should just accept it. Also, we should steam clean the pool table. Now how are we going to get you ready for the school board meeting? What kind of popcorn do you like? Also, do we think Wyatt's brother will be attacking the town hall? I want to know so I know how much popcorn to bring. I've never done a school board meeting. Also, should I bring pepper spray? If there's going to be blood I'll leave Buster at home because he's sensitive, but Jax will be excited. Sometimes he misses the whole 'we're on the run and the world is out to kill him' thing."

Maybe there was a reason he'd never been to a meeting in Bliss. "Uh, if I thought we were in real danger, I would tell the mayor to call off the meeting."

Lucy shook her head as they started walking down the street toward the Trading Post. His day was looking up because if Lucy and River were with him, he wouldn't have to ask Marie about tampons. Or would she want pads? He hadn't gotten around to asking about her menstrual habits.

"Don't call off the meeting," River argued. "I'm never going to be able to join the I Shot a Son of a Bitch club if we go all peaceful and stuff. You would think after years on the run with a paramilitary group I would have shot someone, but nope. And they have all the best snacks. I'm jealous of Lucy's T-shirt. She didn't actually shoot anyone, either."

"We use the word *shot* because it sounds cool. I have, in fact, had a hand in murdering a cult leader who was trying to murder me. Oh, and I helped solve a murder. I mean, Nell figured it out, but she wouldn't have been able to without me." Lucy sighed and smiled. "Life really is better in Bliss."

"Also, part of the meeting is to approve the funds Ms. Leal wants to build the new library. Right now it's a couple of shelves, and I've heard she's not happy with the selection," River explained as they walked along Main, passing Stella's. "Stefan Talbot picked the books himself. I think we might need to talk to him about not getting upset with Sabrina."

Sawyer shrugged. "Nah. She'll take him down and make him pay for the pleasure of doing it. She's way meaner than she looks. And she's the expert. Talbot needs to write his checks and keep his nose out of Teach's business." Watching her filet Talbot with words would be fun. "Do you have any cheese popcorn?"

Lucy had stopped as they came to the corner. Up ahead was the building that housed the mayor's office and all the town's governing boards. To the right was the Trading Post, which housed Marie and Teeny and five different businesses that supplied Bliss with pretty much everything from groceries to sporting goods to fudge.

He could eat some fudge. He should stock up on snacks. Sabrina was a snacker.

"You are in love with this woman," Lucy said, her voice filled with wonder.

River drew her hand over her throat in a quick motion. The universal sign for shut up. "Ixnay on the ovlay, sister. You know he can't handle that word."

He could say he loved baseball. He loved nachos. He was only in like with Stella's waffles. They could be crisper. "I love fucking Sabrina."

Lucy's eyes rolled. "Take one word out and you're there, buddy. So close."

"It's all he can do," River countered. "I'm proud of him. He's coming to a meeting. He talked to people in the sheriff's office and no one arrested him for being an asshole. He said her name and the word love in the same sentence, and he didn't gag. This is progress. Also, when the hell did you get so eager to overshare about your sex life?"

He shrugged and looked both ways. A couple of cars were rolling down the lane. It was a busy day. "I don't know. Everyone is chatty so I thought I should fit in. Come on. Aren't you always on me for not talking? You kind of get on me about it."

Come to this party, Sawyer. Don't work so much. Come to dinner, Sawyer. I'll make your favorite foods.

It had annoyed him but now he wondered. What if it wasn't about annoying him and being in some weird rut where one had to invite their misanthropic childhood friend to things because it was expected? What if... What if Luce and River and Ty were...his family?

This was all Sabrina's fault. She was trying to de-Grinch him, and he was happy not hanging with the Whos. God, he even had a dog now.

Was his heart going to grow three sizes?

How did he know this much about a children's story?

"I think we broke him." River waved a hand in front of his face.

Something had broken inside him. Some wall he'd placed between himself and everyone else. He wasn't sure why it had built up so hard, but Sabrina was making it shake.

You do know, asshole. You don't want to admit everyone is right about you. But maybe if you do, you might find yourself carving that roast beast with all the Who kids this Christmas.

Huh, he wondered if the library had Dr. Seuss or if Talbot had stocked the whole thing with pretentious books about art.

"Nah, I'm just thinking about things." He wasn't about to tell them he was thinking about how fun it could be to have Christmas with them. Wyatt probably could make some kind of dessert, and Sabrina would have to sit on his lap if they were at River and Jax's because they wouldn't have enough seats. And Bella and Buster would run around looking cute and making everyone laugh.

It could be the first nice Christmas he'd had since his mother died. His granddad had tried, but grief had tinged every single one.

He was not doing a therapy thing here in the middle of town. He wasn't doing a therapy thing ever. But he did have tasks to get through. "Hey, would y'all mind coming to the Trading Post with me? Sabrina's staying at our place for a few days, and I need girl stuff."

Lucy's lips tugged. "I think we can help you out there."

River threaded an arm through his. "Definitely."

Why had he ever stayed away from his friends?

"Sawyer," a voice called out.

He glanced over and there was the man, the myth, the legend himself. Stef Talbot was looking casual in jeans and boots and a blue Western shirt. He wore the ensemble often, as if it could make anyone forget he was a billionaire and not a cowboy. Sawyer nodded his way. "Talbot."

Stef hurried across the road, coming from the city building. "We need to talk. A few of us are worried about how recent events could potentially have an effect on county business, and you're at the heart of them. We knew you were coming in this morning to talk to the sheriff's department so we thought we could catch you for an informal chat."

"No." He wasn't going to talk about codes or plans or shit. There was only so far he was willing to go to support Sabrina, and taking a meeting with council people was definitely a bridge way too fucking far. "I have tampons to buy."

He started to cross the street with his friends, who were snorting and proving themselves to be extremely juvenile.

"Then we'll do it at the school board meeting, Sawyer," Talbot said in a deep voice. "We can get this out of the way or we'll do it in public."

He stopped.

"You can't kill him," Lucy whispered.

Oh, he could. But then Sabrina would have lost the biggest donor to her school, and she'd pretty much be pissed at him because he probably shouldn't murder people who annoyed him.

"Fine." He turned. "See you two later. This better be good, Talbot. You just lost me my experts at what heavy flow means."

Stef shook his head as though he wasn't sure he'd heard what he'd heard, and then he was jogging to keep up. "We're in the main conference room."

Sawyer strode through the doors leading to the lobby. It wasn't half bad, though it could use a couple of tables. Maybe some nicely made chairs. This was Bliss. It wasn't supposed to be some arty farty place. It should be homey.

What the hell were they going to complain about now? He'd known the sheriff had handled things too well the night before. Now there would be the actual reckoning. A flare of anger started up. Now they would tell him he was threatening the whole town by having Wyatt around. Or maybe they would simply lump them together. After all, they'd both been members of that fucked-up MC at one point in time.

Sabrina. He forced himself to follow Talbot down the long hallway toward the big double doors dominating the end. Sabrina would be the leverage they used. They would point out all the ways he could hurt Sabrina and her reputation in the town.

And he was going to tell them to fuck right the hell off.

Or should he listen? Had things honestly changed beyond the fact that Sabrina was sexy and mean and could take him down when he needed it?

He still was nothing more than the owner of a seedy bar with questionable connections.

Talbot opened the door and Sawyer wondered who was going to be the town's enforcer. Probably Wright and maybe the mayor, and definitely Mel, who would tell him not to touch his brand-new daughter.

Yep. He stood inside the doorway, and all three of those men were there along with Max and Rye Harper, who sat next to Henry Flanders. The ex-CIA agent was sunny and smiling and had a baby on his chest.

And for a moment he'd thought he might fit in.

Mel stood, a serious expression on his face. "Welcome, son."

Son? "What the hell is going on?"

Talbot closed the doors behind them. "Like I said, it's time we talked."

"Welcome, Sawyer," Mel intoned formally. "This is a Meeting of Men."

Alarm bells went off. This was way worse than a dressing down.

They were going to...fuck...they were going to give him advice.

He tested the doors but they were locked.

So much worse than buying feminine necessaries...

Wyatt was still at the station house. No one would save him.

"Shall we get started?" Mel asked.

Sawyer turned and faced what he was sure would be the most horrifying hours of his entire life.

227

Chapter Fourteen

Wyatt stared down at the report Cameron Briggs had placed in his hands. It was his testimony on what had happened the night before, and he was supposed to ensure it was all accurate and truthful.

It was filled with lies.

Lies he and Sawyer had agreed upon. Lies Sabrina had claimed were necessary.

She didn't want him any more involved with his brother's business than he did. She knew he'd given him the account access he'd needed, knew it was from a criminal enterprise, and she'd told him she didn't think it was a good idea to mention it in this report.

He was dragging Sabrina and Sawyer down.

This isn't your life anymore, she'd said, staring into his eyes. *It's the past, and you handed it back to him. That's all.*

He'd handed his brother more money so he could cause more pain, sell more drugs, kill more enemies.

He was being a coward.

"I'm going to grab some coffee," Cam said, standing. The big blond deputy gave him a smile. "Read your statement thoroughly and let me know if we need to make any changes. You want anything from the break room? Nell sent muffins. They're surprisingly good for vegan."

He'd eaten a hearty breakfast this morning, but now it turned sour in his gut. He shook his head. "No, but thank you, Deputy."

"Cam, please," Cam corrected as he started for the breakroom. "And I'm glad you took care of things. Be careful. The guys from last night have already made bail and processed out. They have some good lawyers. I would hope they would head back to Colorado Springs, but you can never be sure."

Cam strode away, and Wyatt was left alone in Cam's cubicle. The only private office in the entire building was Nate Wright's, and it was adorned with a *Gone Fishing* sign. It was quiet this morning. Sabrina had given her statement first because she was needed at the school. He'd insisted she do it in the closed office since there was a chance the men in the cells might get another look at her.

Gemma sat at the front desk along with a deputy he recognized as the other half of Sabrina's earlier date. The Creede boys. Wyatt could remember the shock on Knox's face when he figured out Sabrina was with him and Sawyer. Sabrina hadn't blinked an eye but Wyatt had watched the deputy, and he hadn't been happy.

"So those are your brother's men?" a deep voice asked.

Speak of the devil. Marshall Lethe wore his khaki uniform with obvious pride. It was perfectly pressed, unlike Cam's, which Wyatt was pretty sure bore the marks of the man's young daughter on his back shoulder. There was a small hand-like print where someone had clung to him. After eating something sticky. Syrup, maybe.

Wyatt put the statement down. It didn't matter. So much of it was lies. It didn't matter if he reread it for accuracy. "He's not my brother anymore."

Marshall was probably an inch or two shorter than Wyatt, but he had way more muscle. The deputy clearly spent time in the gym. He leaned against the cubicle wall, pinning Wyatt with a stare they only taught at the police academy. Or whatever passed for it in these parts. "I overheard the sheriff say you left the Horde last year. I've found it's harder to leave than you would think. If you left, why would he send men to fuck with you?"

This was the part they'd agreed on. A partial truth. "I used to work in one of the legitimate businesses before I left. The dealership. They're coming up on quarterly taxes, and no one knows how to get into my accounting system. He wanted some codes."

"Is that what you call it?" Marshall asked, brows rising. "Accounting? Or was it laundering?"

This was what he'd expected. He was getting as bad as Sawyer, but then Sawyer had been right about most things. "I don't work for my brother, Deputy. You would have to ask him."

"But you did work for him. As recently as last year," Marshall mused. "You know the statute of limitation on money laundering is seven years here in Colorado. You still have six before you can feel like you got away with it."

"Are you planning on arresting me?" Wyatt asked, wanting to get to the real point.

"Just letting you know I'm not naïve like the rest of this department." He looked to the side as though trying to ensure Cam couldn't hear him. "Which is surprising since the sheriff used to deal with people like you all the time."

"People like me?" He hated the sense of shame that washed over him.

"Criminals."

"You know I didn't join the Horde. I was born into it. Not many choices for me, and when I did get into a position where I could decide for myself, I left." Wyatt stood and signed his name to the statement with the pen left on the desk. He didn't have to take this man's vitriol. "Now, if you don't mind, let Deputy Briggs know I'll be around if he has any other questions."

"You're going to get her killed, you know." Marshall crossed his arms over his chest. "Sabrina Leal is a nice woman, and you're dragging her down."

Was this about him or Sabrina? "She's a nice woman who decided she didn't want to see you again."

"Sometimes even nice women make bad choices," Marshall allowed. "They buy into the bad-boy persona and don't understand how much better off they would be with a nice guy."

Wyatt chuckled, though he wasn't even close to being amused. "Bad boy? You know I can't fucking win. My brother calls me a pussy because I don't want to walk around with a gun all the time, taking out anyone who looks at me the wrong way. You think I'm bad because I was born into a family I had a hard time getting out of. I assure you I didn't woo Sabrina with my bad-boy ways. I did it with brownies. See, the key is to use coffee instead of water. Gives the box mix a certain depth of flavor. Oh, and she likes our dog. And I'm reading *Twilight* and discussing my feelings about the whole love triangle with her. I don't see why Bella has to choose. But do go on about how badass I am."

"Well, four men nearly died last night." Cam stood in the hallway, a mug of coffee in one hand and a half-eaten muffin in the other.

In this he wasn't as manly as he sounded. "It was two. Sabrina took the other two out."

"What?" Marshall's eyes had gone wide.

Cam nodded. "That's right, Marsh. She's good with a stun gun, and if I heard correctly, a bottle of vodka."

"Tequila." She'd bashed one of his attackers with a reposado. It was kind of a tragedy since it had been one of the only expensive liquors Sawyer bought. There had been a perfectly cheap blanco sitting right there, but no, she'd gone for the good stuff.

"Sabrina wouldn't..." Marshall began.

Wyatt huffed. "Dude, you don't know her. You're seeing the sweet schoolteacher who would have given you some status in this town, who you likely thought you could set up a nice life with. She could take care of a cabin for you and have supper on the table every night and never give you a moment's trouble. There's a crazy bitch under those cardigans. You couldn't handle her, and I've been told in no uncertain terms I don't get to make the decision whether she should be with me or not. So I suggest you do your job and ensure my brother's men don't come back."

"Dude, she's Elisa's sister." Cam was looking at his fellow deputy like he was a dumbass. "Did you really think she'd be some easy chick?"

"She's a schoolteacher. She's not like El. El is great and all but she's not like..." Marshall began.

"Not like what?" Gemma stood up from her cubicle, reminding everyone she had excellent hearing. She also had a headset on. "Yeah, they're talking about you now. I'm waiting to see if Marshall is going to finish his sentence or crap his pants."

"You called Elisa?" Cam grinned her way. "Damn, I thought you were softening up in your old age."

Gemma's eyes rolled. "Never. Hey, I finally have a woman in this department. Chicks before dicks and all. Elisa and I get along like gangbusters. The only argument we've ever had was when she set her sister up on a date with the Creede boys. You see, I thought they were a bit too traditional."

"I was going to share her with Knox," Marshall pointed out.

"You liked her because she wasn't scary like me or her sister," Gemma shot back. "I hear everything, dude. You and Knox talked endlessly about how scary the women are around here and how soft and sweet Sabrina is. You have obviously never been in charge of a large group of eight-year-olds. She's a badass." She laughed at whatever was being said in her ear. "Yeah, I think he was going to say you weren't wife material, too. I mean he'll make up some bullshit now, but we all know."

"You could be more of a team player, Gemma." Marshall's cheeks were stained with red.

"Oh, I am a total team player," Gemma replied. "You're just not on my team."

"Well, I guess Elisa isn't the woman I thought she was if she's going to let her sister fuck around with criminals." Marshall took a step back as though ceding the argument. "Sabrina's going to get hurt, but I guess she's such a badass she doesn't need our help. Like a lot of women in this town she seems to have forgotten why she needs a man."

"To clean her stun gun. Make sure it has batteries." Wyatt was sick of the macho bullshit. He was surprised he'd found it here since Marshall was right. Most of the women in Bliss were badasses who loved their men but didn't cling to them crying when bad times happened. Nope. They pull out their stun guns and expensive bottles of sipping tequila and go to work. "Also to bring her lunch when she forgets it. Which she did, and it's Nell's day to menu plan, so I'm pretty sure it's like salad she found in the field and maybe some weird bread. I'm getting my baby a burger from Stella's. And that bad-boy Sawyer? You know, the baddest dude in town? He's picking up shampoo and feminine products so she'll be comfortable while she's staying in our cabin. See, I've learned a few things since I left the toxic land I call my childhood. When men talk about taking care of women, they're talking about defending her from vague threats while the women do all of the other work. Most women would rather have a dude who actively participates in the life they share. But that's just my criminal opinion."

Gemma clapped. "Damn straight. I told you he's a keeper."

At least he might have made a slightly better impression on her sister.

"The threats aren't vague, Kemp," Marshall said with a frown. "They're real, and as much as you want to play house, your past is going to come back. I've studied up on the Horde and I'm surprised they let you go. They don't tend to let family leave. Makes me wonder what you have on them. Or if you gave them something so big they know you'll never tell."

Marshall was way too close to the truth for Wyatt's comfort.

"How about you leave it alone," Cam ordered. "Wyatt isn't accused of anything. He was defending himself and Sabrina."

"So the report says." Marshall sighed. "There's something else going on here. I don't know why everyone's burying their head in the sand. No one walks away from a group like that. He's a danger to this community, and I intend to prove it."

"By harassing him?" Cam asked. "I think the sheriff might have something to say. Our heads aren't buried, Marshall. We think everyone deserves a second chance if they work for it. None of us here came from glorious pasts with no trauma or regret. It's precisely why we're here. If you want to know how he paid, take a look at his chest sometime. They wouldn't let him leave with the tattoo they forced on him when he was eighteen so they burned it off his body."

"Everyone knows?" Wyatt was careful to keep his shirt on.

"Doc came in fuming about it the night he went out to Sawyer's cabin to treat you," Cam admitted. "Don't be pissed at him. He was angry for you, and you wouldn't press charges."

"They wouldn't have stuck. My brother had me make a video agreeing to everything he did to me," Wyatt explained. "Pressing charges would have kept me in his world."

"I believe the sheriff said roughly the same." Cam moved to his desk, dismissing Marshall. "You should know the DA is probably going to want to talk to you about a plea deal."

"Whatever makes it go away the fastest," Wyatt agreed. "Honestly, it wasn't like I got hurt. I just want them to stay away. I want to live my life here. It's all I want."

Gemma winced. "Uhm, Elisa wants the death penalty. I don't think that's an outcome we can ask for in a Class One misdemeanor case. You know we should talk this out over the beer you owe me because I was right about your matchmaking skills."

"We'll handle things from here," Cam promised, sitting behind his desk. "You should know one of the things we're going to talk about at the meeting this evening is watching out for you three."

"Watching out for us?" Wyatt asked.

"Yeah. I know it's supposed to be about school, but we don't have a town hall coming up any time soon, so we'll do it there. There's a part of the town halls where we discuss potential threats. Mostly it's Mel talking about coming alien invasions or what to do if you cross paths with a Sasquatch during mating season." Cam shuddered. "He had surprisingly detailed slides. Cassidy is an artist of sorts. But the point is we also talk about human threats. After tonight, everyone will know to watch out for you and Sawyer and Sabrina."

"I appreciate it. Sawyer thinks he's an outsider. It might be a surprise to him," Wyatt said, checking his watch. It was almost lunchtime. He might not be hungry, but Sabrina would be. He could grab her lunch at Stella's and walk to school before her break started.

"Oh, he's learning right now," Cam replied with a grin. "You should know there's a Meeting of Men occurring."

Wyatt gasped. It was a legendary thing around these parts. "He's being brought before the Men's Council? Why?"

"They want to make sure he doesn't fuck things up with Sabrina," Cam replied. "They're not worried about you." Cam's eyes narrowed. "Should they be?"

He suddenly didn't want to get called before the council. "Nope. I'm good. I guess I'll hit the Trading Post as well since it seems Sawyer's got a full schedule all of the sudden."

"See you tonight," Cam said, giving him a wave.

Gemma was still arguing with Elisa over the headset as he walked out of the station house, but the whole way he could feel Marshall Lethe's eyes on him.

The deputy was going to be trouble.

But then he seemed to have a lot of that these days.

* * * *

"Can it be a formal Meeting of Men if there's a woman here?" Sawyer was looking for any way out. She wasn't a woman, exactly. She was a sleeping toddler, but there were rules. Right?

He knew all about the Council of Men. His grandfather had helped form it. Of course back then it was mostly his grandad, River's dad, Mel, Fred Glen, and Brian Bennett meeting out at the Circle G to drink beer and watch football. It was exactly like Stef Talbot to take something simple and turn it into...well, this.

Henry patted the back of the toddler sleeping on his chest. "Don't mind Poppy. She has no interest in the workings of the male mind. She's only here because her mom has lunch duty."

"Don't listen to him." Max Harper frowned Henry's way. "I'm pretty sure he's teaching his baby spy techniques. Nell's been extra nosy lately, and I'm pretty sure it's because Poppy's bringing back intel from playdates."

"Sure, she's getting a ton of intel from her tea parties with the McNamara-O'Malley girls," Henry snarked. "My baby girl will get into intelligence ops over my dead body."

Max huffed and pointed Henry's way as though he'd made his point. "And that's exactly what you would say if you were a spy."

"Little Poppy is welcome," Mel intoned. "She won't cause any trouble at all, but we do need to talk to you, son."

If anyone but Mel had called him son, he would have challenged them. But Mel had been the one to take him hunting when his grandfather's grief had gotten to be too much and he needed to be alone. Mel had taken Sawyer and his brothers camping and fishing. He'd sat up and listened to them talk about Mom.

Mel got all of his respect. Which meant he needed to take this whole thing with some seriousness. "All right. If you're going to warn me off Sabrina, you should know I already tried. I explained how I am and why it won't work. I didn't like try to be charming to fool her. She got a full dose of me, and she's still here. She's...tenacious."

"We're not here to warn you off her." Mel sat down, adjusting his ever-present ballcap. Sawyer could only see the smallest piece of foil poking out. Cassidy had gotten good at tucking it in for him.

"We're here to make sure you don't screw this up."

Well, he hadn't expected those words to come out of Mel's mouth. Did they understand?

"My wife will torch the town if she loses Sabrina," Rye said with a shake of his head. "I'm not joking. Sending Paige to school has made it so much easier to handle the boys. All of that sweet sanity flies out the window if Sabrina runs back to civilization because some asshole breaks her heart. She views Sabrina as a saint and one she will defend bodily if she has to."

"I don't think she would leave town if we broke up." Sawyer was pretty sure she would stun him and explain the town was hers now and he should be the one to leave.

Max leaned over. "Hey, you should warn Wyatt about small, unnamed children who might be out to kick him in the shins. I fear the day Paige gets big enough to kick a man in the…you know…"

Why was Paige going to take out Wyatt's shins? Before he had a chance to ask, Talbot was taking his seat next to the mayor, Rafael Kincaid.

"Sawyer, we felt after what happened last night, we should talk. I know what happened was violent, and you might think Sabrina seeing you forced to attack those men might frighten her. You're probably thinking about taking a step back," Stef began in an oddly soothing tone.

"That would be a mistake," Rafe advised.

"Rookie mistake," Max added.

"Women are more than capable of making their own decisions," Henry counseled sagely while Poppy drooled on his shirt. "Nell was scared the first time I had to kill a couple of assassins in front of her, but we talked about it and she handled it. Our women are stronger than we think."

Rye's eyes rolled. "Dude, you had to sleep on the couch for three whole seasons."

"Guest room," Henry corrected. "She needed some time to think, but the point is I didn't walk away in shame. Sawyer, I know you would never admit it, but I suspect you're actually quite sensitive."

"I'm not." He wasn't in any way. Well, his dick was sensitive to Sabrina walking in a room, but that was about it.

Henry ignored him entirely. "So you're probably feeling shame at having to expose a woman like Sabrina to such male brutality. You have to talk to her. You have to let her know this isn't who you are in your normal life, but the need to protect her brings out your inner beast from time to time."

Sawyer looked to Wright, who was sitting back. He was in jeans and a T-shirt today, a smirk on his face.

"You didn't tell them?" These men were under some misconceptions.

Wright shrugged. "I thought it was your story to tell. They're worried you'll think Sabrina's too delicate to handle all the violence she saw last night."

"I didn't touch any of those men," Sawyer admitted. "I was way too busy trying to get Sabrina out of the line of fire. She's slippery, though. She got away and used a stun gun on two of them. Also, she bashed one of them with the tequila I use to make Jen's margaritas when she and Stef decide to pretend she's a hooker or something."

"Uh, sex worker, thank you," Stef argued losing his smooth tones and sounding more like the Stef Sawyer knew. "It's a little role play, and you have to admit your bar is on the seedy side. It doesn't work at Trio because Zane is impossible. My wife has some specific fantasies, and getting paid is one of them. I'll replace the tequila."

"Wait. So Sawyer didn't beat the shit out of those guys?" Rye asked.

"Nope. Wyatt and Sabrina did all the damage," Wright explained. "By the time Elisa and I got there, Sabrina was talking Wyatt down. Alexei's got his hands full with that one. There's some Hulk in there, if you know what I mean."

Henry nodded as though taking it in and processing the story. "Women can often keep a cool head in the middle of a crisis, but Sawyer might be the one dealing with the ramifications of seeing the woman he...I'm going to stay away from that word...he is seeing because he has eyes and she's often in the line of his vision...in danger."

All right, he kind of liked Henry. But Henry was wrong. "Nah, I was annoyed at first because she's shitty at following directions and apparently loves to throw herself into potential harm, but then she showed me her boobs and I didn't care as much anymore. Y'all are acting like the sheriff left and we all sat around and talked. We didn't.

We had a ton of sex on the pool table, and then we went back to the cabin and fucked some more. I think we all feel better today." He winced because he'd forgotten about Mel. "Sorry. I know she's like your daughter now."

Mel stared at him. "Did she enjoy herself?"

"Like five or six times," Sawyer said with a nod.

"Then good for you." Mel sat back. "As the father figure in her life, I have to ask if you are seeing her only because you have eyes and she's around a lot."

Damn. He was happier talking about the pool table. This was a weird metaphor. How to explain without saying too much or using the word he was avoiding even thinking about? "I...I often look around for her so I can see her. Because I have eyes."

"It's a metaphor," Max whispered to his twin. "I think he's talking about having a heart, but he's Sawyer so he doesn't want us to think he's got one of those. So when he says he's looking for her with his eyes, he's really looking for her with his heart."

Rye's eyes rolled.

Max was an idiot.

"I'm just saying I don't run away when she gets close." Let that be the end.

"Like you did last Christmas?" Rafe asked.

"Look, last Christmas I took one look at her and thought she was sweet and fragile and I knew I couldn't handle her. Or she couldn't handle me," Sawyer began.

"You were right the first time," Henry said. "You were the one who couldn't handle her."

Sawyer would ignore the interruptions. He needed to get out of here. No. He was done lying to himself. He needed to make these men understand. Because if he was going to be with Sabrina, he couldn't be the troll under the bridge anymore. She was a social person. She would want to have friends and go to parties and be part of the town and he would... Could he send Wyatt to all those things?

There were serious advantages to having a partner.

Of course if he wasn't careful, he might not have a partner because his partner was going to be an idiot.

He needed to think this thing through. He couldn't talk about it with Sabrina because he didn't want her to worry.

It sucked to be alone.

Except he kind of wasn't.

His grandfather had been a part of this town.

His grandfather had been broken when Sawyer's mom died.

Would he have taken back all of the love so he never had to feel the grief?

Shit. Was this the question he'd been sitting with for fifteen years?

He was asking the wrong question. Everyone had to make the decision for themselves as to what they were willing to risk. Would he take back going after his brother? Even knowing his brother would end up being a selfish ass who never spoke to him again? Would he go back and tell Wes to fuck himself and leave him with the Horde?

He wouldn't have met Wyatt, wouldn't have been waiting to give Wyatt a safe place to land.

Would he have held back on loving his mom if he'd known she would die so suddenly?

Fuck. Fuck. Fuck.

"I have abandonment issues." It made him vaguely ill to say the words.

Everyone froze, all eyes on him like he'd grown a second head.

"Is this what those sci-fi guys mean when they say they felt a disturbance in the force?" Max asked.

Like Max Harper knew anything about *Star Wars*. He wondered if Sabrina liked *Star Wars*. She looked more like a Trekkie. He could handle a Trekkie. She also looked like a woman who would like Disney movies.

But that was what Wyatt was there for.

It was odd how the world didn't seem as dark as it had mere moments before.

"She didn't abandon you, son," Mel said quietly, putting an arm on Sawyer's shoulder. "She died. Your brothers... I don't think they handled things well, but they grieved, too. We can't know what's truly in someone's heart, but I've found most people do things for selfish reasons and not malicious ones. Thoughtless, but not with cruel intent."

Wes had found a new home, a new world. Jimmy had been gone since he graduated from high school, joining the Army and only coming home for their grandfather's funeral. He'd left and built a new family for himself.

What if he could do the same? He turned to Mel. "I'm worried Wyatt's going to do something dumb."

"This is more words than I've ever heard Sawyer say at one time," Max said with a shake of his head.

He sent Max his middle finger. "You are not helpful, Harper. And I think I might need some. I don't want Wyatt to leave. He's happy here, and if he leaves, Sabrina is still going to want someone to watch home and garden shit with her and she's going to want to talk about the books she's reading and…I don't think I'll be good at that part. I think we need Wyatt."

"Because you see Wyatt, too. Because you have eyes and he's in your line of sight," Henry said with a beatific smile.

"I do not love Wyatt." Except maybe he did. Maybe this weird loosening in his chest when his friend was around was something like love. "Okay, let's just say I'm happy to have him around. And I might…might…that word Sabrina. I mean she's around a lot, and you get real used to someone, and I think they call it that word."

"Love." Rafe had a grin on his face like all of this was some unexpected entertainment. "You're falling in love with Sabrina."

"You know she's only been around you for a week or so." Max pointed out the fallacy in his reasoning. "I don't think you've had time for her to be a habit yet."

Henry shifted as Poppy's head came up and she yawned. "Max, he's working on it."

"Well, I had to tell Rach I loved her real fast or she was going to kill me with a bunch of flowers." Max frowned. "I don't see why Sawyer gets to work around it. It's not fair."

He wasn't listening to Max. But he might listen to the others. "Sheriff, have you looked into the situation with the Horde?"

"You're asking if I've made a study of a potential threat to this town and its citizens?" the sheriff asked. "Pretty much the day after Wyatt got here. Zane and I reached out to some people we know who are still in that world. Wyatt is a solid guy. He would never have been involved if he'd been given a choice. I like the kid."

And if the sheriff liked someone, he would protect them.

Hell, Nate Wright would protect him even if he didn't like him.

"He's in trouble, and I think there are things he's not telling me."

"About how he managed to get out?" Wright asked.

Well, no one ever said the sheriff was a dummy. Except Callie a couple of times. And Zane, but they were partners so it was expected. He could totally call Wyatt a dummy and get away with it. Because they were partners. "Yeah. I can't see Wayne letting him go with nothing more than taking a blowtorch to his chest."

"What?" Max asked. "They torched his chest? Why would they burn him? Damn, that's cold."

"It was hot, and it's because you can't wear the tat if you aren't in the club." Sawyer held up his left arm showing the black block there. "I got off easy, but I assure you Wayne would require more than mere pain from his brother."

"Like what?" Henry asked as Poppy settled back onto his lap. She was awake now and looked around the room as though assessing the situation.

Max might be right about Poppy Flanders. "I don't know."

"He does," Wright corrected. "But he doesn't want to say it. Wayne likely would have made Wyatt do something that would make him vulnerable if he ever talked. He would keep evidence of the crime in case he needed to use it to bring Wyatt back into line. Sawyer, I'm here to help. I'm not looking to arrest Wyatt. He was his brother's accountant, right?"

Sawyer nodded. "Yeah, it's why last night happened. Apparently the new guy isn't as good. I know I didn't go over this in the statement."

Wright held up a hand. "I asked about the physical fight. Anything else is outside of the scope of this investigation. And whatever you say here is in confidence. I need to know what we're up against and how you intend to keep Wyatt safe since we both know he's going to try to martyr himself if the going gets bad."

The sheriff had studied Wyatt well. "It's possible handing over the information stops the threat for now."

"But not forever," Rye added. "I've dealt with some members of the Horde in my time, too. Something will happen and suspicions will start up, and they'll look Wyatt's way. How friendly did you look with Wyatt last night, Nate? They would have been watching."

The sheriff winced. "Well, I am friendly with him. I like the kid, but I get your point. If it gets back to the Horde he's hanging with law enforcement, they might get the idea he's talking. I didn't even think about it. I took one look at Wyatt and wanted to make him comfortable because he'd obviously had a break, and it was easy to see why. I know the feeling."

"I think this was about more than accounts," Sawyer admitted. "I think this was always going to happen. Look, Wyatt's been cagey with me and I understand why. He thinks if he talks, he opens anyone who knows to his brother's wrath. I think if it was only me, he might, but not Sabrina. It doesn't matter how cool she was last night, how competent. He won't ever expose her. It's why we told his brother last night we're lovers."

Max burst into laughter and then noticed no one else was joining him.

Poppy frowned his way. "Uncle Max is rude."

"Hey, I wasn't being homophobic. It's cool if dudes want to do other dudes," Max said quickly. "But you have to admit they would look weird together."

"So body shaming," Henry added.

He did not need this shit. Any minute Nell would show up with a bullhorn. "I don't care. I don't think it's going to work. Wayne is going to talk to those guys and he'll start to think about it, and in the end even if Sabrina is nothing more than a friend, she's an easier target than me. And he knows Wyatt wouldn't be able to sacrifice her to save himself," Sawyer explained.

"So we make her a harder target," the mayor said, sitting up.

"We're going to take care of Sabrina," Mel promised. "And you and Wyatt."

Yep, his chest hurt. He was having a heart attack.

Or feelings, as in more than one. It was weird to have more than one. He wasn't sure he liked it.

But damn he liked not being alone. It was something he could get used to.

Chapter Fifteen

It had been a weird day. Sabrina hadn't known how much weirder it could get. "This is a bounty of feminine products, Sawyer."

He shrugged a big shoulder as Bella sat down beside him. She'd spent most of the day at the bar with Lark watching over her. When they'd picked her up, she'd acted like they'd been apart for five hundred years. "Wasn't sure what you would want. It would have been easier if there were way less choices."

He was oddly sweet, even with a grumpy expression on his face. He couldn't help it. He had resting grump face. "Well, thank you, but you know I could have picked some up when we stopped by my cabin to get fresh clothes."

Sawyer and Wyatt had been waiting for her the minute class was dismissed for the day. Sabrina had walked out to the front drive where pickups occurred, and in addition to the usual moms and dads, Sawyer and Wyatt had been waiting. Wyatt had brought her lunch but he hadn't stuck around to eat with her.

She was kind of surprised he'd been standing there with Sawyer. She'd half expected him to find a ride out of town and not even leave her a note.

"It was his quest today," Wyatt replied, holding himself back a little.

"And what was yours?" Sawyer asked, a hint of challenge in his tone.

Wyatt huffed and started to pace beside the sink. "Beyond trying to figure out why two kids kicked me today and then Sabrina's new dad forced me to eat a beet? I drank the juice. I shouldn't have to do it again. A raw beet, Sabrina. It was disgusting, and I think my teeth are purple."

"He did what?" No wonder he'd been quiet. And she was going to have such a word with Paige Harper. She was sure Paige hadn't lied when she said she wouldn't do it. It appeared she was simply ordering other kids to do it. A menace.

"I was at the Trading Post helping Teeny with their point-of-sale system and Mel walked in. He walked right up to the produce section, picked out a beet, talked to it for a weirdly long time, then held it up for a minute. Teeny sighed and said she'd get me some water to wash it down, and before I could ask her what I was washing down, he was on me."

"Mel jumped you?" Sawyer asked but he sounded kind of impressed.

"Not exactly," Wyatt admitted. "But he did put that thing up to my mouth and told me he would never allow an alien in his family, and then he listed all the exceptions because apparently there are good aliens out there, but that's not as dramatic a way to force a beet on a man."

"So you took the physical beet?" She should have known. "Apparently there's a ritual and it requires eating a raw beet. It means he thinks you're serious about me. When you think about it, it's kind of sweet."

"When I think about it, I have PTSD. It was gross," Wyatt reiterated. "Such a weird day."

"I got called into a Meeting of Men," Sawyer admitted.

"That sounds ominous. Is this a Bliss thing?" She hadn't been around long enough to discover all the quirky things about this town she'd come to love.

"Cam mentioned it. A Meeting of Men," Wyatt said, obviously impressed. "I've heard about those. It's when they call a council of the smartest men in town to discuss whatever problem is facing the town. They shut themselves in a room, and then the women have time to actually solve the problem."

"Sounds like something Marie would say." Sawyer unloaded the rest of the groceries they'd bought. It appeared to heavily favor the things she'd talked about liking. Sawyer had bought her brand-name coffee. Not the generic kind he bought for himself. "It's something my grandfather and Mel and some of their friends started when I was a kid. They would get together and talk about how they can help out the town. Or individuals in town. But this is Bliss, and they need to give everything a cutesy name. There are some dramatic motherfuckers in this town."

He was eyeing Wyatt like those words should mean something. There was a tension between the two of them she hadn't wanted to discuss until they were alone.

Well, they were alone.

"He's not being dramatic," Sabrina said quietly, jumping right in without prevarication. She wanted to get this over with so they could get to the fun parts, the parts she'd dreamed about all day. "He's scared his brother will hurt me, and he's trying to find a way out."

"Out?" Sawyer asked, a brow rising. Bella looked up at him as though she too could feel the tension in the room. "Out of the relationship? I don't think walking away from us is going to work."

"I know it sucks. I basically moved the target from her to you," Wyatt began.

Sabrina felt her gut clench. "You did what? How would you move the target? Also, we don't know there is a target. You gave him what he wanted."

"It's not about that," Wyatt hedged. "Or maybe it is. I don't know. All I know is my brother is pissed off, and he'll take it out on me. And I have to worry…"

He stopped, and Sabrina softened her voice. "Wyatt, why are you worried? We don't know the whole story, do we?"

"You don't have to know the story at all," Wyatt countered, his jaw going stubborn. "All you need to know is I don't want you anymore."

She barely managed to not roll her eyes. "Sure you don't. You finally made it to the magic number of times you've slept with me to hit complete satisfaction? You haven't even given me time to show you what I can really do with my tongue."

"Are we back to this?" Sawyer asked, starting to pace. "I told you it's not going to work."

"Only because you decided to not even try," Wyatt shot back. "What the hell is wrong with you? I thought you care about her. I thought you would want to protect her."

"I love her, but I also know her. She's not staying out of this even if you push her away because she loves you. She won't stop trying to save you, so it's better to stay close so we can protect her when it goes down. Protect her with actual weapons instead of martyrdom. I'm going to leave a review on Alexei's website. He's a shitty therapist." Sawyer sighed and looked her way. "Baby, I said love twice. I need a beer to wash away the taste."

He loved her. He'd told her he loved her, and he hated the word.

She wanted to jump into his arms and make this a super-romantic moment that would have made Sawyer uncomfortable for years to come. But she had another love to save. This lifestyle might be great for her sexually, but twice the men meant dealing with twice the emotions. This was it. She knew it instinctively. She'd thrown Wyatt off last night by taking his keys, but he would find a way if he wanted to leave. So instead of throwing herself at Sawyer, she went over to the fridge, pulled out a beer, and twisted off the cap. Sabrina marched over and handed it to him. "I love you, too."

"I'm glad," Wyatt said, his mouth a flat line but his eyes eating her up. "I want you and Sawyer to be happy. Sabrina, what I said…"

She wasn't going to make him say it again. She didn't want to hear or think about those nasty words he'd spoken in fear. "Was a lie to try to get me to walk away from you. I'm quite emotionally aware, and you are not very good at lying. The next time you say you don't want me, don't stare at me like I'm a steak you want to eat. Don't bother at all because even if you say the most hateful things to me, I won't leave you. Not when you're in trouble."

His shoulders sagged, and it was easy to see the weight he'd been carrying. "You have to."

She didn't, but she wouldn't waste her breath telling him. They'd gotten off the topic. "How did you move the target from me to Sawyer? Is this why he tried to tell his brother the two of you are dating?"

Sawyer's lips kicked up. "He's still betting his brother will believe it. We're lovers, Wyatt and I. You're our cover, the girlfriend we pretend to date so no one ever learns about our illicit love affair."

It had been foolish then, and the idea hadn't grown more appealing. "No one is going to believe it."

"Make fun of it all you like," Wyatt argued, "but it will work. You don't know my brother."

"It won't work," Sawyer shot back.

"Only because you're not doing what needs to be done." Wyatt stared at him as though he could work his will through his eyes.

Sawyer's hands came up. "Hey, I told everyone in town how hot you are for me."

"Asshole," Wyatt said with a sigh.

She wasn't sure how Wyatt had thought it was going to work.

Sawyer sobered. "I told everyone what the plan was. I even discussed it at the meeting. The sheriff wanted us to know they'll do everything they can to protect all of us. They'll say what we want them to say, but I don't know if Wayne will believe it. And honestly, it doesn't matter."

"He won't play fair." Wyatt wasn't giving up.

She wasn't either. "My sister won't play fair. Not when it comes to me. I think the sheriff knows how to handle things. Wyatt, you have to understand. We're in more danger if you leave us than we are if you stay."

He squared off with her. "That's bullshit."

"She's right." Sawyer set his beer down and put a hand on Bella's head. The poor baby could feel the emotions amping up, and she didn't like it. She calmed a bit when Sawyer petted her. "Have you thought this through? You walk away, go off the grid. Hide. You think your brother will look for you?"

"He will," Wyatt insisted.

"But according to you, he doesn't play fair." Sabrina knew exactly where Sawyer was going. "Why look for you when it would be so easy to kidnap me or Sawyer in order to draw you out?"

Sawyer winked her way. "Way easier. So in this very reasonable and likely scenario, they would dial you up and offer a trade. You for us. Except you're off the grid and in hiding, so you can't take the call. I wonder how long he keeps us alive in that case. Hopefully long enough for you to see the story on the news. But more likely you won't know until one day you come back because you won't be able to stop yourself. You'll come back because you were happy here. You'll stand in the shadows, hoping to get a glimpse of her, and maybe she'll be with me, holding hands as we take our five kids out to dinner."

"Five?" Sabrina was intimidated at the thought. Five? Five was a big number.

Sawyer's smirk told her everything she needed to know. "I'll try to hold it to five. My line is good at baby making, as you're about to discover. But back to my point, you won't find us because we'll have been dead all this time. Because you weren't around to save us."

They needed to talk about the baby-making stuff, but she had to be impressed with Sawyer's logic. "When your brother realizes it didn't work, he'll have to get rid of the evidence. Also, there's no way he goes after Sawyer first when I'm a far easier target and he knows you care about me. It doesn't matter if he thinks we're sleeping together or if I'm a platonic friend. It wouldn't matter if you broke up with me on live television and he saw it. He would know you would protect me. No matter what."

"Then I'll kill Wayne before he can do it," Wyatt vowed. "I'm not going to run away, Sawyer. I'm going to stalk my brother. I'm going to figure out what he knows, what he's doing, and then I'll take him out and anyone who stands in my way."

The thought made Sabrina sick. "You'll get killed is what you'll do."

Sawyer had gone grim. "Even if you manage to kill Wayne, the Horde won't stop until they've avenged him. We both knew this could happen. We knew the minute you left he could walk back in at any time. He got what he wanted. He got the accounts. There's zero reason for him to fuck with you now. Unless there's something you're not telling us."

Wyatt stilled, and Sabrina knew Sawyer was right.

There was something neither of them knew. What else had Wyatt been put through? What horrors had he been forced to endure?

"The scars weren't the only payment, were they, Wyatt?" Sawyer asked, the question curling around the room, threatening them all. "Your brother needed more. He needed to make sure you kept your mouth shut."

"Yes. There was more than getting rid of the tat." Wyatt's expression had gone a careful blank.

"What did he make you do?" Sawyer leaned against the wall, waiting for the answer. "He would need leverage on you, and I doubt he would think the money laundering would be enough."

Wyatt stood there, unblinking and absolutely not answering the question.

A million horrible scenarios played through her mind. "You're saying they would have made him do something criminal?"

Sawyer nodded. "I should have thought about it, but Wyatt never said a word. So that makes me think it's bad. How did you fake it, brother?"

"I didn't," Wyatt said, looking around as though making sure they were alone. "I didn't fake anything. I did it." He turned Sabrina's way. "I killed a man, Sabrina. I killed a man who might have been able to testify against my brother. He said he wouldn't, but my brother doesn't like loose ends. I should have let him kill me so I never took another man's life. That's who you're willing to risk everything for."

Did he think this would work? Wyatt was perfectly capable of killing a man. She'd seen him fight, and it could absolutely happen when he was in that state. He could kill a man who threatened the people Wyatt loved. Without hesitation.

But in no world she could imagine did he ruthlessly plan and murder a man who'd done him no harm to simply free himself from the Horde. She knew Wyatt, and he wasn't capable of it. Again, Sawyer was right. Also, when had he gotten so damn chatty? "And I will continue to do so."

"Damn it, Sabrina." Wyatt got into her space, looming over her. "I confessed to murdering a man."

"And I do not believe you." He was trying so hard to intimidate her, but it didn't work. He was kind of hot when he played the hardened criminal. She put her hands on his shoulders, wishing he would stop fighting and let her take care of him. "You found a way. You tricked them. You would not kill a man to get yourself out of a bad situation. You only did it because it got you both out."

His head fell against hers, their foreheads touching as his hands cupped the sides of her face. "You can't ever say that, baby. You can't say it. Not even when we're alone."

She was right. She knew she was, and he was beyond scared. He was protecting more than his own heart. "Just because we don't say it, doesn't mean we can't help you carry the load."

His head shook against hers, but he didn't move away. "I'll get you killed."

"No," Sabrina countered. "If someone kills me, it's their fault. It would be your brother's fault. It's not your fault, Wyatt. You didn't deserve any of this. You did everything you could to survive and get out. You don't have a curse. You have a terrible brother who makes bad choices and who does not get to manipulate your life anymore."

"You were brave when you left, Wyatt." Sawyer stood beside them, a hand on each of them. "Be brave again. I got a whole lecture on what's going to happen if you leave, and it was bad. Sabrina's going to cry and then Rachel Harper will set her assassin six-year-old on you and apparently Poppy, the toddler, will help because she's some kind of spy. Aliens will rain down on Earth. I'm not sure if it's your fault or bad timing, but Mel's pretty certain. The point is, they would rather face down a pack of murderous bikers than have Sabrina Leal even think about needing a fresh start somewhere other than in her classroom. The people of Bliss have had a taste of what it means to be able to put a kid in school for eight hours, and they are not going back."

"I liked it better when you didn't fucking talk so much," Wyatt muttered. He brought his head up, and the worry was still in his eyes, but he hadn't moved away. He looked over at Sawyer. "You think this town can handle the Horde if they decide to punish me by taking it apart?"

"Somehow I think the Horde is going to find out how mean this town can be when their citizens are threatened," Sawyer replied. "These are smart men and women we're talking about, and a whole bunch of them have been in tight spots before and fought their way out. Trust them. Trust in us, man, because I don't think I can do this without you. I just figured out what you bring to the table. You can watch all her home and garden shows, and I don't have to. I can be in a relationship and also be alone because you're always here. This can work."

He was so romantic. "Ignore him. He needs you as much as I do.

250

We need each other. I think we might even love each other."

"I'm never going to say those words often. Probably," Sawyer amended. "But I will say I didn't think I would ever want to do this. The whole relationship thing. But I do, and it won't work without you. Teach and I would butt heads too much, but you handle us both. I don't miss my brothers so much when you're around."

It was as close as Sawyer would ever get to telling Wyatt he loved him. Because he did.

"I don't know what to do," Wyatt whispered, looking into Sabrina's eyes. "I can't lose you. I would rather die than lose you."

"You can lose me at any moment. We don't know how much time we have, but if you walk away, then we won't get any time at all. Wyatt, I would rather die trying to keep my family together than live without it."

Something seemed to break inside him. He leaned over and pressed his lips to hers, devouring her like a starving man. Sabrina could feel the emotion cracking off Wyatt. Fear. Rage. Anxiety. Love. So much love. All those emotions were forming a hurricane inside him, and she had to show him she was safe harbor.

She let her hands find the silk of his hair, pulling him close. "I love you. I don't ever want to leave you, but if it happens, know how much I loved you."

He picked her up and started to carry her away. To the bedroom. Where she would show him why they belonged together.

* * * *

She loved him. She fucking loved him, and in the end it was all that mattered.

Wyatt was trying to protect her, but if he walked away, he was marginalizing her because he knew damn straight if she was in trouble, he would never allow her to go because she worried he might get hurt. He would stand by her no matter what. He would step in front of her to take whatever was coming her way. He wasn't going to allow her to take pain for him, but he got it now.

Love meant risk. Freedom was risk. Life was fucking risk, and the only thing a person could hope for was to have the absolute best humans he could find to risk everything for.

Sabrina and Sawyer were his family. His real family. Blood was an act of coincidence, a roll of the dice that could only be forged into true bonds with love and patience and service to one another. He hadn't found love from his blood relatives, but he'd found it in abundance here.

Damn, but Bliss was his family, too.

He carried her through the kitchen and the living room, moving toward the bedroom. If he could get to the bedroom. Bella was wagging her tail and seemingly trying to get between his legs. Probably because if he was incapacitated, she could love him as much as she wanted. "Sweet girl, I'm going to need some time with your new momma."

"Bella," Sawyer intoned. "Stop trying to murder Wyatt via tripping. Come on. I'll get you a snack and you can have some crate time."

This was what Sawyer had talked about, though he'd used all the wrong words. He'd talked about getting free time since Wyatt was around, but it was more than not having to watch a show he didn't want to watch. It was about having someone else he could count on. Someone who would always stand up for their family. Someone who wouldn't let him down.

"You know why he told you he loved you in the middle of a deeply emotional moment." It also came with a bastard who knew him far too well and didn't mind ratting his best friend out to their one-day wife. At least that's how it was going to be for Sawyer.

Sabrina's lips curved up, her arms tightening around him as he moved into the bedroom. "Because now he doesn't have to talk about his feelings. He knew we would have to settle this thing between us before we could do anything else, and he also knew we would end up in bed, so he thinks he's said it and now it's settled and he'll never have to say it again."

"I'll fix it," he promised. If she was staying, he wouldn't let anything hurt her. Even Sawyer.

She shook her head. "I have what I need. It's hard for him. He's already opened up so much. Give him time. Before you know it, he'll be the most romantic man in Bliss."

"I will not." Sawyer entered, pulling his shirt over his head. "I will be surly and need alone time and I won't talk much, but that's why Wyatt's around. He'll chit chat about whatever book the two of you are reading and I'll..." He seemed to think for a moment. "I'll teach you how to build a table if you want. Or we'll start easy. I get the feeling we're going to need some bookshelves."

He was inviting her into his private life the only way he knew how. It was enough.

"I definitely want some bookshelves," she replied, her eyes soft as he set her on the bed. "Sawyer, I don't need you to say the words."

Sawyer's lips quirked up. "I love you, Sabrina. Now I've said it twice, and he hasn't said it at all. I think I deserve the before double penetration blow job I've been assured someone gets during the final consummation of a threesome. There's a rule book around here somewhere."

Sabrina snorted. It was an inelegant sound Wyatt still found adorable.

And Sawyer was right about one thing. "I do love you. I love you so fucking much."

Sabrina sobered, standing and putting her hands on either side of his face. "Be sure. You've only started to explore the world, Wyatt. There's a lot more of it."

"Not for him there isn't." Sawyer closed the door behind him, shutting them inside. "Don't try to wiggle out of this, Teach. He loves you. He's never leaving Bliss unless you need to leave for some reason. Hell, he was never actually going to leave this cabin. He's like a tick. He's dug in."

"Well, it sounded like he was leaving about five minutes ago," she complained.

"I was going to kill my brother and make sure you were safe. However, I've recently had the stupidity of my plan pointed out to me. So I have to rethink." He tightened his hands on her hips, not allowing her to pull away. "I'm not leaving, but we need a plan to protect you. And the town."

"The men are already working on it." Sawyer moved in behind her, brushing her hair to the side and setting his lips on the curve of her neck.

"I think we need to deal with the Creede boys." Wyatt hadn't liked how Marshall had handled him today. Like they were still rivals and he had a real chance with Sabrina if he could only convince her she'd made a poor choice. "I think they're still interested in her, and they want to fight it out."

"There's no fight." Sabrina's head shook. "I have my men. I'm not about to sit around and wait to see who wins my hand. I'll talk to them if I need to."

"Or I can talk to Nate since apparently we're friends now," Sawyer said with a long sigh. He leaned over and nipped her earlobe, a move that made her eyes close in obvious pleasure.

She liked a little bite every now and then. His body started to heat as lust caught up to emotion. "Good. I think it's great we can talk to Nate, but when we're done here, I'm going to tell you the whole story. I'm going to lay it all out to you and maybe we can decide how to handle it."

Neither of them believed he'd killed for his brother. They had zero reason to believe he hadn't done exactly what he'd said he'd done. Except they knew him. Really knew him. Like no one else on this planet ever had.

This love was worth risking everything over.

He used the hold on her hips to pull her close, rubbing his cock against her so she knew how much he wanted her. And because he wanted to. He wanted to be near her always. Sawyer was right, too. He'd never actually planned on finding his own place. He'd known he was home the night he found his way here.

"I'm glad," she said, her eyes promising him a future. "We'll find our way through this."

"We will," Sawyer promised. "But I was serious about the blow job. I'm addicted now."

Sabrina leaned back against Sawyer's chest, a magnificent smile on her face. "I think you like knowing I can't talk for a while."

Sawyer's hand came around her neck, cradling her head to him. "I love the way you talk. I love listening to you. Sometimes yours is the only voice that grounds me, and I was ungrounded for so long I forgot what it felt like to have someone I can trust. And yes, it gets easier to say the word, but it still makes me want to vomit a little."

"I can say it enough for both of us," Wyatt vowed. "We love you, Sabrina. And I'm willing to take all the shin kicks I have to in order to prove to your army of children that I'm one of the right men for you."

Before she could promise she would talk to them, he fused his mouth to hers. It was time to move past talking.

He unbuttoned her blouse, never taking his mouth off hers. He loved kissing her, loved the slow slide of her tongue alongside his, loved how she moved with him. He could kiss her for hours, simply enjoying the intimacy of her smell and taste and the way she whimpered and moaned.

But he wanted more. He needed her aroused as hell because there was no way they weren't taking her together tonight. Sawyer might be bullshitting about there being a handbook, but even Wyatt knew this had been where they were heading all along.

Sawyer dragged the blouse off her shoulders and expertly handled the bra she wore, tossing it to the side along with the blouse and exposing her gorgeous breasts. Wyatt couldn't help but palm them, rubbing his thumbs over her nipples.

"You are the right men for me," Sabrina said, her hands playing in Wyatt's hair as Sawyer moved behind her, dragging down her skirt. She'd kicked off her shoes the minute they'd hit the cabin so she was left in nothing but a pair of silky undies.

She was the most gorgeous woman in the world, and he'd been offered so many. So many women had come through the clubhouse, looking for something he couldn't give them, offering something he didn't want. He wanted peace. He wanted a woman with a saucy mouth who didn't follow orders when she didn't agree with them. He wanted her quiet strength, her boundless love.

He wanted her everything, including the knowledge that if ever her class thought he wasn't treating her well, they would send an army of six-to-eight-year-olds after him and he would need to be ready.

God, he wanted this life.

When Sawyer moved, dispensing with his jeans, Wyatt pressed Sabrina back against the bed, wrapping his hands around her ankles and flipping her over so her pretty ass was exposed.

"You are not going to need these for a while." Wyatt tugged the panties off her. "Now turn around and get on your hands and knees. Take Sawyer while I get you ready."

She flipped herself around, doing what he'd asked, and before he knew it, her round ass was in the air and he couldn't help himself.

He gave her a smack, satisfied by the way she gasped and wiggled, inviting more. "You need to understand that just because I'm willing to let you take the risk, I will be pissed if you're not careful. You don't go anywhere alone until we figure this out." He gave her a smack to her other cheek this time. "Am I understood?"

"I am more than happy to discuss any and all security protocols you feel we need," she promised sweetly.

He gave her another spank. Not to prove a point. Simply because she liked it. He spanked her ass until it was slightly pink and she was groaning, her fingers locked in the quilt covering the bed.

"She really does like it," Sawyer said, his cock in hand. He'd also laid out what they would need on the nightstand. Condoms and lube. No plug tonight. She was getting the real thing. "Maybe we should think about spending some time in Talbot's dungeon. I've heard along with all the sex toys you can imagine, the fucker serves snacks mid-session. Although I bet it's not like mini corndogs. He probably serves fancy shit."

Wyatt didn't care about snacks. He had his snack laid out in front of him, but he did like the idea of exploring play with their gorgeous girl. "I can bring our own snacks, though I bet our baby here would love canapés and mini tarts along with some kinky play. Spread your knees wide. You take Sawyer. You get him ready to fuck your ass."

Her breath seemed to catch and then she obeyed, her legs making room for him as Sawyer moved into place.

Wyatt watched as Sawyer's big hand came out to cup Sabrina's head. "Take me, baby. I need something sweet because I had to talk to people and have emotional revelations, and I'm worried my heart is going to do this three-size growing thing."

Sabrina snorted. "I think your heart is big enough. Come here. Let me take the terrible sting of emotional honesty away."

He watched as she licked that big cock of Sawyer's. His own tightened at the sight of her sucking Sawyer's cockhead behind her lips. She worked him over, and he could see her tongue whirling around him.

She deserved some, too. He grabbed the condom he would need in a few moments and then shed his clothes, getting where he wanted them to be. Skin and nothing else. They didn't need clothes between them. He could be exactly who he was meant to be with these two people, and this place was their sanctuary.

He got onto the bed, laying on his back and sliding his head up between those legs because he was going to make it extremely hard for her to keep her mind on Sawyer. "Don't lose him."

She needed to understand that she would be taken care of even while she took care of one of them. She was the light in their sky, the center around which they both would orbit.

He gripped her hips and brought her down, rubbing his nose right in her already wet pussy. Yes, this was what he'd needed. He needed this utter intimacy, to know with this one woman nothing was off limits.

"He told you not to lose me," Sawyer was saying. "Keep your mind focused."

"That's hard when he's eating my pussy," Sabrina shot back.

Wyatt gave her a long lick, reveling in her taste and the smell of her arousal. She tasted so fucking good. He measured the strokes of his tongue, not wanting this to be over too quickly.

He held the cheeks of her ass, giving them a squeeze as he speared her with his tongue, going deeper, fucking her harder. She was caught between him and Sawyer, and she moaned and writhed, pressing her pussy to his mouth, obviously requesting more. This was how he wanted her. Wild. He needed to be one of the men who could make the perfectly proper and infinitely competent teacher go wild.

He felt the minute she went over the edge, and he heard Sawyer curse. Sabrina sat back, riding Wyatt's tongue.

"That was close," Sawyer said. "Her mouth is heaven, but I don't want to come in her mouth tonight."

Nope. Any orgasms were going to be had deep inside her. But it didn't mean she didn't get one. He felt the gush of her orgasm coat his tongue and he knew he was close, too. Just from giving her an orgasm. Sabrina stayed in place, her breath rasping from her body.

Oh, she wasn't done. Wyatt quickly sheathed his cock in the condom he'd left beside them and then tugged Sabrina down his body. "Come on, baby. You still have work to do."

She kissed him, shamelessly and totally. She would be able to taste herself on his tongue. If she'd finished Sawyer off, he would taste his partner. It didn't scare him at all. It didn't spark anything but heat.

She broke off the kiss and sat up, staring down at him. "I love you."

He loved her so much. "You, too, babe. Now sit on my cock because the big guy is getting impatient."

"The big guy is fucking dying," Sawyer complained. "I can't wait."

Neither could Wyatt. He pressed his pelvis up, his cock finding her pussy like it was a heat-seeking missile.

He vowed he would hold out because this was the first night of the rest of their lives.

Chapter Sixteen

It had taken every bit of restraint Sawyer had to pull away from Sabrina, but there was something he wanted more than the momentary high. He wanted them all to be together. As they should be. As they would be for as long as life permitted.

He stood watching as Sabrina lowered herself onto Wyatt's cock, the sensual movement of her body a siren's call. He had no idea why this woman did it for him.

No. That was bullshit, and he wasn't going to lie to himself anymore. He wasn't going to be emotionally open or shit, but at least to himself, he would be honest.

She was strong and smart and kind. Her beauty was something he could take or leave. He'd been around many beautiful women, but only Sabrina's soul meshed with his. She filled his empty spots. No. Loving her filled his empty spots. He realized it suddenly. He was complete. He was his own person, and being in this relationship wouldn't steal his individuality. It simply made him a better version of himself. She and Wyatt made him more himself.

Yeah, he was never saying those words out loud, but she would know. Because she saw him.

Actually, now that he'd talked to some of the citizens of Bliss, a surprising amount of people knew him. Maybe he wasn't as impenetrable as he thought he was.

The good news was, she was totally penetrable. As she was about to find out on two fronts.

See, he could do this. He could be slightly emotional and get right back to shamelessly horny in seconds. And he hadn't needed a shit ton of therapy to do it.

He grabbed the lube Wyatt had thoughtfully set up for him while Sawyer had been fucking Sabrina's mouth. Teamwork really did make the dream work.

When was the last time he was so fucking cheerful about sex?

This wasn't a biological need. This was joy.

Sabrina's back arched, her breasts thrusting out as she seated herself on Wyatt. So fucking hot. His cock pulsed at the thought of being inside her.

But he couldn't start fucking her the way Wyatt had. Nope. He had work to do. He put a hand on her back, gently easing her down so her ass was in the air, her chest against Wyatt's. "Stay still. No more orgasms for you until we're ready."

"But I'm so close," she complained.

It was easy to smack her pretty ass since it was right there. She moaned, and Wyatt's hands found her hips.

"Do that again and it won't be Sabrina going over the edge," Wyatt warned. "She feels so fucking good, man. Hurry."

Such impatience. Wyatt usually took his time. But Sabrina was the one, and they were riding on the high of finally getting their shit together. It was natural Wyatt wanted to get to the good stuff.

This felt meaningful. Like once they did this, the whole fate thing he'd felt that night almost a year ago would be done, and he would be firmly in the grips of what it meant to be a husband and a partner.

It didn't scare him the way it had back then. Now all he could see was this—the three of them together.

He pressed his hand to the warm skin of her back, easing her down so her breasts were against Wyatt's chest. "Calm down, Teach. You're going wild on me, and I need a minute to get you ready. Have I told you how fucking gorgeous you are?"

"You make me feel gorgeous," she said, a little breathless. Wyatt was stroking her hair back, kissing her forehead. "You two make me feel like I never have before."

He had zero idea what had been wrong with the men in her life, but he was glad they hadn't been able to see what a jewel she was.

She was his and Wyatt's, and they were never going to let her go. Wyatt could be her happy husband who attended PTA meetings, and Sawyer could be the dude who stood in the back and scared the shit out of anyone who thought about touching her. It was a good role for him.

"You are the sexiest woman in the world." He spread her cheeks, getting a good look at the sweet asshole he was about to fuck. "And your asshole's sexy, too."

Sabrina's shoulders shook as she giggled against Wyatt's chest.

The big bad Doms he knew would spank her, but Sawyer had a sense of humor. "Hey, it's a pretty asshole. I know. I get to see it. Have you ever seen it?"

"Of course I haven't seen it," she shot back.

Wyatt grinned up at him. "We should take pictures."

The joy on his friend's face hit him squarely in the chest. This was something she brought with her. Joy and laughter and the ability to make him feel comfortable in the oddest situations. He hoped he could do the same for her in this instance because he knew she was going to love it.

"We are not taking pict…" she began and then shuddered as he dribbled warm lube over her tender flesh. "Oh…"

He pressed his thumb against her, spreading the warm lube where it needed to go. He played with her for a moment, reveling in the intimacy of being here with her, having access to parts of her no one else ever would. He loved the way she squirmed and moaned as he worked his fingers inside her.

Then it was time to stop playing. He replaced his fingers with his cock, lining up perfectly and starting to penetrate in shallow waves.

Sabrina gasped, but the sound was cut off by Wyatt, who pulled her head down and kissed her like he needed her to breathe. He kissed her over and over, distracting her from the pressure Sawyer was giving her. He was careful, easing in and then out, opening her up slowly, though it took every ounce of willpower he had. She felt so fucking good. She clenched around him and then he was the one moaning.

"Let me in, Teach," he said between gritted teeth. He needed all of his hard-earned control because she was testing his limits. "Relax for me. Let me in, baby. You're going to like it. I promise."

He hoped she did because it was already the best sex he'd ever had. His whole body hummed with anticipation.

"Relax," Wyatt said soothingly. "Let us in. We want to be with you. Did you know I'll be able to feel him when he gets inside you? He'll slide against me."

She took a long breath and flattened her back, releasing whatever tension she'd been holding in. He thrust in gently, his whole cockhead disappearing. He gripped her hips as he gently eased in and out, giving her time to adjust to his size, to the feel of both of them.

Sabrina held on to Wyatt. "I don't know how this feels."

It wasn't a *hey stop*. "Give it a minute. Tell me how this feels."

He was all the way in, his hips flush against her ass and hands holding tight to her. He held himself there, breathing in and out, his cock begging him for more.

"Tight. I feel so tight, Sawyer. I feel both of you," she whispered. "We're all together. I like being together."

"Now tell me how this feels." He wanted more than the emotional connection for her. He wanted her to love it. He wanted her to crave it, to not be able to go too long without having both of her men buried deep inside her body. He eased his cock out, stroking nerves deep inside that had never been touched like this before.

Sabrina's gasp this time wasn't about discomfort. She whimpered and moved against him, trying to get the sensation back. "What was that?"

"Why women let men do this," he said with a chuckle. "I think we have this, Wyatt."

"I think we do," Wyatt agreed. "Come on, baby. Let's see how high you can fly."

He pressed in again, letting himself off the leash a bit as she started to move between them. Sabrina's hips moved in a rhythm, riding Wyatt and then pressing back to take Sawyer deep.

Sawyer's body felt electric as he worked with Wyatt to take her higher and higher. They rode her body, but it was clear who was in charge. Sabrina was fierce. How had he ever thought she couldn't handle him? Hell, there were moments when he was certain he was the one who couldn't handle her.

But he damn straight was going to try. For the rest of his life.

He felt her whole body go stiff as she shouted out and held onto

Wyatt like he was a lifeline. She clenched around him, and he swore he could feel the moment Wyatt filled her. The sensation was a wave dragging him out to sea. He lost control, thrusting into her again and again until he had nothing left to give her and his body knew no other feelings beyond pleasure and contentment.

He fell forward, rolling slightly so they were in a happy heap, he and Wyatt keeping Sabrina between them.

Where she belonged.

Sabrina laid her head on his chest. "I think I can safely say that was a successful experiment."

He kissed the top of her head, his whole body languid and satisfied. "Very successful, and it's not an experiment. It's us."

She smiled at him. "It's us."

Wyatt sat up. "Before we say us…"

He picked up a pillow and smacked his partner in the face. "Shut up, Eeyore. We're not going anywhere." That wasn't right. "Except back into Bliss because we have to tell Talbot he's got a stick up his ass."

"Well, I'm planning on being more subtle," Sabrina admitted, settling down. "Especially now that I know how it feels."

Wyatt dissolved into laughter and wrapped himself around her.

For a moment, they were happy.

* * * *

Sabrina stepped out of the shower and wished they didn't have a meeting to go to. She glanced at the clock and realized they had less than an hour to make the eight o'clock start time.

Would everyone look at her and know she just had wild, crazy, double penetrative sex with two hot men?

Probably, but then most of the women in town were well experienced in the scenario. Including her sister, who would absolutely take one look at her and know she'd done the deed. She hoped Elisa didn't high-five her in front of everyone.

"You okay?" Wyatt stood in the doorway, already dressed in jeans and a Western shirt, though his hair was still wet from the shower the three of them had shared.

Sawyer had gotten in and out, more concerned about dinner than he was in having long, slow romantic time underneath a stream of surprisingly hot water. He had an excellent water heater.

Proving he was serious about his earlier speech concerning partnership, Wyatt had simply stepped up and kissed her long and slow and rubbed his hands all along her skin while he cleaned her up. He hadn't left until she'd washed her hair. He'd kissed her and told her not to be too long.

Because he had a confession to make. One he'd been holding in for so long.

The look on his face told her he was anxious again. She trusted this anxiety wasn't about leaving. They'd settled this between the three of them. No, it was about telling them the truth. He needed to relax because there was no way this discussion of his didn't go well. They were together. They would get through whatever they had to. So maybe a bit of self-deprecation was needed to break the tension. "I was wondering if Elisa will take one look at me and know my asshole is sore."

The admission earned her a high-wattage smile from his handsome face. "Somehow, I think you'll tell her. You're not exactly withholding with your sister."

And the frown was back as he obviously considered what he'd said.

She moved into his space, putting a hand on his chest. "I love my sister. I tell her everything about me, but it doesn't mean I can't keep a secret, Wyatt. I can keep any secret you want me to."

"The trouble is I'm starting to think I was wrong for keeping the secret in the first place," he admitted, dropping his forehead to hers. "I worry I made a poor choice by leaving the MC the way I did. A cowardly choice."

A low groan came from the living room, and Bella bounded in. "Do we have to do the whole 'I should have risked my life to take my brother down' drama right now? I made us PB and J's."

She was going to have to do something about their diet, though she had to admit peanut butter and jelly sounded good after all the physical exertion of the last couple of hours.

Had it only been a few hours since she'd sat in her classroom worried she would lose Wyatt, and now she wasn't at all anxious about this secret he had to tell her. She wanted to get through it so they could make a plan. They would discover she was excellent when it came to planning. She could organize a classroom. She could certainly organize revenge. Wyatt's brother deserved some nasty revenge. Wyatt, however, wasn't thinking straight. He was lost in his own fear and guilt. "Wouldn't taking your brother down have implicated you?"

He hadn't exactly wanted to launder money for his brother, but here they were.

"I could have cut a deal." Wyatt stepped back, giving her space, though Bella danced around them both, taking up her own. "I could have smuggled out records and gone to a prosecutor my brother doesn't own."

Sawyer leaned against the doorjamb, winking Sabrina's way. "Hey, Teach. You're looking good. Need a bag of frozen peas to sit on?"

Sabrina felt herself flush. It actually sounded kind of nice, but she was trying to keep her dignity and she wasn't showing up to a school board meeting with a cold pack against her ass. "I'm fine, thank you. I barely notice."

Sawyer's grin kicked into high gear. "Then I obviously didn't do it right and we need to start all over again." He sighed. "But first we should deal with Wyatt's delusions about how the justice system works."

No one needed a lecture on how hard it would have been to take down the Horde. "He's feeling selfish for saving himself. But sometimes you have to in order to do more good in the world." She dropped the towel and moved to where her suitcase sat, pulling out the clothes she would need for the evening.

"You do not have to put on clothes," Sawyer murmured.

"It does feel like a mistake," Wyatt concurred.

It was good to know she could make them both stop simply by being naked. She stepped into her undies. "What? Being clothed for the meeting in which I have to tell Stef Talbot he knows nothing about stocking a children's library? Half the town will be there to complain about there being a full set of books on art history and only three Dr. Seuss books. Poor little Logan probably gets read Georgia O'Keeffe's biography as a bedtime story."

"I personally think you being naked would make the meeting

way more fun." Sawyer sat down on the bed, Bella between his legs as he stroked his big hand over her head.

"We could have it at Mountain and Valley." Wyatt's eyes watched her as she hooked her bra and reached for the black and blue floral dress she had picked out to do battle with the King of Bliss. It was her favorite since it had the deepest pockets.

"Nah. Then we'd all have to be naked, and I don't like my junk swinging around," Sawyer admitted. "Also, Max Harper gets a little crazy at those parties. Like he thinks it's funny to dress his dick up and make it do tricks. We should have Sabrina explain to everyone she feels more settled naked, and then Nell will chuck her clothes, too, and Henry will lose his shit because he's got extremely firm rules on where his wife's breasts can be free. Then half the women will go bare breasted in solidarity, and Rachel will already be topless because she's breastfeeding again and she'll take the whole thing as an excuse to get rid of the drape she usually uses. And when Rye tries to cover her up, she'll yell if he didn't want her to breastfeed in public, he shouldn't have knocked her up, and she'll use her boob as a weapon. I've heard she can aim. Anyway, I'm only saying it will liven things up, Teach."

Wyatt's eyes had gone wide. "That is the most words I've ever heard him say at one time."

She was taking Sawyer's chattiness as a sign of good things to come. "He's comfortable with us so he doesn't hold back. However, there will be children there, so I shall forego the nudity and the chaos occurring after. I do not need my students knowing what my boobs look like. There's a reason Mountain and Valley is adults only."

"Yeah, it's because it's the only place some of those motherfuckers can get away from all the kids they're having," Sawyer complained. "Have you noticed? It's like kids are everywhere. They're running wild."

"And yet you say you want five." Maybe this would be an easier subject.

"I said if we're not careful, we'll have five." His smirk told her he was fucking with her.

Which made her want to fuck with him. "I don't know. It could be fun. Five kids. Then obviously Bella will need a friend. I'm sure at least one of the girls will want a cat, so we'll need a kitten. Elisa told me she and Hale and Van are talking about adopting, so I would definitely want to start soon."

He stared at her for a moment and then his head shook. "So fucking mean."

He liked her mean. "I think we'll wait a while to have this discussion."

"Well played, and by the way you look lovely," Sawyer said. "I'll stick close to Wyatt in case any of those rogue kids I talked about come for his shins. I would set Bella on them, but we all know how that would go."

Bella would lick the attackers to death. Or at least until they giggled and petted her.

"I can handle the kids." Wyatt frowned. "I think. I hope I can. But I get what you're saying about the situation in Colorado Springs. I would have to have found someone willing to prosecute and put their own families at risk. There's a reason the Horde hasn't been taken down and it's because there are cops out there who work with them and others who are scared of what could happen to their loved ones if they try."

Sawyer sighed as though he didn't really want to have this conversation but was resigned to it. "There's a balance held between them, and there has been for years. It's why I went in. The cops have to show they're trying. And they are, but it can be difficult and extremely dangerous to take down a group like the Horde. On the other hand, Wayne understands the game. The cops need a win every now and then. So Wayne throws them a prospect. A new kid to do some time because it also keeps up the group's reputation."

"He was absolutely planning on using Sawyer's brother to keep the cops off the club. I heard him talking about it," Wyatt explained.

"And Wyatt risked his brother's wrath to tell you," Sabrina surmised. She'd always known there was a strong bond between these two men. It had been forged by their time in the MC and by their willingness to risk for the people around them.

"He did. I was able to mitigate the damage," Sawyer agreed. "If things had gone down the way Wayne planned, my brother would have done at least twenty years. As it was they couldn't get him for more than eighteen months, and he was out in half the time. He left the Horde after and he's...he's good, I think."

Her heart ached when she thought about Sawyer's brother rejecting him. "He's foolish. You did him a great service, and one day he's going to figure it out."

Sawyer stared down at her for a moment, an oddly gentle look on his face. "I wouldn't take it back. Not even to spare myself the pain. I would do it because he's my brother, and I didn't try to save him so he would like me more. I would do it because it led me here, and I want to be here. So if he never speaks to me again, I'm content."

She breathed in the words. He didn't talk this way often, but when he did, oh, she felt every word in her soul. "I'm more than content, Sawyer."

He winked at her. "Yeah, I know. You're sore." He kissed her briefly and turned to Wyatt. "So who did he want you to kill and how did you fake it?"

Wyatt sighed and leaned against the footrest of the bed. "This was supposed to be my darkest secret. Would you like to tell the story?"

"Someone who could have testified against him?" There was a surety to Sawyer's question, like he already knew the answer. He ignored Wyatt, obviously wanting to get to the point.

Wyatt sat down beside Sawyer, his hand going to Bella's back. She probably wasn't joking about more dogs. And she planned on bringing up the idea of classroom pets at the meeting this evening.

"How did you fake...his? Hers?" Sabrina wasn't sure. "How did you fake the murder you were supposed to commit? I assume one of the reasons he would want you to commit murder is having it over your head. I don't understand why he didn't have you do it in front of him."

Wyatt glanced down at his watch. "Do you want the whole story because we're going to be late. It's kind of long, and there's something we need to talk about before the meeting."

"But we're going to talk about it," Sawyer said, leveling a stare at Wyatt.

Wyatt nodded, obviously conceding. "Yes, I promise we're going to talk about it. When we get home tonight, I'll tell you everything you want to know. Or rather I'll fill in all the blanks since you two seem to already know most of it."

She stood in front of him, her hand coming up to stroke his

cheek. "I know you. I could walk into a room and see you standing over a body, and I would ask you what happened."

Wyatt's gaze went steely. "Good, then you'll trust me now. Stay away from those deputies from Creede."

She sighed. They'd been over this. "I'm going to make it plain I've made my choice and they'll back off."

"I'm not sure they will," Wyatt began. "I think they're looking for something to use to discredit me. The way he looked at me this afternoon makes me think he's got plans. He'll come to you at some point with a story about me."

"She already knows everything." Sawyer stood and stretched. "Look, we'll have a talk with them, you and I. I get it. She's gorgeous, and they thought they'd found their girl. Unfortunately, they found our girl, and we're not giving her up. They can back off or we can flip that switch you have and problem solved."

He was not joking. What had happened with Wyatt the other night had shaken her. "We are going to talk about how to make sure he never loses his temper again. Not like he did in the bar. What does Alexei say about it?" He was quiet. "You have talked to Alexei about the fact that you blow a gasket from time to time."

"It hasn't come up," Wyatt tried.

"How can therapy possibly work if you don't talk to your therapist? Do you not trust him?" If he needed another person to talk to, they would find someone else. Alexei seemed like an amazing guy, but she knew the therapist thing was so personal. A patient didn't necessarily match right away.

"Alexei is great. I'm cool with him. He's taken me a long way. I've been so good I thought I was past it. I hadn't had an episode like the one in the bar in years. I thought I was in control," Wyatt said.

"He touched her and you reacted the way you used to, the only way you knew how," Sawyer explained. "You went into survival mode, but I need you to understand you can't do it again. You have to stay in control and trust yourself and us. No matter what happens, we can handle it. I was going to explain that I would have gotten Sabrina out of there and you could have finished what you started without ever having to meet with your brother, but now we both know Sabrina would have stunned someone and there would still have been a fight. I just need it to be a fight where I'm not worried you won't know who you're killing."

Wyatt took a long breath, as though the words Sawyer had said needed time to settle in. "I'll talk to Alexei about how I can start handling it. I think it's going to be easier knowing I'm not alone, but you can't think I won't defend her. Or you."

This seemed to be a talk between the two of them. They both knew she would defend them all. They were well aware she could use a stun gun. They didn't know about the pepper spray or the small pistol she sometimes carried. It was good for a girl to have a couple of secrets.

Sawyer put a hand on his shoulders. "And I'll do the same. Please try to stay with us. You're enough, man. You don't need some Mr. Hyde shit to fight. You're good enough."

She kind of wished they would kiss. They were awfully pretty together. Her sister told her Van and Hale avoided most touching, but that didn't mean all threesomes were so…hetero.

"She's looking at us weird," Wyatt said, staring back.

Sawyer's eyes narrowed on her as though he could see right through her.

Sabrina gave them her most innocent smile. They were absolutely not ready for this discussion, but who knew what could come later? "Just happy we're together."

"I am, too. But I'm serious about Knox and Marshall." Wyatt held a hand out and brought her into their circle. "I want you to stay away from them for a while. I think you'll find they've pissed off your sister, so it shouldn't be too hard. Once we've got you moved in here, I think things will calm down. I'm going to fix this problem with my brother one way or another."

"Not alone," she insisted.

He leaned toward her, brushing his lips over hers. "I promise. Not alone. We'll sit down and talk this out and then bring the sheriff in. We'll do this right and as carefully as possible."

"And if it gets too dangerous and we're truly worried about her safety, we take care of her together," Sawyer vowed. "We make a plan, but we don't ever let them split us up."

"Sawyer, you can't leave here. Everything you own is here." Sabrina was shocked he would even think about leaving. When everyone had left him behind, he'd had this place and the business his family had built. "This is your home."

Sawyer stared down at her, his eyes softer than she'd ever seen before. "Don't make me say it, Teach."

They were his home now. His home had become something far larger than a brick-and-mortar building, more than the land they stood on. Hadn't she learned this? A house never made a home. Not truly. A home was always a place found inside a person's soul. "I won't. But back at you, Sawyer."

"I am not sure what we're not saying," Wyatt admitted. "But I know he won't ever sit here while we're somewhere else. So let's eat something. I'm starving, and we still have a meeting to get through, and then we have to plan how to survive if my brother finds out I didn't murder the witness he ordered me to and the dude's still out there with all the necessary information to force the cops to potentially start a war."

As scenarios went, it wasn't her favorite, but she'd learned to work with what she had. "All right. Food, meeting, and then we talk."

"Naked," Sawyer offered.

She would argue but her clothes did tend to drop off when they were around.

There was a knock at the door and Sawyer frowned. "Who the hell would come up here at this time of night?"

"It's not even seven yet. It's barely night, and it's likely a friend." Wyatt started for the door. "You're going to have to get used to having friends drop by."

Sawyer's expression told Sabrina he didn't like the thought.

He was always going to be her gorgeous grump.

Bella growled a second before Wyatt opened the door.

"Wyatt Kemp," a deep voice said. Deputy Marshall Lethe stood in the doorway, and his partner was behind him. She couldn't help but notice the set of cuffs in Marshall's hands.

Or the fact that Knox had his sidearm in his hand.

"You're under arrest for the murder of Dennis Hill," Marshall intoned.

And Sabrina knew her world was in more danger than she'd ever imagined.

Chapter Seventeen

Wyatt stopped, his whole body going still as he stared down at the gun Knox was holding. He was still out of Marshall's range, but all it would take would be a couple of steps and he would have to decide if he was going to fight.

Hadn't he been waiting for this to happen? Hadn't he been waiting for his brother to push the issue? Somehow he'd thought he had more time. He also hadn't thought his brother would use the cops to get him. Because he had zero doubt his brother was behind this.

His brother wanted him in a place where he had to allow himself to be taken in, to be put in a cage where he was going to be totally vulnerable or fight and put everyone at risk. Even the timing had been made with precision. They took him at the cabin where Sawyer and Sabrina could be collateral damage and not the meeting later this evening where the sheriff might have some say.

He wasn't going to fight. Sawyer wasn't carrying and neither was he. Fuck it all. He wasn't this guy. Maybe he'd heard wrong or this was some kind of asshole joke they were playing on him. "What?"

Marshall had traded the uniform he wore when he worked extra shifts in Bliss for the one he normally wore as a member of the Creede Sheriff's Department. Which explained how this was happening since Wyatt was fairly certain Nate wouldn't have sent them. If Nate had questions—or even needed to bring him in—he would have come himself.

"You're under arrest for the murder of Dennis Hill," Marshall reiterated. "Last year you killed Dennis Hill on the orders of your brother, Wayne Kemp."

"No, he didn't." Sabrina took a step forward.

Sawyer reached out and took hold of her elbow. Wyatt sent up a silent thank you because he wasn't sure Sabrina wouldn't try to attack the police.

They were going to arrest him. Something had gone terribly wrong, and he was about to pay for it. He had to make sure they didn't go down with him.

"Sabrina, stay back." He was going to keep it together for her sake. It was surprising. The urge to fight his way out wasn't pounding at his brain the way it normally would be. He couldn't lose it. No matter what. "Guys, you don't need the guns. I'm not armed. None of us are."

"Yeah, we'll keep our guns," Knox replied with a hardening gaze. "Somehow I think you lie. After what you did in Colorado Springs, no one should trust you. Sawyer, you going to give us trouble?"

"No more than I have to," Sawyer admitted.

Bella moved around Sabrina and Sawyer, growling.

That fucker actually pointed a gun at their dog. "Call her off, Sawyer. We're not playing around. We know exactly who he is, and he's going to pay for his crimes. You're lucky we're not taking you in, too. I think you're probably an accessory after the fact. If not before."

"He knows nothing." Bella came to stand at Wyatt's side, her stare wary on the intruders. She was a sweet baby but she knew how to protect the people she loved. And so did Wyatt. There was a time to fight and a time to call the battle.

"Bella, go to Sawyer." Wyatt took a deep breath as he held up his hands. "No one's going to give you any trouble. There's no reason to hurt our dog."

Marshall huffed. "Do you think we want to hurt a dog? We don't, man, but we also can't let you pretend to be a good guy. I've seen the evidence. You're going to drag Sabrina down with you, and I won't let it happen. Even if she can't care about us. It doesn't matter. I'm not letting a woman like Sabrina get involved with a murderer if I can help it."

"You can help it." Sabrina's tone had gone even, the panic from before shoved down. It allowed Sawyer to let her elbow go so he could reach for Bella's collar. "You don't have to do this. There is an explanation. Wyatt didn't kill anyone."

"That's not what the Colorado Bureau of Investigation says." Knox stood tall, his jaw going tight. "We didn't make shit up. The CBI investigator brought us the evidence, and our bosses in Creede gave us the go ahead to bring you in."

"Creede?" Sawyer asked. "Why would the CBI go to Creede? Bliss is the nearest town."

"You're on unincorporated land," Marshall explained. "CBI decided they would rather work with Creede than Bliss. Nate has a reputation for being difficult."

"Nate has a reputation for being thorough," Sabrina pointed out. "From what my sister tells me he doesn't allow other authorities to walk in and do whatever they want. Did he show you a warrant? Because I would like to see it."

"I don't have to see it. He's CBI. His credentials check out," Knox shot back. "Unlike Wright, I trust my fellow officers."

"Because no law enforcement officer ever went bad," Sawyer said with a shake of his head. "You know this is wrong. Even if we're unincorporated, agencies still coordinate with local law enforcement, and it's not the town a good thirty minutes away. Something is wrong and you can feel it. This is a setup."

"At least take him to Bliss. Lock him up at the station house and let us figure this out." Sabrina sounded so reasonable.

This wasn't a situation where reason would win out. The deputies were too far in at this point. They believed they were saving Sabrina from the big bad wolf, and anything challenging their perceptions would be ruthlessly thrust aside. They thought they were being heroes.

Knox actually seemed to think about it for a moment, but then he shook his head. "No. You feel free to call Nate, but we have a job to do and we're not taking any more time. Wyatt Kemp, you have the right to remain silent."

Sawyer kept a hold of Bella's collar when she started to try to get to Wyatt.

He couldn't hold back Sabrina. She walked right up to him, throwing her arms around him like she could keep him there.

"I'll get you out," she whispered. "I love you."

He was worried there might not be a chance to "get him out." If he thought they would simply take him to a jail cell and let the justice system deal with him, he would go easily. But someone would be waiting for him there in Creede. Or Colorado Springs.

"Sabrina, don't make this hard on us," Marshall warned.

She turned, her eyes going steely. "Hard on you? You have no idea how hard I'm going to make this on you, Deputy. Can't take a no, can you? I owe you something because you thought I was halfway pretty and willing to give you some attention? I didn't owe you anything, but now I do. Now I owe you, Deputy, and I assure you I will make those payments one way or another. Watch your fucking back."

"She doesn't mean it." The last thing he wanted was to get Sabrina mixed up in this. It was everything he'd feared. After the first couple of days, he hadn't truly worried she would walk away from him. He worried she would defend him and die in the process.

"Yeah, she does, and so do I," Sawyer said grimly. "You know this is wrong. You know Nate should be handling this. This is fucked up, and you're playing into their hands."

"I'll call for backup if you don't surrender right now." It seemed Marshall had chosen the hill he was going to die on. "And I wouldn't threaten an officer of the law. We tend to take threats seriously around here." He glared Sabrina's way. "Maybe you aren't the woman we thought you were."

"Damn straight I'm not, and you're going to find out," Sabrina challenged.

"Baby, please." If he didn't turn the heat down, something was going to explode, and he couldn't handle the idea of it hitting his family.

This was what it meant to have a real family. Sabrina and Sawyer and Bella were his family now, and he would sacrifice anything for them. He would also trust them. Giving Sabrina a job to do might help her back down. "Baby, call Nate and let him know what's happening and where they're taking me. Tell him I'll be able to prove I didn't kill anyone."

He offered his wrists to Marshall.

The deputy turned him around with a rough twist of his forearm, bringing his wrists together behind his back.

"Come on," Sawyer complained. "You can't cuff him in front? How scared are you?"

He tightened those cuffs to almost the point of pain. Angry. The deputy was angry, and Wyatt might be able to make use of that. He would have half an hour to try to figure out how much they knew. He would bet not a lot. Maybe the distance from Sabrina would help them think more logically. "It's fine. Sabrina, I love you."

She had her cell in hand. Tears shimmered in her eyes. "I love you. I'll get you out as soon as possible."

"I'll follow them." Sawyer kept his hold on Bella, who was whining now and trying to get to Wyatt.

Marshall put a hand on Wyatt's shoulder, starting to lead him to the waiting squad car. Wyatt had to be fast to not trip.

Knox followed behind them. "Good luck following us, Sawyer. Looks like someone doesn't care much for you. You're down two tires. Noticed it when we came in."

"What?" Sawyer asked. "You trashed my Jeep?"

Wyatt ducked, avoiding taking a hit as he was pushed into the backseat. His heart rate ticked up. Why would someone slash Sawyer's tires if the intention was to get him to jail? In a jail cell, they could do whatever they wanted to him. They could arrange for an accident, or they would find him alone and call it suicide.

But the jail scenario couldn't be countered by Sawyer following them.

"I sure as hell didn't do it." Marshall slammed the door. "It was already done. I know you don't understand this, but I'm a police officer. I follow the damn law. I don't break it. And we'll discuss the threats you two have made at another time."

"Deputy, something's wrong," Sawyer insisted. "I'm not joking. You know this is wrong."

"I know I have a job to do." Marshall slid into the driver's side while Knox buckled in beside him.

"Yeah, Harriet this is Deputy Miller," Knox said into the radio. "We're on our way back with the suspect, but you should warn the sheriff we might have a problem. I think Sheriff Wright is going to try to make things difficult."

Wyatt stared out the window as they pulled away and prayed he would see them again.

* * * *

Sabrina felt sick as she watched the squad car pull away. She took a deep breath, hearing Sawyer talking behind her. Minutes passed and she felt completely frozen in place. Every second took Wyatt farther away.

What had happened? She shook her head, trying to bring herself back to reality. "He thought he would be the one to get me in trouble. It's the other way around. They wouldn't act like this if they weren't pissed I rejected them. I can't believe they took him."

Sawyer moved in beside her, sliding his cell back in his pocket. "Wyatt knew this could be a problem. He should have talked to us, but we can discuss it later. For now, we need to find transportation. I don't want to leave him alone for long. Nate's on his way to Creede. He's taking Gemma with him to act as Wyatt's lawyer. He's sending your sister to pick us up. She'll drive us there, and hopefully we'll see him before they take him to Colorado Springs."

"Will he survive the trip?" A shudder went through her. This was serious, and Wyatt was in real danger. She turned and found herself in his arms. She sank into his strength. "What's going to happen to him?"

"Nothing." Sawyer gently tugged on her hair, bringing her head up so she had to look him in the eyes. There was a hard resolve in those dark orbs. "He is going to be fine, and we're going to make sure of it."

She held him tight, waiting for her sister to show up. They didn't go back in the house, simply stood there, holding on to each other.

His hand smoothed back her hair. "I'm going to beat the shit out of those assholes, though. Fucking with my Jeep. If I hadn't crated Bella, she would have warned us."

She shouldn't have been crated in the middle of the afternoon, but they'd wanted no interruptions to their lovemaking.

Guilt swamped her. She couldn't have waited? If they'd caught someone slashing Sawyer's tires, they might have known something was wrong.

"I can hear you blaming yourself, Teach," Sawyer said, cradling her close. "Not your fault. It's not yours any more than it's Wyatt's. You followed your heart. They're trying anything they can to change your heart's decision. I'm sure that warrant was a gift from the heavens. And now they're afraid of you."

They should be. "I meant what I said. They want a war, I'll fight it."

"Such a savage creature." But he was laying kisses on her forehead. "I'll fight it with you and so will Wyatt, but for now we're going to play this whole thing cool. We're going to go to the police station and let Gemma ask all the questions. If we need to follow him to Colorado Springs, we will. Lark can run the bar for a few weeks. Hell, she'll be thrilled."

It was the second time he'd offered to give up his precious work time. Her heart ached for what Wyatt was going through, but there was a calmness, too. A bit of anxiety had flown away when she'd realized Sawyer was all in. "And I'll do what I need to do. I've got some people I can call to take over for me, but I don't have any vacation time so I might need a job soon."

Sawyer huffed. "You are not giving up your job. I assure you we'll make it work. But it would be best if Nate could find a way to take custody of him. I'm worried about him going into prison while awaiting trial. If he can't get bail, we're going to have to think about...other options."

She wasn't sure she wanted to Bonnie and Clyde it the rest of her life. "You think you can break him out?"

"No," he admitted. "But I think I might be able to figure out where he stashed Dennis Hill. You know they say no body, no crime. Well, they mean no dead body. I assure you when I drag a living one in there, they'll change their minds."

"Wyatt was trying to save him," Sabrina pointed out.

"And now I'm going to save Wyatt," Sawyer promised.

There was the sound of tires crunching on the gravel and Sabrina turned, expecting to see her sister. Instead of the squad car, a small

SUV pulled to a stop, the tires the only sound the electric vehicle made. Henry Flanders stepped out, a smile on his face. "Hey, Sawyer. I thought I'd bring by the wood I found. I think it would make an excellent toy chest. I was hoping you'd let me use your heavy-duty sander. Hey, Sabrina. I'm getting pretty good with making furniture, but Sawyer is a master. Is everything okay?"

Henry went still, his expression going blank as his eyes darted around, taking in the area.

"Wyatt was just arrested," Sawyer explained. "Elisa's coming to pick us up. You should take Poppy home."

Sabrina realized she could see a toddler girl leaning over as though trying to catch sight of the world outside.

"What's wrong with your Jeep?" Henry opened the door to the car and hauled Poppy out, the child wrapping her arms around her father as he settled her on his hip. "Someone slashed the tires? How long ago?"

This was a Henry Flanders she hadn't met. Henry was soft spoken and always gentle. There was a hard edge to the man in front of her she couldn't deny.

"It had to be in the last hour and a half," Sawyer was saying. "I think it might have been the Creede guys. They're the ones who arrested Wyatt. They were working in Creede which I think is awfully convenient."

Henry moved to the porch, setting Poppy on the rocking chair. "Stay there, sweetie. Daddy needs to talk to some nice people."

Poppy's head nodded, and then she was happily petting Bella, who seemed to know where she was needed.

Henry crossed the space, his hand going to the pocket of his jeans and pulling a cell phone out. After a few seconds he frowned. "No one's answering at the station house."

"Elisa was on duty. She's on her way here," Sabrina explained. She knew a bit about how her sister's department worked. "I know when they don't have enough manpower, they set the phones to an answering machine for non-emergencies. 911 still works, but the people they would send are already on their way."

"Are they saying Wyatt killed someone in Creede?" Henry asked. "Because even then they should have called Nate and had him arrest Wyatt and turn him over. I know this isn't technically Bliss, but everyone knows this falls under Nate's territory. Which means this isn't about a murder in Creede. This is about Dennis Hill."

Sabrina felt her jaw drop. "How did you know?"

Henry's eyes were cold as he examined the tires. "Information is the most valuable asset we have, Sabrina. Even out here. Bliss has a high percentage of what I would call vulnerable citizens. Many of our people have pasts that might create problems later on. Some of them violent ones. Nate formed a committee to monitor these kinds of situations so we can handle them properly. I'm on the committee."

"Because you used to be CIA. I like it. You dug into Wyatt's background when he started living here?" Sawyer asked, apparently untroubled with the snooping into other people's lives aspect. "You could have mentioned it at the meeting this afternoon."

"We talked about it and decided it's Wyatt's secret to tell," Henry confessed. "I also thought we had a little time."

"Have you been spying on Wyatt?" Sabrina knew Henry had worked for the Central Intelligence Agency, but even though they joked about him being a badass, she'd thought he was like an analyst or something. The man in front of her hadn't been a paper pusher.

"Spying?" His lips tugged up, and he looked closer to normal, as though he realized his mask had slipped. "I would call it gathering intelligence. What we know would only ever be used to help. Wyatt's brother is dangerous to everyone, but especially to him. Doc asked us to look into his situation after the first night. It was obvious what had happened with Wyatt. So I dug a little further. It stood to reason Wayne Kemp wouldn't have allowed his brother to go without some kind of leverage over him. Wyatt knows far too much. I found the missing persons report for a man named Dennis Hill. He'd been playing around on the outer edges of the Horde for years. The police took him in for questioning about a triple homicide they believe Wayne at the very least ordered. Dennis held the line in the interview. He promised he didn't see anything, but he was scheduled to take a lie detector test three days after he went missing."

"Wyatt wouldn't have killed him." The choices he'd had to make. She couldn't imagine it. He'd had to find the will to break out of the only world he'd ever known.

She couldn't lose him. She loved him. Loved them both.

"I know." Henry's expression had softened as he watched

Sabrina. "I know for a fact he didn't kill Dennis. I know where he stashed Dennis."

Sawyer's jaw dropped. "You do? You know you could have mentioned it."

"Like I said, the information is only ever used to help our people. Up until today, that information was something for Wyatt to deal with," Henry replied surely. "Now I'll use it to get him out of trouble, though I would rather talk to him. I want to let him decide how to handle the situation."

"No." Sawyer's head shook. "You're going to tell the police everything you know and get him out of this."

Henry sighed. "Part of being in charge of an operation like this is holding firm to one's ethics. Before I offered to help, I made everyone involved sign an agreement. The information we have is sensitive and only to be used if the person the information pertains to wants us to use it. Think of it as our way of opening up options to vulnerable citizens."

Sabrina wasn't hearing it. She didn't give a fuck about ethics. She didn't care about Dennis Hill, or honestly whatever Wyatt thought. He was right. He'd put her in this position by making her fall in love with him, and now he had to deal with the consequences. And the men on this committee would deal with her, too. "Henry Flanders, you will take whatever information you have and hand it over to the Creede police force and the CBI, and if you don't I swear I will salt the earth with your bones. Metaphorically, of course, but I swear it will hurt. You think you like to protest? I can do it, too, friend, and I'll ensure your wife knows exactly what you're doing and that you allowed an innocent man to die. That's what we're talking here. If they manage to get Wyatt to jail in Colorado Springs, who's waiting for him in there?"

Sawyer seemed to pick up her line of argument. He stood beside her, a hand on her shoulder. "I assure you there are Horde members serving time right now, and they'll be more than willing to do the boss's business. Or if Wayne wants to keep his hands somewhat clean, this would be a good way to do it. Think about it. What would be better for a rival MC member than shivving Wayne's brother? It's a good way to get some revenge."

So it could be more than Horde members out to get Wyatt.

Desperation surged through her.

Sawyer's hand came off her shoulder and he took her own, giving her a squeeze and letting him know he was there for her. "Henry, I know you have your ethics, but he's my partner. I don't do this. I don't beg, but I will for him. He's going to die in there. Our shot at getting him out is keeping him here in Bliss."

She heard the sound of another vehicle coming up the drive and saw Hale's big SUV turning in. Her sister was out of the passenger side as Henry got back on his cell phone. She heard him mention Stef's name, and then her sister was hugging her.

"Are you okay?" Elisa stepped back and looked her up and down as though trying to find a wound.

"I'm fine." Tears were gathering again. "But they're going to kill Wyatt if we don't get him back."

Elisa nodded. She was in her uniform. Hale and Van slid out of the SUV, standing behind Elisa, offering their support. "Sorry. I had to have Hale drive me up. My county-issued vehicle is in the shop for maintenance. They were about to drop me off at the station when Nate called. Let's get you in the SUV. We can be in Creede in twenty minutes if we haul ass."

"I promise, I'll get us there as fast as we can," Hale said with a nod. "Nate and Gemma are almost there, and he'll do what he can to slow down the whole processing-him-through thing."

Time. They had a little time. Paperwork would be involved. He would likely have to process into the Creede jail, and then custody would have to be changed from the Creede Police to the CBI. More paperwork. They had a real shot at solving the problem if they could use all the bureaucratic bullshit to their advantage.

"Yeah, I think we should make a call here," Henry was saying to Stefan Talbot. "We don't know if they'll let Gemma in. Technically, they can hold him for a while without admitting his lawyer. They could tell her she can see him in Colorado Springs. I think we need to get this ball rolling whether he likes it or not. I know Nate would rather wait, but Sawyer and Sabrina are closer to the situation, so I have to listen to them. Besides, Sabrina promised to tell Nell we're abusing power." Henry winced and looked Sabrina's way. "You don't want to know what he's saying. It's not suitable for children."

So she'd pissed off the King of Bliss. It probably wouldn't

matter because they would likely have to leave.

"Come on." Elisa took her hand. "We'll get to Creede as fast as we can. Sawyer can come with us. Henry, you're letting the rest of the town know? I'm pretty sure Wayne Kemp isn't planning on causing trouble in Bliss since he worked so hard to get his brother out of it, but I want people on alert."

Henry nodded. "I will, and Stef is activating our plan."

"There's a plan?" Sawyer asked.

"Always," Henry assured him, and his cell rang again.

Sabrina rushed into the house to grab her purse. She couldn't stand the thought they wouldn't all be here together again. She had to get control of her emotional state. She'd already threatened two people she had to share a town with. Although once she gave Nate Wright a full dose of her feelings about his part-time deputies, she doubted she would have to see either of them again. Henry was another story.

Deep breath. She would see Wyatt again. She would.

"It's going to be okay." Sawyer wrapped big arms around her. "He'll be back here tomorrow, one way or another."

She sniffled. "He needs to be home. This is our home. I know it's yours, but…"

He squeezed her tight, pulling her against his chest. "This is our home, Sabrina. Yours and mine and Wyatt's. And we'll bring him back here and decide where to go from there. We might have to leave for a while."

She nodded but felt better. How would she get through this without Sawyer? She forced her fear down. "I know. All right. Let's get going."

The faster they got to Creede, the sooner they could get Wyatt back where he belonged.

She held Sawyer's hand as they walked back out to the porch, ready to face whatever came next.

Elisa had her radio in hand, and her skin had paled in a way that let Sabrina know something had gone horribly wrong. "Sabrina, Wyatt didn't make it to Creede."

Sabrina held on to Sawyer because the world suddenly seemed like it was spinning.

Chapter Eighteen

"**D**on't worry about Wright," a tinny voice said over the radio Knox had called in on. "The CBI is going to handle everything. They'll have the suspect back in Colorado Springs before Wright can cause problems. I'll be happy to send over all the paperwork if they insist. We're only doing what CBI requested."

Maybe there was real paperwork and this wasn't some ploy to get him vulnerable. Maybe he'd fucked up when he'd followed through with the plan to save the man his brother required him to kill. The evidence he'd given Wayne had been good, but it wouldn't stand up to real forensics.

What if Wayne had his proof double checked? What if he'd done a DNA sample and realized the body he'd brought back hadn't been Dennis Hill?

Then Wayne would certainly want to have a word. But only after he'd gotten the accounts he'd needed from him. This move was right from Wayne's playbook.

Wyatt's heart rate ticked up. "Guys, I didn't kill Dennis. I need you to check out who the supposed victim is." Could he trust them? The answer was obviously no, but he also couldn't not try. "Dennis witnessed my brother killing three members of a rival MC. Wayne ordered me to kill Dennis so he couldn't ever testify. It was my only way out of the MC. If I killed the witness, I could be free."

"And you decided his life was worth it so you could get out?" Marshall shot the question back through the cage separating them. He drove down the mountainside with the surety of a man born here.

"I didn't kill anyone," Wyatt replied, trying to keep control over his temper. "And I'm trusting you with that knowledge because right now I'm wondering if you aren't working for my brother."

Knox turned in his seat. "You asshole. We wouldn't work for a fucking criminal. We're the good guys here. Even though no one seems to be able to see it. Bliss isn't the right place for us. They don't care about rules. They don't care about laws."

"They care about what's right," Wyatt argued because he did believe they thought they were the good guys. They thought they were saving a good woman from a bad man. They were wrong, but they believed it which meant there might be room to reason with them. "I know you do, too. You don't want a bunch of blood on your hands, and that's what you're going to get if you turn me over to the CBI without looking into their story."

"They don't have a story." Marshall turned right onto the highway. "They have a warrant."

"Did you see it? Did you really look at it?" Wyatt asked. "Or did you just trust him?"

"Why wouldn't I trust a CBI agent?" Knox asked, but there was something in his tone. "Why would a CBI agent lie? And no, I didn't personally inspect the warrant. I didn't have to. I do what my superiors tell me to do."

"Unless they're Nate Wright." He had a chance with them. They reached the bottom of the road and Wyatt watched as they passed the bar. It looked so normal. Dusk was rapidly approaching, and the neon sign was on. The parking lot was fairly empty. It was a weeknight so it would be pretty empty. As they drove past the front of the bar, he got a glimpse of motorcycles on the far side of the building. Tucked away close to the trash bins.

Or maybe he hadn't seen it. Sometimes Gil parked his bike by the bins since taking out the trash was the last thing he did every night.

There had been more than one.

Wyatt forced down his fear. He'd gone by fast. He hadn't been able to ID any of the bikes. Maybe it had been an optical illusion.

"I have never disobeyed an order from Sheriff Wright," Knox replied. "Not once, but I knew he would try to... I don't know. He would try to figure out a way you're not the bad guy. He doesn't see things straight when it comes to this town. He believes all the shit people spout."

"He coddles these citizens." Marshall made another turn. They were following the river out of town. Two more turns and he would be out of Bliss's jurisdiction. "He lets them walk all over the rules. He should take this place in hand and things would be better."

He was sick of listening to them. It was obvious they weren't going to help him. They would mindlessly do their jobs and think they were good guys for never questioning authority. "Better? In what way? What exactly do you take exception to? The everyone looks after everyone else thing? How kind people are?"

"The naked people," Knox said with a sigh. "They skirt the law all the time up there. And then there's Mel. Someone should pick him up and shove his ass in a psych ward."

"You know Sabrina calls him Dad," Wyatt pointed out. "Nice way to talk about the woman you like's father."

"Yeah, well, she turned out to not be who we thought she was," Knox admitted. "And this has nothing to do with her. Not really. I thought she was a nice lady, the kind who might want to settle down."

"She does." Wyatt didn't mind twisting the knife in this case. "She wants to settle down with me and Sawyer."

A nasty chuckle came from Marshall's throat. "Yeah, and that's why she's not who we thought she was. I can't believe they're going to let her teach school."

"You need to stay out of Bliss after this." Even if he couldn't be there, Wyatt knew there were plenty of people who would defend Sabrina. Some of them were tiny, but they had some pointy cowboy boots and could kick a shin when they wanted to. And some of them would simply brush these two off like the pests they were. "I assure you the town isn't going to welcome you back."

"I already planned to let Sheriff Wright know we won't be available for extra shifts anymore." Knox settled but his shoulders were still up around his ears. He wasn't as sure about the decision as he wanted Wyatt to believe. "We won't go back there."

He had one last road he could go down. "No, you won't because whoever the CBI sent is almost assuredly working for my brother, and he'll want to ensure he cleans up all the evidence. You're part of it. You'll likely meet a nasty accident."

"More threats?" Marshall asked, staring at him through the rearview mirror.

"More like predicting your future," Wyatt replied with a long sigh. He sat back as much as he could since his hands were cuffed behind his back. "I know how my brother operates."

"Probably because it's how you operate." Knox seemed to want to say more, but the radio squawked suddenly. Knox picked it up. "This is Miller."

"Knox, there's been a change of plans," the voice said over the radio. "The CBI agent needs to get the suspect to Colorado Springs tonight. They're meeting you at the old gas station on the edge of Bliss. It's closed, but it's a good place to make the transfer."

"Uh, what about the paperwork?" Knox suddenly didn't sound as sure.

"Sheriff okay'd it. You know he doesn't want any of this. Let the CBI deal with it. He doesn't want beef with Nate Wright. He's calling him as we speak to try to settle things," the woman said. "Let me know when the transfer's been made. Boys, this isn't your fight. The Bureau wants this guy. It's best to get him to a facility that can handle him."

"I don't have anyone behind me." This alone should tell them it was a setup. "I left the MC. They won't save me. Unless you're worried Sabrina is going to storm the station house."

"We're on our way and will call back when the handoff is done," Knox said and hung up the radio. "I'm not afraid of anything."

"Think about it." He was getting desperate. He'd thought he would have time, but they were working around all the paperwork standing between him and his brother. "You know something's wrong. You have cop instincts. What are they telling you right now? Don't listen to the whole I have to do what my superiors say. You know damn well there's a time and a place to rebel. What's your gut saying?"

"My gut is saying the sooner we turn you over, the quicker we can get on with our lives," Marshall announced. "Look, it's right up ahead. What do you think they're going to do? Shoot us in broad daylight and take you away? I think someone will notice if we don't make it back."

They obviously didn't have vivid imaginations. He could see the CBI agent up ahead. He was parked slightly behind the abandoned building. It would give him some cover. "First of all, it's not broad daylight. It's twilight, and it'll be dark in moments. Second, he'll almost surely set it up so I'm the one who got hold of one of your guns and killed you as I fled the scene. Then he'll kill me unless my brother wants a word."

"You're paranoid." Marshall shrugged him off.

"He's desperate. He knows this is it," Knox argued as Marshall pulled into the parking lot. The CBI agent motioned for him to pull in further, until the squad car was next to his. And out of sight from the highway. "I'm sorry, Wyatt. You did the crime. You gotta pay for it."

"Don't get out," Wyatt warned. "I am begging you to drive to Creede. Do it there. If we're in front of the station, he can't kill you."

Knox rolled his eyes and opened the car door. "Agent Reese, it's good to see you again. We've got the suspect. He's been read his rights and is ready for transfer."

Agent Reese was a tall, thin man. A somewhat familiar man. He wore a suit today, his badge in clear view, but when he came to see Wayne, he was always more casual, always trying to hide his features with sunglasses and a ball cap.

Fuck and fuck. Worst-case scenario.

"He's on my brother's payroll." He had to try. He didn't like these guys, but he couldn't watch them die without trying to warn them.

Marshall sighed, a frustrated sound. "Sure he is. Give it up, man. It's over. You're not getting out of this."

Marshall stepped out of the car just in time for Agent Reese to pull a gun and shoot Knox right in the chest. Then he turned and popped two into Marshall's chest.

Wyatt felt sick.

"Come on, Wyatt." Another man moved around the squad car. Doug. His brother's enforcer was here. "You've got some explaining to do, son. I'm afraid you're needed in a meeting of the board."

So they wouldn't kill him. Not yet. He would be brought in for what his brother liked to call a trial. Oh, there would be no lawyers or real rules beyond what his brother says goes. There would be no appeals.

The door came open, and Wyatt felt a heavy hand haul him out. "Take the cuffs off him. We've got to make it look like he had a gun on him."

"His prints are on this one." Agent Reese held up the gun, and Wyatt noted the gloves he wore. "I think you'll find this is the gun he supposedly used when he murdered Dennis Hill. He gave it to his brother along with a fake body in exchange for his freedom. Guess what, your parole has been revoked, Wyatt. You've been a naughty boy."

It was worse than he'd feared. His brother was here, and he was going to make him pay. He stumbled, trying not to trip over Marshall Lethe's still body. Both he and Knox had fallen forward. He'd watched as Marshall had put a hand to his chest and gone face first onto the gravel.

"Hey, we need to move," Doug said. "Wayne wants us back. We'll make it look like Wyatt took them out and took you captive."

Agent Reese huffed. "I suppose he's going to beat the shit out of me."

"Well, someone is. Gotta make it look good," Doug vowed as he dragged Wyatt along. "As for you, kid, well, you shouldn't have fucked with the Horde. I think I'll put you out for transport. I'm not going to deal with the berserker again."

Wyatt tried to twist out of his hold but felt a sharp pain in his shoulder.

Drugs. Well, it wasn't like Doug didn't have access to a wide and varied supply.

The world started to go hazy. The next time he woke up he would be in hell.

* * * *

"What do you mean he didn't make it?" Sawyer ground the question out. His whole body had threatened to slump at Elisa's words.

Wyatt couldn't be dead. He couldn't. He'd promised Sabrina

they would all be okay. He couldn't let Wyatt be fucking dead.

"I mean Nate was already on the Creede side of Bliss. He made excellent time and Wyatt's not there, and Marshall and Knox stopped answering their radios a couple of minutes ago." Elisa's hand slipped back toward her gun belt as though she wanted to make sure it was still there. "He said the CBI requested they transfer the suspect at an offsite location. He and the Creede sheriff are heading there now."

"We've got big problems." Henry strode back up, his cell in hand. "I called a contact of mine at the CBI and she says she can't find a warrant for Wyatt's arrest. She found a file about Dennis Hill, but it's a missing persons report, not a homicide case. I gave her the name of the CBI agent the receptionist in Creede gave me, and she says he's under investigation with the department for possibly mishandling a couple of cases involving…you know who…"

"The Horde." Sawyer tightened his grip on Sabrina's hand. "They always have someone working for them."

Sabrina held on, but it was easy to see she'd switched to calm and collected mode. She wouldn't cry. Not now. She would save it for later, for when they were alone. For when they knew what the rest of their lives would be like. "Where would they have taken him? Do we think Marshall and Knox are in on it?"

"I would be surprised," Van said. "I've spent some time with them. They're cool, but they both have big feelings when it comes to rules and laws. They see the world in black and white, if you know what I mean. I would be surprised if they would toss out their whole belief system to get back at one man."

"One man who took what they wanted," Sawyer pointed out.

"I don't think they would risk losing their jobs," Elisa countered. "I've worked with them for months. They live to be cops. They wouldn't. I'm worried they've gotten in the middle of something they don't understand."

And it might cost them everything. He had to pray it didn't cost Wyatt. "We should alert highway patrol. Does the Creede station know what kind of car the CBI agent was driving?"

"I've got his name, and Cam is running his plates. We'll check the traffic and wildlife cams in the area just in case." Henry sounded smooth and competent. "We'll know more once Nate gets to the meet spot, but I'm afraid Wyatt will be gone."

"Not dead." Sabrina took a long breath. "His brother obviously knows he didn't kill Dennis Hill. He'll want that information."

"You should know I'm having Hill moved. If I found him, they potentially can. Though probably not. I don't think these guys are working with hackers on the level of ours," Henry explained. "Still, I can't risk the Horde finding him and taking out our best resource."

The Horde wouldn't merely kill him. They would hide him so no one could ask questions, and then they could control the narrative around Wyatt. He was sure there was some kind of plan in place for the CBI agent to get around the whole authorization issue. Or this was the CBI agent's way of paying his debt to the Horde and getting out.

So many debts made to a man who hurt so many people. "Do what you need to do, Henry, but hiding Dennis Hill won't help us find Wyatt. I assume your CBI contact can have someone watching the clubhouse in Colorado Springs?"

"Yes, but I don't think they'll risk taking him back there. It's a two-and-a-half-hour drive, and there are plenty of cams along the way," Elisa mused. "They'll want to question him someplace close by. How far out of town is this meet site?"

"Not far," Henry replied. "About fifteen minutes north of here. But you can't go. Let Nate do his job. I wouldn't want…"

His gaze trailed to Sabrina. Henry wouldn't want Sabrina to see what could have happened to Wyatt and the deputies. Sawyer didn't want it either. He glanced around. It was time to make some decisions. "I think it would be best if Elisa takes Sabrina to her place for a while."

Sabrina's eyes went wide, and she dropped his hand. "Not on your life."

"I was thinking more about yours and what Wyatt would do if he was the one standing here. I think he would try to get you somewhere safe." Sawyer couldn't stand the thought of fucking up and getting her hurt or killed. But he also hated the thought of choosing for her. Letting some man send her off for her own safety wasn't exactly who Sabrina was. It wasn't who he'd fallen in love with. "I owe it to Wyatt, don't I?"

"You need to figure out what you think is best. Wyatt isn't here. He's not the man I'm dealing with, and I don't want you sitting around wondering what he would do. Yes, he would try to send me away for my own good. It's the part of him I find least attractive."

There was a wealth of warning in those words. He needed to answer his woman properly or he would get his ass crated alongside Bella.

What would he do? He would let her choose. "What do you want to do, Teach? I'm worried about being so isolated here. We could move down to the valley and I would feel more comfortable. There are always people moving around the valley. And we would be close to your sister."

She studied him for a moment and then went on her toes, brushing her lips across his. "That sounds like a reasonable plan. I concur." She kissed him once more and stared up at him. "Thank you."

She was a part of the team. She was the best fucking part of the team. He would never sit her on the bench. "None needed. Go and pack a bag. I'll come in soon and grab Bella's food and her crate. Henry can give us a ride back down the mountain. I need to call and make sure Lark knows what's going on."

He would have her close the bar for the night. And for the immediate future. He wouldn't give Wayne a shot at his employees, and he was going to spend all his efforts to watch Sabrina and keep her safe. He mentally went through his accounts and felt like he could still pay them. For now.

Sabrina walked into the cabin.

"I think we should wait and escort you down," Elisa said. "You'll be safe in her cabin. Which apparently is also your cabin."

The rental. He'd almost forgotten about it. Her rental cabin was the reason they were here. He was going to have to thank the ghost.

He kind of hoped there wasn't a ghost.

"My grandfather owned several properties around town and ten cabins around the area," Sawyer explained. "In addition to the bar. I guess I hadn't realized how much work it really was until Wyatt took some of it off my shoulders."

He couldn't lose Wyatt.

"We're going to get him back," Elisa promised. "They won't kill him. Not until they figure out how to find Dennis Hill."

"Which they won't, and then they'll march back in and start

torturing him again." Henry moved to stand beside Elisa. "I know it sounds bad, but all we can care about now is that he's alive when we find him. If he's the man I think he is, he'll suffer through anything as long as it means getting back home. I should know. I've been in this position. I was the one with information someone wanted, and they didn't care how they got it. Watch Sabrina. They'll want her. She's the one who can get him talking."

"I'm shutting down until we're safe again." Every word Henry uttered made Sawyer think he was doing the right thing. He turned to Elisa. "But I'm going to ask you to keep me in the loop. Don't hide things from us. I want to help. I know these guys."

Elisa nodded, glancing back where Van and Hale were standing close to Poppy, both men watching the area around them.

She'd obviously trained them well. Elisa ensuring her men knew what to do was one of the reasons they would be safe in the valley. Everyone in the valley looked after each other. He loved his mountain home away from everyone, but it was good to know when he was vulnerable, he could shift down to the valley for a while and still be in a place he called home.

He wasn't alone. He could depend on these people. If he called Lucy or River or Ty they would come running to help him.

He totally fucking blamed Sabrina because this feeling welling inside of him had to be emotion, and he didn't have those. Or he didn't use to. Had it been meeting Sabrina that kicked him into rolling down this hill? Or had Wyatt been the one to start the slow roll to Emotion Town? He huffed because he knew where it had started.

When he hadn't been able to leave Bella behind. When he'd decided another creature's needs were slightly more important than his need to stay where he was, to hide in the numbness that had come with losing his grandfather and then his brothers leaving and not coming home. For years after, he'd taken refuge in his reputation, shoving anyone away because all people did was disappoint a man.

And then Bella had stared at him with those big innocent eyes, her tail half wagging like she wanted to think she'd found a good place with him but she couldn't quite believe it. It might have been the drooping tail wag that sealed his fate because something had opened in him when he'd taken her home.

A door. A door leading him to the future. A tiny crack Wyatt had pushed a little further, and Sabrina had blown the hinges off of.

Sometimes all it took to find your way out of darkness was a single crack of light.

Holy hell, he was never going to admit it to anyone but somehow his inner voice had gone all soft on him.

"We're going to find him, and I promise it's not going to take weeks," Elisa said with a certainty Sawyer didn't feel. "We've got all kinds of protocols in place for such an occasion. Nate's been worried about Wyatt since the first day he came into town."

The sheriff, it turned out, wasn't such an asshole. "He really does worry, doesn't he? This isn't some way to investigate him further or anything."

Henry's head shook. "It's not. We care about Wyatt because he's part of the community, and a pretty decent one from everything I've learned about him. And you, Sawyer. I know you've got it into your head you're the outcast of town, but it wasn't ever true."

Sawyer could see a lot more about himself now. It was probably the emotional maturity Sabrina had forced upon him. "I was ashamed. I was ashamed of that fucking tat and ashamed that after everything I went through, my brother still turned away from me. It was easier to distance than to face all those people who might see me as a criminal and not a dude trying to save his brother. So I made the decision for everyone. It was easier, I suppose."

Henry reached out and put a hand on his shoulder. "Of course it was, but it wasn't true. We did not blame you. Your friends let everyone know exactly what was going on. They never abandoned you."

Even after he'd left them. After he'd rejected their offers of companionship.

"I have good friends." He was not getting choked up. Not in any way. It was the weather.

"You do, and more of them than you can imagine," Henry said.

"I'm going to go see if Sabrina needs any help." Elisa stepped away, giving Sawyer a nod before she turned.

"I think moving spaces is a smart play." Henry glanced back, ensuring Poppy was still occupied. She was babbling at Bella while Hale and Van had taken up two different places on the porch, opposite ends where they could watch the road on either side. Van looked out to where most traffic came from—the highway. But if one was coming up from the valley there was a road that wound around the mountain and took the car to the other side. Hale watched that road. It was the one they and Henry had come in on.

"I might have to go further," Sawyer murmured. He didn't want anyone to hear his concerns and have it get back to Sabrina. "They will come after her. She is the person who can make him talk, and no one bought the lie he's not into her. I know I'm supposed to let her choose, but she can't comprehend what they can do to her. In this one case, I have to honor what Wyatt would want. I can't allow her to sacrifice herself for him. They would do…" He couldn't say the word, simply let it hang out there like the bomb it was, waiting to go off. "They would make Wyatt watch. It would break his soul."

"I understand, but I need you to understand Wyatt's soul isn't as fragile as you think," Henry replied. "He was smart enough to figure a way out. He's survived a lot. He can survive this. And if you and Sabrina need another place to stay, somewhere out of the state, perhaps, well, we have friends who can take you in."

He kind of hoped they were talking about that big bastard Taggart, who lived in Texas and knew a thing or two about protecting people. Taggart was kind of a sacred role model to Sawyer. He said the shittiest things, and people loved him for it. "We'll cross that bridge when we get to it. I should go and get Bella's stuff packed up. Let me know if you hear anything."

"Elisa has her radio," Van said as Sawyer started up the steps. "Nate will contact her as soon as he knows something. But he would definitely want us to move Sabrina and you to a safer location. You're too isolated up here if she's in danger. And good job on not getting your head taken off. For a minute I thought you were going to go all manly and order her to safety. Instead you explained and she agreed. I wish Elisa would take that class."

"You like her bossy," Hale said with a shake of his head.

"I do, actually," Van agreed with a grin and then he sobered. "I'm sorry about Wyatt. He's a good man. They'll find him."

Elisa walked back out. "Did Sabrina come this way? I didn't see her inside. She pulled out her suitcase, but it's sitting on the bed."

Shit. "Henry, Sabrina's missing. They must have gotten her

phone number off Wyatt. He had his cell in his pocket when they took him." There was only one reason Sabrina wasn't in the house and Bella wasn't barking her head off. Bella wouldn't have allowed anyone close. It had been his mistake to crate her earlier when they were making love to Sabrina. She couldn't see out the window from her crate. If she had been able to, she would have alerted them to the assholes who'd slashed his tires. Bella was looking up at him as though waiting for something. She wasn't worried or anxious. "They called her and threatened her and she's on her way to turn herself in."

Henry didn't question him, merely started working the case. "She wouldn't have come this way, and she's got to get to a road where they can pick her up. They likely wouldn't know about the path from the valley, so they'll have her run down to the highway."

An awful thought went through Sawyer's brain.

"Yeah, Nate, I think they might have my sister." Elisa's tone was solid, but Sawyer knew she was afraid. They moved around the house until they found the open window. Sabrina had pushed the screen out and jumped. The back door would have squeaked and Bella would have run around trying to figure out who was visiting. Sabrina had been smart and quiet, and he was going to spank her.

Now he stood at the top of the road, and there was no sign of her. He was about to take off when his cell rang. He thought about tossing the thing, but then he noticed the caller's name on the screen.

Wyatt Kemp.

Sawyer turned, sending Elisa a look he hoped told everyone to be quiet, the bad guys are on the line. He knew she'd understand in two seconds. "Wayne?"

Elisa stopped in her tracks and held a hand out toward Henry, who'd been too far behind to have heard.

A low, nasty chuckle came over the line. "See, I always knew you were smarter than you looked. Are you one of the assholes who helped my brother trick me?"

Henry was on his cell, likely trying to figure out if they could track anything at all about this call. Where were they? He didn't sound like he was on the road, but then he likely hadn't gone to capture Sabrina himself.

Sabrina. Fuck. He had to fight to breathe. "Yes, I did. You should tell me where you are so I can turn myself in."

"Just like that?" Wayne asked, suspicion plain in his voice. "You're not going to call in those friends of yours?"

Fuck. Wayne thought there was only one way to his place. He thought the road from the bar to his cabin was the only way to get here. He'd likely been watching the road and from what he knew, only the deputies had been up here.

He could use his reputation in this case. "I don't have friends, Wayne. You know it. I have Wyatt and I have her, and you have both of them. What did you threaten her with?"

He needed to get to wherever Sabrina had gone. Elisa and Henry could figure the rest of it out.

Because he did fucking have friends. He did belong in this weird community. He was the sarcastic bastard who showed up for everyone in the end. Every group needed one. He was it.

"What do you think? I didn't buy the you and Wyatt thing," Wayne said over the line. "I know my brother, and he's into women. So now I have his woman, but I'm thinking taking you in might save me some trouble. We can fix all of this, you know."

Oh, he knew how Wayne would fix it. Wayne would fix it by killing them all.

"I think that's an excellent idea. Where do you want me?" Sawyer asked.

"Come down the road with your hands up. If my men see even a hint of a weapon, you'll be the first one to die," Wayne said.

And Sawyer heard it. There was music playing in the background. Guns N' Roses. He'd had to put it in the jukebox for Taggart, and it had the slightest scratchiness to the sound since he had an old-school juke.

They were at Hell on Wheels.

His stomach churned. Lark and Sid were there. Gil would be there. He prayed they were okay.

"I'm on my way."

"Dump the cell, Sawyer," Wayne warned. "Wouldn't want people able to track you."

Sawyer hung up. They would almost certainly move, but for now Sawyer felt like they had the advantage again. He turned to Elisa and Henry. "They're at Hell on Wheels."

Henry nodded. "I'll let Nate know, and Elisa and I will follow."

Elisa pulled a gun from her utility belt. "Take this, Henry."

Henry's head shook, his hands coming up. "Oh, no. Nell and I have an ironclad agreement. I'm supposed to try to kill in an earth-friendly fashion. I'll use my hands. I'm good with them."

He kind of wished Henry would take the gun, but he'd heard stories. "I'm going to join them. If they're smart enough to watch the cameras, there's one out in the back. I haven't fixed it yet. It's near the bins. You crouch low enough and you can access the back door. It's almost never locked. Gil smokes too much. Hopefully my staff figured out what was going on and got into the office. It's like a safe room. I'll give Elisa the code."

"Uh, have we forgotten the kiddo?" Van asked. "Maybe I should go in Henry's place."

Because the thought of being murdered by MC riders was apparently nicer than being left to take care of Poppy Flanders.

"Let her watch TV," Henry said, starting for the side of the road. "She never gets to and she's fascinated. And no sugar. I'm serious, guys. She turns into a monster. Good luck."

Henry stepped back, and Sawyer would have sworn the man disappeared into the foliage. Elisa followed him but he could still get a hint of her.

He tossed his cell and jogged down the road.

It was time to save his family.

Chapter Nineteen

Sabrina was crying by the time she made it to the bottom of the road. She was still waiting for the sound of Sawyer running after her, but the road was eerily quiet behind her.

Twilight had deepened to night, but there was still enough light for her to follow the road.

All she could see was the photo they'd sent her. She might never get it out of her head. She'd gotten to the bedroom and hauled out her suitcase, and then her phone had dinged.

Wyatt. It had been from Wyatt's number, and she'd known not to answer. Deep down there had been the instinct to treat the phone like it was a hot potato. She should have given it to her sister or Sawyer, but she hadn't. She'd prayed it was really Wyatt.

It hadn't been a call. It had been a text, complete with photographic proof they had Wyatt and could kill him at any moment.

The order had been plain. Come to Hell on Wheels. Don't bring anyone or we'll slit his throat.

They'd had a knife against Wyatt's vulnerable neck, and she couldn't tell if he was awake or unconscious.

She'd panicked. Her hands had been shaking as she'd written a quick note on the notepad on the nightstand. **Come to HOW. Bring**

cops. Nothing more. Had he even found the note? She should have texted, but if she had hesitated for even a few more seconds and Wyatt died, she wouldn't be able to live with herself.

He had to find that note.

She was stupid. Even as she heard someone moving in front of her, she knew she was in so much trouble.

Would Sawyer ever forgive her? Would he even try to understand?

Would it matter because she was pretty sure she was about to die.

Why was it so dark?

She held up her hands as she managed to make her way to the gravel covering the parking lot for the bar, which usually lit up the night, but someone had turned off the big neon sign and all the outdoor lights. She could still see the warm glow coming from inside, but it was quiet. Too quiet.

"Keep those hands up," a deep voice said.

It took everything Sabrina had not to jump when the man touched her. He wasn't alone. A large man in jeans, a black T, and a leather vest moved in front of her.

"Stay calm," the big guy advised. "No one's going to hurt you."

"Not yet," the asshole behind her said as he slid his hands over her sides as though looking for weapons they all knew she didn't have. This was intimidation.

And perhaps a promise of things to come.

She was here to get Wyatt to talk. Sabrina bit her bottom lip as the jerk slid his hands over her ass. Sawyer had told her. He'd explained all of this to her, and she'd still run without thinking. She'd still put them in this position, and he would be right to never talk to her again. She was going to get them all killed.

She gritted her teeth as the asshole's hands came up under her breasts.

"I don't think she's got any weapons on her," the man said, and she could smell liquor on his breath. "But I could check some more. You sure she took down a couple of men? I heard a rumor."

"She did not," came the terse reply. "She's just some dumb bitch Wyatt's fucking. Get her inside."

She winced as she finally recognized the man who'd called her a bitch. She had taken him down with a stun gun and likely didn't want anyone to hear that particular story again. "I'd like to see Wyatt."

She was here, and she had to calm down. Panic had gotten her into this terrible situation. Calm and logic would be her tools to get out. To get both of them out. Sawyer would work it from the outside, but she couldn't stand the thought of Wyatt being all alone with the wolves.

"You'll see him soon enough," the guy said, taking her arm.

She was jerked back and nearly stumbled as he dragged her along.

What shape was Wyatt in? Was he conscious or would she have to try to protect him while he was vulnerable?

She would do her best. She would give him as much time as she possibly could because Sawyer would figure this out. He would come looking for her, check her phone, and know what she'd done. Then he would call in everyone. Once he figured out they were here at the bar. Elisa would wait for backup and then come in, and her sister and Sawyer would save them.

The door to the bar opened, and she was hauled in.

The bar where she'd made her stand and claimed her men was now taken over with Wyatt's worst nightmare. The jukebox was playing an old Guns N' Roses song, and there were burly men shooting pool on the table where she'd... Well, they probably didn't want to know how she'd christened that particular pool table. They were drinking beers, and she caught sight of Lark moving through them.

Lark's eyes widened as they hauled Sabrina in. She gave Sabrina a shake of her head which Sabrina decided meant she wanted them to think they didn't know each other.

"Sit." The guy pulled out a chair and shoved her down. "The boss is making a call. He'll be with you in a minute. Hey, waitress. This one needs a drink. We need to loosen up for what we're going to do to her."

The other asshole winked down. "Don't try to leave, darlin'. We'll have to punish Wyatt if you do, and I don't think he can take much more."

Sabrina's heart threatened to seize but she sank down to the chair.

"What the fuck, Sabrina?" Lark leaned over, her voice going low, and then she spoke as she normally would. "What can I get for you? Mostly I want to pour the pickle juice we keep over your head, bitch. We'll see you get what's coming to you for taking my man."

Uh, it seemed like she should be the one asking what the fuck. Lark had never once come off like she was into Sawyer. Sabrina hadn't been around her much, but she'd seemed sisterly toward Sawyer. Annoyed sister most of the time.

Was Lark working with them?

How far did the betrayal go? How would Sawyer handle it? His staff were the only people in the world he truly trusted outside of Wyatt and herself. Would this send him right back into the cage he'd built? Or would her running have already made him decide none of this was worth the heartache?

"I'm sorry." She wasn't sure what to say, but Lark seemed to require a response. "I didn't know he was yours."

Lark glared down at her. "Yeah, well, you should have asked, rich girl."

Rich girl? Lark knew she was a schoolteacher. It wasn't like they were known for their free-flowing cash. "What the..."

Lark slapped her and pushed her back, the chair she was in hitting the concrete floor hard. Pain arced through her, but she'd managed to keep her head up. In the background she could hear the men starting to take bets, chuckling about whores and skanks and how this was the way women were. Lark was on top of her, and Sabrina put out her arms to ward off the attack.

"Scream," Lark whispered directly in her ear. "When I lift my head, you scream and don't move your right leg too much. I slipped you something. Scream, Sabrina. Now."

Sabrina pushed at Lark and screamed. "Get this crazy bitch off me."

For some reason Lark wanted them to fight. Wanted to hide what she was about to do. As Sabrina halfheartedly pushed at Lark, the waitress got one good smack in before she got carted off Sabrina.

She didn't have to pretend to be shocked. She still wasn't sure what had happened, but she felt something against her right thigh. Lark had shoved something into the deep pocket of her skirt. Something hard and maybe metal.

A knife. Lark had given her a small knife, likely a paring knife she would use to slice limes and lemons for drinks.

A shot. That was what Lark had given her.

"Sorry." A big man came into view. A man who looked like a rougher, older version of Wyatt. "I didn't realize that little honey was so mean. Guess she was serious. I thought cash would buy me a couple of Sawyer's employees, but it turns out she just wants revenge."

She wanted none of the kind, but Lark was smart and resourceful, and she would do what it took to survive. If she complied, she bought herself and the others time.

Where were the others?

"Did you pay off the rest of the staff? Sawyer's going to be so betrayed." The last bit was tossed Lark's way.

"Well, he picked you over me, so I don't care." Lark could have been an actress. Or there was some truth to what she was saying. Sabrina wasn't sure. She only knew Lark was playing a role, and that meant Sabrina had one, too.

Wyatt's brother offered her a hand up. She wanted to spit in the man's face, but was Lark trying to tell her something? To be the opposite of what they were expecting? Wayne hadn't seen her, and from what she'd heard from her sister the men she'd taken down denied it. None of them wanted to think a schoolteacher could hurt them.

So she was going to play into all their stereotypes.

She let her fear show through, putting a shaking hand in Wayne's. When he gently hauled her up, she made sure to shift to her left in case he could see anything. The skirt was one of her longer, more voluminous ones, and it was a darker color so she might be able to pull this off. "Thank you. I didn't know. I'm not the kind of woman who would try to steal someone's man."

Wayne had a bushy beard with hints of gray sliding between the honey color of his hair. He picked up her chair and offered it to her, sitting down across from her. "Well, for what it's worth I don't think old Sawyer there ever gave the girl a ride. I'm pretty sure the attraction is all one sided, but I know how to use an advantage when I find one. She was the only one who didn't run. Did you know Sawyer's got the equivalent of a safe room in his office?"

She hadn't spent much time in the bar, so she shook her head, relief flooding her because it meant the others were safe. "I didn't. I've only been with Wyatt and Sawyer for a few days."

But they'd been serious days. They'd been days spent wholly in each other's company, days where she was wrapped up in them while the world outside didn't matter. She didn't need years to know these were the men for her.

"So you're not pretending." Wayne stared as she took the seat he'd offered. "My brother thought he could get me to believe it was Sawyer he was interested in."

"He was trying to protect me." If there was one thing she wanted this man to believe, it was that he'd been smart to take her. If he didn't think she could help, he would get rid of her. He needed to believe she was the only person in the world who could get Wyatt to talk.

And then she would take as much pain as she had to until Sawyer found a way to save them.

Wayne turned his chair around and straddled it, staring at her like he was trying to figure her out.

She was too calm. She needed to let some of her fear show. She sniffled. "Can I see him?"

"What the hell do you see in Wyatt? Is it the schoolteacher thing? Men aren't attracted to you and so the one who shows interest gets all your attention?"

Sure. Because men didn't have schoolteacher fantasies. Yeah. She reached out for a napkin, dabbing at her eyes. "I love Wyatt. I fell in love with him, and Sawyer was part of the deal."

The last thing she wanted was the dude to decide getting Sawyer was a good idea.

"You prefer my brother over Sawyer?" Wayne asked.

She loved them both equally. It was odd because she could no longer see one of them without the other. "Sawyer is handsome, but he's not my type. Wyatt is sweet and cares about the people around him. Sawyer can be a selfish prick, but he's good in bed. Wyatt and I are going to leave him. Wyatt thought he owed Sawyer, but I think we've more than repaid him. We were going to tell him once we found a place to live."

Best to let him think Sawyer didn't matter at all.

"You listening, big guy?" Wayne looked over his shoulder toward the side entrance. "You tore down that mountain like she means something to you and guess what? She was playing you to get to little brother."

Sawyer was here. Two big men were on either side of him, his hands together in front of him bound by a zip tie they'd definitely gotten too tight. Her heart sank. What had happened? He'd heard her say shitty things, and it would ruin them. And she couldn't take them back without making them even more vulnerable.

"Yeah, I heard." There was a dull note to Sawyer's tone that made her ache. "I should have known. I guess I didn't think Wyatt would do that to me."

Wayne pushed his chair back and stood. "You don't know my brother the way you think you do. My brother is a traitor. He's a liar. He cheats. He's not the kind of man you risk everything for."

But he was, and so was Sawyer.

"I don't suppose you can let me go and we'll call it all even?" Sawyer asked. "I have zero problems marching right back up to my cabin and putting them both out of my mind."

"Sure. And you wouldn't call anyone," Wayne mused. "You should know I took out the phone lines and have a cell phone jammer working now. Your safe room isn't going to help."

"Well, I don't see the rest of my employees here, so it must have done something," Sawyer said with a smirk.

"Yeah, they're locked in," Wayne admitted, "but they can't get a message out. I made sure of it. As for letting you go and brood over the fact that no one's ever going to want you as part of their family, I'm going to have to pass. I will admit, I thought bringing you in might help. I wasn't sure the lady here is going to be able to take as much pain as I'm going to need to inflict in order to get my brother to talk. I thought you might be an extra go to when it comes to torture, but it seems he wants you out of the way."

"I love you, Sawyer. You don't have to be with her," Lark said.

Sawyer's eyes widened in obvious surprise. "Really?"

"I'll take care of Sawyer." Lark nodded Wayne's way. "I mean it feels like you owe me for not giving you trouble."

Wayne stalked over to her. "Not making you part of the torture is payment for what I owe you. See, my brother has many flaws, and one of them is caring too much. I was thinking about starting with you and seeing if I even have to bring out the big guns."

Lark had overplayed her hand.

"Hey, you don't have to do any of this," Sawyer said, pulling slightly away.

That was when he suddenly had a gun leveled at his face, and it took everything Sabrina had not to throw herself in front of him. Wayne moved in, stepping beside his guard. The whole place had hushed though the jukebox was still going. It felt like everything slowed down, and she reached for the knife.

"Stop," Wayne said. "This isn't the time to start shooting, boys. Sawyer, you want to tell me what you know about Dennis Hill?"

Sawyer's expression went blank. "No idea. It happened long after I left the Horde."

"Ah, but you still had influence over my brother, didn't you?" Wayne Kemp hissed the question out. "You were still talking to him."

"We played games online sometimes," Sawyer admitted. "But Wayne, if you think I invited that little asshole to show up on my doorstep, you're wrong. I liked living alone. I wasn't looking for a kid brother. I've had enough of those in my life. And you need to seriously think about what can happen when you hurt her. You haven't done your due diligence when it comes to her kidnapping. You know she's the schoolteacher, but you didn't connect her to Deputy Leal? You honestly think you're going to kill a cop's sister and they'll let you get away with it? Wright will take exception, and he'll have more firepower behind him than you can imagine. They won't be satisfied until they burn down everything you care about."

"I don't believe a word of it. Bliss is a town of hippies and perverts," Wayne said with a shake of his head. "They're just good at mythmaking. And I'll handle Wright if I need to. He's been out of the DEA for too long. He's nothing but a fat cat who spends half his time fishing."

Okay, well, some of that was true. At least according to her sister. What was Sawyer trying to do beyond irritate the hell out of the man they should be trying to soothe? "He's not going to hurt us. He won't have to. I'm sure Wyatt is going to tell him what he needs to know."

And then he would kill Wyatt, but she was buying time.

"Sabrina, he doesn't know anything," Sawyer said, enunciating each word like she was a child who didn't understand.

They were past this now. "I don't know what he knows, but if he knows something, he'll tell his brother."

"Well, we should find out." Wayne gestured toward Sabrina. "Bring him over here. I want them both in one place. Lark, another round. I'm afraid you're going to have to settle for no one else having your man. I don't think he'll survive the afternoon."

Lark sniffled but turned and went back behind the bar.

Sawyer was shoved Sabrina's direction, two big men forcing him down into the chair. They stepped back.

"Now go and wake up my asshole brother," Wayne said, smiling like this was all one big party and he was having the time of his life. Lark brought him a bottle of beer, and he tipped it Sabrina's way as the two giant assholes walked toward the back of the building. "Tonight, the Horde accepts payments for the debts of my brother."

A cheer went up, and the Horde started partying. They'd brought a couple of women with them. At least Sabrina hoped they weren't women who got caught in the bar. They seemed perfectly comfortable with a bunch of men treating them like blow-up dolls.

"We're going to have to do such a deep clean."

She could barely hear Sawyer over the loud music but he sounded...not how she'd thought he would. Anxiety pounded at her. She wasn't sure who she should be more worried about, and then there was the horrible things Sawyer had heard. She leaned over as far as she dared. There were still eyes on them. The fact that they gave them some space basically told Sabrina they didn't think they had a chance if they tried to run.

Wyatt definitely wouldn't have a chance.

"I didn't mean it," she whispered Sawyer's way.

He leaned over. "Didn't? I can't hear you, babe. I'm serious, though. What just happened on the back pool table? I don't think we can use it anymore."

Why was he talking about this? "Sawyer, I didn't mean it."

"But I do. We're going to have to clean," he practically shouted before leaning in again and his voice going low. "Henry's here. So is your sister. Hang tight."

Henry? They couldn't get Nate? "I left a note. You didn't find it?"

"I don't know about a note, babe. Keep calm," Sawyer whispered.

Sabrina took a deep breath and vowed to do whatever it took to get them out of here.

* * * *

Wyatt lay on the floor, the concrete cold under his cheek, but it barely registered compared to the throbbing in his head.

That asshole had hit him, but not before he'd murdered two police officers and probably made it so it would look like it was him. Everyone would believe it. No one would want to believe the former MC member over a trusted law enforcement officer.

It was so fucked up, and the only thing he could be slightly happy about was Sawyer had Sabrina, and he wouldn't let her out of his sight. Sabrina would be safe no matter what. Sawyer would make sure of it.

Where the hell was he?

"Keep it down, buddy," a low voice said. "I think if they don't turn on the lights, they might mistake me for the guy I killed. Sawyer keeps a surprisingly clean supply room. I'm going to mention to Nell he's using very earth-friendly products. I always knew he was a good man hiding behind a wall of misanthropy."

Yeah, his head hurt, and he wasn't sure what Henry Flanders was saying. And why was Henry Flanders in Sawyer's supply closet, and why did it seem like there was some kind of dance party going on outside? Every muscle he had ached. He opened his eyes, trying to let them adjust to the low light, and the first thing he saw was a foot. Like a dead foot. At least it looked like it wasn't going to be moving again.

Despite his unusual upbringing, he hadn't been around a ton of dead bodies. It freaked him out, and he shoved himself up, palms flat on the floor.

"Oh, sorry. Thought I got him wholly behind the paper products," Henry said with a low chuckle as he dragged the dead dude back so Wyatt couldn't see him. "He's a slippery fucker.

Sometimes I wish rigor mortis set in earlier. Of course other times it happens way too fast like the time I had to stuff a Russian operative into a suitcase. It was rough going. How are you?"

"I don't... What's happening?" The last thing he'd known he was being taken to his brother. Now he was at Hell on Wheels. And he might throw up.

"Okay, I've got to be quiet because I'm pretty sure they're going to be in here any minute, unless your brother is a monologuing son of a bitch, and then we've got some time." Henry knelt down, and Wyatt could see he'd put on the guard's leather vest. He was roughly dressed the way the other man had been, so he did have a shot if no one looked too closely. "Nate is on his way, but he's got to be careful because of the hostages. Elisa and I are in the building. We came in where the security cams are down. She's making her way to the office where she hopes the employees took shelter when they realized what was happening."

Happening? What was happening? "We're at Hell on Wheels?"

He asked the question despite knowing the answer. It was all around him. He was in the supply closet, and they were talking about Sawyer's beloved bar being taken over by his brother and a bunch of criminal assholes.

Sawyer was never going to forgive him. Sawyer loved this bar. It connected him to his grandfather. It was his hiding place from the world.

Henry winced and moved in closer, his voice barely above a whisper. "Yes, we're at Hell on Wheels. From what I can tell in the brief time I've been here, I believe Wayne thinks everyone is going to be so freaked out by you not showing up in Creede they won't think to look here. He's going to see what he can get out of you in the next hour or so, and then there's an SUV coming to transport you back to Colorado Springs."

So his brother intended to spend some quality time with him, likely in one of the Horde's many safe houses. He would be too smart to take him to the club house. Sabrina and Sawyer would look for him starting there.

"They took my cuffs off." He wasn't sure why he pointed out something Henry could easily see himself.

"Yes, they likely left them behind at the scene of the crime,"

Henry said grimly as he moved to the door of the large closet. It was at the back of the building across from the office where he prayed everyone had gone and locked themselves in. The door was secure, and when they felt like it was safe, they could find the hidden ladder leading to the roof.

Sawyer's grandfather had told Sawyer he liked sitting on the roof and watching the stars, but Wyatt thought the old guy also liked to have a way out.

He hoped Lark and Sid and Gil had taken it.

It was supposed to be a slow night, a night where they could likely close shop early.

He'd fucked it up for everyone.

"I guess the deputies are dead." Despite the fact they hadn't liked him or listened to him, he felt guilt at the thought of their murders. They'd tried to do the right thing. They just hadn't understood how his brother's world worked and that right meant shit here.

Henry eased open the door, stealing a peek outside. "No idea. Nate hadn't gotten to the scene before my cell dropped out. I think they've got a jammer somewhere. It's not a great one. Not much range, but it'll do the job in here."

He wasn't worried about his cell. "They shot the deputies, so I don't hold much hope. Why are you here, Henry?"

"Because I was the closest one, and I couldn't let Elisa go in without backup. Van offered but he's not much of a... How do I politely say the dude would get killed? Because he would. I'm honestly a little worried about Elisa, but at least she's got training. I told her not to fire unless she absolutely has to. I'd rather get all the hostages out before the gunfire starts."

"No gunfire," Wyatt said, struggling to his feet. "Henry, you have to let me distract my brother. While he's paying attention to me, you can get the staff out."

Henry stepped back into the shadows, his eyes on the tiny slit where the door wasn't quite closed. "I'm not worried about the staff. And you know the term is torture. Not attention. But I believe you, Wyatt. I believe you would do whatever it takes to save a couple of people you haven't known for very long. I'm an excellent judge of character, and I've always known you're a good guy."

He wasn't so sure, but Henry was right about one thing. He

wasn't leaving the staff to pay for his mistakes. Sawyer had them trained. They would have gotten to the office and locked themselves in. And that meant Elisa was going to...what? Knock? "The staff would go to the office and put it in lockdown. Elisa can't get in."

"She's already in," Henry replied. "Sawyer gave her the code before we came down the mountain to save you and Sabrina. Elisa's going to wait until she can get them up on the roof and maybe out of here. Van should have called Nate by now and warned him about where we are. It won't take long for Nate to figure out they've got jammers and hostages. I'd like to hand over as many to Nate as I can before this thing goes down. I overheard this asshole confirming someone from the MC will be here with a suitably large vehicle they can transport you across the state in. It better be big. Not that we're going to allow them to take you."

There was something about what Henry said that caught Wyatt's attention, but then a spike of pain went through his brain. "Is that what we're waiting for? A driver? And how about you do a guy a solid and you give me your gun and then get the hell out of here. You're a dad. This is dangerous."

"So is fatherhood, and I don't have a gun, son." He held his hands up. "I promised my wife if I had to kill anyone else, I would use my hands. A knife is acceptable if I can't do the deed in the neatest way possible. But if she asks, you remember me talking to him and asking him if he wants to reconsider his life choices. I offered him help, right?"

Nell was a woman of mysterious ways. In this he would absolutely back up Henry. "I don't think he would have been swayed... He wasn't swayed by your logical and kind arguments as to why he should give up his life of crime. But a gun really would help."

A rowdy shout went through the bar, and he wondered if the entire Horde was here. It slightly shook the floors. They were happy about something. Most likely his upcoming torture.

"Sorry," Henry offered. "But I promise we're going to get you out of this. Nate won't let them get away. Unlike your brother, Nate knows all the roads. There won't be anywhere to go. Gosh. I should have texted Van about the babysitting rules. I worry she's going to get hungry and Van will give her a ham sandwich, and then she's almost certainly going to break her mother's heart and become a rabid carnivore. What was I thinking?"

Henry was questioning his parenting choices, but Wyatt would rather know why he'd come into a den of vipers without so much as a gun. And he'd managed to take out the man who'd earned the nickname Brutus. Bru was a nasty piece of work. "Are you sure he's dead? And how exactly do you kill a man quietly with your bare hands? I would think a fight like that would attract attention even though they've got the music too loud."

In Wyatt's experience, fighting was a loud thing. It was something that took time and spent blood, and he didn't see a drop of Brutus's on the floor or on Henry.

Henry turned to him, a serious expression on his face. "I know you think I'm a mild-mannered dad, but I haven't always been. The CIA operative is still in here, though he's happily controlled through love and sex. John Bishop gets to come out to play when things go wrong. You assume he even knew I was here before I got my hands on his head, twisted in the exact right way, and internally decapitated him. He didn't have a chance to scream or fight or even pray to whatever god he worships. He threatened my town, and I took him out. I do not need a gun, Wyatt, and you don't have to worry about me. I assure you I've seen and dealt more death than you can imagine."

Okay, Henry was scary as shit when he wanted to be. He was glad he wasn't Van because he probably would give that kid a ham sandwich.

But something Henry had said finally sank in. "What do you mean save Sabrina? Sabrina's already safe. Sawyer would have made sure of it. Why would someone need to save Sabrina?"

Henry sighed. "Because when she went in to gather her things, apparently she got a call or a text from your brother and it scared her enough she took off without asking Sawyer's opinion. The good news? Your brother has no idea Elisa and I were even there, so we've got the element of surprise on our side."

Panic threatened to overtake him. The only fucking reason he'd been calm at all had been the fact that he knew Sabrina and Sawyer were safe. If Sabrina was here… "Tell me he stayed behind. Tell me he's waiting for Nate."

Henry stepped over the mop bucket. "Of course he didn't. Wayne asked him to turn himself in and he did. He's out there watching over Sabrina and waiting for us to make a move."

A move? A move could cost Sabrina her life. It could cost her everything, and it would be all Wyatt's fault.

"Hey, calm down." Henry's tone was low and soothing, sounding more like the man who normally wore Birkenstocks and sold his zucchini bread at the weekend market in town. "They are fine right now, and we're going to ensure they stay fine. Sabrina came because she couldn't stand the thought of being the reason you died. Sawyer came because he loves you both, though he'll never say it. So let him believe he came down and offered to sacrifice himself because he thought it was rude he would get left out of the torture. The point is, they need you calm and rational."

How the fuck was he supposed to...

Breathe.

It was the first thing Alexei Markov had taught him.

Breath is essential. It's a safe space for us to go to when the world overwhelms us. Breathing recenters our focus. Allows us to calm the central nervous system.

Four seconds in. Hold for six. One. Two. Three. Four. Five. Six. Exhale for eight.

And again.

"Good. Keep it up," Henry whispered. "But I'm going to need you on the floor like you're still passed out. Someone's coming. We're out of time. Please stay calm, Wyatt."

He didn't want to. He wanted to let the psychotic asshole who lived inside him out so he didn't have to deal with this. The psycho didn't care about anything but his own survival.

Except the psycho loved Sabrina, too. The psycho was fighting because she needed him.

He dropped to his knees. Breathing. One. Two. Three. Four. Hold. The part of himself that fought and fought had been essential when he'd been alone. When he was the only one fighting, the piece of himself that wanted so badly to survive came out to protect him. He wasn't some enemy to fight. He was part of Wyatt, and the piece of himself had figured out he wasn't alone anymore and he had to be the best partner he could be.

Exhale for eight.

He heard the door open, and the light got flipped on. When the door opened the music blasted through the small space, and he could hear the raucous party. His brother thought he could get away with all of this because no one would come for him. Because in his brother's mind he was useless and weak, and so were all the people in the town down below the mountain. They wouldn't care what went on up here because Wayne never once gave a shit about his neighbors. He was treating Bliss like it was a Horde world and everyone lived in it.

Wyatt had learned the citizens of Bliss made their own rules.

Another breath and he let his whole body go limp. He was vulnerable but it was okay because he trusted Henry Flanders and his apparently deadly hands. Shit. He was putting his and Sabrina's and Sawyer's lives into the hands of a man who spent most of his time with a baby strapped to his chest. And sometimes he wore socks with the Birkenstocks. Breathe.

"Hey, Bru, it's time to bring the…"

He heard a snap and then a big body fell to the floor beside him. Wyatt flipped over in time to miss his brother's now dead enforcer falling on him. But that asshole hadn't come alone. Wyatt got a great view of Murphy standing in front of Henry Flanders.

"You're not Brutus," Murphy said, a sneer on his face. He pointed a gun Henry's way. "Who the fuck are you?"

Henry didn't reply, merely knocked the gun to the side and brought the heel of his palm up, striking Murphy's nose. Another crunch sounded through the space and then Murphy too slid to the floor, his eyes glazing over.

"What the fuck was that?" Wyatt got to his feet. They probably had a couple of minutes. They would expect Murphy to wake him up. Probably why the other guy had been carrying a cattle prod.

"I broke his nose in such a way it sent cartilage into his brain and killed him," Henry explained matter of factly. "But see, no blood. Cleaning blood requires an enormous amount of water and cleaners, and some people use bleach which is going to end up in the ground water. But this way, no mess. Earth friendly."

He wasn't about to debate which type of killing was best for climate change. He did, however, pick up the cattle prod the asshole had expected to use on him.

"Oh, you should totally get the gun," Henry explained, shrugging out of the vest like he didn't need it anymore. He was willing to show his true face to Wyatt's brother. He pointed to Murphy's body. "He's got two on him. You might pick up the other one and give it to Sawyer if you can. I know he can shoot, and I don't think Sabrina cares how he kills the people who are after him."

He wasn't wrong. "The cattle prod is for Sabrina. I'm not sure if I'm going to give it to her so she can defend herself or use it on her because she shouldn't be here and she knows it."

Let Henry do with that what he would. Wyatt had a few dark secrets, too.

"I think cattle prod is pretty advanced. Sabrina is probably still getting used to spankings. You should start out with a violet wand if you want to try electricity play," Henry replied as though he'd been talking about something perfectly normal.

Such a weird place, and he wanted it for his home.

"Could we stop talking about my sister's sex life and get this party started?" a familiar voice asked. Elisa stood in the doorway, staring down the hall, though she spoke to Wyatt and Henry. "I took out the jammer. Nate knows where we are, and he's on his way. I sent Sid and Gil up to the roof, but they're super worried about Lark. She stayed so they had a chance to get to the office."

"How far behind is Nate?" Henry asked, flexing his hands as though readying them for battle.

"He's ten minutes out," Elisa replied.

"It's too long." Wyatt knew his brother. "We can't take down the Horde with a couple of guns and Henry's hands."

"Oh, he can kick people, too," Elisa assured him. "Henry's solid."

"Against how many? In a small space?" Wyatt needed to point out all the problems with the three of them running without backup.

Henry frowned. "It's less likely. Did you check the security cams? How many are we up against?"

Elisa's jaw tightened. "I think they brought most of their members. It's at least fifteen, and I'm pretty sure there's more coming, though they should get here after Nate."

"So I need to hold them off for ten minutes." Wyatt took another long breath. This would be the performance of a lifetime, and if he didn't sell it, they could all die.

"Wyatt, they want to kill you," Elisa pointed out quietly. "Aren't they going to question how you got out?"

"My brother knows I have skills, and he'll believe his guys can fuck up. And yes, they want to kill me, but first they want to cause me pain. I'm going to make sure I take the pain and not your sister." He needed a plan. "Cut the power when Nate gets here. That way I'll know when the bullets are going to fly and I can cover Sabrina. Henry, get to Lark. She won't know what's coming."

"Are you sure? Your brother is angry," Henry said.

"My brother is always angry." He'd been born with a rage inside him, and getting him even angrier would likely spare Sabrina and Sawyer. His head still ached, but he couldn't hide away. This was a job only he could do.

Face the monster who'd never bothered to hide under the bed. Wayne had been the monster in his life since he'd been old enough to take a beating. When he'd displeased their father, Wayne had been the one to serve his punishment. His father had said it was because one day Wayne would be Wyatt's president, and he should get used to doling out the punishments no matter who it was to.

"Thank you, Wyatt," Elisa said as he passed her by. "I promise I'll cut the power the minute Nate gets here. He's coming in without lights or sirens because he doesn't want to tip your brother off, so don't expect to know ahead of time. I'm pretty sure he's bringing most of the Creede department with him. They're pissed."

Because two of their officers were down, and Nate had apparently made them believe it wasn't Wyatt's fault. Or they would arrest him and he would start this whole cursed night all over again.

Henry stopped him, his eyes going down to the cattle prod in his hands. "I think you have to go out there without weapons. If you're stalling, you need to give them not a single reason to open fire. Are you sure they're going to believe you could take those men out on your own? If not, then we might need to just use the element of surprise. They're not expecting us."

"I have a certain reputation," Wyatt said, his gut clenching, but he knew Henry was right. If he took the cattle prod, or worse, one of the guns with him, they would take him out quickly, and Sabrina could get caught in the cross fire. He handed the weapon over. "I assure you, my brother knows I can perform violent acts when I need to."

Breathe.

He started down the hall.

Sometimes he could hear his father telling him he was nothing. Wyatt was too weak to be his son. He wouldn't survive and he shouldn't because he was as useless as a daughter. A daughter, he'd been told, could at least be married off to gain something for the club.

But he heard other voices now as he forced himself to take each step.

He heard Sabrina telling him she loved him.

Sawyer telling him they're brothers. Though grudgingly.

He heard Alexei telling him he did not have to follow the life script handed to him at birth. Alexei had told him how brave he'd been to break free, to have taken all the abuse and still be a decent, loving human being.

Because he was unbreakable.

Four in. Hold for six. Exhale for eight.

He could do this.

But his performance had to be good. He knew exactly what would catch his brother's attention.

He stumbled the last of the way to the main floor. For the briefest moment, no one saw him, but he was able to take in the scene in front of him. Lark was behind the bar. Good. He hoped she stayed there. Sabrina and Sawyer were seated at a table in the middle of the room. Where anyone could get to them. It wasn't ideal, but he had to trust Sawyer would know what to do.

Sabrina's eyes came up and lit on him, widening as she started to stand, but Sawyer reached out and caught her arm. His hands were in zip ties but at least they weren't behind his back. His brother wasn't as by the book as the deputies had been, and Wyatt hoped it was about to cost him.

Wyatt watched as Sabrina's hand went into the pocket of her skirt, showing him the hilt of what he prayed was a knife. It didn't look large, but it would get Sawyer's hands free.

If the crowd was distracted.

"Wayne Kemp," Wyatt yelled out.

The whole place went still, and sure enough every eye turned his way. He hoped he looked pathetic. He knew there was blood on his shirt. It was sticky where he'd bled from the head wound.

His brother moved from the pool table, hands on his hips as he stared at Wyatt. "Where the hell are Murphy and Kick?"

He hadn't known the other guy. "I killed them. And I'm going to kill you."

Wyatt started for his brother and prayed they all survived the experience.

Chapter Twenty

Sawyer watched with a tight gut as Wyatt stalked toward his brother. His friend looked like hell, with blood staining his shirt and a defined bump on his head. Also matted with blood.

Wyatt had killed two men? Had he lost it? He didn't look like he had. Sawyer had seen Wyatt's dark part many times, and this wasn't it. He appeared calmer than he'd ever seen him in a situation like this. His eyes were clear, and he looked over at Sabrina as though telling Sawyer silently what he wanted him to do.

Save her.

He would if she would freaking let him. They were going to have such a talk after this was over. Stef was right. He was going to slap a collar around her neck and follow her constantly because she was trouble. So much fucking trouble. Her ass was going to learn the word trouble.

"Sure you are, little brother," Wayne said with a derisive chuckle. "I'm also pretty sure you didn't kill anyone. You're too calm to kill anyone. You can't do it on your own. Did you give them the slip? I'm surprised."

Sabrina leaned over, her hand coming out to touch his thigh.

He cautiously glanced down and saw she held a paring knife. He was pretty sure it was Lark's. She was particular about knives and always complained about the state of the ones in the bar. So Lark was playing along like Sabrina was. Good. The women were smart.

"Well, head down there and count the bodies, asshole," Wyatt challenged.

Did Wyatt know he was being surrounded? The other members of the Horde were circling like a pack of wolves.

And no one had eyes on him and Sabrina. Even the asshole they'd put on the door was watching Wayne and Wyatt.

Sabrina leaned in as though afraid. She cried and put her head down. The sight in front of her was simply too much for a small-town schoolteacher.

She used the ruse to start in on the zip ties.

Even in this situation he thought she was so fucking hot. He wouldn't blame her if she had cried out of pure fear, but no, his honey pretended so she could give them an important advantage. Lark pretended to be in love with him to give Sid and Gil a chance to run.

If they had an army of daughters, he would be cool with it. They could take over the world, and he would be there to fix them a drink after their long days of taking down the bad guys.

"Go and check the supply closet," Wayne said, nodding to two of the men in the back. "It's obvious someone fucked up."

Where Henry and Elisa would even out the odds a little more. They'd gone in the back, and it was obvious they were already at work. He kept his eyes up, but worked his wrists over the knife Lark had managed to get to Sabrina.

Something was happening or Elisa wouldn't have allowed Wyatt to come out and face his brother. She would have tried to buy them more time.

Elisa would have gotten into the office and sent Gil and Sid to the roof and then down to safety. She would find a way to let Nate know what was going on.

Nate was going to be here. He would come in guns blazing because there was no other way to handle this situation. They'd mitigated the damages as much as they could, but they were outnumbered.

He had to protect Sabrina and figure out how to get Wyatt away from his brother. If Wyatt was close when the shit went down,

Sawyer knew his brother would rather not go out alone. He would try to take Wyatt with him.

That son of a bitch had ruined Wyatt's life enough. He wasn't going to take him down. He wasn't going to take Wyatt. Sawyer needed Wyatt because Wyatt seemed like a man who wouldn't mind changing diapers, and Sabrina was obviously a career woman who would need support.

No one was taking Wyatt because he was a part of Sawyer's family.

And the diaper stuff. He wasn't sure how good he'd be at the stinky part, but he was ready to face it because he wasn't alone.

He would be if Wayne murdered Wyatt.

"You want to tell me where you actually stashed Dennis Hill and maybe we can talk about how fast I kill you," Wayne offered.

Sawyer felt the zip ties start to give. He kept his hands under the table, hoping no one could see Sabrina sawing away.

"I don't know what the fuck you're talking about." Wyatt sounded strong and sure. "I gave you his body."

"You gave me someone's. As I recall it was too burned to be recognizable. At the time I bought your story about him starting the fire when he realized what was happening, but now I wonder."

Sawyer was almost there, almost all the way through the zip ties when the big guy named Doug approached.

"Hey, you sit up," he ordered Sabrina's way.

Her head lifted, and she sniffled. "I can't watch. You can't expect me to watch you hurt him."

"Leave her alone," Wyatt ordered, and there was a little shake to his voice. Rage. He was fighting it.

"Hey, she's fine," Sawyer said. "Babe, you need to sit up and let him see you're fine. He's on the edge."

She sniffled and managed to move the knife to her side, slipping it under the folds of her skirt. "I'm not fine. I can't watch them hurt him."

He kept his hands under the table. Sabrina had sawed through enough of the hard plastic bindings that he could break them when he needed to, but they weren't ready for an all-out assault. They needed a distraction.

How long before Nate made it here?

Wayne grabbed Wyatt by the neck, a vicious hold on him. "You think I'm going to hurt you? You can take pain, little brother. I taught you how to do that a long time ago. Daddy taught us both how to take it so we never open our mouths to the cops about the Horde. He taught you not to betray your family. I guess the lesson didn't take."

He needed to get them all out of here. He needed something that would make these guys panic. In the chaos he might be able to get Sabrina and Wyatt out.

But it might cost him. Would cost him if he did what he was thinking about doing.

He glanced over at Lark, who had been watching him as though she'd known he would have a plan.

It was good to have people who had faith in him. It was funny since he would have said no one viewed him as a steady presence, but he guessed he was for his employees.

He really had been looking at the world through poop-colored glasses. Once Sabrina had ripped them off his eyes, he could see far more clearly, and that was why it was okay to lose what he was going to lose.

It was something they joked about. If joking about a building being a fire hazard was something to find humorous. He was up to code, but the truth was anything burned if you threw enough firepower at it.

He had a whole bar full of accelerants. All he needed was a chance to light it up.

"I didn't fucking betray you," Wyatt was saying. He was on the edge. Sawyer could see it, but he seemed to be holding on. "Whatever you think I did, I didn't. You wanted me to kill Dennis Hill. I did."

"And I know for a fact you didn't," Wayne growled back.

"Is he going to kill Wyatt?" Sabrina asked the question in a whisper, tears rolling down her cheeks.

Fuck, he was going to kill every single one of these motherfuckers. They made Sabrina cry. They made her afraid in a place where she should fucking be safe. This was his bar, the business his grandfather built, and it should be safe for her.

He'd thought he'd felt rage before, but it was nothing like what blazed through him now.

"He's not going to kill Wyatt," Sawyer managed between

clenched teeth. "I need you to stay calm. I need you to be the woman you were the other night. Calm. Cool."

"I want to say something to you," she began.

She thought they were going to die. He couldn't let her believe it. "I don't want to hear it. Not now. After."

Wayne released Wyatt, who stumbled slightly but managed to catch himself on the edge of the pool table. "Where the hell did Greg and Maverick go?"

Wyatt turned slightly and looked over Sawyer's way, sending him a knowing look.

He'd definitely seen Henry and Elisa. And they'd likely killed or incapacitated two more of Wayne's men. Unfortunately, that left them with ten versus four. He didn't count Sabrina, since she did not have her trusty stun gun, or Lark. They would be hiding if they needed to.

He hoped.

Women were unpredictable creatures.

Lark moved into his space. She had a couple of beers on a tray because these assholes demanded service. They were lucky they'd brought their own women because if they'd tried to… He wasn't going to think about what could have happened. Lark had played her role, and she'd done it beautifully. She didn't know yet but she was getting a serious promotion.

If they lived.

Lark passed him and handed out the beers to the men hanging around the pool tables.

They would have one shot.

Damn, but he needed some cover. He couldn't talk to her openly, and he needed Lark to make this insane plan work.

Wyatt turned and faced his brother, his hands in fists. "Do you understand what the sheriff of this town is going to do to you? You killed those deputies."

Sabrina gasped, and it took everything he had not to reach for her. He'd known they would be dead the minute he'd found out the CBI agent was dirty.

"I did nothing of the sort," Wayne replied with a smirk. "I think you'll find you're wanted for killing those boys and for kidnapping a CBI agent. You took him out to the woods and nearly beat him to death, but you won't be surprised to find he's survived. By now your face is likely all over the news. Everyone will be looking for your ass, little brother."

There were many flaws in the plan, but he wasn't going to point them out. Lark was slowly making her way back, and it might be his last chance.

"Are you going to pin our murders on him, too?" Sabrina asked in a shaky voice. "Is that your plan? Because I can see some problems with it. My sister won't believe it."

"Your sister?" Wayne nodded toward one of the men by the pool table, and he stalked over, brushing past Lark and slowing her down. "Are you talking about your cop sister? You think she can save you from me? You better stay sitting, Sawyer. Or I'll have to find a new place for you."

His heart rate tripled because they were going to start in on Sabrina. They were going to make her hurt in order to get Wyatt to talk. He couldn't let this happen. He couldn't.

Sabrina looked his way and put a hand on his arm. "I'll be okay. I will. I can handle it. Please, Sawyer, don't make this worse."

The man reached down and hauled Sabrina up. Wyatt started toward her, but two more of Wayne's men grabbed him and held him back.

Please don't let him lose it. If Wyatt lost it, Sawyer wouldn't be able to work his plan. Wyatt wouldn't care the world was on fire. All he cared about in that state was taking out anyone in front of him.

He would have to risk it because there was no way he was leaving Sabrina in their hands for long. He knew she was tough, knew she could handle a lot. But the reality of watching her get hurt was far fucking too much for him. She might be strong, but when it came to this Sawyer was delicate.

She gasped as they drug her away, one of her kitten heels coming off as she tried to stay on her feet.

"You leave her alone," Wyatt yelled.

Lark stopped at the table, her eyes on the scene in front of them. Exactly where everyone's eyes were. Wyatt was causing a scene, and he was good at it. "What should I do? We can't call out."

He kept his tone low. "Deputy Leal and Henry Flanders are already in the building. Nate's on his way, but we're going to need to avoid a hostage situation. Nate being outside won't stop them from holding us inside, and then they'll get desperate. We need to get everyone outside."

"How?" Lark breathed.

"Torch the whole place, Lark," he said. "By now Elisa and Henry will have gotten the rest of the crew out. Make some Molotov cocktails. No one is watching you. When they're ready, light this place up. They'll be forced to run."

"Sawyer," she began, finally looking at him even as Sabrina was held away from Wyatt.

"Do it. Try to hit the curtains in the back. The ones my granddad wouldn't get rid of because he was so cheap." They were out of place. Filmy and delicate in their own way.

They would go up quickly.

Wayne would have to make some hard choices.

"He doesn't know anything because he didn't do it," Sabrina was saying as Lark moved away.

A loud smack went through the room, and Sawyer felt frozen in place. Wayne. He'd hit Sabrina. He'd fucking slapped her, and there was a hand mark on her face, and he was going to make this man eat his own colon.

Wyatt pushed at the men holding him, his face red. But he seemed to be holding on. There wasn't any glassiness to his eyes. Just normal rage at men harming someone he loved.

Time. He needed time. "Hey, Wayne, your guys are taking too long back there. How do I know they're not stealing my shit?"

Wayne looked over, his eyes widening as though he'd forgotten Sawyer was there for a moment. He glanced back down the hallway. "Hey, anyone here? Come out right now."

Sawyer watched as Lark made her way around the bar, leaning so no one could see what she was doing.

Only a couple of minutes and he would have the chaos he needed. "They better not be fucking with my stuff, Wayne. I'm not joking. I don't care what you do with those two, but you mess with my bar and we'll have trouble."

Wayne was about to understand he would burn the whole place down for them, for his family. But for now, his former occupation of complete misanthrope came in handy.

"How you like hearing that, Wyatt?" Wayne asked, getting into his brother's space. "Your best friend doesn't care about you. Did you think anyone would?"

Wyatt turned his way, a bit of desperation on his face. "I suppose I should have expected it from you. All you care about is money and power."

Okay, they were going to have to work on his dialogue skills. Wyatt was obviously a reader and not a writer, though he had caught on quickly. They were going to have to act a little. Play out a drama to give Lark time. Wyatt wouldn't know what he was buying time for, but he'd caught the line Sawyer had thrown out. "What did you think I would do, Wyatt? Burn down the bar for you?"

Wyatt's eyes widened as though to say, *you sure that's the way we're going*? But he turned and looked his brother directly in the eyes even as he spoke to Sawyer. "No. You would think I would have learned the lesson a long time ago. Brotherhood means nothing."

"Brotherhood is everything," Wayne insisted. "You are the one who broke the bonds. And now you'll be the one to pay the price."

Wayne drew back his fist.

"Still no idea where your men got to?" Sawyer tossed the question out before Wayne could hit Wyatt. "There's no good help these days. How many have you lost so far? Is it four or five? How dumb are your men that they can't find their way around a small building?"

Wayne stopped, his expression changing to something in between rage and trepidation.

He was starting to understand things weren't going to go as planned.

Wayne turned to Sawyer. "Who's back there?"

Sawyer shrugged. "They're your men. I don't know their names. I would probably call them something offensive like Bloated Asshole and Dude with No Hair."

It's what he did call them in his head.

Wayne's eyes narrowed. "I mean who is back there and what are they doing to my men?" He looked over at the pool table bikers. "Tiny and Ed, go and make sure the jammer's still working." He snarled when they hesitated. "And kill anyone you find."

Sawyer felt comfortable neither Tiny nor Ed would be able to find Henry and Elisa if they didn't want to be found. But they would have been watching and listening.

The men strode to the back.

Two more down. The odds were getting better all the time.

"I don't know what you think you're going to find, but I hope it's not your men wrecking my stuff," Sawyer insisted.

"My men are well trained, Sawyer. You should know since you used to be one," Wayne reminded him.

"I was there for one reason and one reason only." Sawyer kept his hands down. The zip ties were holding on by a thread thanks to Sabrina's help. If there weren't so many guns involved, he would wrap his hands around Wayne's throat and squeeze until the man turned blue.

"Yeah, you were there for a brother who no longer gives a shit about you," Wayne pointed out. "So you thought you could take mine. Here's the truth, Sawyer. You shouldn't care about your shit because you're not going to be alive to enjoy it. I was never going to let any of you live. I'm going to torture the two of you until Wyatt can't take it no more and gives me what I want. Then I'll put him out of his miserable existence, and I won't think about him ever again. I thought I would start with the teacher, but you've pissed me off enough. I think we'll begin with you."

Sawyer was perfectly content even though he knew the next few minutes were going to hurt like a motherfucker. The pain would be his and not Sabrina's. He could handle anything as long as she was safe.

He felt movement behind him and got ready to take whatever they threw his way.

And then something was being thrown, though it wasn't a punch. It was a bottle of... Was that the good vodka? Damn it. Lark could have thrown the cheap stuff, but no, she had to pick the French vodka Taggart's wife liked.

It hit the back wall and sort of exploded, the drapes going up as quickly as he'd expected.

"Wyatt, cover her," he yelled as he kicked back in the chair, pulling his hands apart and hitting the guy straight behind him. It caused him to stumble to the side which turned out to be a good thing since he narrowly avoided the bullet flying by him. He felt a slight burning sensation but no blinding pain.

Wayne was done playing. Sawyer heard another bottle slam against the far wall and someone screamed. The lights went out. Henry and Elisa had apparently been making plans. The darkness gave him some cover, though he could hear the bullets starting to fly.

Two walls were clearly on fire now, and Sawyer rolled to his right, getting under the table he'd sat at with Sabrina. He needed to figure out where Wyatt had her. He would do whatever it took to get Sabrina out. Blue lights suddenly made a ghostly appearance through the smoke.

Nate. Nate was here, and now all they had to do was get the fuck out with their lives and this would be over.

"You should probably try to get out the back," Sawyer yelled at Wayne over the chaos. The front door had already been thrown open as several of the bikers and the women they'd brought with them started to run. Sure enough, a couple took off for the back.

The bullets were flying all around them.

Sabrina was out there. She could get hit. Damn, now that he was here, fear took over. Not for himself. He was terrified he could lose her or Wyatt.

Then Sawyer felt the chill of metal at the back of his head.

"You get up real slow now," Wayne warned. "Otherwise I might accidently blow your fucking head off. I need a hostage if I'm going to get out of here, and the little lady has left the building."

A wild sense of relief swept through him. Sabrina was safe. He wasn't, but it didn't matter. The people he loved were safe, and that was everything. The rest, well, he would trust Nate and Elisa and Henry to get him out of the current shitty situation he found himself in. The heat was starting to pulse through the bar like a dragon breathing fire. Smoke rolled in, threatening to choke him.

He got to his feet, hands held up.

"Damn, I don't know how you're still moving, but you start to make for the exit and know if I see anyone coming, I'll kill 'em if you don't get them to back down," Wayne explained, his voice shaky.

He wasn't sure why he shouldn't be moving, but it was suddenly harder than it had been a moment before. His chest ached but he didn't touch it since he had his hands in the air trying to show Wayne he wasn't a threat.

"Move it, asshole," Wayne said. "You should know when I get out of this, I'm going to find your bitch and I'm going to show her what a real man is like. I'm going to..."

A loud *thunk* ended whatever Wayne had been planning to say, and Sawyer spun around, his head getting light. Wayne slumped to the floor and there was Sabrina. His Teach was standing there with the fire extinguisher in her hands.

Wyatt ran in. "Sabrina. Damn it, I told you..." He looked at Sawyer. "Oh, no. Sawyer..."

They were okay, so now he could deal with the bullet he'd taken straight to his chest. Yep. It had been adrenaline that kept him upright, and now he slumped down, vision beginning to recede.

Wyatt caught him and he heard shouting, saw Sabrina's desperate eyes. She looked really pretty in the firelight.

It was a good way to die.

* * * *

Sabrina stood as Wyatt entered with two cups of coffee in his hands. The waiting room of the small hospital in Del Norte was packed with Bliss citizens. Henry's wife, Nell, had joined them, bringing muffins and some incense she claimed would calm them all down, but the hospital had said no. Which earned them a slot on Nell's protest schedule.

Elisa and Van and Hale were sitting close. Elisa had a couple of scrapes but had already been cleared by the EMT who'd come to the bar with Nate. He'd ridden in with the Creede department at his back, and they'd managed to take down everyone that Henry and Elisa hadn't.

Including Wyatt's brother, who was now in custody and likely dealing with a hell of a headache.

"Here you go," Wyatt said, passing her one of the cups.

"Any word?" She knew she'd asked the question a hundred times, but she couldn't quite stop herself.

"On Sawyer, no." Wyatt slumped down beside her. "On those dipshits who started this clusterfuck, yes. I met Sawyer's friend Ty down in the cafeteria. He was on call when they found Marshall and

Knox. Who luckily had both worn vests because they were worried I would kill them if I had a chance. So they're alive. Nate fired them, though. Said he wouldn't be able to trust them again."

She knew she wouldn't. "I'm still glad they're alive. They can testify against the CBI agent. He lived, I suppose."

She didn't care if he died.

"They only wounded him," Henry said. He sat across from them, Poppy laid out on her father's chest sleeping away. "From what I heard, he was extremely surprised when he called in your escape and the sheriff from Creede arrested his ass." He winced. "Sorry, baby. They arrested him."

Nell sighed and leaned against him. "I don't think she's listening." She gave him a smile and her hand went to her belly. "But this one might be."

She'd heard rumors Nell was pregnant and being careful about it.

She wouldn't be able to even tease the thought of having Sawyer's babies if he didn't pull through.

He had to pull through.

Wyatt reached out and threaded his fingers around hers. "It's going to be okay."

She wasn't sure since he'd had a hole in his chest.

"Hey, Sabrina," a feminine voice said. "I'm Lucy and this is…"

"River." She'd seen pictures of these two along with Ty. They ranged from when they were kids to a picture at a wedding where Sawyer had stood in the back and looked utterly uncomfortable in a suit. Lucy and River and Ty were Sawyer's cobbled-together family. "It's nice to formally meet you. I've heard a lot about you from Sawyer."

River sank down to one of the seats. She looked like she'd hurried to get here. She was still in PJ pants, but she'd thrown a hoodie and her sneakers on. "How long has he been in and is it true the bar is a total loss? I heard those bikers went crazy and started throwing Molotov cocktails around."

"Oh, that was…" Wyatt began.

But Sabrina knew a couple of things. "Yep, that's exactly what happened. When they began to realize they weren't getting the answers they came for, they wanted to burn it all down. I'll let the sheriff know I'm willing to go on record. Sawyer is going to need a police report if he's going to be able to get insurance to pay out."

Which they wouldn't if they knew it had been Sawyer's own employee who'd tossed the bombs.

"Yes, I heard it, too." Ty strode in, taking a place beside Lucy, his hand holding hers. "Michael is parking, and Jax is going up to Sawyer's to pick up Bella. She can stay with River and Jax for a few days."

"For tonight it's fine, but I want her with me at home," Sabrina said. "I'm sorry. I didn't mean to sound rude. I don't like the idea of Bella not knowing where we are."

River leaned over, putting a hand on hers. "It's okay. We'll keep her overnight since I doubt you'll be leaving."

The only way she would leave tonight would be if he...

Caleb Burke walked in. He'd been with Nate, too, and had ridden in the ambulance with Sawyer. Now he walked toward them in scrubs, looking beyond tired.

Sabrina stood. "He looks upset."

Henry waved the thought off. "Nah. That's just his face. He's got a perpetual look of doom on his face. Sawyer's good."

"He is," the doc said. "He's going to need some rest, but he's a tough bastard."

A wave of relief flooded Sabrina, and she slumped against Wyatt, clutching him like she would never let him go. She couldn't stop the tears that had been building up. He was okay. He was alive.

Would he ever forgive her for the terrible things she'd said? She'd been so afraid he would die thinking she didn't love him with all of her heart.

She looked up to Wyatt. "I said things..."

Wyatt squeezed her. "What things, baby? Don't cry. Everything's going to be okay."

"I said I didn't love him. I told your brother I was only with him because I loved you and you were a packaged deal. I never thought he would hear me," she admitted.

Wyatt sighed and stroked a hand down her hair. "Baby, you were playing a role. I also accused him of only caring about money and power."

Lucy snorted. "Power? Sawyer tries to avoid being placed in any position of power. It would mean talking too much."

Wyatt forced her to look at him. "Baby, do you remember when he said he didn't care what happened to us? Only to the bar? And then he proceeded to do something we will never talk about in front of insurance agents. He didn't mean it any more than you did. Now I do believe he's going to want to talk to you about sneaking away from safety and running back into a burning bar to save him."

"Yeah, I might talk to her about running into danger," her sister said with a shake of her head.

"Well, do all of that on your time. For now, Sawyer's out of surgery, and we're moving him to one of the Bliss suites. I assume you're staying." Caleb pulled his scrub cap off.

"There's a Bliss suite?" Wyatt asked the question she was curious about, too.

"Oh, yeah. A couple of years back Stef built a wing of the hospital, and now we get this big old suite with overnight privileges for two instead of one," Lucy explained. "We have to use it way more than you would think."

River had her cell in hand. "We'll get back home now that we know he's okay, but you should understand life is about to change. We're done waiting for him to decide he wants to come out of his shell. We're pulling him out. You're about to get a bunch of invitations, and I hope you'll accept them. He has a family that loves him, and we'll love you, too, if you let us. We'll start with dinner at my place next week, but you should remember the holidays are coming up."

Sabrina gave River a watery smile. "Yes, we would love to be invited. And we'll be there for dinner as long as Sawyer's able."

Caleb shrugged. "He'll make it. He's strong as a damn ox. I should be able to let him go home tomorrow if he promises to rest. Were they able to save any of the bar?"

Sawyer's employees had stayed behind, helping with the volunteer fire fighting team trying to save Hell on Wheels. Lark had texted her when they'd finally gotten the fire out. "It's pretty bad, but the structure held. We've got a ton of work ahead of us."

It didn't scare her. She only hoped Sawyer wouldn't be too upset about the bargain he'd made.

Hours later, Sabrina came awake to the feel of a hand squeezing hers. She blinked in the early morning light and for a moment she was disoriented. She was in Del Norte. In the hospital. She'd fallen asleep sitting next to Sawyer, praying he would wake up because despite all the doc's promises, he looked so vulnerable.

"Hey, Teach," he said with weary eyes, but his lips were curling to a smile. "You okay? That was a killer swing."

She sat straight up, putting his hand to her chest. "You scared the hell out of us. Don't ever, ever get shot again. I swear I can't handle it."

Wyatt rolled over on the second bed that was in the room. He'd fallen asleep at some point, and now he rubbed his eyes and got to his feet. "Damn, man. When you want to cause some chaos, you can cause some chaos. I barely managed to get Sabrina out. Everyone panicked. The ones who took off out the back got caught by Elisa and Henry, and Nate and Cam picked up the ones who ran out the front."

"And when did you lose track of her?" Sawyer asked, his voice a little gravelly. "I caused chaos so you could protect her."

"She's slippery," Wyatt pointed out.

"If I hadn't gone back for you, you would…" She couldn't even say the words.

Sawyer's hand squeezed hers. "Shh, Teach. I'm all right, and we're not going to have to worry about Wayne Kemp again."

"No, we won't because I talked to Dennis," Wyatt said. "He wants to testify, and he's got proof. He was afraid for a long time, but he wants to come forward now."

That was news to her. Maybe she had fallen asleep before him. "You called him."

"He called me," Wyatt explained. "Henry really did know where he was and had him moved. Apparently he also talked to him and convinced him the only way to be safe is to put Wayne behind bars for life. I know I'm going to testify. You should understand I might have to spend some time away."

Sawyer groaned. "No, you won't. Nate'll make sure you get a deal in exchange for giving up the club."

She would feel better when Wayne was safely behind bars. Forever. She held a hand out to Wyatt. "We're not letting you go to jail. Neither one of us is great at cooking. If you leave, we'll starve."

"And I have a bar to rebuild," Sawyer said with a chuckle that made him wince. "I can't do it alone."

"Somehow I think you'll have plenty of help." Sabrina held both their hands. "Sawyer, you know what I said…"

His dark eyes rolled. "You mean your lies so they didn't immediately start beating me? Yeah, babe. I got that. But Wyatt needs to work on his bad dialogue. I only care about power? Who the fuck am I?"

Wyatt grinned, the expression lighting up her world. "I thought it was pretty good myself." He sobered. "It was touch and go, but I stayed calm. I never want to do that again. Let's be the most boring threesome this town has ever seen."

Sawyer nodded. "I think boring sounds fine to me. I think I want to build the booths for the new bar. That's the most excitement I want. I want to build something new, something for us and the town."

She couldn't think of anything better.

The door came open and her adoptive dad strode through, Cassidy behind him. She moved in and opened her arms.

"Come here, sweet girl," Cass said, wrapping her arms around Sabrina. "We were so worried when we heard. I'm sorry this is the first chance we got to come in. It was our night watch out on the highway, and Mel is serious about keeping the lines of communication open."

Her dad nodded, putting down the bag he'd been carrying. "It's almost time for breeding season again. Got to keep a watch out. Now Sawyer, how are you feeling? We stopped by the house and brought you some snacks."

Sawyer frowned. "Like chips? Or beets?"

Mel shrugged. "Why not both? Beet chips. They'll keep you healthy, son."

Sawyer sent her a look. Yeah, there probably wasn't a lot of moving her dad. Beets were his love language. And alien hunting. Sawyer and Wyatt probably had some training in their futures.

The futures she would share with them.

"I think River is bringing us breakfast, but we're happy to have some nice snacks, Dad," she said, hugging him, too.

"Damn, did he already bring the beets?" Her sister strode in dressed in civies and carrying a couple of bags with her. "I thought you might get a day or two."

Mel winked Elisa's way. "You know aliens like to plant their seeds when a man is at his most vulnerable, daughter."

Sawyer frowned. "I think I'll take those beets now."

Wyatt stood by his partner. "Yeah, I don't want any seeds planted in me. I'll eat the beet chips. Maybe they'll go with the breakfast burritos River's picking up." He looked down at Sawyer. "I mean not for you, buddy. You're on a hospital diet for a couple of days."

"What?" Sawyer put a hand to his chest. "I should have killed your brother. What a fucking asshole."

It did not surprise her he was more pissed off about the loss of breakfast burritos than nearly dying. She turned to her sister. "Hey. How are you this morning?"

Elisa hugged Cassidy and then joined Sabrina. "I'm good. Henry is scary, by the way. Like do not piss him off. I went in thinking I would have to protect him. Nope. The CIA did a good job. He might not have killed a son of a bitch recently, but he definitely remembers how. I drove by the bar this morning. Lark and the others are already working to save what they can. It's going to be a long haul, but it's salvageable."

She wasn't afraid of some hard work. "And the school? I didn't even think about it. I didn't call and make arrangements."

"You were going through some things," Cassidy said. "There's nothing for you to worry about, sweet girl. Del is stepping up. Rachel and Jen and Callie are helping today, and Laura, Nell, and Holly will take care of tomorrow. They hope you'll feel like you can come back later in the week. And Stef was so freaked out you might leave after nearly getting murdered that he's giving you a blank check for the library and promises he won't make a single suggestion. I could have told him our girl is made of stronger stuff, but I thought you would appreciate the check. Maybe if you cry, he'll throw in a gym. Your dad and I have been discussing how to train the next generation."

Oh, she hadn't even thought about the fact that her adoptive parents would view alien hunting as something to teach in public schools. She was going to have to find a way to turn it into a fun PE class. The idea of Paige Harper learning how to use various weapons scared her. "I'll see what I can do."

The next few years would be all about building. Rebuilding the bar. Building the school system.

Building her family.

The good news? She wouldn't be doing it alone. Not even close.

Cassidy started to explain how she made the beet chips to Wyatt and Sawyer, while Mel nodded and agreed with her, looking on with all the love in the world on his face.

And Sabrina's world went watery. "How did we get here? We shouldn't be here."

Her sister's hand slid into hers. "Because of history? Sure, maybe our history set us up to be too afraid to ever take a chance. Maybe the woman who raised us wanted us to never leave home, to stay stuck in the life she chose for herself, but she made a mistake."

"She met your bio dad," Sabrina said quietly. "And it gave you the courage to completely change your life. And you gave me the courage to change mine."

Elisa's head shook. "No. You gave me that gift, little sis. You're rewriting history. You found Mel. You tracked him down. You did it because I was failing. I'd beaten cancer but I didn't care. I did it because I had to. Because I couldn't leave you. Today, I would do it because I don't want to leave any of this. Because I love this life you led us to. I might have been brave enough to follow the thread you passed to me, but don't ever think I don't know what it could have cost you. We've never talked about this. Were you afraid?"

"Was I afraid you would come out here, find a new family, and I would lose you?" Sabrina asked. "Yeah. I was terrified, but I knew I could also lose you to Mom's never-ending darkness. I think if we'd stayed in that house, we wouldn't have left again. We would have lived out our lives there like she thought we should. Instead, you came here and you found Van and Hale."

Elisa's eyes were bright with tears as she leaned against Sabrina. "And you found Wyatt and a big, gorgeous asshole."

"I heard that," Sawyer said from across the room. And then he grinned. "It's accurate. Proceed."

Sabrina realized everyone was watching them.

Wyatt sniffled a little. "I'm glad you got out, baby. And I'm glad I did, too. I'm glad somehow, someway we all found our way to this town."

"I was born here," Sawyer added needlessly. "I didn't have to like take a journey."

"Well, I was born here, too, son," Mel said. "But then I was taken to the planet Araxia, and that was quite a journey."

"I was born in Del Norte," Cassidy offered. "But I was happy to find Bliss, too. And so happy to share a beautiful family with the man I love. I don't think you should be so hard on your momma. I think maybe she had a disease she couldn't deal with. I choose to believe she's somewhere better, somewhere happier, and no one is prouder of her girls than she is."

The tears flowed freely now, and she found herself wrapped in a hug from her sister. Then Wyatt joined, putting his head against hers and whispering that he loved her. Mel and Cassidy worked their way into the best bear hug she'd ever received. Only one thing was missing.

"Finally a good reason to be shot," Sawyer snarked from his bed. He gave her a thumbs-up. "You go, Teach. I'll be here when the sappy stuff is over and you need an or..." He seemed to remember they weren't alone. "Some more affection."

Mel snorted and stepped back. "Sure, son. That's what you're talking about. You won't be getting any affection for a while. You have to rest."

Sawyer's expression went beyond sad. "But I wasn't shot in my dick."

Wyatt seemed to think Sawyer was hysterical, and River and Lucy and the gang chose that moment to make their entrance complete with breakfast burritos and coffees and tons of stories about what it was like to grow up in Bliss.

Sabrina listened and dreamed of her own blissfully ever after.

Epilogue

*E*very citizen in Bliss loved Christmas a lot
Except for the misanthrope Sawyer, who did not
He didn't believe in candies and treats or a tinseled-out tree
He thought Christmas cheer shouldn't be given away for free

"Hey," Sawyer said with a frown, looking up from his place by the fire. "I give nothing away for free, kids. Just because it's Christmas doesn't mean we throw capitalism in the trash."

Nell stood. "I believe that is exactly what we're supposed to do at Christmas time, Sawyer."

Sabrina should have known this part of the annual town holiday celebration would go a bit wild. She'd planned to read the kids a Christmas story, but it turned out to be way more fun to write one herself.

"Well, I've got candy for every kid here," Wyatt announced. He sat beside Sawyer, with Bella in between them. Wyatt was dressed for the festivities in a green and red sweater someone—likely Teeny—had embroidered with the words *Happy Blissmas*. There was a decent rendering of Maurice the Moose wearing a Santa cap. "And hopefully that will make everyone stop kicking me in the shins."

Wyatt knew how to bribe a kid, though Sabrina noted Paige

338

seemed to be reserving judgment.

"I think we should talk about your views of late-stage capitalism," Nell challenged.

Max Harper groaned as he looked at the two cowboys across the room. "No, Nell. We don't need to talk about economics. We need to talk about those two asshole cowboys Stef is letting stay out at his place. Does no one remember the chaos they caused a couple of years back?"

Stella snorted. She stood at the pie station. "Seriously? Are you talking about Shane and Bay?"

Max stood, nodding Stella's way. "Damn straight. I'm talking about those two ass...cowboys who ogled my wife and tried to buy her for the night."

"You know Rach was in on that," his twin pointed out. "Besides, she's not going anywhere since you knocked her up again. You know what you're getting for Christmas? The old snip snip, and I'm not taking no for an answer."

Max seemed to shrink back. "Well, it's got to wait since Brooke's here. My baby sister doesn't need to hear talk about her brothers cutting off each other's balls. It's not family-like."

Sawyer guffawed. "That's right, Harper. Protect those balls."

"Why is everyone talking about Daddy's balls?" Paige asked. "Which ones? He's got lots of sports balls."

And it was time for her to take charge. Maybe a story wasn't what they needed. Maybe a bit of exercise was required. "I think it's time for a Christmas dance off."

Sabrina got the music going, and the kiddos were happily dancing and spinning around and Charlie Hollister-Wright was intent on proving he had zero rhythm. Good thing he was cute.

Her sister brought her a mug of mulled wine. "I hear Nell was in charge of the entrée for tonight. Who thought that was a good idea?"

"You know it was mine. No one ever asks Nell to cook, and she's pretty good. I hear her tofurkey is...edible," Sabrina shot back, her eyes trailing to where her men were sitting. Michael Novack sat in the same general vicinity, and every now and then Sawyer would tip his beer Michael's way or Michael would nod his.

They might be best friends now.

The Christmas season seemed to have put everyone in a good

mood. Just yesterday she'd opened a Christmas card from Sawyer's brother's wife. It wasn't more than a picture of his brother, wife, and their child gamely smiling at the camera, and she was almost certain his wife had sent it. She'd made note of the address and sent one of their own as well, detailing how Sawyer was doing.

It was a start, and no matter what happened, Sawyer had a family right here in Bliss.

"Don't worry," her sister admitted. "Van snuck in a ham, and I'm pretty sure Stella puts bacon in everything. I mean everything. Hey, I caught sight of those two cowboys Max is complaining about earlier. I don't want to give him credit, but those two boys are trouble. I'm not sure if they're in trouble, but they absolutely *are* trouble." She winced. "If I had to bet, though, I'd definitely say they're in trouble, too."

"Well, isn't this kind of the place to be then?" Wyatt leaned over and kissed her cheek, winking her sister's way. "Isn't Bliss where we all go when we need a place to hide and then, oops we're getting married and having kids and suddenly we're old and getting our balls snipped."

Sabrina had to laugh. "I think I'll likely be using your balls before we let doc give you a snip. We're a couple of years away. Though I probably won't be making any babies until I'm married."

Wyatt's lips curled up in the sweetest smile. "Well, it is Christmas. It's the season of miracles." He frowned. "Not that getting married would take a miracle. It's the over-the-top romantic proposal I'm talking about. But I'm working on it."

She knew damn well he was working on it. Bliss wasn't a place where secrets got kept. Well, except for the whole Henry Flanders was a former CIA operative, and they'd only managed to keep the secret for a couple of years. The fact that Wyatt and Sawyer were planning on making the grand reopening of Hell on Wheels super special hadn't gotten past her.

Her men were going to ask her to marry them, and she was going to say yes.

"Hey, we're heading to River and Jax's place after dinner for the after party," Wyatt announced with a smile. "That's a party after the party. Doesn't it sound like fun? If I can get Buster to stop sniffing around Bella." He got an outraged dog-dad expression on his face.

"Jax, your dog is fixed, right?"

Callie stepped in, looking over to where Sawyer sat with Michael. "They are so quiet. It's like they're trying to prove who best resembles a statue. And I think they're happy. Sawyer even gave me a nod as I walked by."

Yup, her guy made big impressions.

"Mom, Zander says Santa is an alien from outer space," Paige announced.

"Oh, Dad is handling this one." Elisa shook her head. "He is a menace. You relax. You're not working tonight. I'll snag us a table, and we can enjoy the chaos. Max and Rye's sister walked in a few minutes ago, and Shane and Bay are watching her like hawks with a particularly sweet rabbit. Max is going to lose more than his balls when he figures out they're into his sister."

It sounded like a perfect way to spend the night.

She glanced out, and the snow had started to fall as they announced dinner was ready and everyone got to moving.

Sawyer came over and slipped an arm around her waist. "I had the best time with Michael. I like that dude. Lucy chose well. I mean she also chose Ty, but she's got a real winner in Michael."

"You didn't say more than two words to each other," she pointed out as Wyatt joined them.

Sawyer gave her a satisfied smile. "I know. It was wonderful. We're going to not talk at the after party, too. I'm thinking about inviting him over. He might be soothing to have around while I work on the new tables. Wyatt's always asking questions."

Wyatt groaned. "Because I'm a normal, curious human being. Unlike you, weirdo."

"Hey, are you looking at my sister?" Max Harper said from across the room.

Sabrina took her seat, happily in between her men.

It was going to be a fun holiday season.

The whole town of Bliss will return in *Brooke's Bliss*, coming November 2025.

Author's Note

I'm often asked by generous readers how they can help get the word out about a book they enjoyed. There are so many ways to help an author you like. Leave a review. If your e-reader allows you to lend a book to a friend, please share it. Go to Goodreads and connect with others. Recommend the books you love because stories are meant to be shared. Thank you so much for reading this book and for supporting all the authors you love!

No More Spies

Masters and Mercenaries: New Recruits, Book 4
By Lexi Blake
Coming March 18, 2025

Kala Taggart has known she was in love with Cooper McKay since she was a young girl. But her wild-child ways sometimes clashed with Coop's apple pie, all-American persona. After the worst night of Kala's life, she decided to give up on having any kind of normalcy. She focused on her future and let the idea of Cooper go.

Cooper knows he screwed up with Kala when they were young, but the adult Cooper is unwilling to let their past rob them of a future. He joins her CIA team not for the thrill of the job but to be close to the woman he's always loved. He spends night after night with her at the club, trying to fulfill her needs, to prove he doesn't need some perfect partner. All he needs is her.

When Cooper and Kala are assigned to a mission in Sweden, they find themselves locked together and forced to face their problems. As the truth of that long-ago night slowly comes to the surface, Cooper has to admit that Kala might be further from him than ever. And all his plans come crashing down as the elusive terrorist they've been hunting makes a move no one is expecting, but the real threat might come from within.

About Lexi Blake

New York Times bestselling author Lexi Blake lives in North Texas with her husband and three kids. Since starting her publishing journey in 2010, she's sold over three million copies of her books. She began writing at a young age, concentrating on plays and journalism. It wasn't until she started writing romance that she found success. She likes to find humor in the strangest places and believes in happy endings.

Connect with Lexi online:

Facebook: Lexi Blake
Twitter: AuthorLexiBlake
Website: www.LexiBlake.net
Instagram: AuthorLexiBlake

Sign up for Lexi's free newsletter!